BLIND ALLIANCE

Book Three of the Blind Series

by

Linda Riesenberg Fisler

Published by Linda Riesenberg Fisler

DBA Kit-Cat Press, Middletown, OH

ISBN: 978-0-9967479-8-1

Author's Note:

This is a work of fiction. Names, characters, places, and incidents either are the product of the author's imagination or are used fictitiously, and any resemblance to actual persons, living or dead, events, or locales is entirely coincidental.

Many thanks to Sonja Sweeney, Editor

Cover design by Linda Riesenberg Fisler

Published by Linda Riesenberg Fisler

DBA Kit-Cat Press, Middletown, OH

ISBN: 978-0-9967479-8-1

Author's Note:

This is a work of fiction. Names, characters, places, and incidents either are the product of the author's imagination or are used fictitiously, and any resemblance to actual persons, living or dead, events, or locales is entirely coincidental.

Many thanks to Sonja Sweeney, Editor

Cover design by Linda Riesenberg Fisler

Other books by the Author

The Blind Series:

Blind Intention (Available as a free download at www.LindaFisler.com)

"This is a great primer to get readers to fall in love with the characters and want more. I'm so glad that I read it. I purchased Blind Influence right away after reading this." –M.E.

Blind Influence-Three-Time Award-Winning novel!

"Interwoven plots of international intrigue propel the storyline through all the twists and turns; the author uses solid dialogue and three-dimensional characters to keep the pages turning! This is a visual experience in the words that demonstrated her other talents. Linda is equal parts writer and artist—a rare combination that brings her story to life!" –A.M.

"I just read this book while on vacation. My only complaint is I couldn't put it down to do anything else! The author has written a gem. The characters are compelling and the plot engrossing and fully fleshed out. "It and They" pull the reader in and don't let you out! Looking forward to reading the prequel now…and every book in this series as they appear. Please don't make us wait too long! -M.D.

Blind Persuasion- Award-Winning novel

"Suspenseful, moving and kept my attention. I did not want to put the book down. Intertwined characters & anxious to know how their relationships change in book 3. The author did great research to provide authenticity" -M.F

"I have already finished Blind Influence and now this book. Had to read it straight away. Could not wait. Lots of action and twists. Will read the next book." -R.A.L

Want more Blind Series?
Want Behind the Scenes information,
access to author readings, podcasts,
and special secret meetings?

You can become a field agent on
Linda's Patreon page and receive all
that and more!

www.patreon.com/LindaRiesenbergFisler

DEDICATION

To Thomas, Angela, Mel, Jamie H., Joanna,
Jamie M., Kim, Frances, Gwen, Deborah, and the Fem Dems for their
gracious support and always asking "Is it done yet?"

To my readers everywhere
who I may not know personally (yet) and hope to
meet in the near future

And
To my editor, Sonja, whose suggestions
are priceless and greatly appreciated.

"It is probably not love that makes the world go around, but rather those mutually supportive alliances through which partners recognize their dependence on each other for the achievement of shared and private goals."
--Fred Allen

"When we believe in lies, we cannot see the truth, so we make thousands of assumptions and we take them as truth. One of the biggest assumptions we make is that the lies we believe are the truth!"
--Don Miguel Ruiz

CHAPTER ONE

April 1980

London, England

"Sean," the nurse whispered. Nicole and Sean were asleep in her hospital bed, lying side by side, Sean holding Nicole as best he could. While her breathing tube, respirator, and other life-support machines were no longer supporting her existence, she was still hooked up to her IV. Her shoulder and neck were in a brace. She was still weak but was growing stronger with each passing day.

The nurse had learned to carefully wake Sean over the course of Nicole's stay in the hospital. When touched or frightened awake, Sean's impulse was defensive. It usually resulted with the nurse pinned to the floor before Sean realized who it was. Even though Sean felt terrible and apologized profusely, he was still embarrassed whenever he saw her. "Sean," the nurse whispered again before touching his shoulder and then quickly backing away.

Sean opened his eyes but didn't move. His eyes darted about taking in the information around him. He lifted his head and looked at the nurse who was now standing five feet away from him and close to the door. He smiled, then saw the concerned look on her face. "Is something wrong?" Sean asked as he wiped away the sleep from his eyes.

"Senator Jenkins is on the phone. He said it was urgent," the nurse told him as she walked out of the room.

Even though the nurses expressed their concern about Sean lying on the bed with Nicole, he disregarded their rules. Nicole seemed to rest better when he was by her side. Sean tried not to wake her as he slipped out of bed. It was a valiant effort, but not successful.

"Sean?" Nicole questioned, still in a light stage of sleep.

"Go back to sleep. Bobby's on the phone. I'll be right back." He kissed her gently on the forehead and turned away from her as she fell into a deep sleep again. He walked to the nurse's station where the nurse handed him the phone. "Hello?"

"Hold for Senator Jenkins, please," Chris said as he put Sean on hold and buzzed the senator's line.

Jenkins didn't greet Sean with his customary greeting. He was too excited. "Sean, tell Nikki that Tony Shafer is alive!"

"Alive?" Sean questioned.

"I can't wait to hear what he has to say."

"I don't understand. What exactly happened?" Sean listened as Jenkins explained that he just received a call from Tony and that he dispatched Thompson to the Old Ebbitt Grill to bring him back to his office. "Are you sure it was Tony Shafer and not someone playing a trick?"

"Yes, I'm sure. Shafer told me he wants to testify how he obtained the tape and why Stevens ordered a SEAL team to kill him," Jenkins finished the explanation. "I know his voice, Sean. It's him."

Sean's emotions were raging. "I don't understand why you are so excited," Sean responded. "If anyone should have exposed that tape to the public, it should have been Tony. To me, he is nothing more than a coward hiding behind Nicole's skirt."

Jenkins was quiet. He hadn't considered the possibility that Tony used Nicole in the way that Sean just described. "How is she?"

"Sleeping," Sean informed coldly. "I'll tell her when she wakes up."

"Do you seriously think that Shafer planned for Nikki to take a bullet for him?"

"I don't think planned is the appropriate word. Obviously, Tony knew going public would put his life in danger. He just told you Stevens ordered a SEAL team to kill him. In my view, it doesn't take a brave man to put a woman's life in danger like that. He knew what he was doing, and he knew Nicole would not be able to remain silent. You knew that too. So, tell me, why should either of us be as excited as you to learn that he is still alive?"

Jenkins sat quietly for a moment pondering Sean's question. "He wants to testify. I think he deserves a bit more credit."

"He doesn't deserve shit. He could have testified to your committee without involving Nicole. Like I said, I'll tell her, but he isn't getting anywhere near her. In my mind, he is just as guilty as the person who pulled the trigger." Sean looked back at Nicole's room. "It's late. I'll talk with you later, Bobby." Sean handed the receiver back to the nurse, who replaced it in the cradle.

Sean thanked the nurse, turned, and walked back to Nicole's room. He walked over to the bed and sat on the edge of it. The movement

15

woke Nicole, and she opened her eyes. She turned her head slightly, the brace hindering her movement, to see Sean looking at her. She smiled at him, but he didn't return her smile.

"What's wrong?" she asked, sleep still apparent in her voice.

Sean turned to face her, still sitting on the bed. He reached his hand to hers. "Bobby wanted me to tell you that Tony Shafer is alive."

Nicole's brow furrowed. "What?" She couldn't believe her ears. "Am I awake? Did I hear you say Tony is alive?"

"Yes, to both questions."

Nicole released Sean's hand, raised it and scratched her scalp, her face showing confusion. She wasn't sure how she felt about this news. "He has to be mistaken," she mumbled. She looked away from Sean, who could tell that she was processing a range of emotions. She looked back at Sean. "Alive? Really? He's sure it's Tony?"

"Bobby said that he recognized Tony's voice. He sent Thompson to pick him up. Tony said he wants to testify before Bobby's committee."

Nicole's chin quivered. Sean took her hand again, squeezed it, and gently stroked the top of her hand with his thumb. Nicole felt betrayed. "Why would he do this to me?"

"I don't know. Bobby was pretty excited. I, on the other hand, feel like you do. I look at it as a betrayal of your friendship." Sean watched Nicole's chin quiver once more.

Nicole was tired, but she fought back her feelings. She needed to think this through logically. She needed answers. "Should I think that Tony did this on purpose? Do you think he planned this whole thing?"

"You know the man better than I do, but I do know this. He knew that you would not remain silent after you received that tape. He knew that you would do exactly what you did. In my opinion, he is a coward, and he used you." Sean moved to lie down next to her and placed his arm around her waist. "It will be a cold day in hell before he gets close to you again."

"I just can't believe that he would intentionally put me in that kind of danger."

"Intended or not, I think he knew what he was doing." Sean playfully brushed Nicole's cinnamon-red hair from her face with his free hand.

"I feel so deceived," Nicole stated, still trying to work through the emotions this news brought her. "Do you think Tony thought that Bobby would listen to me and announce the tape?"

"I don't know. But it doesn't matter now, does it?" Sean asked. "The tape is out there. The hearings are going to begin, and Tony is alive and well. Meanwhile, you were shot, asked for asylum, and your reputation has been questioned by people in a country you can't return to currently. You don't owe Tony a damn thing."

Nicole smiled at Sean's protective instincts. "You know that I will want to know why he did what he did."

"You have more important things to worry about," Sean replied, as he laid his head on the pillow. "We have to figure out who pulled that trigger and why. Until then, we need to determine a place where you will be safe."

"And then you'll leave me?" Nicole asked, looking up at the

ceiling.

Sean's confusion showed on his face. He rolled over, lifting his head to look her in the eyes. "Leave you?" Nicole nodded slightly. "I'm not planning on leaving your side ever. Why would you think that I'm going to leave you?"

"To go after Kent," Nicole whispered.

"I've told you, Kent will come after us. You are, unfortunately, stuck with me, sweetheart." Sean smiled and kissed Nicole's forehead.

Although Nicole's mind was racing, she held Sean's arm around her waist tightly. The security of his arms and his affection was in great need. She thought briefly of her dependence on him. If any other man acted this protective of her, she would have immediately declared her feminist independence, insisting she could take care of herself. Instead, she welcomed Sean's overprotectiveness. She would have never let Jenkins act this way with her. There was nothing in her body or soul that rejected Sean's behavior. Was it because Sean had proved he could protect her in the past? Her thoughts turned to Tony again. How did she feel about that? A thought came to her, and she needed to ask Sean a question.

"Sean," she started, hesitating for a second. "Do you think that Bobby could be playing us?"

Sean's initial response was to deny it. He had known Bobby for a little over ten years and had always known him to be brutally honest with him. They thought of each other as confidants and good friends. Sean contemplated Nicole's question. Could Jenkins be playing them? Could Jenkins have known all along that Tony was alive? Was his excitement genuine, and why didn't Jenkins think about the possibility that Tony played Nicole in regards to revealing the tape? Sean sighed. "I don't know."

"That's not very comforting," Nicole responded.

"There is a part of me that wants to believe that Bobby is not playing us. But there is also a part of me that says he could be doing just that. I've never known him not to be honest with me, though."

"That night we called him before the campaign rally and put this plan in place, maybe there was more at stake for him than just exposing the conspiracy. Maybe there is something else going on that we don't know about."

"Like what?" Sean asked, intrigued.

"I'm not sure. We've both witnessed the change in Bobby's demeanor during his speeches before I exposed the tape. I don't believe that had anything to do with me leaving, especially if he was having me followed. I just have a weird feeling he isn't telling us everything."

"You've had that feeling for a while now," Sean noted. "In any case, we still don't know for sure who shot you. If it was Kent, then we have to be especially careful. I can't believe that Bobby would want to harm you. I saw him looking at you long before you staged my intervention in North Carolina."

"What do you mean?"

"After Carol's murder that night in the nightclub and you ended up back at Bobby's condo, I could tell that he was very interested in you then. I just don't want to believe he would intentionally harm you."

"I use to think that about Tony." Nicole's brow furrowed as she started to recall the events that landed her in the hospital. She remembered walking out of the building and how close Sean was holding her. She remembered turning around because she heard a familiar voice. "Oh my God…"

"What?"

She looked into Sean's eyes again. "When I spun around outside the television station, right before being shot, do you remember?"

Sean closed his eyes. Of course, he remembered.

Nicole could tell he still blamed himself. "You didn't fail me, Sean," she said, interrupting her thoughts. "If anything, you saved my life again. I remember you pleading with me to stay. Your voice anchored me. I wanted to stay with you."

Sean gave her a weak smile and leaned forward to kiss her. Nicole tried to raise the hand of her injured shoulder to touch Sean's cheek. She winced, and Sean reached for her hand midway, taking it into his. "Thank you for that," he said softly. "What are you remembering?"

"I spun around because I thought I heard a familiar voice. I thought I heard Tony."

"What?" Sean asked in disbelief.

"I remember now. I distinctly remember hearing what I thought was Tony's voice calling my name."

"Did you see him?" Sean asked.

"No. Everything happened so fast. I don't remember." Nicole thought for a moment. "What would it mean if he was there?"

"I don't think it changes anything," Sean replied. Nicole wanted him to continue. "If he played you, he may have decided to come down to the station to thank you."

"Oh, that is just harsh," Nicole responded, with a bit of a chuckle in her voice. Sean laughed at her sense of humor.

"Maybe he came down to apologize?" Sean questioned. "Or, maybe he was part of the plot, getting your attention and whoever was doing the shooting is just a bad shot."

"Ouch!" Nicole replied, grinning at Sean's harshness. "That's pretty cold. What would Tony have to gain?"

Sean managed a devious smile. "Seriously, Nicole, you can't figure that one out for yourself?" Nicole thought for a moment. Sean sighed. "His freedom—he would be completely free. He would no longer be a threat to Stevens and the others. That link back to him would be gone. The conspiracy would be exposed, and we both know that Stevens won't survive this. Eventually, Stevens will either be prosecuted or at the very least removed from office. As far as anyone else would know, Tony would be dead, so Tony has his total freedom to start his life over again."

"Then why would he expose himself now?" Nicole asked.

"Good question," Sean responded. "I didn't say the man was intelligent. There could be one reason he is making himself available to certain people. He may want to make sure you are dead or to make sure to finish things off."

Nicole didn't like the sound of that. "Finish what off?"

"Getting Stevens convicted," Sean responded, still thinking. "If the plan was to get the tape exposed and that was it, you'd be expendable. If it included removing Stevens from office, you are not so expendable because they would need you to continue to make appearances, keep the attention on Stevens."

"Whose plan?"

"Bobby's and Tony's," Sean stated flatly. Nicole recoiled as best she could when she heard Sean speak their names. She seemed to sink into the bed, trying to disappear.

"But you said that you didn't think Bobby would harm me." Nicole's response was almost a whisper. "And you said that he was excited that Tony was alive."

"There's a lot we don't know, sweetheart," Sean admitted. "This is all just speculation. We can't prove anything." He nestled his cheek on the top of her head. "It just reinforces that we need to get you somewhere safe."

{II}

Washington, DC

Thompson parked his car outside the Old Ebbitt Grill and began to walk toward the restaurant. Even a couple hours after the prime eating hour, patrons were coming and going. Thompson sauntered up to the door, just as a man in his late thirties exited the building. His crew cut and physique were somewhat familiar to Thompson, who was holding the door open for him.

"Kevin," the man questioned. "Is that you?"

"Yes," Thompson confirmed with a confused look on his face. He studied the man closer. "Kenny Wilson?"

"In the flesh," the man responded, grinning. "It's been ages. What have you been up to lately?"

Thompson closed the door to the restaurant and stepped to the side so as not to block the entrance. "I'm working for Senator Jenkins. I'm conducting some investigations for him."

"Didn't you work for the FBI?" Wilson asked.

Wilson and Thompson had been football teammates in high school. They had lost touch when Thompson graduated ahead of Wilson. Thompson was not as skilled as Wilson at the game, having to pay for his college education majoring in criminology. Wilson, on the other hand, was awarded a scholarship to the University of Southern California.

"I used to. I left in November to work on a special investigation that Senator Jenkins is heading up," Thompson explained. "What about you? Are you still playing football?"

"No. I'm a Navy SEAL," Wilson responded, then looked down.

"A SEAL? That's fantastic!" Thompson wasn't surprised to hear of Wilson's accomplishment. While being the most skilled football player on their high school team, Wilson possessed all the qualities needed to pass the SEAL tests with flying colors. Still, Thompson knew turning pro was Wilson's desire. "What happened to football?"

"I didn't get drafted. It's hard to find a job when you have a degree basket weaving," Wilson joked. He fully realized that he had squandered his opportunity for a great education by partying and playing football through his college years. He truly did want to become a professional football player, but the odds were against him. It never occurred to him that he wouldn't make it to the pros.

"Damn, Kenny; I'm sorry to hear that. I know that meant a lot to you. But hey, a SEAL, that's not something to sneeze at, you know. Congratulations!" Thompson could sense Wilson's dismay

23

at not making it into the pros. Always the mentor to Wilson in high school, Thompson felt he needed to provide some sort of approval for his accomplishment.

Wilson smiled at Thompson's cheerleading. "Hell week was rough. I'm sure I do more for my country than I would have done on the football field." Thompson agreed with Wilson. Wilson's smile turned serious as he asked Thompson, "You said you work for Senator Jenkins?"

"Yeah, I don't know if you heard about the big scandal—" Thompson started.

"Shit, who hasn't?"

"Well, I'm doing some of the investigation on that."

"No shit." Wilson's mind started churning.

"Well, I'm kind of late for a meeting." Thompson reached into his back pocket for his business card. "Give me a call, and we'll grab a beer sometime."

Wilson took the card. "Kevin," he called as Thompson started to move away from him. "There's something I need to get off my chest. I think Jenkins would be interested in hearing this also."

Thompson stopped, turned, and walked back to Wilson. He took him by the arm and walked him further away from the restaurant entrance. "Are you implying that you know something that could be helpful to the investigation regarding the president's assassination?"

"I think so, but I'm not quite sure how it fits." Wilson lowered his voice. "It regards a mission we were involved in—it just didn't feel right—and I think I need to come forward. With Jenkins being a former SEAL, maybe he would understand what I'm going through and help to protect me. What do you think?"

Thompson thought for a moment. "I think he'd be interested in hearing what you have to say. You have my card. Think it over and if you still want to talk, call me. I can arrange something."

Wilson looked at Thompson's card. Both men understood that if Wilson were to talk, he would be breaking the code, as well as an order. Wilson nodded his head. "Thanks, Kevin. I'll give it some serious thought and call you either way in the morning."

"Good. It was good to see you again, Kenny. Take care." Thompson shook his hand and turned to enter the restaurant.

Tony, the once debonair, wealthy, highly sought-after attorney, was sitting in the corner of the bar area waiting for Thompson. He had no idea what Thompson looked like, so it was going to be a challenge to hook up with this man. To Tony's left were two plastic bags filled with containers of takeout food. He had mentioned to Jenkins that he would buy them dinner. Tony was hoping the conspicuous bags would be the tip-off to this Thompson fellow.

Thompson walked into the restaurant and scanned the tables. He looked over in the corner and saw a man in a knit hat, dark clothes, and a white beard and mustache sitting with food-laden bags beside him. Thompson chuckled when he saw him. The man couldn't look more out of place. He started to walk toward him when Tony stood up and grabbed the bags. The movement of the peculiar man caught several people's attention.

"It's about damn time! Where the hell have you been?" Tony snapped in a loud, obnoxious voice. He looked at a couple sitting to his right and said, "Told my son to pick me up here a fucking hour ago."

Thompson smiled at Tony's acting job and decided to play along. "C'mon Dad, leave these nice people alone." Thompson walked up and took his arm. "The nursing home is really worried this time." He couldn't resist tossing that into the conversation. "You know you aren't supposed to leave the building without an escort."

"I don't know why the hell you think I need to be there," Tony shot back.

Thompson looked at the couple and smirked, "I think that's pretty obvious." The couple laughed at Thompson's comment. "I'm sorry if he was bothering you. C'mon Pops, let these nice people enjoy their dinner."

Thompson and Tony headed to the door of the restaurant, Tony grumbling the whole way to carry off the ruse. When they reached outside, Tony looked at Thompson. "I assume you are Kevin Thompson?"

"Yes. That wasn't very smart."

"I think it went pretty well," Tony snapped. "What took you so long?"

"I got here as quickly as I could," Thompson said as walked over to his car. He opened the door for Tony to get in. "I sincerely hope that you have food in those bags."

"I do," Tony confirmed.

Thompson walked around the car, got in, and started the engine. He pulled away from the curb and headed back to Jenkins's office.

"Can I ask you a question?" Tony asked.

"I think you just did," Thompson replied, sardonically. When it was apparent Tony was waiting for a more well-mannered response, Thompson added, "Sure, go ahead."

"How's Nikki?" Tony asked.

Thompson looked over at Tony, then turned back to the road. "You'll have to ask the senator."

{III}

Washington, DC

Chris, Jenkins's senior aide, had stepped out for a few minutes to attend to nature's calling. Jenkins was sitting at his desk looking over a document and making notes on a pad of paper. The notes were questions that he wanted to ask Tony when he arrived with Thompson. He was so deep in thought that he didn't hear the outer door to his main office open and close.

"What has your undivided attention there, Bobby?" The thick Texas accent of Senator Larry Barker broke the silence and Jenkins's concentration. Barker was leaning against the door frame to Jenkins's inner office with his arms folded in front of him. When Jenkins looked up, Barker gave him a devilish grin.

Jenkins felt the grip of fear in the pit of his stomach. Their last encounter did not end well and Jenkins, with the help of Senator Daniel Mercer, had since avoided all interaction with Barker. He didn't know what Barker wanted, but he knew it could not be good. Using all his Navy SEAL training, he pushed down that initial feeling of fear and replaced it with confidence. "What can I help you with, Senator?" His southern charm was evident as he placed his pen on his desk and flipped over the pad of paper. Jenkins stood up but did not move from behind his desk.

27

Barker didn't move. "I have a mind to forgive you for your power play in Kansas with Senator Mercer if you do me one favor."

"That might be quite generous of you. Of course, it depends on the favor." Jenkins was crafty at negotiating, something Barker admired and, at times, lacked.

"Put me on the committee," Barker demanded. The committee he was referring to was the Select Committee on the Investigation of the Assassination of President Andrews.

"No deal," Jenkins declared confidently and quickly.

"I don't think you understand," Barker started. "I have no problem hurting you, your reputation, and all those you care for," he said, smiling. Jenkins swore he saw a sparkle in Barker's eyes. It confirmed that Barker enjoyed this part of politics.

Jenkins knew the *"all those you care for"* comment included Nicole. She and Barker had had many arguments when Nicole accompanied Jenkins on the campaign trail. He had not realized how many until Thompson recounted them the night following the attempt on Nicole's life. He remembered how brave Nicole had been on several occasions, never backing down from Barker's threats. "I clearly understand what you are saying." Jenkins moved out from behind his desk and walked slowly up to Barker. Barker was well over six feet tall, and Jenkins was an inch or two shorter, measuring in at six feet two inches. Jenkins wasn't about to give into Barker's demands. Standing very close to Barker, Jenkins started, "I believe it is you who doesn't understand. Your intentions for being on the committee are not in line with the committee's objectives. I'm leading this committee, not you. Your presence has not been asked for and not needed."

The door to the outer office opened, and Chris walked in, surprised to see Barker standing in the doorway of his boss's office. He quickly moved to it. "I'm so sorry, Senator," Chris said to Jenkins.

"It's OK, Chris," Jenkins said, addressing his aide without taking his eyes off of Barker. "The senator was just leaving."

"No," Barker responded, pushing past Jenkins to a chair by Jenkins's desk. "I think you should close the door, Bobby. We're just getting started."

Jenkins heard the outer door to his office open. He looked to see Thompson with Tony in the hallway. Jenkins grabbed the door to his inner office and gestured to Chris to get Thompson and Tony away from there. Chris quickly moved to fulfill Jenkins's unspoken order. After securing his office door, Jenkins walked slowly back to his desk. Barker was already sitting down, but Jenkins chose to stand, as a way to demonstrate his command of the situation.

"I certainly don't think you want me leaking what happened in Vietnam," Barker started.

"That nightmare has haunted me for years. I served honorably. If you want to blame someone for my Medal of Honor, blame my commanding officer and his superiors, who didn't wait to speak with me before filling out their reports," Jenkins explained. "If you think that continues to be a threat to me, then you don't know me."

"You certainly saw it as a threat when I first mentioned it."

"Yes, well, times have changed," Jenkins said. "You are not going to hijack this committee with your presence or your bribes. Too much is at stake, and if you decide to ruin me, so be it."

Barker studied his former apprentice. He wasn't sure if Jenkins sincerely meant what he said. "You are willing to lose all this,"

29

Barker responded, opening his arms to indicate Jenkins's Senate office and infer his status in Congress.

"And more," Jenkins added. "You don't intimidate me anymore. As Senator Mercer implied, we are not afraid to let your secret out as well. Are you willing to throw away the upper hand the Democrats will have for years to come by spreading gossip?" Barker stood up and started for the door. He was clearly angry. As he reached for the doorknob, Jenkins added, "And Senator, the next time you want some of my valuable time, I suggest you call for an appointment." Barker didn't turn around. He walked out of the office, slamming the outer office door behind him. Jenkins sat down and exhaled a sigh of relief.

Chris walked into his office. "Are you okay?"

"Yes," Jenkins said, replacing a lock of his disheveled brown hair. "Get Senator Mercer on the phone and then go find Thompson."

"Yes, sir." Chris returned to his desk and dialed Mercer's number. "I have Senator Jenkins for you, sir," he said into the receiver.

Jenkins didn't wait for Chris to put Mercer on hold and picked up the phone. "Dan, guess who was just in my office threatening me again. He wants a spot on the committee."

Mercer didn't hesitate. "I hope you told him no."

"I did. It was the same threat," Jenkins added.

"Well, our plan remains the same. Are you all set for *Newsweek Tonight* this Sunday?"

"Yes, I am." Jenkins paused. "Are you sure this will get buried?"

"The media will put its focus on the committee hearing. It's the bigger story. As for Barker, I'll pay him another visit. You keep focused on the evidence for the hearing."

{IV}

Washington, DC

Barker was like a steam engine barreling down a steep hill with white smoke puffing from its stack and high-pitched horns alerting all to its presence. His arms pulsated from side to side, and his heels hit heavy on the hard floor, sending deafening thuds with each step throughout the corridors. Those who happened to be in his way moved quickly to hide from the obviously angry and powerful senator.

He opened and slammed shut the outer door to his office. He had sent his aides home early, knowing the Senate's agenda in the coming weeks would yield very long days. He briskly walked into the sanctuary of his inner office and headed directly to the bar. Barker took the top off the crystal decanter that cradled his favorite bourbon. The senator was about to throw the top, catching himself before committing the livid act. He set it down while his other hand reached for and secured the etched glass decanter. This Waterford crystal collection was his father's, and it meant too much to him to abuse it in a fit of rage. As he poured the tawny, amber-colored nectar in the matching glass of his prized collection, he snarled aloud, "I've taught you well. But I didn't teach you everything, Jenkins." Barker picked up the glass and downed the bourbon. He grimaced as the warmth attacked his throat and made its journey to his stomach. He poured another and then walked to his desk.

He sat down in his oversized, leather desk chair, contemplating his next steps. The bourbon was tempering his anger, clearing his mind, and helping him to focus. No one had been able to tell him the condition of Jenkins's girlfriend. Without knowing how Nicole truly was, as he had just discovered, he couldn't use her to intimidate Jenkins. He recalled how Jenkins didn't flinch when he mentioned her. Was their relationship over? Jenkins had been effectively dodging that question during media interviews.

Barker took another sip of the bourbon. It seemed to placate him as he licked his imaginary, self-inflicted wounds. The phone rang, and Barker fully expected it to be a call from Mercer. "Damn it!" he cursed, realizing that his foolish interaction with Jenkins did nothing but strengthen their position. Barker grabbed the phone and shouted, "What the hell do you want?"

There was a brief silence, and then a woman's mysteriously husky voice asked, "Senator Barker?"

Caught off guard, Barker found the raspiness of the woman's voice attractive. The voice was calm, yet something about it pleased his ear. Was it the British accent the woman was failing at in her attempt to cover it up? He smiled as his well-used and demeaning phrase "pretty little filly" came to mind. He cleared his throat and composed himself. Two words and the voice were already intriguing. He wondered why he was captivated, as he began to speak with his Texas charm oozing with every word. "Well now, I'm terribly sorry for my abruptness of my reply. I was in a bit of a disagreement with someone and didn't expect this call to be you."

Barker could almost hear the smirk in the woman's voice. "I highly doubt you even know who this is."

"That is true. Who am I speaking with?"

"This is someone who can get you back in the game, Senator. I think we have a mutual interest in having someone...." There was a small pause as the woman searched for the proper words. "Shall we say, removed from causing us problems in the future?"

Barker's brow wrinkled. He sat back in his chair admitting that he had never thought of having Jenkins assassinated. That thought intrigued him, albeit only briefly. He cleared his thoughts and turned his focus to the caller. "That depends on who we are talking about."

The woman scoffed at Barker's feeble attempt to have her identify the intended victim. "You know."

Barker sat back and smiled. He prided himself on this kind of game. "I don't know who you are referring to, my dear."

"You know, Senator," she emphatically charged. "I've heard the rumors, and we have mutual friends. We want to know if you want to work with us."

Barker laughed. "Work with you? I don't even know you."

"We thought you might say that. Tomorrow, an envelope will arrive registered mail to your home. Inside you will find a key and a note containing further instructions. If you are interested in wrestling back your power, I suggest that you follow those instructions."

"I don't take orders from people I don't know," Barker stated adamantly.

"There are times, when being anonymous is helpful," the woman replied. "It will become clear when you receive and read the information."

The phone line went dead. Before Barker hung up the receiver, he took the last, long drink of his bourbon while reflecting on the conversation. He desperately wanted back in the game. What possible information did this woman have that he didn't already have? But more importantly, was it worth the risk to find out?

{V}

Washington, DC

Jenkins looked up from his phone conversation to see Thompson and Tony standing in his doorway. He gestured for them to enter his office. "I will. Thank you, Senator," he said into the phone and hung up. "It's quite a surprise to see you, Mr. Shafer," Jenkins said as he stood up and extended his hand.

Tony shook his hand and removed his knit cap revealing, his sun-bleached white hair beneath it. He started to sit down as Jenkins asked his next question.

"What makes you think that President Stevens sent a SEAL team to kill you?"

"Before we get to that, may I ask how Nikki is?" Tony inquired, now sitting. Thompson followed suit, as did Jenkins, who hesitated with his response to Tony's question.

"That's a rather difficult question," Jenkins said as he interlaced his fingers and rested his hands on the desk in front of him.

"Is she alive?" Tony pressed.

Jenkins smiled. He recalled the conversation he had had with Sean; the conversation in which Sean voiced his concern that Tony put Nicole in danger intentionally. Jenkins couldn't help but wonder now if Tony had indeed sent that tape to Nicole for her to take the bullet for him. Jenkins sat looking at Tony, scrutinizing what kind of friend he truly was to Nicole.

"Is she?" Tony asked again, more forcibly.

"Mr. Shafer, I find your inquiry rather peculiar."

"Peculiar? Why is that?" Tony was confused by Jenkins's choice of words. "She is a good friend. Why would I not be interested in how she is doing?"

Jenkins drew in a breath as he prepared his response. "Mr. Shafer," he exhaled as he spoke. "What I don't understand is why you chose to send the tape to Nikki. You knew she would not be able to wait to expose the conspiracy. You not only put her life in danger, but you also exposed a tape that was not ready to be viewed by the public. We were working to verify the tape's accuracy. We are now rushing through this process because of the public outcry. This situation isn't the best position to be in, as you know. We must be careful not to make mistakes."

Tony smiled and sat back. "I sent it to Nikki for that very reason. I knew she would come to you first and, obviously, you decided to do something that Nikki couldn't accept."

Jenkins knew he bore some of the responsibility for Nicole's actions, but he resented Tony's attempt to blame him fully. Jenkins also knew anything short of exposing the tape to the public was not going to be acceptable to her. "Faking your death put Nikki in a frame of mind that was very hard to deal with so I would be very careful placing blame at my feet," Jenkins warned. "If you would tell me why you think Stevens tried—"

"Is she alive?" Tony interrupted.

Jenkins sat back. "I'm not at liberty to discuss Nikki."

"Why is that?" Jenkins didn't respond. "Senator, we are in a position to help each other here."

"Are we?" Jenkins asked his doubt showing. "Mr. Shafer, I have a copy of the tape. I have information, and we are establishing a timeline with the help of those who want a plea bargain agreement. Davis, Engle, and Jefferies will be appearing before my committee. I can't see how what you have to say will be any more damning than what those three men have to say."

Tony knew Jenkins was right. "Then I guess we are wasting each other's time." Tony started to stand up.

"Did Stevens order the SEAL team out to kill you?" Jenkins asked for a third time.

"If you won't tell me how Nikki is, you don't get to know what I have to tell you." Tony started for the door, fully expecting Jenkins to cave into his demand. He kept walking when Jenkins didn't speak. He walked into the hall and shut Jenkins's office door behind him. He cursed to himself that he knew nothing more about Nicole's fate.

Jenkins looked over at Thompson, who shook his head once as Tony walked out of his office. When Tony shut the office door, Jenkins asked, "Why did you shake your head?"

"On my way into the restaurant to get Tony, I was stopped by an old friend. He's a Navy SEAL, and he said he has some information you might be interested in hearing. He's going to call tomorrow morning, and he may want to talk about a mission he was on recently. He said it doesn't feel right to him—I think he was on the raid to kill Tony. If so, we don't need him." Thompson tilted his head toward the outer office door, indicating it was Tony whom they didn't need. "Until we know who is responsible for Nikki's injuries, I think we keep her condition to ourselves. Unless the BBC reports something, I don't think we should."

"Are you sure this SEAL wants to talk?" Jenkins was skeptical, knowing the code that existed between these men, their commitment to silence, and the support of one another.

"Yeah, I'm pretty sure. My friend said that with your SEAL background, you'd understand that he would need to keep this quiet."

Jenkins nodded his head. "In the long run, Stevens ordering Tony's death isn't as important as the assassination plot on the president. I doubt Tony would have anything more to offer except to testify to the tape's legitimacy."

"And can he say it is legit any more than you or Nikki? He wasn't there when Sipes recorded it," Thompson added.

"Let me know if you hear from your friend. If he asks, I am willing to hear what he has to say, and if it is something that we would like to include, we can do so without identifying him." Jenkins looked at the papers spread across his desk. "I have a lot of work to get through. Thanks for running over to get Tony."

Thompson stood up. "There's some food in the other room. He did buy us dinner," Thompson informed him. Jenkins stood up and followed him into the outer office. Thompson stopped and turned to Jenkins. "I just had the strangest thought. You don't think he was intentionally trying to get Nikki killed, do you?"

Jenkins gave Thompson a look with an air of confusion. "Why would he want her dead? I mean, he clearly knew that Nikki would go public, something he obviously wasn't willing to do himself but to have her murdered is totally different."

"I don't know. That thought just popped into my head," Thompson admitted. He looked at Chris who was standing by a table next to his desk, arranging the containers of takeout food. Thompson finished his thought by saying, "I guess his persistence in wanting to know Nikki's condition set off an alarm bell."

Jenkins picked up a paper plate and started to put some of the food on it. "I doubt he knows any snipers." Jenkins finished loading his plate by grabbing one of the sandwiches. "It is an interesting thought, though," he added, pondering the possibility.

CHAPTER TWO

End of April 1980

London, England

The hospital was quiet even though a shift change was occurring. Nurses were exchanging pleasantries and information on patients. The muffled whispers splattered with some occasional laughs were the only indication of the change. Spending all of his time by Nicole's side, Sean had become familiar with the schedule.

A few days had passed since Jenkins had called. Something was bothering him in the days following that phone call. He was sitting in a chair watching Nicole sleep and running scenarios through his mind. While he still had not quite forgiven himself for Nicole's injury, he had stopped torturing himself, mostly at Nicole's insistence. He had retrieved all the information he deemed useful from the shooting, and it was time to let it go. His father reported that SIS was conducting ballistic tests on the bullets they found and confirmed there were two shots fired. The second shot missed everyone, hitting the wall of the building. Sean smirked at the thought that Kent was bad at some things, but he knew shooting someone from a distance wasn't one of them. Sean began to think that Kent had not perpetrated this attack after all.

He looked over at Nicole. The nurses had removed the brace and shoulder harness two days ago. Nicole had been instructed to begin to gently use her right arm and shoulder as well as turn her head. Her wounds were healing, and she was gaining strength with each passing day. The doctors were suggesting that Nicole could leave the hospital in two or three days.

Earlier in the evening, Nicole had been in some discomfort, resulting in the nurses giving her a strong painkiller. When the medicine kicked in, Nicole became drowsy and the comfort the medicine provided allowed her to finally fall asleep. She started to dream. She was back on the campaign trail in South Carolina with Jenkins. She saw everything in the dream through her eyes. She walked into a room to find Senator Barker standing with Jim Carson, Jenkins's campaign manager, and a Barker ally. Jenkins had just finished a speech and was addressing questions from the local press in another room.

Nicole felt happy as she entered the room, recalling that Jenkins had amended his speech to include a progressive passage on civil and equal rights, which she had suggested. The passage was met with cheers from the people of color who were watching from the hillside. Although there were some prominent black businessmen among the predominately white faces in the crowd, it was nevertheless evident that the South was still deeply divided. Nicole had observed the divisive nature of the crowds at prior rallies. Her sensitivity to these improprieties had heightened during her work in the attorney general's office in the mid-1960s. She was in Mississippi when three CORE volunteers were killed. Goodman, Schwerner, and Chaney were working for the Congress on Racial Equality (CORE) during the Freedom Summer campaign by attempting to register African Americans to vote. Nicole assisted in the discovery of all three of their bodies from an earthen dam. She knew all about discrimination, having faced her fair share at Harvard as part of the first integrated male/female class to attend Harvard Law School. More than 560 men let their displeasure be known to the twenty-two females who had been accepted and were a part of the class of 1964. Nicole barely escaped being sexually violated by one of those men. Her father had prepared her well, and she was thankful for his instruction on how to escape the unwanted grip of a man. Her roommate, who was not as fortunate, committed suicide when she found out she was pregnant. An unfortunate outcome of a violent crime was how the university chose to address her roommate's suicide. Nicole had fought all her life for civil and equal rights under the law, despite the consequences to her safety. She felt good about the passages in the speech that Jenkins had added, and she was ecstatic that Jenkins shared her views.

Barker, on the other hand, was not at all amused with the control he felt Nicole had over his prodigy. He moved toward her as she entered the room unattended. His body language made it clear he was angry. The words started to flow, and before she knew it, she was face-to-face, toe-to-toe with Barker.

"If Jenkins loses," he started to hiss. His hatred of her reared its ugly head. "It won't be because of his stance on civil rights! It won't be because of his stance on the Middle East, hostages, or drilling for oil in the ANWR! It will be because of you! You are destroying this campaign! Instead of being the pretty thing by his side, taking care of his every need, you think you have some superior knowledge that this campaign can't do without. Worse yet, you have him thinking you, a woman, can think and knows more than his advisors. Your manipulation of him costs us money and support. You should be nothing but a piece of ass to him!"

Barker took in a breath and shouted, "I AM GETTING TIRED OF YOUR SHIT!"

Nicole wondered if her hair blew back from her face as Barker yelled the words. Nicole didn't back down. Calmly, she said, "I've got news for you old man. If you think for one moment that Jenkins is going to make you his vice president, then you don't know him at all. If you want to continue to think I'm stupid and nothing more than a piece of ass, then you go right ahead. Don't think for one minute that I don't see the games and the power play you are making behind his back. I have and will continue to bring those to his attention." Nicole paused with her eyes locked in a stare with Barker's. His face became gnarled, and his eyes showed only a hint of the encompassing hatred he felt for her. But Nicole saw it. She held onto the courage she had mustered, knowing she was the only female in the room and began to speak with a strong conviction. "You don't scare me. You never have. It irritates the crap out of you that I have his ear." She paused and raised her eyebrows giving a telling smile as she spoke. "I have more than his ear, you pathetic old man. What I have you'll never be able to take away from me. He'll never trust you, and if I have my way, you will have no part in his administration. That will never happen as long as I'm around."

Barker started to recoil like a rattlesnake preparing to strike. He had once found Nicole to be a beautiful woman, but now her intelligence, strength, and foresight had ruined that for him. His face contorted, and his upper lip curled as his disdain for her seeped forth from him. He pronounced each word distinctly so it would be understood and its hatred felt clear to the bone. "Don't think for one moment that I haven't thought of getting rid of you. You are expendable. You have no idea how insignificant you are to him and this country. You are here because I allow you to be here.

You are a detriment to him, and I will see to it that your role in his decisions diminishes. I will see to it that you won't matter to him any longer."

Nicole tossed and turned in the bed, trying to get away from the figure of Senator Barker in her dream. It felt so real that her body was tense, her breathing had increased, and she started to sweat from the fear and adrenaline that was now coursing through her sleeping body. Sean noticed Nicole's movements and got up from the chair, moving to her side.

The dream continued. Barker now seemed to be towering over Nicole. "I own Bobby. I trained him, and he is mine! He will do as I say or he will not be president. I will be standing next to him, and I will be his vice president. And you—you will only be a part of his life if you are seen and not heard. I will and can make you disappear if you don't just fuck him when he needs it and keep your mouth shut. Don't think for one moment that I don't have it in me. I have done everything I have needed to do to get to this place. I won't let a slut destroy that." Nicole didn't think it was possible for Barker to get any closer to her face, but he did manage to do so. In a vile whisper, he finished his threat. "I sincerely hope you understand me. I'd hate to see a pretty little filly like you put down."

Nicole sprang up in bed, her hand shooting up to her chest. She gasped for breath as the fear that she had felt when Barker made that threat returned. Her eyes were wide open, and she continued to draw in deep breaths and exhale forcibly. She grasped her hospital gown by her heart, gathering it into a tight fist. "I can't breathe!"

Sean arrived at her side just in time to grab her in his arms as she sprang up in bed. He brought her to him with one arm and engulfed her fisted hand at her chest in his. "It's all right, Nicole," he started. "I have you. You're in the hospital. You're safe." He kept reassuring her until she settled down and her breathing returned to normal.

Nicole took a few more breaths and then felt the pain that her actions had caused. She grimaced at it in a way that made Sean chuckle. "It's not funny," she chided him. She started to lie back down, Sean assisting her as best he could.

"I know it isn't, but the look on your face," Sean started, then stopped when he received another look from Nicole. He decided his best defense was to change the subject. "Were you dreaming of the Serpent?"

"No, it wasn't the Serpent." She paused. "I don't want to talk about it, and besides, it doesn't matter anymore. It was just a dream." Nicole brushed her hair from her eyes. "I'm all right now. Don't worry about it."

"You're sure you don't want to discuss it?"

"I'm sure," Nicole replied. She decided that since she was absent in Jenkins's life, the threat made by Barker, even though it was real, was no longer needed. Barker got what he wanted. She was no longer influencing Jenkins's campaign. She was in a foreign country and certainly not welcome to return to the United States anytime soon. She wondered if Barker was in full dictator mode with Jenkins now. She wondered if she would ever advise Jenkins again.

"Try to get some rest," Sean said as he sat on the edge of the bed. "My dad will be by shortly."

Nicole closed her eyes and fell back asleep. Some time later she woke to the sound of Peter's voice.

"I think it would be a perfect place for you and Nicole to hide out," Peter said in a low voice. Sean was looking out the window of Nicole's hospital room. "The cottage is walled, and there is a post for security guards."

"Where is the cottage?" Nicole asked, now looking at the two men standing by the window.

Peter turned and smiled at Nicole. He walked to her side, bent down, and kissed her cheek. "Good morning. It's in Guildford."

"I have no idea where that is." She looked at Sean. "Would it be safe enough?"

Located southwest of London, Guildford was a rather large town. Its Saxon roots were evident in the historic buildings and also in its proud residents.

"It's not far from here really," Peter started. "Guildford is—how should I say this—in Surrey. You may recall a pub bombing in 1974."

Nicole was adjusting her bed, pushing a button on the controller to a more upright position. "Sorry, I didn't follow IRA bombings much."

"Right, it certainly was of no concern to you back then," Peter replied. He turned to Sean. "We can get enough security in place." He turned back to Nicole. "There isn't much of a woman's touch there, I'm afraid."

Sean chuckled as he walked away from the window to his father. "I'm sure Margaret had her say on things."

Margaret was Peter's chief of staff and close friend. Peter smiled, detecting Sean's dislike for the close friendship. "Sean, I know that you have begrudged Margaret's role in helping me—"

"To some degree, but I'm much older now," Sean said with a laugh.

"Well, I feel compelled to say that she had always been faithful to her husband."

Nicole's eyes darted from Peter to Sean. Did Sean think that his father was sleeping with his chief of staff? Nicole felt like she should excuse herself, but she had to admit that she didn't want to miss out on this conversation.

"Dad, I could have gone a lot longer without that statement."

"I only mention it in case that was the reason for your dislike of her."

"No, Dad, I don't dislike her. I just resented how she swooped in on the heels of Mum's death." Sean sat on Nicole's bed. "After all these years, I know you asked her to help. I just need to realize that she was doing what you asked."

"Yes. I couldn't have done a lot of things without her help."

"You never remarried?" Nicole asked.

"No, Brighid was the only one for me." Peter smiled to cover the loss he still felt. "But don't you worry about me. I am happy with my books, my position in Parliament and my work there, as well as supporting my children in as many ways as possible. Of course, with Sean's chosen profession, Geoffrey has received more of that support."

Nicole smiled. "I'm glad you love your work."

"I love it, yes, and my family," Peter said, looking at Sean. "So, would the cottage be acceptable?"

Sean thought for a moment. Was it possible that Kent knew about it? He probably did. He liked the bonus of a few security guards. He was continuing to weigh the pros and cons in his head when he turned to noticed Peter was looking at him waiting for an answer.

"I hope that you wouldn't mind me dropping by once and a while. I do like to disappear from London on occasion." Peter added, "But if that is a problem, I wouldn't have to do so."

"Don't be silly," Nicole said. "It's your cottage. Don't let us keep you from using it." She looked at Sean who was giving her a disapproving look. "That is if Sean thinks it's OK."

Sean laughed. "My concern isn't whether my father visits. It has to do with how well known the property is. It will do for a short while." He sighed, and he looked at his father. "We need to determine who did this, Dad," referring to the attempt on Nicole's life.

"I know, Sean. Jack has assured me that he is doing all he can. I've also put pressure on the police as well. The lack of evidence seems to be slowing the process."

"Is there any information on Kent?" Nicole asked.

"Jack hasn't mentioned anything about him. As far as they know, Kent is in France." Peter cleared his throat and changed the subject. "I'm glad that you'll be using the cottage."

"For now," Sean added.

"You know, Sean, she can't leave the United Kingdom."

"Yes, I know. But at some point, we might have to take our

chances."

"Well, I guess we shall cross that bridge when we come to it."

"I'd like to go back to my apartment and pack some things. Can you entertain Nicole while I attend to that?" Sean asked. "You can tell her more of your stories that she loves to hear."

Nicole smiled at Sean's cynicism.

"I would be happy to tell her more about our family," Peter said. He thought for a moment then added, "Mainly because it irritates you."

Nicole laughed as Sean walked over to kiss her. "I'll leave her in your hands even if I have to endure a few hours this evening hearing how we are so alike."

Peter looked at Nicole. "Sean and I are alike? You genuinely think so?"

Sean gave Nicole another kiss. "I'll be back before you know it."

"Be careful," Nicole said as he walked away from her. She looked at Peter. "And yes, you two are very much alike."

Peter gave a disbelieving scoff, "I don't see that at all."

"You aren't the only one, Dad," Sean said as he left the room. Nicole just smiled.

{II}

Washington, DC

Jenkins entered the conference room as the journalists scampered to their places. The photojournalists started snapping photos of

Jenkins when he reached the podium. He opened the leather-bound folder that contained his notes, looking over them quickly. He tapped the microphone to make sure it was live.

"Good afternoon," Jenkins began. Each day since returning from Kansas after Nicole had released the Sipes confession tape, he had held a press conference. Mercer was correct in his assumption that the committee hearings would afford Jenkins more coverage than the campaign trail. His numbers were climbing, and early polls showed that the majority of Americans, regardless of which political party they belonged to, felt Jenkins was trustworthy and appeared presidential during this crisis. While Jenkins had every right to gloat, he never took the opportunity. He knew too well that his party could be in the same situation as the Republicans. It only took someone like Barker to bring it down.

"Thank you for waiting, and I apologize for the delay. The committee hearings will start this coming Monday. We are still gathering information and have a couple more important interrogations to conduct with those arrested. As you know, President Stevens still refuses to meet with the committee. Stevens's dismissal of the evidence gathered and the witnesses' testimonies are concerning. The others mentioned in the confession tape are all cooperating. I wanted to take a moment and announce the committee members." Jenkins turned to Chris who uncovered a poster board that listed the names of the committee members. The journalist started writing the names down.

"The Select Committee on the Investigation of the Assassination of President Andrews is now officially announced. The members of the committee are Senator William Anderson, Senator Kenneth Smith, Senator Brian McNair, and Senator Thomas Westendorf. These distinguished gentlemen are the Republicans on the committee. The Democrat members are Senator Andrew Kerr,

Senator Patricia Samuelson, Senator Benjamin Hopkins, and Senator Steven Watson. Of course, I am chairing the committee. All three networks have agreed to air the committee hearings live, and the session will start promptly at ten o'clock Monday morning. I believe the committee will not rush to judgment, but I don't expect this to last very long. The preponderance of the evidence, in my most humble opinion, supports the assertions made by Mr. Sipes. I can take a few questions now."

The journalists' hands shot up in the air. Jenkins pointed at a journalist in the second row. He stood to ask his question. "Thank you, Senator Jenkins. After Ms. Charbonneau and the BBC had exposed the tape, there was an attempt on her life. We, the press, haven't received any word on her condition since the initial reporting. Can you tell us how she is doing?"

"I'm not at liberty to discuss Ms. Charbonneau's condition," Jenkins declared.

"But you were dating her. Are you still together?" The journalist followed up.

Jenkins paused for a moment. He took a deep breath. "Ms. Charbonneau sought and obtained asylum in the United Kingdom. While I see no reason to charge her with espionage, some of my counterparts don't agree. I believe Ms. Charbonneau has paid a high price for bringing this information out in the open. I admire her courage. While I still consider her a close friend, our relationship ended the day she exposed this conspiracy."

"Have you been in contact with her?" another journalist blurted out.

"I have not," Jenkins replied quickly. "I have not even had time to check on her condition. The British government is providing information on Ms. Charbonneau on a need-to-know basis."

"Why is that?" shouted another journalist.

"That's a question you'll have to ask the British government," Jenkins said.

One journalist was skeptical. "Senator Jenkins, you are chairman of the Intelligence Committee. Are you trying to tell us that the British government isn't talking to you?"

"No," Jenkins said, smiling. "I'm trying to tell you that I don't know anything about Ms. Charbonneau's condition and, even if I did, I probably wouldn't tell you."

The journalist laughed. "So it's a matter of national security?"

"I'm not sure how national it is, but it is a matter of security, yes," Jenkins confirmed. "I think we can move on to other things."

"Why are there only nine members on the committee? Senator Barker requested more members, and he also asked to be on the committee, but you turned that request down."

"Until a few days ago there was only one member of this committee: me. And the majority of the Senate thought the investigation was unwarranted and a waste of taxpayer money. The tape surfaced, and now everyone wants to be on this committee. Do I need to mention that it is an election year? I chose these nine members because I have worked closely with each of them in the past and, even though we may have disagreed at times, we were able to talk about our differences and reach a compromise. The very nature of this topic demands that all members of this committee be able to look beyond this and see the irreversible effect the finding will have on this country. Every member of this committee is highly respected and has served admirably, to my knowledge. While I welcome Senator Barker's knowledge and wisdom, it is not the time for grandstanding or to be overbearing in our judgments. Senator Barker has a great deal of work to do, and he will have his opportunities to present his ideas and concerns to me or even to the press since it seems he is not shy about talking with you. No one is saying he can't watch the proceedings on television just like the rest of the nation. I felt a committee larger than nine would be bogged down and would lack the flexibility needed given the situation. We aren't changing any laws. There will be no amendment introduced or change to the Constitution recommended. We are investigating whether or not the allegations of the confession tape are true and, if so, we shall call for impeachment hearings, and we will ask for President Stevens to be arrested."

There was a silence in the room. Jenkins's comments were honest and to the point. For the first time in history, a sitting president could be arrested, disgracing the office with his actions. In the silence, Jenkins closed his leather folder. He was about to leave the podium when a very shy, female voice asked, "Do you think he did it?"

Jenkins looked out at the sea of reporters. "Excuse me? Who am I addressing?"

The female journalist stood up. "Anita Cameron, Associated Press. Senator, you have all the evidence. President Stevens claims that the Democrats are framing him. Do you think he did it?"

Jenkins swallowed but did not blink an eye. "I will let the evidence presented to the committee deal with that question. Thank you very much." Jenkins walked out of the room amid more questions yelled by the journalists.

{III}

Washington, DC

Jenkins returned to his office after the press conference. He looked at his watch and knew that he was going to be late for the meeting with the *Newsweek Tonight* host. "Chris, can you call Steven Harrigan and tell him I'm on my way?"

"Yes sir." Chris dialed Harrigan's number.

Thompson, sitting at his desk, hung up his phone and walked into Jenkins's office. "I just got off the phone with my friend, the Navy SEAL. He would prefer not to meet in your office and asked if he could join you on the campaign trail."

"I can understand not wanting to meet me in my office, but why out on the trail?" Jenkins asked.

"I think he wants to be out of state when he talks to you. I suggested that you would be in Raleigh tomorrow at a rally. I can make arrangements for him to meet with us discreetly," Thompson offered.

"What time are we leaving tonight?" Jenkins asked.

"Whenever we get to the airport."

"He couldn't join us on the plane?" Jenkins was throwing some folders into his briefcase.

"I wouldn't recommend that. My friend believes that the team is being watched. I just need to tell him the hotel, and he'll worry about getting there and not being seen."

"If that is the way he wants it, then that's fine." Jenkins started for the door. "But Kevin, make sure he understands that if this

54

information is so important that he needs to share it with me, I may have to call him to testify." Jenkins opened the outer door to his office and started into the hallway.

Thompson started walking with him. "What part of Sean's order that you don't go anywhere without me did you not understand?"

Jenkins stopped, turned, and looked at Thompson. "I'm meeting Steven at a hotel bar. I doubt he'll be carrying a knife or gun. I was a Navy SEAL myself. I truly doubt I'll be in any danger."

Thompson walked out of the office, joining Jenkins in the hallway. "Out of the two of you—Sean or you—I fear Sean's wrath more than yours," Thompson whispered as he closed the door behind him. "I'll call our friend about the meeting from the hotel."

They arrived at the Four Seasons Hotel and walked to the bar. Back at the corner table sat a board shouldered man named Steven Harrigan. Although Harrigan was of Irish descent, his hair was a dark brown, but when caught in bright sunlight had a reddish sparkle. As Jenkins moved to the table, Harrigan stood and extended his hand. Jenkins shook it. Thompson stopped and strategically positioned himself at the bar where he could see everyone, including Jenkins and Harrigan.

"I'm sorry for the delay, Steven," Jenkins said as he unbuttoned his suit jacket and sat down. "I hope Chris was successful in telling you I was running behind."

A waitress moved to the table and asked what the Senator wanted to drink. Jenkins responded that he would like a scotch and Harrigan ordered another whiskey. The two engaged in small talk until the waitress returned with their drinks. When she was out of earshot, they began their conversation.

"Bobby, I have always liked you, so I have to say that I'm a bit worried about your welfare."

"My welfare?" Jenkins questioned.

"Yes," Harrigan confirmed. "I'm not sure this program is the best thing for you to do right now."

"This is a sudden change. What has you spooked, Steven?"

Harrigan looked around the bar. He leaned in and in a low voice asked, "Are you familiar with Operation Mockingbird?"

"I'm chairman of the Intelligence Committee. Of course I have heard of Operation Mockingbird. You do know that the current CIA director has shut that operation down."

Operation Mockingbird was a convenient way for the CIA to control the propaganda that it pandered to the citizens of the United States and countries abroad. By paying journalists to spread the carefully devised stories that could influence the outcome of many events including politicians' careers, the CIA was in control of the future of prominent and influential individuals regardless of the country in which they lived. The operation was in full swing during the McCarthy years, toppled the Iranian and Guatemala governments, and it lasted well into the 1960s. During the seventies, the discovery of the operation occurred, and the CIA was ordered to stop the payment to journalists by its new director, Stanley Coburn. The Intelligence Committee was informed of the CIA's activities and found that their manipulation of the press was so out of hand that it threatened democracy itself. The decision to stop Mockingbird happened just before Jenkins's appointment to the Intelligence Committee.

"He has?" Harrigan questioned with a sardonic smile on his face.

"He was ordered to do so by my committee just before my chairmanship," Jenkins responded confidently.

"It's not shutdown," Harrigan asserted.

"What makes you say that?" Jenkins asked.

"Who was your predecessor on the Intelligence Committee?"

"Larry Barker, but he is no longer on the Intelligence Committee."

"Did you ever stop to think why Barker stepped down from one of the most powerful committees ever formed by Congress?" Harrigan took a sip of his whiskey, finishing off the last of his first glass.

"He said he preferred the Ethics Committee."

"Where he could bribe members of Congress to achieve his ambitions and still keep Mockingbird in operation with a few, strategically placed bribes to the media." Harrigan watched as Jenkins realized what he was saying.

"Barker," Jenkins swallowed, "has journalists in place to bring me down?"

Harrigan looked down. "Not only journalists, but he also has some network big guys on the payroll, including the CEO of my network." Harrigan took another drink. "We were fed the story of what happened to you in Vietnam a few days ago. I hadn't told anyone what we discussed. I have only shared the hard-hitting questions on the assassination committee with my management. No one knew we were going to expose what happened in Vietnam on the show, Bobby."

Jenkins felt his blood pressure rising. "Who approached you?"

"I was called into my CEO's office. He told me that he had a lead on you and then told me to use it to destroy you. I'm not supposed to tell you I know. I didn't let on that I already knew about this." He watched Jenkins take a drink of his scotch. "One more thing, the story is a bit different than yours. While you blame your commanding officer for filing a false report, Barker's version says that you filed the report, and John Spencer, who was your second in command, ordered the massacre." He paused. "Which is the truth, Bobby?"

Jenkins looked at Harrigan. He sat back, his mind racing trying to determine Barker's next step. There was no time for dishonesty. "My commanding officer submitted the details of that raid before I woke up in the hospital hundreds of miles away. John Spencer, my second in command and best friend, was by my side. John was the one who told me about the report. This report wasn't my commanding officer's first false report. He is a highly decorated admiral, very respected." Jenkins sat forward again. "Do you have time to confront this admiral?"

"It depends on where he lives. I can tell you that my chain of command will not support me," Harrigan informed him.

"Are you on Barker's payroll?" Jenkins asked bluntly.

Harrigan looked at him and gave a quick laugh. "Bobby, I'm a liberal, and I believe wholeheartedly in the freedom of the press. My actions might get me fired, but I believe the American people deserve the truth. We just need to figure out how we are going to tape this show and get it on the air without my superiors pulling it."

"You realize your life is in danger." Jenkins took another drink of his scotch.

"So is yours."

"Can we deceive them?" Jenkins asked. "Can we do the interview live?"

"You want your confession to be live on Sunday night?" Harrigan was shocked at the suggestion.

"Yes. Tell your superiors that you told me that Barker has the goods on me and that I want to confess to it live. Play along with their ploy. When we are live, I will tell the story, the true story, of what happened that night." Jenkins never took his eyes off of Harrigan, who was observing the young senator's body language.

Harrigan shook his head. "By God, you have balls."

"Do you believe me?"

"Yes," Harrigan confirmed. "But it is your word against Barker's."

"Not if you have done your homework and not if you can get an interview with my former commanding officer. I was hoping we could keep him out of this, but Barker just upped the ante." Jenkins sat for a moment. He then reached into his suit jacket pocket and produced his small, pocket-sized notebook. He flipped open the leather top flap and took his pen out of his other pocket. He started writing something down. He tore the paper out of the notebook and handed it to Harrigan.

Harrigan looked at the note. On the top of the piece of paper was the name of Jenkins's commanding officer, the man who had filed the report while Jenkins was in the hospital. Under the officer's name were listed other key offensives that this commanding officer was in charge of directing. He looked at Jenkins.

"If you check those reports, you will find that they also lack certain information, the same information that my report didn't contain. There is a clear pattern, and you'll see it now that you know what you are looking for." Jenkins downed his drink. "We are going to do this live, and you are going to do your homework." Jenkins stood up. "If you need any help, call me."

Harrigan sat there in shock as he watched Jenkins walk out of the bar, followed by Thompson.

{IV}

Raleigh, NC

The next morning Jenkins awoke in a hotel room in Raleigh. He turned off the alarm and wiped the sleep from his eyes. He attached his prosthetic leg, grabbed his robe, and walked to the bathroom. His mind went back to only a few weeks prior when he was sharing his bed and life with Nicole. He truly missed her.

A few minutes later, there was a knock on his door. Jenkins walked from the bathroom, still in his robe. "Who is it?"

"It's me, Thompson."

Jenkins opened the door to find that Thompson was not alone. He quickly opened the door wider so that Navy SEAL Kenny Wilson and Thompson could enter quickly. Jenkins shut the door and locked it. The three men moved to the table located near a small bar area. "I haven't had the chance to make coffee yet."

"I hope I won't be here that long," Wilson replied.

Jenkins moved to the table and sat down. "Kevin said that you had something to tell me."

"Yes sir," Wilson said, sitting forward. "You being a former Navy SEAL, you know what could happen to me."

"Yes."

"I have your word that you won't name me?"

"I will do my best."

Wilson frowned. "I'm not sure if it means anything."

Jenkins stood up and walked to his briefcase. He opened it, removed a pad of paper and pen, and walked back to the table. "Just tell me what you came here to say, and we'll go from there."

"My unit was ordered to go out on this mission over the Caribbean. We were ordered to scuttle a yacht, kill those on board, and then plant some drugs. We were told to stage it to look like it was a drug deal gone wrong. The problem was when we got there, the yacht had already been scuttled, and the guy aboard was already dead and so bloodied that we couldn't ID him. We planted the drugs, and we dropped his body farther out to sea. The yacht was the Vita Mea, and from the news report, I learned that the body was that of Tony Shafer. The next day, I heard my commander saying that the order for this mission came from POTUS himself." Jenkins stopped taking notes and looked up at Wilson. "I just thought that someone should know. I don't get all this political stuff, but given that the guy was supposed to be a good friend of POTUS, I thought that someone should know."

"Were you given the man's name before your mission?" Jenkins asked.

Wilson reached into his shirt pocket. He threw a folded-up picture on the table. Jenkins reached for it and unfolded it. He looked at the picture and back at Wilson. Jenkins showed the photo to Thompson. "Can I keep this?"

"They haven't asked for it back, so yeah. I don't want it."

"You said there was a body on board when you got there. Was it Shafer?" Thompson looked at Jenkins. They both knew it wasn't Tony.

"The guy's face was so bludgeoned we couldn't make a positive ID. He had white hair, and he was the same size and build. We assumed someone beat us to the punch and we didn't care. He was dead. We completed the rest of the mission and headed back to base. The commander was looking for something. He never found it."

"What was it?" Thompson asked. "What was he looking for?"

"I don't know. My commanding officer never said," Wilson replied.

"Would it be in the mission report?" Jenkins asked.

"I don't think there is a mission report. After the mission we debriefed, and nothing was written down." Wilson looked down. When he looked up again, he told Jenkins the mission name. "You can check to see if there is anything about it since you are on the Intelligence Committee. Of course, if you do that, they will know that someone talked."

Jenkins made a few more notes. He stood up. "I'll have my aide type this up. Read it over and make sure that I have captured it correctly." He handed the pad of paper to Wilson, who did as instructed.

"Yeah, you got it."

Jenkins offered his hand. "We'll include it in the materials, but it will only identify you as an unidentified soldier. We'll redact the report, of course. I appreciate you coming forward. It does collaborate with another witness's testimony. We'll call that person to testify if we get that far."

Wilson shook his hand. "Thank you, sir."

"Want me to walk you out?" Thompson asked.

"No. Thanks for breakfast and the cover." Wilson walked to the door, opened it, and looked up and down the hallway before he left the room.

"So, Tony was telling the truth," Thompson said to Jenkins after the door had shut.

"Yes, it appears so," Jenkins said as he placed the pad of paper in his briefcase. He sat down on the bed. "Where does this end?"

"What do you mean?" Thompson asked.

Jenkins looked at Thompson. "If Stevens ordered a SEAL team out to dispose of Shafer, did he order the assassination of Nikki too?" "I think it's possible. Do you think Jefferies could have gotten in touch with an assassin before we arrested him?"

"I don't think we can rule that out. I'm assuming the commander was ordered to find the tape. With the tape missing and the BBC running the promotion that Nikki was going to be on their morning show, Stevens put two and two together."

"There are only two people who can answer that with certainty: Jefferies and Stevens."

Jenkins nodded in agreement. "As long as Stevens is in the White House, Nikki isn't safe."

"As long as Stevens is in the White House, none of us are safe," Thompson corrected him.

CHAPTER THREE

May 1980

Guildford, Surrey, England

S ean had his arm around Nicole as they walked from the car to the cottage. Peter had stayed in London needing to finish some work. He had dropped a key off to Sean just before Nicole was discharged from the hospital. When they reached the front door, Sean redeemed the key from his pocket to unlock it. Nicole entered first, and Sean was right behind her. She stopped and looked around. It was a quaint little cottage, spotlessly clean, with large windows that allowed the outdoor light to stream into the living room and kitchen. It was a stark contrast to the home that Peter occupied in London. She could understand why Peter would want to escape here.

"Have a seat on the couch, and I'll retrieve our luggage," Sean said, as he started back outside.

Nicole slowly moved to the couch and sat down. She realized the car trip had taken more out of her than she liked to admit. She began to wonder when she would fully get her strength back. She hadn't even removed her jacket before she sat down. She felt like she didn't want to move again. She closed her eyes, only to open them a few minutes later when Sean reentered the cottage.

"Sorry, I was a bit longer than I wanted to be." Nicole didn't notice. Had she fallen asleep? Her eyes darted around the room to discern if the light had changed. "Dad was on the spot. The security guards just arrived. I had a chat with them, you know, to check them out."

Nicole smiled. "In one encounter you're able to tell if they are on the up and up?"

"Not totally, but I can tell which one I would trust more," Sean said as he took their suitcases into the master bedroom.

"Sean, that's your Dad's bedroom."

"So, it is," Sean confirmed, continuing into the bedroom.

"We can't sleep in there. I won't put your father out of his room," Nicole shouted after him, leaning forward on the couch.

Sean returned to the living room. "I don't think you could climb those stairs," he said and motioned to the staircase off the kitchen. He walked over and sat down next to her. "At least not now. Besides, Dad said that we should take it."

"Wait," Nicole said, as Sean started to remove her jacket. "Your father said that it was OK for us to use the bedroom together? You and I in the same room?"

"Yes," Sean replied, a bit confused.

Nicole wasn't quite sure what to say. "That's…pretty…amazing."

Sean laid Nicole's jacket in his lap. His confusion was now evident. "Nicole, I just spent over two weeks not leaving your side in the hospital. He knew we were together in my flat before that. I would imagine he put two and two together and figured I wouldn't be leaving your side here either. In addition to that," Sean stood up and walked to the closet to hang up their jackets, "I don't think you are in any condition to do anything at the moment." He gave her a sheepish grin. "I doubt my father could think any less of you. In case you haven't noticed, he adores you."

"Well, good to know I have his approval," Nicole replied.

Sean returned her sheepish smile with a wink. Nicole did win Peter's approval and stole his heart much like she had stolen Sean's. Geoffrey had only been around her a couple of times in the hospital, but he liked her as well. The only family member with whom Sean could see any trouble was Elizabeth, Geoffrey's wife. He hoped that he wouldn't have to deal with that anytime soon.

"Today is Sunday, right?" Nicole asked.

"Yes." Sean walked back to the couch.

"We should call Bobby and tell him where we are. I also want to wish him well tonight," Nicole said. She watched Sean's expression change. "He asked us to let him know, remember?"

"Yes, I remember," Sean said. "What made you think of that?"

"The clock," Nicole pointed to the clock on the mantel. "He'll probably be leaving for the studio soon."

"I see."

"You do know how hard this is going to be for him," Nicole stated, noticing the concerned look on Sean's face. "You of all people should understand. You were never asked to go before your whole country to talk about your demons."

"OK, I get it." There was a hint of irritation apparent in Sean's voice. He wasn't annoyed, and he wasn't jealous. He couldn't put his finger on it, but he knew he just didn't like the way this felt.

"Sean you have nothing to be jealous about," Nicole said, misreading the look on his face.

"I'm not jealous," Sean responded. "I think it is more of not wanting Bobby to get any ideas. I don't want him to think that he could steal you back."

"Steal me back? You didn't steal me from Bobby." Nicole smiled at the comment. "Unless, of course, this is some male thing that you have to think that. Is it?"

Sean looked at her. "Male thing?"

"Yeah—you know, some kind of machoism or something."

Sean laughed. "Machoism? Really?"

"You're the one who used the word *steal*, not me."

"Machoism," he repeated, laughing. "I don't even know how to respond to that one."

"I think you are doing a pretty good job," Nicole said.

Sean tried not to laugh again. "It's not that."

"What is it then?"

"I don't know." Sean shrugged his shoulders. "I just don't want him getting the wrong idea."

"I care for him, Sean. Is that giving him the wrong idea?"

"Nicole, I understand that you care for him. You two were lovers, so I do understand that. But let's think back to the hospital when he called to tell us that Tony was alive. If he knows he can play the care card with you, he may be able to keep things from us. He might be able to disguise things all bundled up in a tidy little care package."

"I know him. I would be able to tell when he is lying."

"Oh, you would? Just like when you thought he threatened your life?"

"Oh, shut up," Nicole said as she picked up a pillow and threw it at Sean's face.

Sean caught the pillow and brought it down to reveal a smile. "We'll call him and wish him well. You need to keep your senses sharp. While we worked all this out before that Kansas rally, a lot has changed. To be honest, I don't want to believe he had anything to do with the attempt on your life or the possibility that he may be playing us, but those options exist."

"Wow," Nicole said. "Someone being that cold and calculating, I just can't imagine that."

"Politicians have ruthless bedfellows. I've been around this all my life." Sean turned and pulled the phone off the table, which was behind the couch where they were sitting. He picked up the receiver and thought for a second. When he recalled Jenkins's home number, he dialed it. Nicole was impressed, and it showed on her face. Sean gave a little chuckle and shook his head. "Hello, Bobby, it's Sean."

"Hello, Sean," Jenkins greeted him. "How is everything?"

"It's all good. I wanted to give you the number of the place we are staying at for now. I'm not sure when we'll move again."

"Let me get a pen," Jenkins said. He picked up a pen that was lying on the table next to his favorite chair and grabbed his black book from his inside jacket pocket. He opened it to a blank page and said, "OK, I'm ready." Sean rattled off the number, and Jenkins wrote it down. "Thank you for passing that on. How is she doing?"

"She is doing very well. She wants to talk with you. Here," Sean passed the receiver over to Nicole.

"Hello, Bobby," Nicole said. "How are you feeling?"

Jenkins smiled when he heard Nicole's voice and her concern. "It is so like you to worry about everyone else. I'm doing all right."

Nicole could hear the nervousness in his voice. "Just tell the truth, Bobby. If you tell the truth, they can't catch you in a lie."

Jenkins smiled. He paused a moment trying to decide if he wanted to say what came to his mind. "I wish you were here with me. I could use your counsel and strength."

Nicole smiled. "You will do just fine. You love politics, and it will come naturally to you."

"No, Nikki. Politics is my service, it's my duty. I love *you*, and it will be a long time before I can close the door on that." Nicole was stunned. She wasn't sure how to take his comment. "Nikki?"

Nicole shook her head to clear it. "I'm here." She paused and looked at Sean, who had a confused look on his face. "Bobby, as long as you are truthful with me, you'll always have my counsel." She watched Sean roll his eyes. He gave Nicole a disapproving look, knowing Jenkins was tugging at her heart.

Jenkins knew her response was a diplomatic one. "Just your counsel?"

"Bobby, a lot has happened and you know I'll always care for you, but…" her voice trailed off. "I'm sorry if I hurt you, but you had to have known that I couldn't stay with you."

"Everything you ever wanted, Nikki, is happening. We have the

Investigation Committee convening in the morning. The tape has been made public. In all likelihood, Stevens will stand trial and—"

"Bobby," Nicole interrupted in an attempt to make him stop. She was uncomfortable with his comments, and she knew where he was going with them.

"Everything you asked of me, Nikki," Jenkins paused. After a long silence, he cleared his throat. "Nikki, I know I would be stronger and a better person with you by my side. I also know that I wouldn't want you by my side if you loved another man."

Nicole looked at Sean. Sean knew Bobby was trying to win her back and he was starting to get angry. He grabbed the phone. "Bobby, Nicole's really tired. It's been a long day."

"Sean, we were in the middle of—"

"I know you were," Sean interrupted. "She's really tired, and she doesn't need to make any decisions right now. Besides, half of your Congress wants her extradited back to your country to stand trial as a spy. She has asylum here because of that. I don't think playing the relationship card is the correct move right now."

"Relationship card? That is an interesting choice of words," Jenkins quipped. "Sean, as I told you before, she's not going to be extradited. No one is going to bring those charges against her." Jenkins sat a moment and then in a cold voice asked, "Since when do you give a fuck about anyone, Sean? Does she even realize who she's getting involved with? A cold-hearted killing machine isn't exactly her style."

Sean smiled at Jenkins's attempt to manipulate him. "It will be a cold day in hell, Bobby, when a politician can play mind games with me. Maybe I should remind you that I'm not the only cold-hearted bastard on this phone call." He watched Nicole's mouth drop in disbelief.

She tried to grab the phone from Sean who wouldn't surrender it. "Stop it—both of you!" Nicole said loudly enough to be heard by Jenkins.

Sean ignored her. "Obviously, you haven't heard the news. I'm no longer part of SIS. I'm between occupations." Sean grabbed Nicole and pulled her toward him to thwart her taking the phone.

"Then you aren't in the position to protect her after all, are you?" Jenkins replied. "I'd like to say goodbye to Nikki if you don't mind."

Sean handed the receiver over to Nicole. "Bobby," she said, "this kind of talk between you and Sean, I won't have it. We had made a pact before I was shot and I won't stand for these mind games. Stop this or you will never—"

"I just wanted to wish you a good evening, darling," Jenkins interrupted. "Is it OK with you if I mention that you are recovering nicely? The media and people on this side of the pond still think we are together."

"I don't think it would be a good idea to mention me at all."

Sean grabbed the phone. "You know better, Bobby. No mention of Nicole like we discussed when she was in hospital, recovering from a bullet wound that almost killed her. The only thing you know is that she is alive and you have only spoken to the British Government." He gave the phone back to Nicole. "Wish him luck and tell him good-bye." Nicole's confusion showed on her face. Sean mouthed, "Please."

"Send us a tape of the interview," Nicole said staring into Sean's emerald-green eyes.

"I wouldn't know where to send it," Jenkins responded flatly.

Nicole rolled her eyes. "You can send it to Lord Peter Adkins. I'm sure he'll want to see it as well. Let us know how it went. I'll talk to you soon. Good-bye." She handed the receiver to Sean. Jenkins's voice could be heard calling her name as Sean hung up the phone. "He still thinks of us as a couple."

"Of course he does."

Nicole scratched her scalp and ran her fingers through her hair. "But I don't."

Sean acknowledged her comment with a quick nod. "That's good to know."

"What was all that cold-hearted talk about?"

"He doesn't think I'm your type," Sean informed her as he put the phone back on the table. "Nicole, in some ways, Jenkins and I are very much alike. He's a trained Navy SEAL. He has the killer instinct."

"I know," Nicole responded, not at all happy with the current conversation.

"I think he is right about one thing."

Nicole looked into Sean's eyes. "What would that be?"

"I'm not sure either one of us is your type."

"How could you say that?" Surprise overtook Nicole. Sean turned his head, so he didn't have to look at her. "Sean, how can you say that?" she repeated.

"I am a cold-hearted person. I kill for a living."

"You aren't cold-hearted. You aren't a killing machine." She could tell Sean didn't believe her. "How many people have you killed?"

"Nicole, don't." Sean clearly didn't want to tell her.

"Tell me," Nicole insisted.

"No," Sean resisted.

"Is it confidential? Is that why you won't tell me?"

Sean was getting angry. "I don't want to discuss it."

"Hundreds?"

Sean let out a sigh trying to quell his anger.

"Thousands?"

"No!"

"Then tell me."

Sean sat there, thinking, as he closed his eyes. "It wasn't hundreds. There probably weren't more than thirty."

Nicole was shocked at how small a number it was. "Really?" Sean looked at her. "That few?"

Sean gave a sardonic chuckle. "That was more than enough."

"I would be willing to wager that each life you took was necessary for you to accomplish the missions you were sent on."

"And in your mind, that justifies it."

"What's in my mind doesn't matter."

"It obviously does because you are the one who wants to know." Sean shook his head and looked away from her.

"Sean, I know you don't like to talk about it, and in some cases, you aren't allowed to talk about it. I know you can take a life. I was there when you had to do it." Sean looked at Nicole. "The fact that you aren't proud of it is reassuring to me." She reached over to caress his face. "I have seen how capable of loving someone you can be. When I was in the hospital, and you were at your flat packing for us, your father told me about your childhood. How you rescued animals and how loving you were before your mother died. I didn't see you with Sarah and Kate, but I can only guess that they meant the world to you."

"No," Sean said quickly. "I mean, yes, I loved them." He hesitated. He knew what he wanted to say he had never said to anyone. Did he want to admit it to Nicole? "It was different."

Nicole wasn't sure what Sean meant. "I don't understand. What was different? Was Sarah an agent? Was it all—"

"No, Sarah was not an agent. She was lovely and kind."

"Then I don't understand."

Sean turned so that his whole body was facing Nicole. "I don't know how to describe it. I loved Sarah and was happy with her. I never realized, until I met you, that there are different kinds of love. The way I feel when I hold you when we make love..." Sean's voice trailed off. Was he embarrassed to admit it? Nicole patiently waited for Sean to finish. "When we were in the car, and you were fading, you told me you loved me. And I realized in the hospital, when you were recovering and unconscious, I never told you that I loved you."

"It's OK."

"No, it's not. The nurse wanted me to talk to you and I couldn't. I wanted to scream in agony for what had happened to you. A part of me was dying, torn from me with your struggle for life. I don't know if this is true, but the nurse encouraged me to hold your hand, and when I did, she showed me how your heart rate jumped at my touch. She said it doesn't happen often. Did you even know I was there?"

Nicole moved toward Sean, wrapping her arms around him. Sean accepted her and started to lie back on the couch. She whispered, "Of course I did. It was strange. I could feel your presence in the room."

Sean just held her for a few minutes. "It is different with you, Nicole. I didn't love Sarah the way I love you."

"I know. I've never felt this way with anyone either. I think some people refer to it as soulmates."

Sean chuckled. "I've never believed in that kind of thing. I have seen so much ugliness, how people can be so ruthless that I don't believe there is this thing called a soul." He gently stroked the cinnamon-red hair he had grown to love. He pulled her hair back so he could see her eyes. "All I know is that I want to tell you that I should have said I love you then. I just don't know how to tell you how much I love you."

Nicole gave him a squeeze and moved her head to kiss him. "I feel the same way. You kept me here, Sean. I saw visions Carol and my parents—I wanted to go to them. But I heard you calling me and begging me to stay, and I wanted to be with you more. You have to know that I wouldn't fall in love with someone who is as bad as you make yourself out to be. You have always been a conundrum to me. How you can be ruthless when you need to be. But what you don't know is how ruthless I have had to be in my past. It wasn't easy. I think everyone has things they aren't proud of and I accept that." Nicole gave a little laugh. "Right now, I'm glad you have a gun."

"Maybe I should teach you how to use a gun."

"I don't like those things," Nicole was adamant.

"We'll talk about that later. It wouldn't be a bad idea," Sean suggested. "Right now, though, I doubt you'd be able to stand when you fired it."

"I'm not so sure that's the case," Nicole insisted.

"We'll talk about it later." Sean snuggled her closer. After a few minutes, they both fell asleep.

{II}

Washington, DC

The time had arrived. Jenkins's live appearance on *Newsweek Tonight* was about to start. The day before, Jenkins had discussed his concerns with Senator Mercer. Jenkins felt the network executives could cut the live feed with a simple phone call if they didn't like what was occurring. Senator Mercer volunteered to commandeer the control room, intercepting any calls from the network. Neither were sure what would happen if that phone call came, but Jenkins felt better knowing that Mercer was in attendance.

Harrigan had done his homework and met with Jenkins the day before. There were not going to be any surprises during the interview and Jenkins, although nervous, projected an air of confidence to all he came in contact with prior to walking onto the set.

Arriving on the set amid controlled chaos, Jenkins sat down in the chair that faced Harrigan's empty seat. The sound technician attached the microphone to Jenkins's lapel and adjusted the wire that ran behind Jenkins's jacket and out of the camera's eye. Harrigan arrived, sat down, and the same technician performed the same task on him. Neither man spoke. The crew gave their instructions and left to assume their positions.

"Hello, Senator," Harrigan finally greeted Jenkins. "Are you ready?"

Jenkins smiled. "As ready as I can be."

"Just talk to me," Harrigan coached him. Jenkins acknowledged his comment. "How's Ms. Charbonneau?"

Jenkins looked at Harrigan. "I haven't spoken to her," Jenkins lied easily. "But I'm told she is doing well." Jenkins cleared his throat and leaned in toward Harrigan. "Nikki's condition and the status of our relationship are off limits in this interview. I thought that I made that clear."

Harrigan looked up from his notes. "It's clear. I was just chatting to calm you down," Harrigan straightened his notes. "And your mic is live."

"Meaning what?" Jenkins asked.

"Meaning that everyone in the studio can hear what you are saying," Harrigan informed him.

Jenkins didn't respond. He was aware that his microphone was live from his experience on the campaign trail. He hadn't said anything he didn't want to be heard.

"We're ready to go live in five, four, three..." the stage manager finished the count silently and pointed to Harrigan.

"Good evening and welcome to *Newsweek Tonight*. I'm your host,

Steven Harrigan. Tonight we talk with Senator Robert Jenkins during this historic live broadcast. In addition to his senatorial duties, Senator Jenkins is running for president and is chairing the Select Committee on the Investigation of the Assassination of President Andrews. He is also chairman of the Senate Select Committee on Intelligence. We are very honored to have Senator Jenkins on our show to discuss many topics, most importantly, the historical and unprecedented situation our country finds itself in presently. Welcome, Senator Jenkins."

The red light on the camera that was trained on Jenkins's face illuminated. Jenkins knew he was now on every viewer's television screen. In his charming southern accent, he responded, "Thank you. I'm honored to be here."

"The country is in waters it has never navigated before, if the Sipes confession tape is true. When did you take possession of the tape?"

Jenkins took a deep breath. "I took possession of the tape, or rather it was delivered to me, the day after the murder of Norman Sipes."

"So that was back in November of 1979?"

"Yes."

"Why are we just hearing about this tape now?" Harrigan asked.

"Because of an unfortunate leak to the media, but let me assure you that doesn't mean I wasn't acting upon its information. My office was gathering evidence, myself included, immediately after its receipt. My lead investigator was tracking down sources and gathering financial information of those named in the tape. The accusations made by Mr. Sipes on the tape were extraordinary. Before disclosing it publicly, I wanted some reassurance that the claims were true."

"Do you think you have a pretty good case? Are they true?"

"I think we need more than a pretty good case. As you mentioned, this is an unprecedented situation and to remove a sitting president without incontrovertible evidence would be wrong. This investigation and its findings are setting a precedent that has implications for our country's future. God forbid we have something like this occur again. In some ways, this was almost a coup," Jenkins paused, choosing his next words carefully. "I would like to add something here. When I first viewed the tape, I, like many Americans, was in shock. Almost to the point of, how should I say this, not being able to think or process what I had just witnessed. The thought that someone could be so blatantly cold in their attempt to secure the Oval Office was astonishing to me. The very conception of this plot—" Jenkins stopped and just shook his head. "Words escape me. *Inconceivable* is one word that comes to mind, but that doesn't cover it. With the cold-blooded pull of an assassin's trigger, the vice president and his accomplices allegedly dismissed the Constitution; the very document we are sworn to uphold." Jenkins looked away from Harrigan for a moment. His last statement fanned a flame of anger he had not quite extinguished in the months leading up to this time. He turned his thoughts to the question of the tape's validity. "Having said that, I'm very confident in the evidence we have gathered to prove Mr. Sipes was at the center of this plot and that those he named are also guilty of conspiracy, treason, and murder. As you noted, the process starts tomorrow morning."

"You seem angry, Senator," Harrigan asserted. "Are you?"

"Yes," Jenkins confirmed. "But the time calls for cool heads. This situation isn't the time for politics as usual. We must put that aside, put our anger aside, and do what is just."

"What can the American people expect to see during these

hearings?" Harrigan asked, checking off another question.

"Between being on the campaign trail and my duties as a senator and chairman of this committee, it's been a rather hectic time, so forgive me if I announce something not previously announced—"

"That's what being live on the air is all about, Senator. We hope to bring something new to our viewers," Harrigan interrupted.

Jenkins smiled at his comments. "Yes, well, the committee will call former FBI director Michael Jefferies first to testify. We have deposed Jefferies, and he has confirmed what Sipes has confessed."

"Then why not go directly to trial?"

"There is a process we are bound to follow. We are starting that now, and I would say, based on this evidence, the process will not take very long."

"Is the White House, specifically President Stevens, cooperating with the committee?"

"No," Jenkins declared. "President Stevens has refused to appear before the committee and has been adamant that he was not involved in the plot despite the evidence and the depositions from Jefferies and Davis. We have asked for the deposition of the president, but he has refused."

Harrigan established the tape's delivery to Jenkins and the hiring of the Serpent. Jenkins declined to answer specific questions regarding the hiring of the assassin, noting national security reasons. As for the delivery of the tape, he only noted that a man who previously represented Sipes personally delivered the tape to him. Jenkins also noted that President Stevens knew the man who delivered it.

"Should the average citizen be shocked at the corruption?"

"I don't think the average citizen will be shocked at a corrupt politician. In some instances, you may hear them say that it is more of the same." Jenkins paused. He looked at his watch and realized they were running long on time. He wanted to clarify his last comment. "I mean regarding conspiracies or conspiracy theories, the average citizen may think it is the same; however, I believe this goes beyond theories and does show blatant corruption."

"We need to pay a few bills, Senator. When we return, we'll continue our discussion with Senator Jenkins." The red light on the camera went out, and Harrigan reached down for the glass of water sitting on the floor by the front leg of his chair. He motioned to Jenkins, pointing to the floor by Jenkins's chair. "It's going well."

"Thank you," Jenkins said. He grabbed his own water, took a quick drink, and set the glass back down on the floor.

The stage manager began to count them back into the live program. He pointed to Harrigan as the red light on the camera illuminated again. "Senator Jenkins, some have called for the election to be postponed, citing that these extraordinary circumstances will heavily sway the election. What do you think?"

"I should disclose that I am a presidential candidate in case anyone out there has been asleep for the last few months." Jenkins chuckled along with Harrigan.

"Yes, and you declared your candidacy before this scandal hit. Some say that was an interesting coincidence."

"I have heard the accusations that I planned all of this. Announcing my presidency, then arranging for the tape to be released, and so on." Jenkins paused, trying to find the appropriate words. "Some have accused me of plotting the release of the tape with Ms.

Charbonneau. I did not do that, and in fact, Ms. Charbonneau's decision to release the tape was hers and done so without my counsel, which has resulted in a very painful and, I dare say, permanent end to our relationship. To be clear, I would have continued gathering evidence before I announced this tape to the public. In hindsight, I can't with certainty say when that announcement or the forming of the committee would have occurred. I would have still launched my candidacy. I would have still chaired this committee. The only unfortunate circumstance is the premature announcement by Ms. Charbonneau, who felt it needed to be released as soon as possible."

"Since you brought up Ms. Charbonneau, did you work with her in any way before her making the tape public?"

Jenkins looked at Harrigan, letting some time pass before he responded. "Nikki and I had a disagreement about how to handle this. I respect her decision to do what she did, even though it has cost us both." Jenkins shifted in his chair. "That's all I'm going to say on that."

Harrigan paused. "Senator, when looking into your background in preparation for this interview, I found some interesting information. In fact, you approached me and said you wanted to talk about your service in Vietnam." Jenkins nodded his head. "You told me, Senator, that it involved your Medal of Honor, which you received for the night you lost your lower leg on a Navy SEAL mission."

"That's correct," Jenkins confirmed. He waited for Harrigan's question.

"Would you like to tell us what happened that night?" Harrigan wasn't exactly sure how to start into this portion of the interview.

"I'm not sure where to begin except to say that another colleague has been using this information, lauding it over me for his gain. With that in mind and with good counsel, I decided the only way that this will stop haunting me is to tell the American people what happened that night. May I?" Jenkins felt the need to hesitate, hence the question.

"Yes, of course," Harrigan responded.

"My team was given orders to infiltrate and capture key officials of the Viet Cong. We had intelligence that these high-ranking officials, officers really, were in this particular area. We launched our mission and deployed from a swift boat at the foot of a very tall cliff." As Jenkins started to tell his tale, it reminded him why he wanted to serve his country. His mind took him back to his childhood, particularly, his father spinning the swashbuckling tales of his efforts in World War II. As a young child, he listened with his head resting on the spindles of the stair's handrail. The tale was better than any "B" movie at the theater. His father's tales made war glorious in Jenkins's mind. Only when Jenkins was in Vietnam did he shockingly discover how abominable it truly was. "With water of the river lapping at our shoes, we started our climb. With the climb behind us, we walked a few miles into the jungle, when I came upon a small boy. He couldn't have been over ten years old." Jenkins blinked and swallowed back the metallic taste of adrenaline that was beginning to flow. In his mind's eye, he could now see the images as if it was playing out before his eyes all over again. He paused, trying to gain control of his emotions. "To my utter surprise, he had in his possession an automatic machine gun. He fired first, and the kick of the gun was too much for him to handle. He shot up my lower leg, and I could no longer stand on it. I fell to the ground, bleeding profusely from the wounds, and radioed my second, Lieutenant John Spencer. The medic did some first aid, and I ordered him to go with my other men. Although immobile, I continued to command the raid by radio, and by the time the raid was over, I was about to pass out from the loss of blood. Lt. Spencer found me and carried me to the evacuation rendezvous point, or so I am told. I was not conscious at that time."

"You pretty much just told us what is on your Medal of Honor commendation," Harrigan interjected. Jenkins cleared his throat and repositioned himself in his chair once again. "I can see this isn't easy for you, but there is more. Isn't there?"

"Yes. The boy that I mentioned was a threat to our surprise attack. He ran in the direction of the hooches we were targeting. We couldn't let him report my team's presence to the village or our lives would be in danger." Jenkins was beginning to realize that talking about this out loud was harder than he thought it would be. He tried to keep his composure, but the thought of killing that young boy haunted him every night, even though he did not pull the trigger himself. He brought his hand up to his mouth, his index finger resting on his lips. "He was killed by one of the men in my command."

Harrigan waited for a few seconds, unsure if he should continue. "Were there others?"

Jenkins looked at Harrigan. "Yes. We came across the village—"

"We? You were not with your men. Is that correct?"

"No, I was not physically with my men, but I had radio contact, and I was still in command. So I think of this as my sole responsibility. I take full responsibility for the orders I gave and their execution." Jenkins paused at the words that had just left his lips. "In the village, in the hooches, it was initially reported that only women and children were present. The team gathered them in the center of the village, and questioning began. My men took fire and scattered to take cover. After a short time, we detained four men who had been firing at my men and determined they were the men we were looking for on this mission. The men were extracted from the village, an area of only five or six huts, and taken to the rendezvous point. I was told that Lt. Spencer went looking for me and ordered the others to take the men to the chopper. I was told afterward when we arrived at the chopper, we left. I was taken immediately to a surgical unit and Lt. Spencer accompanied me. When I was in stable condition, he returned to our base camp. I awoke a few days later and found Lt. Spencer at my bedside."

"What did you find out then?" Harrigan shuffled a card and then looked at Jenkins.

"John was a good friend, and he reported that our commander had put in a commendation for the Medal of Honor. The four men we extracted provided key intelligence for an upcoming offensive. It proved to be very helpful."

"But that wasn't all, was it?"

Jenkins swallowed again. "There isn't a day that goes by that I don't wish for a different outcome than what occurred under my command. It haunts me every day. I can't say with certainty who killed those women and children. I did not order their deaths, but I can't be sure during the exchange of gunfire that we did not kill them."

Harrigan paused for a moment. He looked at Jenkins's pained face. "You didn't explicitly order their deaths?"

"No. I did not order their executions," Jenkins repeated.

Harrigan called for another commercial break. During this break, the stage manager approached Jenkins. "Senator Jenkins, I just wanted to let you know that Senator Mercer informed the network bigwigs that we wouldn't be taking the show off the air. It helps to have friends on the Commerce Committee." He paused, then shifted his clipboard to his other hand. He checked his watch. The stage manager then extended his hand. Jenkins took it. "I was in 'Nam. I don't think many will understand the demons we face every day, except for those who served. I watched a nine-year-old, innocent girl walk up to my buddy with a flower. When he reached into his pack to give her some chocolate, she exploded, killing him, and injuring two other of my fellow soldiers. She had no idea that she was a walking bomb. I had no problem killing the son of a bitch that strapped the bomb to her and detonated it. You have my vote, Senator." He turned and walked back to his place beside the monitor while counting down to the live interview again.

Harrigan had a blank stare on his face. In all his years working with the stage manager, he couldn't remember him telling any stories of his service. In fact, Harrigan didn't even know he had served. He turned his attention back to Jenkins. "Senator, the killing of civilians in a war zone isn't new. What I mean to say is that civilians have been killed, not purposely targeted, but it isn't the first time something like this has happened. Why now and why is this so difficult for you?"

"The report that earned me the Medal of Honor was falsified. It was written without my account of the raid and was false in its claim that we did not take one civilian life." Jenkins paused. "My dad served in World War II. I used to listen to his swashbuckling tales peering through the stairs at night when he gathered with his war buddies. John Spencer and I remained close friends until he was murdered. We never talked about Vietnam. All war is awful, and that word doesn't come close to describing it. I don't hear a lot of veterans talk about their experiences in Vietnam. I don't know if it is my generation's way of coping or maybe the wounds are still too fresh. For me, I just couldn't continue to have this lie lauded over me and used to make me do things." Jenkins paused. "Used as a form of manipulation. It's out in the open now, and people can judge me whichever way they want."

"Wait," Harrigan interrupted, blinking his eyes and not sure he heard Jenkins correctly. "Your aide, John Spencer, was murdered?"

Jenkins looked at Harrigan. "Yes, I suppose that is another surprise in this live telecast. I had sent John to the ANWR to gather some evidence for me that the Sipes Oil Company had started to construct and wanted to begin drilling illegally. When he secured the evidence, I ordered FBI director Jefferies to dispatch a plane to bring John and the evidence to me. My new aide and a former FBI agent, Kevin Thompson, managed to find evidence that the director ordered the plane to be deliberately sabotaged. John and the two pilots died in that crash. Mr. Jefferies will discuss this in the committee hearings, and I will be turning that evidence over to the Justice Department and the attorney general for prosecution. What President Stevens and Mr. Jefferies didn't realize was that my ever cautious friend, John, mailed a copy of the information to me. The information John carried with him on the plane went mysteriously missing. As I said, John mailed a copy of the information to me and the Inuit people we worked with also have a copy safely hidden in case something should happen to me."

"Where does this end?" Harrigan asked.

"The tape is just the tip of the iceberg, and now you understand why I asked Ms. Charbonneau not to come forward and to wait until the completion of a thorough investigation." Jenkins looked at Harrigan. "If you were the vice president and you ordered and participated in the plot to assassinate your superior, your commander in chief, wouldn't you go to extraordinary measures to make sure that no one found out? Of course, you would. The only thing these men did not take into account was Mr. Sipes's reluctance to take the fall for all of them. He explains that on the tape."

Harrigan nodded. "Let's go back to your falsified report. Who wrote that report, Senator?"

"My commanding officer, whom we know today as Admiral Jonathan Weston, wrote and submitted the report before I regained consciousness."

"The same Admiral Weston, who is a joint chief?"

"Yes." Jenkins shifted in his chair again, obviously uncomfortable. Before Harrigan could ask the next question, he started, "That was only one inaccuracy in the admiral's report. He also states in this report that these incidents happened in Vietnam—South Vietnam. In truth, this offensive was conducted fully in the country of Cambodia." Jenkins's head began to clear, and he took a quick look at Senator Mercer in the control room. Through the window, he could see that Mercer was on the phone. Jenkins glanced at the stage manager and then looked at the camera and saw the red light still illuminated. They were still on the air.

"Admiral Jonathan Weston was your commanding officer?" Harrigan asked to get Jenkins's attention.

Jenkins looked at Harrigan. "He wasn't an admiral at the time. He was close to being promoted. He was on the fast track, and he wanted to make sure nothing and no one got in his way." Jenkins paused and then asked, "Did you look into the other offensives?"

"Yes, and we talked to Admiral Weston. He denies it."

"I'm not surprised. He would be facing a court martial and instant retribution."

"However, we didn't stop there. We did look into those other offensives you gave me. In all accounts, Admiral Weston specifically states no loss of civilian lives occurred. We spoke with the Vietnamese and Cambodian governments. They are checking into a few of the offensives. There were two on the list that they noted civilian casualties. They have filed a complaint on these two previously and did extensive research to support that complaint. They have, in fact, sent us photographs as proof." Harrigan nodded to Jenkins to look at the monitor. The American public was now witnessing them. "Senator, I'm curious, you are in the middle of a run for president, investigating a sitting president and you are a very powerful member of the Senate. Why come clean now?"

"You make it sound like all of the sudden I'm trying to clear my conscience. I assure you, this is not the case. If you look at any photograph of me from the time I came home from Vietnam until this very day, I have never displayed that medal. In the weeks leading up to my medical discharge, I had tried to return that medal and correct the report. I've never been proud of that mission."

"But you've used it in your campaigns," Harrigan charged.

"Have I?" Jenkins asked. "Other than the fact that I served as a Navy SEAL, which I am proud of, by the way, I made no claim or comment about this mission. I was awarded other medals before that, and I wear those medals. I'm proud of those missions and what we accomplished without loss of innocent lives."

"Hypothetically, let's say you are elected president in spite of all we have learned this evening. Just how are you going to change things?"

Jenkins reached down for the water glass, took a drink, and placed it back on the floor. "That's a very good question. There is so much that needs to happen, and I don't think the American people understand who controls the government. We know, for example, that Joseph Engle, financier and allegedly a co-conspirator according to the Sipes tape, was a huge contributor to the campaigns of many senators and representatives—all legally done I might add. I received no money from Mr. Engle." Jenkins smiled when he said this. "But you can look at various campaigns and determine who owes Engle favors. There are so many things that need to change. Campaign financing is just one of them. It is the reason I don't accept soft money." Jenkins thought for a moment, struggling to answer Harrigan's question without sounding like he wanted to wipe the government clean and start over. "Let me put it this way. I came here today to put something that was wrong, that I did wrong, out in the open so that it could not be held against me any longer. Washington is about power and who controls the power and the powerful. We are dangerously close to losing control of our government to a few nonpoliticians and a few very powerful politicians on both sides of the aisle. If we aren't careful, this place we are at will decay our position as a world power and render us in a caustic internal battle that does no one any good. I want to try to change that course and, short of a revolution, establish campaign finance rules that prohibit large contributions from corporations, individuals, or investment firms—"

"Are you talking about Wall Street?"

"Yes, Wall Street and others. There is a shake-up that needs to occur at the FBI, and a sharper eye kept on the CIA and the NSA. There are things that I'm not at liberty to share, being on the Intelligence Committee, which quite frankly frightens me and also goes to the heart of privacy for our people. If we don't provide some boundaries, future generations are going to pay dearly with a huge impact on their privacy and possibly their pursuit of happiness. We could very easily erode a healthy middle class that is essential for capitalism and democracy to succeed. Our country could become a country of haves and have-nots, with those who have money and power not caring about the plight of those who do not. That is not the America I fought for, and it is not the America my father fought for either."

"Can we expect to see a comprehensive plan from you on what you would do in your first one hundred days of your presidency that would address these issues and more?" Harrigan asked, realizing they were running out of time.

"Oh, I think I can write that up within a couple of hours between the committee hearings." He gave a bit of a laugh, and Harrigan joined him. "Seriously, now that the information that was being used to get someone else's message out there is exposed, you will see a change in my campaign and its message. I will be working on what my first one hundred days would address. However, the most important thing for me and this country is to bring to justice those responsible for the assassination of President Andrews, leaving no stone unturned. His murder is not a pardonable act. If I do one thing right for my country, it is to get to the bottom of this conspiracy no matter what it costs me. As a result of that commitment, you won't see me on the campaign trail this week or in the coming weeks, for however long it takes. The American people deserve a thorough investigation in regards this horrendous act."

Harrigan smiled at how Jenkins sidestepped his question. The show was out of time. Harrigan extended his hand to Jenkins. "Thank you for coming on the show. I wish you all the best in your endeavors."

Jenkins shook Harrigan's hand. "Thank you for giving me the opportunity."

{III}

Washington, DC

The nervous voice of Stevens's secretary greeted vice president Dan Blackwood's abrupt hello, the receiver barely reaching his mouth before she started speaking. "President Stevens is demanding airtime on the major networks to address the nation in regards to Senator Jenkins's live interview," she said, her voice cracking.

Blackwood, formerly the speaker of the House of Representatives before Stevens asked him to be the vice president, was at Blair House where he and his wife had watched the interview. There was no new information shared on the program. Jenkins had prepared him in advance. There was no reason to go on air with a rebuttal. Blackwood sighed. "I assume by the tone of your voice that he is a raving lunatic right now." It was more a question than a statement.

"I've never seen him like this," she said, her voice still quivering. "I don't know what to do, sir."

"I'll be right over. Don't do anything." Blackwood slammed the receiver down, turned, and walked to the foyer. His wife followed him. "I need to go to the White House. I don't know how long I'll be." He opened the door. "Don't wait up," he said as he walked out.

The barrel-chested Blackwood arrived at the Oval Office to greet the president's secretary who was in tears. She had a box on her desk, and she was gathering her personal items.

"What are doing?" Blackwood asked as he approached her.

"He fired me because I wouldn't phone the networks."

"You aren't fired. That's not your job. That's the job of the press secretary. Is he still in there?"

"Yes, should I announce you?"

"No." Blackwood walked to the door of the Oval Office and entered without knocking. "Mr. President, I think it is time you and I had a talk."

Stevens was standing, looking out the window. "I don't want to talk to you. Get out!" Stevens yelled.

"Like it or not, you are going to," Blackwood demanded. Stevens didn't move. "Sit down!"

Stevens turned and looked at Blackwood. "I'm still the president, and you will not talk to me like that." His voice showed the sinister person he could become as he spit out every word.

"You are a murderer, and everyone knows it. You are going to give this office back its dignity by removing yourself, or I, along with Senator Jenkins, will have you forcibly removed. Picture this image: the Sergeant of Arms arrives at the White House with your arrest warrant and then handcuffs you. The reporters are outside as you are taken away from the White House in a squad car to the jail." Blackwood paused. Stevens moved to his desk chair with a defiant look on his face. "That's the way it will happen, Mark. Jenkins has looked it up and so have I. All he needs is the order."

"You're a traitor," Stevens hissed.

Blackwood laughed. "I'm not the traitor. I didn't kill Andrews, you did." Stevens didn't move. His eyes were boring holes into Blackwood. In a strange way, Blackwood felt like Stevens had lost his mind. He stood there, looking at Stevens and wondering what it was going to take to get him to resign. "You can't stay here. You need to step aside. The latest polls are showing that the American people have lost their confidence in you and this office. We are on—"

Stevens stood up and thrust his fists in the air as he shouted, "I am the president, and you will not bully me!" This rant was the beginning of the one that Stevens had held inside for weeks. "I will not let Jenkins remove me from this office. You heard him—he didn't earn his medal. He has no right to judge me. I'll have him locked up. That's what I'll do." Stevens sat back down as he started mumbling details of how to arrest Jenkins. "No, no…I can't have him arrested. He shouldn't be allowed to live. Yes. Maybe it's time to remove him from this all together." Stevens was looking around the room, his eyes searching for someone. They never focused on Blackwood. It was as if Blackwood wasn't there. He just kept murmuring about killing Jenkins and expanded his thinking to the members of the committee. Stevens opened the top drawer of his desk and removed his personal directory. "I should call him now. It takes a while to plan these things out. The sooner, the better—"

Blackwood watched in disbelief. He backpedaled to the door, opened it, and addressed the secretary. "Get his doctor," he instructed. Blackwood closed the door and waited. He continued to watch Stevens unravel before his eyes.

When Stevens couldn't find the phone number he was looking for, the phone number he never had, he started to bang his fist on the desk and then began to have a breakdown. He violently shook his head, and then he said in an evil voice, "He can't do this! I won't let anyone do this! I fought my whole life to be here, and I won't leave. They can't make me leave. Damn Jenkins! Damn that little whore of his! Damn them all! I am not leaving this office."

Blackwood watched Stevens look around his desk again. A few minutes later there was a faint knock on the door. Blackwood walked to the door and opened it. It was the doctor.

"We need to sedate him," Blackwood said, as the doctor entered the room and walked up to Stevens.

Stevens's depression was now showing on his gnarled face. He slumped over his desk, his arms bracing his head. The doctor addressed him. There was no response. Blackwood looked at the secretary, who had entered behind the doctor, and said, "Assemble the cabinet."

As the secretary was leaving the room, Stevens looked at the doctor who was now rolling up the sleeve of his white shirt. "What are you doing here?"

"It's time for your weekly checkup, Mr. President," the doctor lied. Stevens wiped his face with his free hand while the doctor took his blood pressure. "Your blood pressure is high. I think I need to treat that." The doctor looked at Blackwood, who nodded his head. The doctor removed a syringe and a small vial of phenobarbital. He injected the drug and then placed a cotton ball over the injection site. As the doctor secured the tools he had just used, Blackwood opened the door and called for the Secret Service standing outside the door. "I need you to take the President to the private residence—to his bedroom. Stand guard outside it." Blackwood turned to the doctor. "Would you stay for a moment, doctor?"

The unconscious Stevens left the room—just as he said he would leave—carried out feet first as the detail executed Blackwood's orders. The doctor walked up to Blackwood, who started to tell him what he had witnessed. The doctor nodded his head.

"I saw something similar the other day. If you are looking for a medical reason to remove him from office, I'll supply that."

"Thank you, doctor. I think it would be wise for you to be at the president's side in the residence. Keep an eye on him. I'm gathering the cabinet. I may just need that letter." Both men left the Oval Office parting in different directions.

Blackwood waited until the cabinet was gathered in the Roosevelt room before he left his own office. There were a few inquiring comments as Blackwood entered, which he ignored until he reached the head of the table.

"If you will take your seats, I'd like to fill you in on the latest developments." Blackwood waited for everyone to sit down. "President Stevens had a bit of a...well...meltdown. I don't believe he is fit to carry out his duties as president. I rang for his doctor, who administered a sedative. I think we should proceed with his removal from office."

"Can we do that?" one of the cabinet members asked. "I mean, under the Twenty-Fifth Amendment, can we legally do that?"

"It's late, and I've not had the time to write up the necessary letter. I will do that in the morning. But what I need to know is if you will back me in this action. The amendment states that a majority is needed for me to proceed. All in favor, raise your hand."

He didn't need to count the hands; all but a few were thrust high in the air. All were quick to abandon the president now, wanting distance between them and Stevens. Blackwood started for the door. He stopped when he reached it, turned, and said, "This meeting is confidential. You should plan on gathering here at 10:30 in the morning to sign the letter. I'll deliver it to the House and Senate." He opened the door and left the room.

He walked back to his office. He wanted to get a first draft written so that he could review it in the morning. He had a nagging thought that told him to call Senator Jenkins. He reached his desk, sat down, and looked at his phone. Blackwood had worked with

Jenkins on many pieces of legislation and, even though they were in different parties, they worked very well together. Blackwood laughed at the thought that each was open with each other. They both had secrets—everybody did. Maybe they were better at conveying the need without divulging the reason for the stance. He looked at his watch. It was after midnight now, and he wondered if his colleague would mind the late-night phone call. He reached for the phone, only hesitating once. He dialed Jenkins's number and waited.

"Hello," Jenkins greeted the caller. He obviously was wide awake.

"Hello, Bobby," Blackwood said. He took a deep breath. "I saw your interview this evening. That took a lot of courage."

"I don't think courage had anything to do with it," Jenkins retorted. "Besides, I doubt a call this late has to do with the interview."

"It doesn't. I wanted to get you up to date with what is happening here," Blackwood started. "But you have to promise me that you will keep this quiet until afterward."

"After what?" Jenkins asked confused.

"After Congress gets the letter," Blackwood added. "Stevens has cracked up. The doctor is sedating him, and I'm evoking the Twenty-Fifth Amendment to have him removed."

Jenkins sat forward in his favorite chair and placed his glass of scotch on the table next to him, which was helping to soothe the demon that would not let him sleep. "I won't let him bypass the committee by pleading insanity." There was quiet on the other end. "Danny?"

"I understand," Blackwood affirmed. "He's not fit to serve."

Jenkins snickered. "He never was."

"Are you drunk?"

"No," Jenkins started. He wasn't drunk; he just found Blackwood's statement funny. "You have to admit that he was never a great candidate for president."

"Yes, true. Stevens would never have been elected," Blackwood agreed. "Look, Bobby, the doctor is sedating him. To have him removed, I have to say that he is unable to perform his duties because of his heavy sedation. There's no way around this."

"Have him resign," Jenkins blurted out. "If he resigns, he bypasses my committee and spares the Republicans the embarrassment. Your attorney general can then pursue him on conspiracy, treason, and murder charges."

Blackwood thought for a moment. "He'll never sign the letter of resignation."

"He is sedated. Don't let him read it," Jenkins suggested. He took a sip of his scotch.

"That doesn't feel appropriate. You want me to lie to the President?"

"I don't care how insane he is; I will call him in front of my committee. In fact, an insane Stevens appearing before my committee is better for the Democrats." Jenkins waited for Blackwood's response. He heard a heavy sigh.

"I thought we were above this kind of shit," Blackwood bemoaned.

"We're never above this kind of shit," Jenkins responded sardonically. "Resignation is the only way to spare your party more embarrassment than it will receive with Jefferies's and Engle's testimonies."

"What about Davis?" Blackwood asked.

"What about him?" Jenkins returned.

"Are you calling him?"

"Yes, he will appear before the committee as well." Jenkins took another sip and waited.

"I'll see what I can do," Blackwood lamented dejectedly.

"You have to see that this could be worse. Having Stevens resign and pursued outside the office makes it look like your party is trying to do what's right. You'll return dignity to the party quicker if you have him resign." Jenkins was truly trying to help Blackwood's party avoid additional disgrace.

"What if we don't announce the resignation until after some of the testimony is out publicly?" Blackwood asked. "We use your committee to make the case to the American public that Stevens should resign."

"Danny, I'm using my committee to impeach the president and have him tried for murder." He paused a moment. "What are you going to do about the Twenty-Fifth Amendment?"

"I'll work that out behind the scenes. I'll have to tell the cabinet that—"

"You have already informed the cabinet he is under sedation?"

"Yes."

Jenkins let another snicker escape his lips. "You can't wait then. There is no way you can work behind the scenes with the cabinet knowing that you are acting as president."

"I'll talk with you tomorrow, Bobby." Blackwood hung up the

phone. He sat back in his desk chair and brought his hand up to his mouth. He thought about the conversation he had just had with Jenkins. He honestly didn't know what to do and the thought of another person taking the reins—the third president in six months—paralyzed him. Jenkins was right. If the Republicans wanted to salvage anything from this situation, it would look better if they forced Stevens to resign and then pursued him for the murder of President Andrews. It was no secret that Blackwood detested Stevens. The only thing Blackwood couldn't determine was why he was hesitating now. After a few more minutes of contemplation, he took a pen and pad of paper from his top desk drawer. He drafted two letters, both of which invoked the Twenty-Fifth Amendment. One stated that Stevens resigned and the other that Stevens was unfit to act as president. He locked them in his safe and decided he would read them over in the morning. A few minutes later, he left his office for Blair House.

{IV}

Guildford, Surrey, England

Lord Peter Adkins was smitten. He hadn't felt that feeling for a long time. Nicole had entered his son's life, and Peter couldn't be happier. Nicole, in Peter's eyes, was charming and he had to admit that the attention she gave him when he told his stories made him love her too. Their love was different, of course. Peter thought of her as hopefully a soon-to-be daughter-in-law. In truth, the thought of seeing Nicole again always lightened the load of his legislative duties, and even Margaret noticed his mood change when he would talk about her. He wasn't in love with Nicole, he just simply loved her like any father would love a daughter.

His driver stopped at the gate of his Guildford home and announced his passenger to the security guard. The gate had already opened when the guards recognized the car approaching.

After the required check of the car, it rolled up the drive. Peter urged his driver to join him in the house, but he refused. He showed Peter that he had brought lunch and the paper, fancying a sit outside to soak up some of the sun's rays. Peter smiled his approval and walked to the door. He paused a moment, wondering if he should knock on the door of his own house. He gave a few light raps and opened it.

Sean had heard the car pull up and was about to open the door when he heard the raps. He was drying his hands with a dishcloth when the door opened. "Hello, Dad. You don't have to knock. It is your house after all."

Peter smiled. "I didn't want to surprise anyone."

Sean chuckled at his father's insinuation. "Nicole's in the shower. That was something she was looking forward to doing all alone." Sean turned and walked toward the kitchen. "We just finished lunch, but I can fix you a sandwich if you like."

Peter followed him to the kitchen, stopping to put down the two small packages he had brought with him. "No need for you to fix it, Sean. I can manage." He walked into the kitchen and gathered some bread, cheese, fruit, and a glass of water. "How is she?"

Sean turned and looked at his father. He could sense the concern in his voice. He finished drying the last dish and placed it in the cabinet before speaking. "She is doing well actually." Sean closed the cabinet door.

"Honestly, Sean, there is a dishwasher here."

"It gave me something to do." Sean smiled, changing the subject back to Nicole. "Yesterday's journey was more tiring than we thought it would be, and I think she was aching more than she let on to me. She woke up mid-morning, probably due to the painkiller I made her take last night." Sean studied his father as Peter took a bite of the apple. "You know, I don't think I ever saw you act this way with Sarah."

Peter looked at his son. "You know I cared about Sarah and I adored my granddaughter."

Sean acknowledged his father's statements with a crooked smile and raised eyebrows. "But…" Sean said, encouraging his father to continue.

"Well, my son, if you can't admit that Nicole isn't the most enchanting woman you've ever met, then that is not my problem."

Sean laughed at his father's admission. "No worries, Dad. She thinks the world of you as well." He could almost hear the sigh of relief his father exhaled. "Of course, she did say she was a sucker for an English accent." Sean laughed again when he saw an ever-so-slight slump in his father's shoulders.

"All kidding aside," Peter started. "I barely know anything about her. What about her parents and how serious are you?"

Sean shook his head. "Dad, it's not the right time. There are too many unanswered questions to start making regular people plans. I do love her, and she loves me. I'm rather happy about that. Can we just leave it there?"

"I didn't expect you to say that you were ready to get married, Sean. I was just curious how serious you might be."

"They're dead," Sean stated, changing the subject.

"What?"

"Her parents are dead. I don't know how and we don't talk about the past that much." Sean heard the bedroom door open. He turned, looking in the direction of the bedroom. "Dad's here," he called to Nicole.

Nicole emerged from the bedroom a few seconds later, dressed and brushing her long, cinnamon-red hair. "I'm sorry; I didn't hear what you said."

"I said Dad's here."

Nicole smiled as her eyes moved to Peter, who had just finished eating the apple. "Good afternoon, Lord Adkins."

Peter walked toward her. "Why so formal? Give me a hug." Sean shook his head and walked out to the living room. Nicole gave Peter a quick hug, feeling a bit embarrassed. While she adored him and his stories, she continued to keep everyone at a distance. Everything seemed to be moving so fast and she, like Sean, had no desire to analyze or discuss any plans.

"Dad, which of these is the tape of Bobby?" Sean called.

They both walked into the living room. "The one in your left hand," Peter told Sean as he walked to his favorite chair. He placed his plate, which contained some cheese and bread, on the table next to it.

Sean walked up to the VCR located next to the television, turning on both devices. He walked back to the couch to sit down, motioning for Nicole to join him. They sat down, and Sean put his arm around her. Sean picked up the remote and pressed the play button. The television screen came into focus, and the program began.

Nicole was shocked to hear the details of Jenkins's heroic raid. She couldn't imagine living with that nightmare. She had never been in an actual war. She remembered back to that time and the impression she had formed from various news reports. It was not uncommon that people who were considered civilian were Viet Cong soldiers. She thought back to the reports on guerrilla warfare and how it was different in Vietnam. She remembered reporters like Harrigan who were reporting from the trenches. Every night America ate dinner while seeing body bags and the ravages of war on the news. She knew she couldn't judge him, just like she could not judge Sean for the men or women he had killed. She sat quietly when the show ended, deep in her own thoughts. The only thing she knew for sure was that Jenkins was brave to bare his soul on this show and that seeing him speak so candidly made her realize that she still cared for him.

Peter was the first to speak. "That was interesting. What could he possibly hope to gain?"

"Freedom," Nicole replied, still looking at the television, which was now displaying the typical snow that occurred when a tape ended. Sean stood up to turn the devices off.

"Freedom?" Peter questioned.

"He was being blackmailed. Barker was using it to control him. He wanted it to stop," Nicole explained.

"He may have just ended his career," Peter baited.

"No, his advisors threw this story out with the trash," Nicole replied. "The news the committee hearings will generate will keep the focus on Stevens."

Peter smiled. He had wondered how astute Nicole was at politics and he wasn't disappointed. He had talked to Mercer, who happened to be a good friend, the week before. Peter had his answer now. "Very good, my dear."

Nicole looked at Peter, confused by his statement. "You knew?"

"Yes. I'm afraid it is time for me to come clean. I'm very good friends with Daniel Mercer. He told me a week ago what the plan was. I was just curious if you could figure it out for yourself."

Sean laughed. "There was nothing to figure out. We talked to Bobby about this weeks ago."

"So you are still in communication with him?"

"Yes, Dad," Sean confirmed as he sat down on the couch. "Bobby knew we were going to expose the tape even though he said he didn't on the show. We knew he was going to tell this dark secret."

"I see," Peter acknowledged. "Hand me that manila envelope behind you, Sean." Sean gave it to him, and Peter began to open it. "We, or I should say Jack Kensington, have some information on who tried to kill Nicole."

Removing his arm from around Nicole's shoulder, Sean sat forward. Nicole did as well, wondering if Jack had some intelligence that pointed to Jenkins. Nicole's brow furrowed as she waited for the other shoe to drop. She almost couldn't stand it. Peter seemed to be taking his time opening the envelope. Sean sat patiently with his elbows resting on his thighs; well aware of his father's flair for the dramatic. Nicole slipped her arm around the closer of Sean's arms, reaching for his hand. Sean turned his head and kissed her forehead while grasping her hand in his. "Dad, what do you know?" Sean finally asked, hoping to speed the process along.

Peter finished opening the envelope and produced the contents that were inside. He handed them to Sean. Photographs and a typed one-page report, all stamped classified, were paper clipped together. "I know it wasn't Kent who tried to kill you," Peter stated as Sean took the papers.

Nicole was reading the paragraphs along with Sean. When Sean finished the report, he paged through the photographs, all supporting the report's findings.

Sean looked at Nicole. He handed the materials back to Peter. "Are we sure this report is accurate?"

"Jack is very sure," Peter said with a sigh. "It was confirmed by another source who is tracking the Serpent as well."

Sean cocked his head and looked at his father. "Jack doesn't trust Maggie?" Nicole made a face when Sean mentioned Maggie. She recalled the meeting in Charlie's office. Maggie was the agent that MI6 was dispatching to engage and, if MI6 ordered it, kill Kent.

"He didn't come right out and say that," Peter said. "Maggie is a little green, and he wanted her tailed for a while. It evidently has paid off. We know that Kent was in Spain at the time of your attempted assassination. Maggie made her first connection with Kent in Spain and was with him at the time of the attack on you. A bullet found at the scene doesn't match any records of known weapons used by the Serpent. As you can see by reading the report, we don't know who ordered your attack or who wants you dead." Peter finished putting the information in the envelope and put it on the table next to his chair. "We are waiting for the ballistic report, but I'm afraid, other than ruling Kent out, we are no closer to determining who shot you."

"Are you sure that Bobby was the only other person who knew you had a copy of that tape?" Sean asked Nicole.

"Tony knew. Bobby, Tony, and I were the only ones who knew. At that time, we thought Tony was dead. Could Tony have orchestrated this whole thing? Could he have been working with

Stevens?"

"At this point, we can't rule that out," Sean replied.

"No, we cannot," Peter confirmed. "I need to get back. I'll let you know when I hear anything that I think might be of interest." Peter stood, gave both Sean and Nicole hugs at the door, and departed for London.

Nicole sat down on the couch after Peter left. She turned on the television when Sean announced that he was going to have a look around the property and check in with the guards. She flipped through the stations, nothing grabbing her attention until she came upon a news channel that had Senator Brian McNair on the phone. McNair was a familiar figure to Nicole. Tony had represented him in the past and seemed to be friends with him. Not sure why, she listened to the interview with great interest.

McNair was up to his usual tricks, being one of the most vocal Republicans and a staunch conservative. She smirked as the man who was calling for the opportunity for Stevens to explain himself never took the time to inform his constituents of his many sins. There was a reason why she saw him in Tony's office so many times. He was no saint, even though he invoked Christianity at every opportunity.

She only caught the end of the interview. She turned off the television and started to look for the newspaper they had received earlier in the day. She found it on the table behind the couch and began to page through it, trying to acquaint herself with current events in the United States. Her health had prevented her from doing this in the hospital, and she honestly didn't have the desire until now. She chided herself for becoming dependent on others to feed her information. She knew it was time for her to grab her life with both hands and be a part of the decision making. To do that, she had to be knowledgeable. She had to look at the data and make informed decisions.

She found a few articles interesting, and she began to run various scenarios in her head. If Kent had not tried to kill her, who had? This little exercise made her feel empowered. It made her feel like she was getting stronger and she liked that. She continued to search through the paper and contemplate. She started to connect some dots, but there were still holes. She needed additional information—and that was going to take some time.

CHAPTER FOUR

May 1980

Washington, DC

J enkins took a deep breath and exhaled as he gaveled the hearing to order. The only thing he knew for sure was that there was no turning back now. The room was full of spectators, anxiously waiting for the hearing to begin. Some were standing, engaging their colleagues in conversation, while others sat quietly. Between the average Americans, who were lucky to get a seat inside the chamber, a table stood. Glasses encircled the two pitchers of ice water on an otherwise barren table. The confessions of the co-conspirators would originate from here. Located between the table and the committee was the press. Perched above everyone in the room were the committee members. Their perch was intentionally constructed to mirror the superiority their egos demanded. Throughout the hearing, they would be looking down upon the witnesses already prosecuted in the press and deemed guilty. Due process takes many forms.

"The Select Committee on the Investigation of the Assassination of President Andrews is now in session. Before we call our first witness, I would like to address those on the committee, those present in the room, and those of you watching at home. We are at a precarious time in our government's history. The evidence about to be shown and the testimony of our first witness may be distressing. It will cause our nation to pause and ponder its future. It may even cause further distrust of politicians. I am concerned about the toll this evidence will inflict upon the citizens of this great country. I encourage my colleagues to ask questions for the purpose of understanding and of making our government more responsive in and responsible for its actions. We will not be judging these men. This hearing is not a court of law. Gentlemen and Gentlewoman of this committee, we are at the point of a possible revolution. Our constituents are angry. Our nation is divided. It is now up to us to restore our government to one that is truly representative of the people, for the people, and by the people. To the people of this land, you are about to witness a full disclosure of what we consider a matter of national security. However, the need for transparency is vital to building our nation's future. Sweeping the actions of these men under a rug will not be permitted, and we are seeking full exposure. Our dark path cannot be walked down without consequence. For that reason alone, this public hearing is forthcoming. Thank you." Jenkins opened his binder. He took another deep breath. He was about to speak when Senator Brian McNair interrupted.

"Senator Jenkins," McNair started. "May I ask a point of order?"

Jenkins noticed the breach in etiquette in addressing him as a senator and not chairman. He chose to ignore it. Jenkins and McNair tolerated each other. Neither man could stand to be in each other's presence for very long. Hence they hardly ever attended the same function at the same time. To say the men hated each other would be an understatement, but at the same time, both admitted to others that they recognized their love of country and their devotion to their party's ideology. Once, on a Sunday morning political show, McNair even publicly acknowledged Jenkins's love of country. Jenkins remembered the comment, but also recalled how every senator told him about it the next day. McNair rarely had a positive thing to say about any Democrat.

Jenkins turned his head to look at McNair. He wondered if he would regret selecting him for the committee. Jenkins knew that leaving him off would only distract the media and, he wanted the country's full attention on the facts. Jenkins also knew that he would have to address any issues McNair had and decided the best way to manage that was for him to be on the committee.

"The chair recognizes the distinguished Senator from Missouri," Jenkins said with a tone of voice that indicated to everyone in the room the breach of etiquette by McNair.

"Thank you, Mr. Chairman," McNair said, leaning into the microphone. "I assume that the honorable chairman will allow questioning and comments from the rest of the committee, or are we just window dressing?" McNair gave an evil-eyed stare to Jenkins.

"If the distinguished Senator from Missouri is concerned about the ability to address the conspirators in a way that would provide a better understanding of their motives, he shouldn't worry. However, this chair will not condone political speeches designed to devalue the consequences of these gentlemen's actions," Jenkins declared.

"I thought one was innocent until proven guilty," McNair shot back.

"And as I stated in my opening remarks, Senator, this is not a court of law. These men have cooperated with this committee and may face lesser charges for their testimonies here—"

"Has that most gracious offer been afforded our President?" McNair interrupted, trying to purposely irritate Jenkins.

"It has not, and it will not. If you had read the first page of the binder of information given to you a few days ago, you would understand the purpose of this committee is fact-finding. As you know, sir, the legislative branch is not capable of trying an individual. That power falls to the judicial branch of our government." Jenkins sat for a moment. "The question before us is this: is there enough information to impeach President Stevens and recommend to the attorney general that he investigate and charge these men? If you have a problem with that condition as I discussed with each member of this committee before today, yourself included, I wish you would have mentioned it to me then. You are more than welcome to step down from this committee, Mr. McNair, if you can't abide by that."

McNair eyed Jenkins once again. "I was just asking if we were going to be able to cross-examine the witnesses."

"And again, sir, you are confusing the branches of government. This hearing is not a trial. We will not be cross-examining anyone. As stated on the first page, every member of this committee will be allowed to ask questions of each participant."

"My, my, Mr. Chairman," McNair baited. "Already hot under the collar, and we haven't even started yet."

Jenkins smiled. "I'm not hot under the collar, Senator. Piddling around explaining the three branches of government to such a distinguished member of Congress is disappointing. Wasting our time on points of order clearly written on the first page of the information of the binder is indefensible. My only error was believing that you would comprehend it." Jenkins was delighted when the gallery laughed, although he didn't show it. He gaveled a couple of times to regain order. "May we continue?"

McNair nodded his head as he sat back in his chair. Jenkins looked at the back doors of the hearing room and spoke into the microphone.

"This committee asks former FBI director Michael Jefferies to come forward."

The spectators in the room began to mumble. Jenkins gaveled it quiet again. Escorting Jefferies into the room were his lawyer and Thompson, who was trying hard to keep a stoic look on his face, despite the fact that inside he was smiling. Jenkins's eyes followed them both to the table. After delivering Jefferies to the witness table, Thompson moved to an open seat in the first row of the gallery. Jefferies's lawyer stood on his right. He was sworn in and took his seat.

"Good morning, Mr. Jefferies," Jenkins started in his polished southern twang. He addressed him quickly after the solemn declaration as McNair sat forward. He knew McNair wanted to ask why Jefferies was being sworn in and the obvious reason was to ensure that Jefferies would tell the truth. Jenkins didn't want to waste more time over every trivial point that McNair would try to suggest.

"Good morning, Senator," Jefferies answered. He adjusted his glasses, pushing them back up his nose.

"Good morning, Mr. Pruett. I must say I didn't expect you to be making an appearance," Jenkins addressed Tony Shafer's law partner. Jenkins was truly surprised that Pruett was defending Jefferies. In all his visits to the jail, Pruett was never present.

"Good morning, Senator. I realize this may be unusual. I was not available on the days on which Mr. Jefferies needed me, so I sent one of my associates to the depositions. I beg the committee's pardon."

"Are you up to date on all that has occurred and the information sitting before you in the binder?" Jenkins asked. He knew full well that Pruett thought himself above gracing jails with his presence.

"I am, and so is Mr. Jefferies," Pruett confirmed.

Jenkins paused for a moment. "I'd like to start with the playing of the confession tape that Mr. Sipes filmed before his death. From there we will try to establish a timeline with your help. Chris, if you would be so kind as to play the tape." Carrying an envelope that contained the Sipes tape, Chris walked to the television and VCR, which sat on a cart, facing the witness table. He turned both on and waited. "For your convenience, I took the liberty of having what Mr. Sipes says in the video transcribed. The transcript resides on page five of the binder." Jenkins opened the binder to that page and nodded to Chris to play the tape.

Chris took the tape from the envelope and put it into the VCR. He selected the play button, and Norman Sipes's voice echoed in the committee chamber. With each accusation spoken by Sipes, the Republicans on the committee lowered their heads. Jenkins sat back to watch the reactions of those on the committee and those seated in the gallery. The Democrats on the committee were almost salivating at the chance to be the ones to hammer the last nail into the Republicans' coffin. Could America ever trust the Republican Party again? The Republican Party murdered one of their own. Jenkins, however, found his colleagues lust for blood disgusting. If the circumstances were reversed, he knew the Republicans would be unrelenting in their accusations. But Jenkins knew something else that the others seemed to have forgotten. This assassination did not reflect badly on the Republicans only; it reflected badly on all politicians and America as a whole.

The tape came to an end. Chris walked over to the VCR, ejected the tape, and turned the television and VCR off. He placed the tape back in the envelope and walked it back to Jenkins. Jenkins took the tape from Chris, who then sat down behind him.

After the tape had ended, there were some whispers in the room. The tension began to rise as everyone waited for the first of what they thought would be many admonishments. Jenkins sat forward to speak into the microphone in front of him. "If the room would come to order, we'll continue." He waited for the mumbling to subside. "I can't help but notice everyone's reaction to the tape. It doesn't matter how many times you have seen it—what Sipes said and what allegedly occurred are incomprehensible. Yet, President Andrews was assassinated. I want to caution my fellow Democrats and also say to my Republican colleagues that this committee is here to establish the truth and the timeline. We are not here to laud over our colleagues the grievous errors made by a few. As chairman of this committee, I will not stand for rhetoric that implies that the same could not have occurred within any political party in which greed and lust for absolute power command them to such action. Select your questions carefully, committee members, because I will not allow grandstanding or admonishments. The actions of these men do not just reflect on the Republican Party, but they reflect on every politician and this great country. If you feel no shame for what has occurred, then you are part of the problem."

There was one person, sitting in the back, who took the opportunity to start the applause from the gallery. Jenkins quickly gaveled the room to order again, squinting to try and see who had started the applause that engulfed the gallery, but to no avail. He took a drink of water and then glanced around at the committee. His Democratic colleagues were glaring at him with their nostrils flaring. Caught off guard were his Republican colleagues, but they appeared thankful for the admission that either party could be guilty of this injustice. Jenkins also knew that outside this committee room, there would be plenty of opportunity for finger-pointing and admonishing over the months to come.

"Mr. Jefferies, I would like to establish a timeline and a motive for the president's assassination. When were you approached and who approached you?" Jenkins asked.

Jefferies cleared his throat, adjusted his glasses and in a pitch higher than normal, he responded, "I was approached initially by Norman Sipes."

"Initially?" Jenkins questioned. "Please explain."

Jefferies cleared his throat again. "Sipes came up to me at a dinner party. He was drunk and asked if I could get him in touch with an assassin. I didn't think he was serious, so I laughed it off. The next day, fully sober, he called me at home and asked again," Jefferies related.

"When was that?" Jenkins asked. "What day and month?" Chris stood up and placed a note folded in half in front of Jenkins. Jenkins acknowledged it and pushed it aside.

"It was in March of last year." Jefferies pointed to a binder sitting in front of Pruett. "May I consult my notes?"

"Yes, of course," Jenkins confirmed. He took the time to open the folded note. It had the familiar header from Senator Mercer's office. It contained two sentences. "Watch it. You better believe we will be admonishing our friends on the other side of the aisle." Jenkins took great pride in ripping up the note and handing it back to Chris, whispering, "Dispose of that note in the shredder, please." These hearings were Jenkins's hearings to lead. He would run them the way he saw fit.

"Here it is," Jefferies said. "It was Saturday, March 10."

"When did you take this request seriously?" Jenkins asked. He reached for a pen to jot down a note.

"It was a few weeks later. Then Vice President Stevens invited a few friends over to Blair House to watch the basketball tournament. I was asked to stay after the party had broken up along with a few other people. It was then that I was told to find an assassin that Sipes could contact. The date was around March 24."

"Who gave you that direction—to find an assassin?" Jenkins asked.

"It was Vice President Stevens," Jefferies replied quickly, clearing his throat again, his nervous habits proving annoying to all who had to watch him.

"Who else was in the room at that time?"

"Stevens, Sipes, Davis, Engle, and me."

"Was a reason given as to why they wanted the president assassinated?" Jenkins asked.

Jefferies looked over his personal notes. "At that time, I don't believe there was one specific reason given."

"You didn't ask?" Jenkins looked at Jefferies. His brow curved downward presenting a rather confused look on his face.

"No sir, I didn't ask. I was stunned and couldn't believe what I was hearing. I waited until everyone had left and then I asked Stevens if he was serious or if he was just placating Sipes. In other words, I wanted to give him the opportunity to tell me not to do such a thing."

"Did that happen? Did President Stevens tell you not to find an assassin?" Jenkins leaned forward.

Jefferies bowed his head. "No."

"I'm sorry, I didn't hear you. Please speak into the microphone," Jenkins instructed Jefferies.

"I said no, it didn't happen."

"When was the reason given to you—the reason they wanted the president killed?" Jenkins asked again.

"I believe it was in June. I didn't follow up on finding an assassin until then. At that time, President Andrews had started to change his positions on key legislation. For instance, Andrews was starting to change his mind on the act that would allow drilling in the ANWR. He was for it initially until he made a trip there."

"That was the only reason?"

"No, that was Sipes's and Engle's reason. That was part of the reason for Stevens too. He and Engle, they owned a large share of stock in Sipes's company. Stevens, however, knew that Andrews would run for reelection and Stevens knew he couldn't challenge a sitting president. He looked at it as a way to show the public how good he could be as president. If he had to wait to run until after Andrews termed out, he felt that it wouldn't be a sure thing for him to be elected president after eight years of the same party."

Jenkins closed his eyes trying to follow Jefferies's accusations. When he opened them again, he asked, "Are you telling us that Stevens felt that if he had Andrews assassinated and finished out Andrews's term as president, that he would assuredly win the election?"

"He didn't say that in so many words, but, yes, he felt that way," Jefferies confirmed.

More mumbling swept through the gallery. Jenkins picked up his gavel, striking the pad to silence the voices. He quickly formed his next question. "Did you then search for an assassin and make the first contact with that person?"

"I never spoke with the Serpent—that was the assassin who was hired."

"Who did the actual hiring?"

"Norman Sipes," Jefferies stated. "He made all the arrangements and payments."

Jenkins swallowed. "Do you know what the Serpent's fee was?"

"It was hefty. Since the Serpent had never traveled to the United States, he asked for a million dollars." There was another reaction from the gallery.

"Was that fee split among all five accomplices?" Jenkins asked.

"Objection!" Pruett yelled.

Jenkins smiled and tried not to roll his eyes. "This isn't a court of law, Mr. Pruett."

"I don't like the inference of the word accomplice," Pruett stated firmly.

Jenkins didn't hesitate. "Aiding a person who commits a felony is punishable by the law and could be construed as an accomplice depending upon how much aid the person provided. If Mr. Jefferies provided the contact information of the assassin who killed the president, I would say that he aided them in a very thorough and successful way. Would you prefer coconspirator?"

Pruett seemed to sink into his chair. Jefferies leaned over to him. Pruett sat up and put his hand over the microphone while Jefferies asked his question and Pruett provided his counsel. Satisfied,

Pruett removed his hand, and Jefferies provided his response. "No, it was not split between all of us."

"Who did not participate in the funding of the assassin?" Jenkins's hand was poised to flip to another marked section of his binder.

"I did not," Jefferies stated.

"Are you sure about that?" Jenkins asked. He flipped to the section of the binder that contained a copy of Jefferies's bank account statements. "If you would turn to page thirty-five, you will find a withdrawal from your account of $200,000 on November 7, 1979."

"Yes, that's right," Jefferies confirmed without hesitating. "That money was given to my daughter for a down payment on a house."

Jenkins looked at Jefferies. "You gave your daughter $200,000 cash?"

"Yes," Jefferies replied.

"Were you compensated in any way for your help in contacting the Serpent?" Jenkins asked. "And by the way, that was a very nice gift to your daughter." Jenkins didn't believe it. He spun his chair around to instruct Chris to follow up. Chris left the room to make a few phone calls.

"I don't consider that I was, Senator."

"Please explain that."

"I was given a large amount of preferred stock options in the Sipes Oil Company. Those options and certificates are worthless today."

"But had you and the other accomplices succeeded, and if Sipes Oil Company had started drilling in the ANWR, those options and certificates could have become a small fortune. We both know ANCILA is making its way through Congress again and it is scheduled to be on the president's desk before November. Do you still have the certificates?"

"Yes, they are in my safe deposit box."

"Is it safe to assume that all five of you did not pay equal shares for the assassin's services?"

"They did not. As I told you, I didn't pay any money. Engle's did pay some, and so did Davis. I'm not aware of President Steven's participation, if he did at all."

"Don't worry, we'll find out," Jenkins replied. Laughter came from those sitting in the gallery. Jenkins looked at his watch. Chris returned with a couple of notes for Jenkins to read. "Excuse me one second." Chris handed him the notes. The first was that, indeed, Jefferies had helped his daughter buy a house, and the second was that Mercer requested all senators to be present for a vote in fifteen minutes. The vote had nothing to do with the hearings; it was a vote on Veterans' benefits. Jenkins swung his chair around. "I have one more question. Was your involvement only to provide Sipes with a name of the assassin? In other words, you did no further planning on the day on which the assassination would occur?"

"That's correct. After supplying the name to Sipes, I did nothing further. Sipes felt a need to keep me informed, but I offered no other assistance," Jefferies replied. He seemed proud that he had done nothing else.

Jenkins noted his attitude. "That may not make you any less guilty, Mr. Jefferies." There were a few chuckles. Jenkins looked at the committee members. "Senator Mercer has sent a note that an important piece of legislation is about to be voted on and has requested our presence in the Senate chamber. Mr. Thompson, please escort Mr. Pruett and Mr. Jefferies to a secure location. This committee will resume in twenty minutes." Jenkins struck his gavel twice before he stood up to leave.

{II}

New York City

Harrigan was filling a box with his personal items when his phone rang. His first inclination was to just let it ring. He didn't want to have another conversation about how what the network was doing was wrong or how proud someone was that he had stuck to the journalist code to expose the truth. His superiors had betrayed him. He had no doubt that Operation Mockingbird, in some form, was alive and funded handsomely. He was not an untouchable. He crossed his management, and no one likes a rogue reporter. He expected his fate, and he accepted it.

On the seventh ring, he picked up the phone. "Steven Harrigan," he spat out.

"Want to get back in the game?" A woman's voice asked.

"What?"

"I said, do you want to get back in the game?"

"Who is this?" Harrigan's interest was piqued. The voice was intentionally seductive yet sounded familiar.

"Hmm, I'm not sure I want to tell you that right this minute," the woman teasingly replied. "Are you still employed by CBS?"

"No," Harrigan said. "In fact, I'm packing up as we speak."

"Good," came the response. "You have nothing to lose then."

Harrigan was getting a little irritated. "You think?"

"I don't want to talk on this phone. Go to the Waldorf Astoria and ask for your room key. I'll call you there in an hour." The woman hung up the phone.

Harrigan looked at the phone. He depressed the buttons breaking the connection and dialed the operator. "Yes, this is Steven Harrigan. Is there any way to tell where my last phone call originated?" The reply was no. "OK, thanks." He quickly finished his packing and left for the Waldorf Astoria hotel.

With only a few minutes to spare, Harrigan walked into the room that had been reserved for him. Elegantly decorated, the small room seemed to glitter. He set his box on the bed and sat down waiting for the phone to ring. He wondered if he was being foolish. He wondered if he was being set up. Was someone out to kill him? He started to get nervous, and he glanced at his watch. Almost exactly sixty minutes from the last call, the phone rang. He grabbed it on the second ring. "Hello?"

"I see you are interested in getting back into the game," the same woman's voice said.

Harrigan was trying to place where he had heard the voice. "I am interested in what you have to say. I'm also curious if I have to pay for this room."

"No. It's our treat." The woman cleared her throat. "I have some information that you might find useful. Are you willing to track some leads down and make some waves?"

"Yes," Harrigan replied. "Am I going ever to know who I'm talking to?"

The woman ignored the question. "Brian McNair."

"What about him?"

"McNair was cleared of any wrongdoing in the attempted murder of a prostitute in November of 1979. He never appeared in court; it was all handled in the chambers of the judge. He also was cleared of illegal drug use related to the case."

"Why are you telling me this?" Harrigan asked. "Who are you?" There was silence. "Look, I have no affiliation with any news agency. I doubt anyone would believe me. I need to know who you are. As a source, I would protect your identity." The line went dead. "Hello?"

{III}

Guildford, Surrey, England

Sean had returned from a quick dash to the grocery store earlier in the day. Now, Nicole was sitting on the couch watching the second day of Jenkins's committee hearing live on the BBC. Sean was preparing their dinner when the phone rang.

"Nicole, would you mind answering that? My hands are full. It's probably Dad," Sean called from the kitchen.

Nicole stood, turned the volume down on the television and hurried over to the phone. "Hello?" she said standing in front of the table behind the couch. She waited to hear a voice on the other end. "Hello?"

Sean noticed Nicole's confusion. He grabbed a dish towel and began to wipe his hands. As he walked to the living room, he heard Nicole's next response.

"How did you get this number, Kent?" Nicole asked. She felt the grasp of fear catch in her heart and throat. She heard Sean quicken his pace to her.

Taking the phone from Nicole, Sean listened to Kent's response.

"The first attempt on your life was clumsy. So clumsy that now there is more than just one person who wants you dead."

"Is that so," Sean said calmly. "Tell me, Kent. How long did you work for the Serpent? Or should I say Saverio as we knew him? All those years that you pretended to be my best friend, was that all an act?" Saverio was the Serpent's given name.

"I should have known you would be by her side," Kent returned, ignoring the questions.

"And did you help Saverio murder and mutilate my wife and child?" Sean shot back. Nicole looked at Sean with concern in her eyes. Sean put his arm around her and pulled her to him. He looked out the window, noticing the absence of the guards.

Kent was quiet for a moment. "I'm not the only one who wants your new love dead." Kent enjoyed playing mind games. He looked at his watch, calculating how much time he had left to speak.

Sean knew Kent better than he knew any other assassin. Kent's mind games were nothing new to him and not up to the torment Saverio could inflict. "Who might you be referring to?"

Kent laughed. "You know the Serpent never tells who he kills for and you know he kills in many ways."

Sean still didn't see any of the guards. There was no movement at all. Then he saw it: the front gate was slightly ajar. Sean's instincts told him to duck. He dropped to the floor, taking Nicole with him, shielding her with his body as he rolled them as close to the couch and under the table as he could. Only a few seconds later a small, loud, and effective bomb exploded, shattering the glass window and blowing open the front door to the cottage. The curtains around the window caught fire.

Sean cursed as he realized he had left his gun in the kitchen. He looked at Nicole, whose eyes were wide open with fear. Both their ears were ringing, and both were shell-shocked. Sean looked around, wondering if Kent might be making an entrance through the front door. He shook his head to try and rid himself of the irritating ringing in his ears and clear his head. Slowly, he stood up and surveyed his surroundings. He motioned to Nicole to stay where she was. Kent was not in the house. He walked cautiously to the kitchen to retrieve his gun and holster. He shook his head again while he put it on and walked back to Nicole. He helped her up, and they moved quickly to the carport through the kitchen. The fire was spreading to nearby furniture and up the wall. Smoke was beginning to billow out of the shattered window and throughout the room. Just before exiting, Sean grabbed their jackets from the pegs that hung next to the door.

When they got outside, the ringing in Sean's ear started to subside. He could hear the police sirens in the distance, and they were closing in fast. They moved to his car and then he thought better of it. "No, don't touch the door!" he shouted to Nicole, stopping her hand. "If he isn't here, he could have rigged the car, knowing we would try to flee in it. This way," Sean said, taking her hand in his as he quickly walked through the back gate of the property. They reached the sidewalk and Sean turned away from the crowd that was gathering. "We need to find a phone."

Nicole held Sean's hand tightly as they wandered the streets of Guildford looking for a phone. News trucks were starting to arrive as they rounded a corner and a familiar red phone booth stood before them. Sean reached into his pocket and produced some change. He brought Nicole close to him in the booth without closing the door. He deposited the coins and dialed his father's office. "Margaret, it's Sean."

"Oh thank God! Jack called us and said you weren't at the

cottage." She exclaimed, indicating some time had passed. Sean had lost all sense of it as they walked through the streets. "Your father is beside himself. I'll put you through."

"Sean!" Peter exclaimed, the relief evident in his voice. "How are you? How is Nicole?"

"We're fine," Sean informed him. "Dad, I need a car."

"What's wrong with yours? Where are you?" Peter asked, confused.

Sean was looking around to gather his bearings. "I don't know if my car has been wired to explode." Sean turned, looking behind him. He noticed the train station located in the next block. Peter was firing questions that Sean neither took notice of nor answered. "Listen, there's a train station just down the street. We're going to take the first train out of here. I'll be in touch."

"Yes, of course. We'll wait for your call," Peter responded to an already dead phone line. He hung up the phone and looked at Margaret who was now standing in front of his desk. "I'm not good at this," Peter told her, wrought with worry.

"Let's go." Sean put his arm around Nicole as they started for the train depot. All of his senses were on edge.

As they got to the station, Sean could see two police cars rounding the corner. He realized that the police's assumption would be that the IRA was behind the bombing. The logical next step would be to secure the town and stop any trains from leaving the station. Sean quickened their pace. When they entered the station, Sean hurriedly looked at the board to see which train was about to leave. He grabbed Nicole's hand, and they dashed through the station to the appropriate platform. Nicole was breathing hard, but the adrenaline in her body from the bombing was still pumping, motivating her every step. Sean could tell she was still dazed. As they reached the top step of the platform, Sean saw the conductor starting to board the train. He quickened his pace. Nicole struggled to keep up. He reached the door, letting go of Nicole's hand momentarily. As he opened the door, the train started to move. He hopped on board, keeping the door open with his body as he turned. He reached for Nicole's hand, noticing that she was starting to fall behind as the train gained speed. He leaned farther out the door, snatched up her hand, then her arm, and quickly pulled her up to him. With Nicole now in his arms, he turned, allowing the door to close. After a few seconds, he lifted her head to look into her eyes. "Are you hurt?"

"No," Nicole replied. "You?"

"I don't think so." Sean looked around. "Let's go sit down." They moved to two open seats.

"Sean," Nicole whispered. "We don't have tickets."

"We'll buy them from the conductor."

"Kent," Nicole muttered.

"Not just Kent," Sean lamented. "I'm not sure who else, but he made it clear that someone else wants us dead."

"Us?" Nicole questioned. "Or just me?"

"Us," Sean confirmed. "Because they won't get to you without killing me first."

The conductor appeared at their seats. "Tickets," he said reaching out his hand.

"I need to buy two, please," Sean said.

"How far are you going?" The conductor asked.

"That depends," Sean started. "Where is the end of the line?"

"Edinburgh."

"Does it stop in London?" Sean inquired as he reached for his wallet.

"Only for a few minutes to take on some passengers."

Sean acknowledged the conductor's response. "Two for Edinburgh." Sean paid the fee, and the conductor handed him two punched tickets. The conductor tipped his hat and moved on to the next person.

When the train pulled into the London station about an hour later, Sean woke Nicole who had drifted off to sleep. They stood and exited the train. When they were in the hustle and bustle of the station, Nicole asked, "I thought we were going to Edinburgh."

"That's what I hope Kent will think in case someone saw us in the train station," Sean explained as they headed for the door. "We're going to catch a taxi to Dad's and then figure out where we go to next."

"Won't Kent think we would go to your…"

"With the bombing of Dad's home, there will be so much security around him that we won't have to worry about that." Sean waved down a taxi when they got outside. As he opened the back door for Nicole, he added, "I'm just glad bomb-making is not one of Kent's strong points."

"You think he's in England then?" Nicole asked as she slid across the backseat of the taxi.

"I don't know," Sean was clearly frustrated at his lack of intelligence on Kent. "That's something I'll have to ask Jack." He leaned forward to speak to the taxi driver and rattled off his father's address.

Sean told the taxi driver to pull over a few blocks away from Peter's home, and paid him as they exited the cab. As anticipated, security guards surrounded the flat. A guard approached them from a block away. After a few checks, Sean and Nicole were allowed to pass and enter the house.

Sean and Nicole walked into the living room. Peter stood and greeted them both with hugs. As Peter hugged Nicole, she remembered fondly the story Peter told about his wife, Brighid. It seemed like it happened yesterday. A smile briefly crept across her lips. Now, she felt she was always on the run.

"Do you have some headache powder?" Sean asked Peter. "I have a headache from the blast." He looked at Nicole, realizing her pain medicine was back in Guildford. "How are you feeling?"

"My ears are still ringing a bit. I think I could use some aspirin too," Nicole said as Peter went in search of the headache powder. He returned with the powder and two glasses of water. Aspirin in powder form was a first for Nicole, so she watched Sean, following his lead.

Sean drank down the headache powder solution in one gulp. He looked at Nicole who was hesitating. "It's better if you take it all in one shot."

"Would you like more water?" Peter asked them, standing up.

Nicole downed the solution as instructed then made a rather funny face as a result of the sour taste. "Yes, please," she was able to choke out. Nicole's face looked like she had just sucked on a lemon. "I think I like the pill form better." She and Sean handed Peter their glasses.

When Peter returned from the kitchen, Sean asked, "Dad, who knew we were at your place in Guildford?"

"I've been thinking about that. Aside from Geoffrey and Jack Kensington, no one else knew. Of course, I have no idea if Jack told anyone else."

"Then I'm going to need to talk with Jack in the morning," Sean said as he tilted his head back to rest it on the couch.

"What happened Sean?" Peter asked.

"Kent called just before the bomb went off. Since the bomb was outside the front door and window, I can only assume he meant for us to run to my car and get in, and that is where he meant to kill us. The bomb in front of the house wasn't strong enough to hurt us." Nicole looked at Sean with disbelief written on her face. Sean saw her look out of the corner of his eye. "It wasn't. It was meant to scare us."

"It accomplished that," Nicole replied.

"I'm just glad my head cleared fast enough to realize that car was the real trap."

"Well," Peter started. "Evidently you were right. A short while ago, the Guildford Police called to report that the car in the carport was indeed wired to explode. They did a controlled detonation on it before they called me."

"Great," Sean quipped, perturbed that they had destroyed his car. "Now I need a car and to talk to Jack."

"He called here this morning with a piece of news that I was to pass on to you." Peter stood and walked over to a cart where he kept his liquor. He opened the gin bottle and poured three glasses of straight gin. He didn't add any ice or tonic. He handed Sean and

Nicole each a glass. "You may need this." Peter sat down and took a drink. "The US Government ordered Nicole's assassination attempt. It's been confirmed."

"Who?" Sean asked without skipping a beat.

"It wasn't Stevens if that's what you are thinking."

"No, I wasn't thinking that," Sean denied, irritated and not interested in a guessing game. "Just tell me who ordered it."

"The evidence seems to be pointing to Senator Jenkins," Peter said looking at Nicole.

Nicole set her glass down on the table without taking a drink. "I want to see the evidence."

"I'm afraid that can't be done. It's highly classified. I haven't even seen the report," Peter confessed.

She looked at Sean. "I'm a lawyer. I've worked on murder cases, some of which were pretty gruesome. I know when someone is concocting evidence. I'm sorry, but I can't believe that Bobby would want me dead." She paused. "If I can't see the evidence, then I want to talk to Bobby directly."

"I'd like to see that evidence as well, Dad," Sean chimed in.

"Why don't you call Jack? Maybe he can tell you the whole story," Peter said.

"It's rather late," Sean said, raising his head off the back of the couch to look at the clock.

"I'm sure he is up," Peter said.

"Fine," Sean replied as he stood and walked over to the phone. He dialed Jack's number. "Hello, Jack."

"How are you, Sean?" Jack asked. Sean assured him they were fine. "Do you have any idea who set the bomb? Do you think it was the IRA after your father?"

"No, we know it was Kent. He called right before the explosion." Sean paused. "I doubt he is in England unless you know something that would say otherwise." Sean's tone reflected the frustration he was feeling.

"I've no data that would suggest that Kent is here. He is too well-known here. Maggie is due to report in the next day. We'll get that confirmed."

"I agree that Kent is too well known to security forces to come here himself. If he had a strong enough network to bust him out of England, that network is strong enough to do his dirty work here." Sean paused for a brief second. "Who put out the hit on Nicole?"

"Evidence is strongly pointing to Senator Robert Jenkins," Jack replied flatly. "I won't share the report until I have a second confirmation but the sniper was military. Sean, we've seen this sniper before," Jack explained some of the sniper's history and that he was waiting for additional information. "Some of this is sketchy, so that is why I'm asking for more information."

"That's it?" Jack confirmed it was all he was going to share at this time. "Ok, thanks. I'll be in touch."

"Who?" Nicole asked.

"They waiting for additional information, but the order seems to have come from the military."

"The military?" Nicole questioned. "I don't understand."

Sean cleared his throat. "Jack said the sniper was military. This particular sniper has been used by the United States before. He usually works in the Middle East. Jack said he is waiting for more details. He's waiting to hear back from the CIA now that they have the tests that match the bullet to that sniper's gun. Given the history and the circumstances, they are beginning to believe that there is evidence that points to Bobby."

"I won't believe that," Nicole said. "I can't believe that."

"He has the access, Nicole," Peter added. "It could have been a joint decision. With all the chaos in your government right now, something like this could've easily slipped through."

Nicole shook her head. "It could just as easily be Stevens."

"It could," Sean said. "We'll just have to wait more information."

"Are they going to ask Bobby directly?" Nicole asked.

"I'm not sure how they will confirm it," Sean conceded. "They could. It all depends on how cooperative some people want to be."

"Can't we just call Bobby?" Nicole questioned, almost pleading.

"No," Sean stated. "We need to find safe haven now that Kent is back on our trail. It's late. SIS will do what they can to find out who was behind it. We need to focus on keeping you alive."

"You know I don't like that plan," Nicole said.

"I know," Sean replied. "But I'm not risking a phone call to Bobby if he is indeed the one who ordered it."

"It's not him," Nicole declared. She stood, walking to the stairs. "I know it isn't him." It was the only defiant comment she could make as she ascended the stairs. She was confident that Jenkins had not ordered her assassination.

{IV}

Washington, DC

It was midmorning when minority whip Ron Sullivan, a Democrat from Massachusetts, entered the House of Representatives. He had met with Jenkins the night of the first day of the committee hearings, and the two formed a strategy. The men knew what to do, and that timing was critical. Blackwood had not delivered the letter announcing that Stevens was invoking the Twenty-Fifth Amendment as he had informed Jenkins the previous Sunday night that he would do. Jenkins called in a few favors that kept Blackwood busy. Now it was Representative Sullivan's turn to capture the attention of the House. Sullivan walked to his desk in the chamber and motioned to the Chair. Recognized by the Speaker, he began his speech.

"I urge the Speaker to invoke the Articles of Impeachment," Sullivan demanded. "As I have told the Speaker in his office, I know that Senator Jenkins is dispatching the Sergeant at Arms with a subpoena for President Stevens to appear before his committee. Ex-Director Jefferies has implicated Stevens in, dare I say it, a coup orchestrated by your party." There was a negative reaction from the Republicans who were on the House floor. Ron Sullivan was an experienced member of the House of Representatives, having served for five terms. He was eyeing a seat in the Senate and was all too happy to help Jenkins lower the boom on the other side of the aisle. If Sullivan could keep the heat up on the House floor, Jenkins promised his support when the term of the junior senator from Massachusetts was up for reelection.

The Speaker of the House, just newly appointed due to Blackwood's ascent to fill the vacant position of vice president, smacked his gavel on its pad. "Order," he called as he gaveled again. Once quiet, the Speaker began. "As the gentleman knows a resolution needs to be drafted and deposited in the hopper. Does the gentleman have a resolution?"

Sullivan lifted a trifold document. "I do," he said before he walked to the hopper. He deposited the resolution into the hopper and then walked back to the podium closest to him. "I would urge the Speaker to quickly advise the House Judiciary Committee, that they have an urgent investigation to conduct. I'm sure the Senate Select Committee on the Investigation of the Assassination of President Andrews would be happy to share its findings." Sullivan waited as a few Democrats laughed at his suggestion. "Given the nature of this rare situation we find ourselves in, we may want to dispense with the usual process. No one can deny what has occurred."

The Speaker gaveled the chamber to order once again. "I understand the urgency that this resolution requires and will now meet in committee to determine the appropriate process." The Speaker leaned over to one of the clerks and instructed him to retrieve the resolution from the hopper. The clerk then handed it to the Speaker. "The Speaker summons the chairman of the House Judiciary Committee to accept, investigate, and return its findings to this body as quickly as possible." The chairman of the committee rose and accepted the resolution from the Speaker. He then left the chamber to call his committee into session. The remainder of representatives returned to their offices to prepare their speeches.

Sullivan walked out of the House and was greeted by one of his aides. "Go tell Jenkins that the resolution is in committee and the process of impeachment has begun." The aide dashed off to do as instructed. Sullivan walked quickly back to his office and waited. There was nothing else for him to do. Every Democrat in the House of Representatives wanted Stevens impeached, removed from office, and tried for his crimes. There was no whipping of votes needed. Sullivan had no doubt his Republican opponents wanted this process to end as quickly as possible so that they could move on to rebuilding their party and repairing the damage done by one sociopath.

Sullivan's aide entered the committee room and whispered in Chris's ear. Chris acknowledged the aide and dismissed him. He opened his notebook, wrote down a message, ripped the paper from its bindings, and folded it. He inched forward and touched Jenkins's arm. The senator turned his chair slightly and took the note from his aide. He opened the note and saw the words: *Sullivan did it. The impeachment process has started in the House.* Jenkins folded the note and deposited it into his trousers pocket. Members of the committee were taking turns questioning Jefferies, who in turn thwarted every attempt to trip him up. Jefferies simply told the truth. Hearing the truth spoken was annoying enough, but having it done with Jefferies's nasally voice and other irritating nervous habits was almost unbearable for some to endure.

Jenkins listened to a few more questions and then turned back to Chris. In a whisper, he asked, "Did the Sergeant of Arms deliver the subpoena yet?"

"He left thirty minutes ago, immediately after I handed it to him," Chris confirmed.

"Thank you," Jenkins said. After Jefferies had responded the last question, Jenkins leaned forward to the microphone. "Gentlemen and Gentlewoman, I believe we have asked as many questions in as many different ways as possible. I believe his role and the order he gave is crystal clear. I want to inform the committee of two things. The first is that the House of Representatives has started the process of impeachment of President Stevens. The second is that President Stevens is being served a subpoena to appear before this committee." There were a few members of the committee who started to voice their disapproval of Jenkins's actions. "Looking at the hour, I suggest we break for lunch before we resume the hearing. This afternoon, we'll call Representative Davis. Mr. Jefferies, thank you for your honesty and your patience. Mr. Thompson will escort you back to prison." Jenkins gaveled the committee to a close. He stood up and stretched before he gathered his binder and a legal pad. He walked out of the committee room and back to his office pleased with how the events were unfolding.

Jenkins was surprised to see Harrigan waiting for him when he arrived. He shook Harrigan's hand and invited him into his inner office. "I know Chris called you, but you didn't have to come over," Jenkins said as he closed the door to his office.

"I know," Harrigan said. "I told Chris that I wanted to talk to you in person. He didn't think you would mind."

"I don't mind at all," Jenkins confirmed.

"I suppose you called because you heard I am no longer employed."

"Yes," Jenkins confirmed. "I have a call into Theodore Warner. He's starting an all-news network. I know they would love to have you be a part of it."

Harrigan smiled. "How do you know that?"

"You would give them credence. You would also be a great role model for the young reporters they will inevitably be hiring. Frankly, they could use your expertise and experience."

Harrigan thought it was very nice that Jenkins cared enough to try and find him another job. "You know this wasn't your fault. You don't need to do this."

"What we did didn't help you," Jenkins responded. "I'm setting up an interview for you. Go to it; don't go to it. The decision is yours. If you do go and get hired, there are no strings attached. I won't call in any favors in the future. You owe me nothing." Jenkins noticed Harrigan's surprise.

"I find that hard to believe."

Jenkins wanted to laugh but didn't. "I appreciate what you did, and you can take what I said to the bank—I meant it. I will defend the freedom of the press as long as it is fact-based, researched appropriately, and presented to the masses without bias or opinion."

"Not many feel like you do, Senator," Harrigan admitted. "Thank you." He paused and fidgeted in his chair. "Senator, I received the most curious call. I trust I can keep this between us?"

"Of course," Jenkins assured him.

"A source gave me some information on McNair that I am researching. Do you think that Mr. Warner would be interested in being the first news network to report my findings?"

"That depends on what you were going to report. Does it have something to do with me in some rather backward way?" Jenkins gave a little laugh considering what they had just discussed.

"I'm not sure. What do you know about McNair?" Harrigan asked.

"That he's a pain in the ass," Jenkins quipped without hesitation. "I trust that comment was off the record."

"You aren't the first to say that. According to my source, McNair was cleared of attempted murder and an associated illegal drug use charge. I can't find anything on it in the usual places," Harrigan spat it out. He somehow felt saying it as quickly as possible would make it seem true. Jenkins didn't show any reaction, which scared

Harrigan more than any other possible reaction Jenkins could have had. "Do you have any idea where I could go looking?"

Jenkins's eyes were darting about as it processed the many thoughts that were flashing through his mind. "Did the source say I was connected?"

"No."

"I see," Jenkins replied. "I need to think about this. I have no knowledge of McNair's indiscretions. However, I might be able to ask a few questions of a trusted colleague. It would be off the record of course."

"Of course," Harrigan confirmed. He stood up. "If you talk with Mr. Warner, tell him I would like to speak with him." He extended his hand.

Jenkins stood and shook Harrigan's hand. "Where can I get in touch with you?"

"I'll leave my contact information with Chris," Harrigan said as he walked to the door. "Thanks for your help, Senator." He started to leave when he turned back around. "The hearing seems to be going well. I hope it continues to go that way."

Jenkins acknowledged his statement as Harrigan exited. He sat down and brought his hand up to his mouth. He could only think of one firm who would have handled the case of a Republican senator who had a drug habit and had an attempted murder charge dropped. The firm had to be Rosen, Shafer, and Pruett. How was he connected to this? Other than the intelligence committee, he had no association with McNair.

Jenkins's phone buzzed. He snapped out of his thoughts and picked up the receiver.

"Senator," Chris started. "The Sergeant of Arms has returned with your subpoena. It appears your presence, along with all the other senators, is requested in the chamber."

"What?" Jenkins asked, not sure what he had heard. Chris repeated himself. Jenkins slammed the phone down, stood while grabbing his jacket, and briskly walked past Chris and the Sergeant of Arms.

Jenkins walked into the chaos of the Senate chamber. Both sides of the aisle were voicing their opinions, yelling over each other. It was obvious to Jenkins, not to mention the American people, that Stevens was guilty of conspiracy, treason, and murder. There were some who were steadfastly defending their president. The tape left little room for interpretation. Nicole left little room for conspiracy theories. Stevens needed to be removed from office and tried for his crimes. There were no other options and as much as the Republicans wanted to deflect these facts, it was not going to happen. Nicole put her life on the line to reveal that tape and Jenkins felt he owed it to Nicole to bring Stevens to justice. Of course, there was a small part of Jenkins that hoped his actions would bring Nicole back to him.

As Jenkins walked to his seat in the Senate chamber, many senators stopped him to ask what was going to happen next. Jenkins patiently informed them that the Sergeant of Arms had been dispatched to subpoena President Stevens and had returned, the subpoena still in his hands. He respectfully added that he knew nothing else and his confusion matched theirs.

Jenkins was surprised when Vice President Blackwood entered the Senate and marched directly up to the President Pro Tempore seat, taking the gavel from the residing leader. He gaveled and called for order in the chamber. Most senators moved quickly and quietly to their seats. A few senators remained standing on the floor of the Senate but turned to listen to Blackwood. As Blackwood gaveled once more to attain the silence he wanted in the chamber, it was then that Jenkins noticed the paper in Blackwood's other hand. Jenkins fell into his seat and closed his eyes. A few seconds later with clenched teeth, he shook his head in disbelief.

"Order," Blackwood said. "I call this chamber to order." He had waited a few more seconds before he made his announcement. Blackwood started as he held up the paper. "I have just left the House of Representatives where I gave them this letter. I have here President Stevens's resignation. I also have a statement issued by his physician that states President Stevens is not fit to either govern or face any criminal charges against him at this time. The President's physician has ordered him to St. Elizabeths Hospital, the Government Hospital for the Insane, and tests conducted."

Jenkins slammed his fist hard on his desk. The loud bang echoed in the Senate chamber and caught Blackwood by surprise. There was an eerie reverberating echo throughout the chamber. Jenkins stormed from the Senate. What happened next surprised Barker and Mercer alike. As Blackwood continued his comments, both Democrats and Republicans who wanted the president to appear before Jenkins's committee and held accountable for his actions, stood and followed Jenkins out of the chamber in protest. Mercer watched while half of the Senate walked out. Mercer waited for five senators to walk past him, and then he joined the line. As he walked up the steps, Blackwood furiously pounded the gavel calling for the senators to return to their seats.

Mercer looked up and saw Barker sitting at his Senate desk, his right hand to his mouth. There was no mistaking the smile that shown through his parted fingers. Mercer knew at that moment that Barker was part of the deal to keep Stevens from being escorted from the White House, sparing Stevens the public humiliation for his sins. Mercer made no indication of his anger or that he knew Barker was somehow involved. He knew he would be able to get the information he needed and that he would personally see to Barker's expulsion from the Democratic Party leadership over time. In Mercer's eyes, Barker had just committed treason against his own party. But more importantly, he had denied the American public the closure and the truth they deserved.

Mercer started up the steps again and out the doors of the Senate chamber. When the procession ended, less than a third of the Senators, mostly Republicans, remained to hear Blackwood's closing remarks.

"By the Twenty-Fifth Amendment, I am now President of the United States. I have delivered this letter to the necessary people, and the process has begun. I will address the nation later tonight, and I will immediately work to fill the vacant offices within the Stevens administration." Blackwood looked at the gavel in his hand. There was no one to hand the gavel to as most had walked out of the Senate. He cleared his throat and said, "I suggest the absence of a quorum." It was the most accurate statement spoken aloud that day.

Jenkins stormed into his office, not stopping to respond any of the questions the press was badgering him with as he walked from the Senate chamber. He was angry, and he was not about to say something he knew he would regret later. He needed to regain his composure and think about his next move. Chris stood as he entered. Jenkins whisked past Chris and into his inner office. He slammed the door behind him.

The press flooded into Jenkins's outer office. Chris held up his hands to try and get their attention. He didn't yell, he just stood there, arms in the air and palms open. As the reporters realized their questions went unacknowledged, they started to quiet down. Chris took this opportunity to address them. "We don't have a statement at this time. If you would leave the Senator's office, we can get back to work. Until then, we have no comment."

The reporters mumbled and walked out of the office. Chris closed the door when they were in the hallway. He locked the outer door, restricting access. Walking back to his desk, he sat down. He knew Jenkins would be calling for him, but he also knew that would not happen until Jenkins settled down.

Jenkins was pacing inside his office. He knew Blackwood was under a lot of pressure to clean this mess up quickly and Jefferies's testimony had not helped. Jenkins wanted to get Stevens before his committee. For once, there would have been the opportunity to document exactly what happened. There would have been no cover-up and no conspiracy theories invented. At the very least, Stevens could spend the rest of his life in prison if he testified. Jenkins stopped pacing and finally sat down in his desk chair. He told himself there was no reason why he couldn't continue the questioning of those subpoenaed to appear. Who could he contact to get these criminals in court? His mind was racing.

Chris knocked on the door, and Jenkins beckoned him into his office. "I thought you might be interested in this," Chris said, handing him the newspaper. Circled on the page was a small article in the Washington Post. Jenkins started to read the article, his eyes widening as he read further. He looked at Chris. "Was Lord Adkins there?"

"No, but somebody was."

"What do you mean?"

"There's a car in the carport." Chris pointed to the photo. "But later in the article, it says that no one was at the residence at the time of the explosion." Chris pointed to the spot in the article that Jenkins had not read.

"I see," Jenkins replied, clearly deep in thought. "Thanks, Chris."

"Do you need me to do anything, sir?"

"Not yet," Jenkins replied. Chris left the office, closing the door behind him. Jenkins reached into his jacket pocket and removed his little notebook. He thumbed through the pages until he came upon the number given to him by Sean. He picked up the phone and dialed it. He was dismayed when he heard that the number was no longer in service. Hanging up the phone, he walked to his office window. He had so many emotions running through him: it was hard to focus. He was angry, concerned, and anxious. He needed to gather his thoughts.

Jenkins was looking out the window, still trying to calm himself. He had the elbow of his right arm propped against the side of the window pane. He was biting the nail of his thumb, something he only did in the privacy of his office or at home in times of deep concentration. His mind was racing, and he couldn't seem to break through his anger to think clearly. His eyes darted back and forth, searching for the answers. What was Blackwood up to and how did he get Stevens to resign? Should he continue the committee hearings? What should be his next steps?

His phone buzzed, catching his attention. With a calm voice, he picked up the receiver. "What is it, Chris?"

"Senator Mercer is on the line. He said it is urgent."

"Thank you," Jenkins said as he depressed the phone button to speak with Mercer. "Senator, what can I do for you?"

"Barker's behind this Twenty-Fifth Amendment deal," Mercer blurted out.

"He said that. He admitted it?" Jenkins was surprised that Barker would admit to his dirty dealings.

"He didn't have to. The smile on his face in the Senate chamber was all the proof I needed," Mercer explained. "Who have you shared your schedule with? Did you share it with your campaign staff?"

"I only shared that I would not be on the campaign trail during the hearings. I didn't share any details. Carson could get a detailed schedule from Chris if he asked. Why?"

"I'm wondering," Mercer started. "If Carson is informing on you to Barker, that would allow Barker to have information to undermine your work."

Jenkins thought for a minute. "Barker wanted me to hire Carson. He wasn't my first choice. Carson takes a lot of direction from Barker and certainly had no problem running to him if I didn't do what he wanted me to do."

"I think it is time to clean house," Mercer said. "It's up to you, of course, but I think you should fire him and hire your own staff. We have to neutralize Barker and having access to you via Carson may be more damaging. I don't know what he is up to, working with Blackwood, but it can't be good."

"I agree," Jenkins replied. "I'm sure Chris didn't intentionally do something—"

"Chris is very loyal to you. I'm not questioning him at all," Mercer interrupted. "If anyone's loyalty is being questioned, it is Barker and Carson."

"I'll have Chris call him, and we'll get that process started," Jenkins responded. He had to admit that he didn't like working with Carson. He didn't care much for Keaton, the treasurer, either.

His next actions felt like a preemptive strike. It would certainly send a signal to Barker. "I'm concerned about how much Barker knows."

"About what?"

"Well, not so much what he knows, but what he could plant that would show me in a bad light."

"I'm working on that," Mercer said. "I'll find a way to immobilize him. You worry about the hearings and your campaign."

"I will," Jenkins confirmed. "Thank you for your help, Daniel."

"You're welcome. I will check in with you later." Mercer hung up the phone.

Jenkins buzzed for Chris to enter his office. He explained the situation to Chris and how he needed to retrieve his schedule and any other vital information that Chris may have shared. After accomplishing that, he wanted Chris to order Carson to his office.

Carson pushed past Chris when he heard Jenkins's voice telling Chris to show Carson into his office a few hours later. "What the fuck is going on here?"

Jenkins motioned for Chris to close the door. Jenkins studied Carson for a moment. He slowly smiled. "You tell me. Have you been reporting to Barker behind my back?"

"What? No," Carson denied.

"Jim, it's clear that you and Senator Barker are good friends. You have sided with him on just about everything, and I feel like I have had to fight you on every issue. This campaign isn't the campaign I wanted to run. It would be Barker's campaign if he ran."

"I won't disagree with that," Carson acknowledged. "But I have no idea what he used against you to get you to agree with everything we suggested until you went public with it. Was he using Nikki in some way to keep you in check?" Jenkins laughed. He shook his head and broke his eye contact with Carson. "I need to know."

Jenkins looked back at him. "Go ask him." Jenkins took a deep breath. "While it appears like Barker is somewhat supportive in public, I want to take this campaign in a different direction. I want someone who doesn't have the allegiance to Barker that you have."

"You're firing me?"

"Yes, I'm afraid so. Thank you for everything you have done." Jenkins extended his hand, and Carson reluctantly shook it. "If you hadn't shown your loyalty to Barker, which I can admire in different circumstances, this might have been different. I just can't trust you."

"I can't say that this doesn't leave me with some hard feelings toward you."

"I understand," Jenkins replied.

"Everything I did for you, it's the reason you're leading."

Jenkins smiled. "The reason I'm leading is that the Republican Party is in shambles. They are regrouping, and I want someone at my side whom I can trust." He depressed a button on his phone, which signaled to Chris that Jenkins had completed their meeting. "I wish you the best."

Chris opened the door, and Carson left without saying another word. Chris looked at Jenkins.

"Get me Nelson Keaton. Tell him to bring the books with him," Jenkins instructed Chris.

Keaton arrived with the books that disclosed the financial information of the Jenkins for President campaign. Jenkins fired Keaton in much the same fashion as he had fired Carson. Jenkins noted that neither man seemed very upset about it. Jenkins spent the rest of the day talking with personnel in his field offices after he placed a call to his old friend Fred Whittaker. Whittaker ran Jenkins's successful campaign for the Senate, and he knew he could trust him. He offered Whittaker the job and, without hesitation, Whittaker accepted. Whittaker recommended the treasurer whom they had worked with on the Senate campaign and Jenkins agreed. Benjamin Hook was his name, and he accepted the offer as well. They planned to meet in Jenkins's office the next morning.

The firing of Carson and Keaton proved to be a diversionary tactic, keeping the press guessing as to why Jenkins would do such a thing. The official response from his office was no comment. Jenkins would address the press after he determined what excuse would benefit him the most in the next few days. However, the story sidetracked the president's resignation and kept reporters wondering if Blackwood's rise to power had anything to do with Jenkins's actions. All the speculations were helping Jenkins, and he didn't want to stop that news cycle anytime soon. Representative Sullivan made himself available to the press to keep the story of how Blackwood helped the president sidestep persecution alive. He had no problem steering the discussion back to the now failed impeachment. Sullivan asked all the right questions that threw doubt and promoted a lack of trust in regards to Blackwood's motives. The press was elated at the number of different scenarios they could easily dream up in the absence of the opportunity to interview Jenkins.

CHAPTER FIVE

Mid May 1980

London, England

It was pouring down rain outside. Peter walked into his office with his raincoat soaked and a dripping umbrella in one hand. He deposited the umbrella into its designated bin and tried to rid the rainwater from his hand. As he took a step forward, a white-haired, suntanned man stood up and called to him.

"Lord Adkins," Tony said, walking toward him.

Peter stopped. He turned to his security guards, who quickly got the hint that Peter did not know this man. They positioned themselves between the two men.

Peter's secretary, Margaret promptly stood up and walked to Peter's side. "My apologies, Lord Adkins. I have been trying to tell this gentleman that patience is a virtue."

Peter was not amused. "And who is this person?"

"I'm Tony Shafer," he replied, resenting the treatment he was receiving. "I'm a friend of Nicole Charbonneau."

Peter smiled. He thought for a moment. "Well, obviously you are not as close a friend as you may think you are. After all, you are in my office."

"I've been trying to find out information on Nikki for weeks. I understand she has sought and received asylum with your help."

"Is that so," Peter replied. He looked at his guards and dismissed them with a quick motion of his hand. He began to walk to his office, cutting in front of Tony. "I don't see what in the world we have to talk about. I'm sorry, what did you say your name was?" Peter knew his name but wanted to give the appearance that he was not impressed with him.

"Tony Shafer. Look, Lord Adkins, I'd just like to talk to Nikki."

Peter, hearing the concern in Tony's voice, stopped just outside his inner office door. "What is it you would like to say to her?" Tony's face showed his surprise. "Ah," Peter started, Tony's reaction telling him what he needed to know. "I don't think that speaking with Ms. Charbonneau will be possible. Go home, Mr. Shafer."

"I'm getting sick and tired of everyone telling me that I can't talk to my friend," Tony asserted.

Peter cocked his head. "Frankly, Mr. Shafer, I don't care." He turned and walked into his office. Margaret walked in behind him, catching the wet raincoat before it hit the chair on which Peter had tried to toss it. He put his briefcase down on the desk. He looked up to find Tony standing in front of him. "Oh, you again," he remarked, annoyed. Peter sat down. "I suggest you leave before I have you escorted out. If Ms. Charbonneau wanted to talk to you, she would have found a way to do so. I'm certainly not in the business of reunions."

"I'm not leaving until you put me in touch with her."

"You do know who you are threatening, Mr. Shafer?"

"Yes. By the way, how is Sean?"

Peter studied Tony for a second. "Guards," he called calmly. "Escort Mr. Shafer out of my office and make sure he is comfortable and well within sight of both you and Margaret." As the guards moved into position, Tony started to walk outside Peter's inner office. Peter, who had moved to the door of his office, shut it behind the guards and walked back to his desk. He sat down, contemplating whether to call Sean or have Tony thrown off the premises. He picked up the phone and called his flat.

"Hello," Sean greeted the caller.

"Sean," Peter started. "I have the most peculiar news."

Sean always chuckled at Peter's flair for the dramatic. "OK, what is it?"

"Tony Shafer is sitting outside my office and is demanding to speak with Nicole."

Sean looked over at Nicole who was sitting on the couch. "That is peculiar. Did he say what he wanted?"

"No, and when I asked he got a surprised look on his face. What should I do?"

Sean thought for a moment. "Keep him there. Nicole and I will stop by on our way out of town."

"Do you think that is wise?"

"We have some questions we'd like to ask him," Sean countered. "We'll be there as soon as we can."

"I'll see you soon," Peter said as he hung up the phone. He opened his briefcase, taking out the papers within, and sorted them according to importance. He worked on various things until he heard Tony call Nicole's name. It was obvious that Sean and Nicole had just arrived. He walked to his door, opened it, and saw Sean standing between Tony and Nicole.

"Shall we all get comfy in my office?" Peter asked.

Tony turned and walked into Peter's office, realizing Sean was not going to let him anywhere near Nicole. Sean and Nicole followed. Peter shut the door and told everyone to find a chair. After taking a seat, Sean tried to take command of the meeting.

"What can we do for you, Mr. Shafer?"

"Are you OK, Nikki?" Tony asked, ignoring Sean and staring at Nicole.

Nicole wasn't going to say anything but then decided to cut to the chase. "What were you doing outside the television station the day I was shot?" Sean slowly turned his head to look at Nicole, surprised at her boldness.

Tony was shocked to hear that she had seen him. He couldn't find the words.

"Tony, did you try to kill me?" Nicole followed up.

"No!" Tony emphatically exclaimed. "I wanted to tell you that Stevens knew you had the tape."

"Of course he did. The promos were running over here for a few days. It wouldn't have taken long for the intelligence community to figure that out and inform Stevens," Nicole shot back.

She was right. Before the promos, Stevens had no idea where the tape was. Tony looked down. "I wanted to tell you that I was alive and that Stevens found out that I had the tape. He ordered a SEAL team to kill me. I guess I wanted you to know that I was OK."

Nicole shook her head once. "Mission accomplished," she responded coldly. "Why did you set me up?"

"Set you up?" Tony repeated. "I don't understand."

"Why did you intentionally send me the tape, knowing that I would expose this conspiracy, all while you played dead?"

Sean looked at Peter, quite proud of Nicole's resolve. He imagined just how precise and deadly Nicole's questioning in a court of law must have been. He waited for Tony's response.

"It wasn't like that at all. I didn't expect you to expose it. I wanted you to get Jenkins to do something," Tony pleaded. "Nikki, you have to believe me. I just wanted you to help Jenkins nail Stevens. I didn't expect you to expose it the way you did. What happened when you told Jenkins you knew about the tape?"

Nicole smiled. "What do you think happened?"

"He didn't want to do anything." Tony frowned at his failure to motivate Jenkins. "I'm sorry, Nikki. I never wanted you hurt."

"Really?" Nicole asked. "You dragged me into this mess. You knew I wouldn't keep quiet. How else did you hurt me?"

Sean sat back in his chair, realizing the lawyer in Nicole was quite up to par. Peter was also enjoying the exchange. He caught Sean's eye and smiled. Peter muttered aloud, "How thoroughly delightful." When he caught the look Nicole was giving him, he cleared his throat.

"Tony?" Nicole turned her attention back to her last question. "How else did you hurt me?"

"I'm not sure." Tony paused as he searched for the proper words. "I feel responsible for putting you in danger."

"Do you know who shot me?"

"No," Tony stated.

"Was it Stevens? Did he order it?" Nicole pressed.

"I don't know. All I know is that it wasn't me," Tony shot back.

"Did Stevens find out that you sent me the tape before I went public with it?"

"I don't think so. I was hiding out and saw that you were going to go public with it. I tried to get to you but didn't know where to start. I was hoping I could talk to you before the interview, but stage manager wouldn't let me into the studio."

Nicole looked at Sean. "We're done here."

"Nikki, you have to believe me. I didn't want any of this to happen."

Nicole stood up. "Then you should have never sent me that tape. You knew I have a strong dislike for Stevens. You knew I wouldn't keep this a secret, and you most certainly knew that Bobby wasn't going to do anything about it." Sean was now standing next to her. "You may not have wanted me to do anything other than talk to Bobby, but in the back of your mind, you knew I wouldn't allow for this to be swept under the rug and dealt with through backdoor meetings on Capitol Hill. Like it or not, Tony, you played me." She looked at Sean, who started to move to the door. Nicole took a few steps then turned around to face Tony. "And true friends don't do that. Good-bye, Tony." She started to walk out the door.

Tony stood up and walked toward Nicole. "Nikki, how can I make this up to you?" he pleaded.

Nicole turned back to Tony and, with disdain in her voice, said, "You can't. Bobby doesn't need your testimony, and I need to find another life." She looked at Sean. "Let's go."

"Dad, we'll be in touch," Sean said as he allowed Nicole to walk out of the office first.

Tony watched them leave. He didn't know what to say. He looked at Peter, then back at the outer office door that was now closing. "Where will she go?"

"That is none of your concern. Good day, Mr. Shafer. It was nice of you to pop by." Peter was intentionally sardonic. "Margaret, would you be so kind as to show Mr. Shafer the door?"

Margaret stood up from her desk and walked to the door of Peter's inner office. "Mr. Shafer, this way, please."

Tony didn't say a word. He just watched someone he truly cared for walk out of his life forever. His mind took him to the many times they had gone sailing, the White House dinners, the evenings working on cases at the law firm. He could see her smiling and laughing. Now, he knew that she was gone. As he left Peter's office, he was still trying to figure out how he could make this up to her. He was heartbroken at the idea that his actions may have caused her all this pain. But Nicole knew that wasn't the case. Nicole knew her actions, her predictable actions led to her current arduous situation.

{II}

London, England

Jack Kensington was sitting behind his desk at SIS headquarters. The rain was pelting his window, and he had just returned from a debriefing. There wasn't any pressing news. The gray day stirred up a memory of someone he had loved and lost. He wasn't sure why his thoughts turned to her now. He glanced down at his calendar and noted the date. Maybe that had something to do with it.

He sat back in his chair and allowed the memory to play out before him. It was morning, and Jack had done something foolish. Although he was married, he fell asleep after he had made love to his secretary at her apartment. It wasn't the first time they had been intimate, and he knew the young woman was in love with him. He recalled every curve of her body. She wasn't extraordinarily gorgeous, but what her face and body lacked, her personality made up for once she warmed up to you. Her laugh was infectious, and her blonde hair was long and thick. She always had it pulled back or swept up on her head at the office. Jack recalled how he loved running his fingers through it. Her steel-blue eyes were piercing, yet inviting. He ached at her absence now.

He let his mind travel to the last time he had seen her. They had met up late in the evening after Jack explained to his wife that he had some work he desperately needed to finish at his office. Having something important to tell Jack, the young woman pleaded with him to meet her at her flat. When he arrived, they poured a drink, talked small talk, and before they knew it, they were in the throes of passion. Jack never denied his love for her. He realized now she was the only woman he had ever truly loved. But Jack was ambitious, and his wife, Mary, had all the right connections.

Mary and Jack were happy for a few years. Mary lost their first baby through miscarriage—an occasion Jack missed due to an important meeting with the prime minister, for which Mary never forgave him. They tried a second time, but the pain of losing the first child was too great. Both of them mourned the loss separately. When Mary demanded they try again, their lovemaking became emotionless, passionless, and solely an effort to create a child that Mary felt would replace the one she'd lost. When she became pregnant, she shielded herself from Jack and focused entirely on the pregnancy. While out shopping one day, she decided to pop into a restaurant for a bite. She accidentally discovered Jack with his secretary. Jack had no idea that Mary was going to be in town that day, let alone go to the same restaurant as him. Jack had secured their customary booth, in the back mostly out of sight of the other tables. It was, however, in clear view if one walked to the bar or restrooms. In dismay, Mary watched Jack smile and fondle his secretary. Instead of yearning for Jack to be that way with her again, she became resentful.

Jack smiled as he heard the familiar laugh of his former secretary in his mind. He reminisced how he had threatened to take her hair down right there in the booth of the restaurant. He remembered the look on his lover's face when she saw Mary staring at her, the hate for her obviously displayed all over Mary's face. Jack recalled her gasp. He looked up to see Mary and could only muster a disaffected, cold response. He simply picked up his glass as if to toast his stoic wife. He smiled and then took a sip. Placing the glass down, he returned his hand to caress his lover's jaw and turned it to meet his lips. He then kissed her, looking out the corner of his eye to see Mary's lack of a reaction. That was the day the uncaring Jack crushed whatever feeling or love Mary had for him.

So when his lover begged him to come to her place the following evening to discuss a matter of grave importance, he didn't hesitate. When he arrived, he wasn't in the mood for a serious discussion. She seemed dismayed about something and all Jack wanted to do was console her. Her youthful inexperience played right into Jack's fantasies as she stroked his ego and made him feel dashingly handsome. They had some drinks, and then it happened. She asked Jack if he would ever consider leaving his wife. Liquor always got the better of Jack—one reason why he would not have made a great field agent. He promised her that he would leave Mary in the following weeks. It was a drunk's foolish answer. He never intended to leave Mary. Her money and family connections saw him rise quickly through the ranks at SIS. His good friend Peter Adkins was supportive as well. Jack knew he needed both in his corner to become director. Mary had made it clear if he ever wanted to leave her, she would make sure that his career would be over. Mary had her lovers, just as Jack had had his over the years. This young woman was not his first affair and would not be his last. But she was the first one to question if he could stay with someone he didn't love. He wondered if her inexperience helped him fall in love with her—a love he had never felt with anyone else.

The next morning they awoke, both with headaches and the realization that they had fallen asleep after their lovemaking. Jack quickly got dressed and was barking orders at her. As he started to leave, he paused to kiss her.

"We messed this one up," he said, after kissing her. "I hope no one notices me leaving."

"Jack," she called. "Did you mean it? You're going to leave your wife for me soon?"

Jack stopped by the door and slowly turned to look at her. "Leave Mary?"

"Yes," she confirmed. "Last night you said that you would."

"Last night I was obviously too drunk to respond that question honestly." Jack opened the door. "I can't leave Mary. You knew that when we got involved." He saw the tears welling up in her eyes. He put on a fake smile and said, "It doesn't mean that I don't love you madly. I do." He blew her a kiss and added, "I'll see you in the office. Wear that blue dress that matches your eyes. You know I can't keep my eyes off you when you wear that dress." With that, Jack dashed out of her flat.

She never came to work that day. In fact, Jack never saw her again. To this day, he never knew what happened to her or why she vanished. It broke his heart. He wondered if she ever considered that. He told himself that she was too self-centered to let it enter her mind. Her absence had turned his feelings for her to animosity. His memories of her only made him feel empty now.

The phone rang on his desk, jolting him back to the present. He cleared his throat before picking it up. It was back to business as usual now.

{III}

Washington, DC

A few days after Blackwood's delivery of the president's resignation, Chris entered the inner office and announced that Jenkins would want to see what was occurring on the White House lawn. He flipped the television on, and as the screen cracked to life, there was President Blackwood with McNair by his side.

"We have work to do," Blackwood said. He looked uncomfortable and repeatedly glanced at his notes. "Late last year, Mark Stevens declared his candidacy for president. Now, due to unforeseen events, he is no longer in the race, and I'm announcing my candidacy."

Jenkins noticed the clumsy phrasing. He knew Blackwood never wanted to be president and now, without a doubt, he was being pressed into service. It was the only clear choice the Republicans had.

"As you know, Senator Brian McNair has also expressed an interest in running. Since there is nothing customary about this year's campaign, I'd like to announce that Senator McNair has agreed to be my vice president and will join me on the ticket." Jenkins looked at Chris. Jenkins's mind was spinning. "We believe that this announcement will go far in mending a shattered party." He looked at McNair. "I believe, Senator, you asked for a few minutes to address the press."

McNair walked to the podium as Blackwood stepped aside. McNair gave a disingenuous smile as he stood before the crowd. He placed his notes on the podium and cleared his throat.

"Watch out," Chris warned. Jenkins sat down in a chair without saying a word.

"A little while ago, I attempted to make a few comments at Senator Jenkins's committee meeting." Jenkins had decided that the testimonies of Davis and Engle were too important not to be voiced. McNair took every opportunity to thwart the progress of the committee, questioning its relevance given Stevens's resignation and condition. "If you watched, you'll agree that Senator Jenkins is not affording me the opportunity to speak. In my opinion, this investigation into the assassination of President Andrews is woefully one-sided. The Democrats, led by Jenkins, plan to use this as a means to divide our great nation with no other purpose for it." Jenkins rolled his eyes at the suggestion. "I believe that additional evidence exists that could prove that Norman Sipes planted the tape to topple President Stevens. Anyone who has attended dinners at the White House can attest that Norman Sipes was an alcoholic." McNair took a breath. "There are so many questions that remain unanswered in my mind. I believe that Senator Jenkins intends to keep me and others from knowing the actual truth. He is protecting some information about that tape. Based on intelligence that has come my way, I believe what I am about to tell you is the reason why. The intelligence I have just received claims that Senator Jenkins may have ordered the attack on Nicole Charbonneau—"

Jenkins shot out of the chair he was sitting in and screamed, "WHAT?"

"I think it would be in the best interest of the United States to again call for Ms. Charbonneau to be extradited. Her side of the story needs documenting before anything happens to her. I, myself, would see to her personal safety."

"I bet you would you son of a bitch!" Jenkins yelled at the TV. Jenkins's office phones began to ring. "There is no fucking truth to anything that bastard just said! Not one fact of it is true! It's like he's making this up as he goes along!" Jenkins was pacing like an angry, caged tiger.

Chris shut the door to Jenkins's inner office. "No comment is our response," Chris stated calmly. He saw Jenkins walk toward his desk, still violently angry. "Don't touch that!" Chris yelled to him, putting his hand on the phone. "Let me do that, sir."

"Are you handling me, Chris?" Jenkins spat out in anger.

"You bet I am," Chris shot back. "You're angry! Sit down! Collect yourself!" Chris demanded. He turned the sound down on the television before continuing. "You know anything you say in anger will only hurt you."

Jenkins knew Chris was right. Jenkins straightened his tie and tugged at the cuffs of his shirt to regain his composure. "No comment is our official response for now," Jenkins reiterated.

Chris turned, opened the door, and walked out of Jenkins's inner office. The two other aides looked at Chris, waiting for instructions. "Senator Jenkins is not in the office at this time," he announced with a wink. "The Senator has no comment at this time." Chris walked over to his desk and picked up the phone. "Thank you for calling Senator Jenkins. How can I help you?" He sat down. The other aides were taking their cue from Chris. Messages were taken and never returned. The calls died down after the press realized that Jenkins was not interested in responding to McNair's accusations.

{III}

Washington, DC

Harrigan was depressed. The information that was passed on to him by the mystery woman was a dead end. He had just returned to his apartment when the phone rang. He was hopeful it was the source calling with more information. Instead, it was Theodore Warner, a billionaire who was growing tired of what he considered the conservative press. Warner wanted to launch a cable news network channel. Others admired his successful launches of entertainment cable channels. Warner obtained his fortune through real estate deals and smart investments in small entrepreneurial companies on the verge of immense success. He was growing tired of what he considered to be the one-sided nature of the news, feeling that its message was too controlled. He longed for a news channel that only reported the facts and expected its viewers to draw their own conclusions.

Harrigan picked the phone and was surprised to hear Warner's voice. "Is there something I can help you with?"

"I understand you're looking for gainful employment?" Warner was an older Southern gentleman and a recluse. He never attempted to refine his Georgian accent because he rarely talked in public. "I'd like to tell you about a cable news network that is about to go live."

"A cable news network?" Harrigan repeated, smiling. "I believe Senator Jenkins has been in touch with you."

"Yes," Warner confirmed. "It will be all news and on the air twenty-four hours a day. I'm tired of filtered news controlled by the broadcasting stations. I want reporters who will dig for the truth and present facts to the American people. I'm looking for people like you. I understand your bosses weren't happy with you because you decided to let Jenkins tell his story. Well, I say, good for you! Come work for me and keep digging for the story that needs telling."

"Where will the station be based?" Harrigan asked.

"Atlanta and you'll have a team of researchers to help you."

"Researchers?" Harrigan asked. "I usually do the research myself."

"Pick your team. Pick the people you trust the most," Warner encouraged him. "Tell me who they are, and I'll get them on the payroll."

Harrigan paused for a moment. "Mr. Warner, I'm flattered that you want me to work for you, but I have a question, and in a way, I'm sticking my neck out here." Harrigan needed to know the answer to the question he was about to ask before he even considered the job offer. "Have you ever heard of something called Operation Mockingbird?"

"No," Warner barked. "What the hell is that and why would I give a damn?"

Harrigan laughed at Warner's directness. Warner's abrupt nature wasn't totally due to his lack of time, but more his lack of patience. "In short, Operation Mockingbird is a CIA directive. The CIA has used this directive in the past, and they own high-ranking personnel at all the networks as well as some reporters and anchors. Essentially, they pay them to report CIA propaganda."

"Are you serious?"

"I'm very serious."

"Are you part of this operation?" Warner asked. The doubt was obvious in his voice.

"No. I was fired because I didn't play by their rules."

There was dead silence on the other end of the phone. After a few seconds, Warner spoke. "Are you telling me the CIA controls all the news agencies in this country?"

"Not all of them, just the big, important ones—you know, the ones that people most trust," Harrigan asserted. "If you like, I can fly down to Atlanta and fill you in on the circumstances of my firing and about Operation Mockingbird. At least, what I have found out about it so far."

"I think that sounds like a fine offer," Warner replied. "I'll have my plane at National in an hour. My limousine will meet the plane in Atlanta and bring you to my office, and we'll have an interesting conversation that I hope ends with you being my star anchor."

Harrigan was taken aback by how quickly Warner wanted to meet with him. "Yes, sir. I'll leave for National now." They bade each other farewell, and Harrigan hung the phone.

Harrigan changed into a suit and got ready to leave for National Airport. He grabbed his briefcase, filling it with all the information on Operation Mockingbird he had accumulated over the last few weeks. He was amazed at the names he had discovered—some reporters who were the most trusted and their reputations considered spotless. In Harrigan's estimation, even though Jenkin's Intelligence Committee called for an end to Mockingbird, the CIA propaganda machine was still at work.

As he waited for Warner's private jet to arrive, he started to wonder why the CIA had never approached him. He thought back to the stories over the years that had been killed by his network bosses. His stories were always thoroughly researched and fact-based. His hero was Edward R. Murrow, and he believed in the power of the pen and the freedom of the press just as Murrow had. He wondered now if those stories were killed by Mockingbird because they would have revealed too much information. He also pondered just how much information he should give to Warner.

The plane arrived and whisked Harrigan off to Atlanta. As promised, Warner's limousine was waiting when he landed. Shortly after arriving in Atlanta, he was sitting outside Theodore Warner's office. The executive secretary offered Harrigan coffee or a soft drink, both of which he declined. After a few minutes, there was a buzz emanating from her phone. The secretary announced that Warner would see Harrigan now.

Harrigan stood, clutching his briefcase. He walked through the now-opened office door. Warner's standard office attire consisted of blue jeans, cowboy boots, and a polo shirt. He stood as Harrigan entered his office and began to walk toward him with his hand extended. "Steven Harrigan, it is a pleasure."

"The pleasure is mine," Harrigan responded as he shook Warner's hand.

"I guess I should have told you on the phone the suit wasn't necessary," Warner said, laughing at his omission.

"Wearing a suit to me is like wearing blue jeans for you," Harrigan joked, taking the seat that Warner pointed to as Warner walked back behind his oversized desk and chair.

"So, this Mockingbird Operation," Warner began as if their conversation had never ended. "Is that something that could be exposed, and what kind of danger would we be in if we did expose it?"

"I guess that depends on who we piss off," Harrigan proposed. "I had heard about the operation when I was doing a story on a Korean War correspondent who had passed. At that time, I didn't think anything of it. I just figured that the CIA was controlling the information about the war itself, even after it had ended. But when I recently interviewed Senator Jenkins, something interesting happened. You have to understand that Senator Jenkins and I were discussing his Vietnam incident way before the network bigwigs were involved." Harrigan wished he hadn't used the *"bigwigs"* description. He cleared his throat. "Senator Jenkins came to me and told me he wanted to come clean and wanted it to happen in our interview. He asked me to keep it between us, and I agreed."

"Are you and Senator Jenkins good friends?" Warner interjected.

"Not really," Harrigan replied. "I respect him. I knew he was giving me an exclusive and I was fine with his request. Working in Washington, you learn not to ask too many questions."

"I'm glad you respect Jenkins. My son was in his unit. Jenkins saved his life over in 'Nam. Damn fine man no matter what that jackass Admiral did to him." Warner buzzed for his secretary. He held up a finger, causing Harrigan to pause. When the secretary opened his door, he said, "I'd like something to drink. Can you rustle up two Jacks?" The secretary nodded her understanding and closed the door. Warner was known for his taste for Jack Daniels, although no one ever spoke about it to his face. Harrigan deduced that Warner didn't care if anyone knew about his drinking habits.

Harrigan had to admit, it fit the man's character. Harrigan determined that the Jack Daniels bottle had to be nearby because, within a minute, the secretary returned with two stiff drinks. Warner prodded Harrigan to continue after he had sipped his whiskey.

Harrigan had to think for a moment before he started up again. "A few days before the interview, I was informed by my boss's boss that he wanted me to surprise Jenkins with information on the very incident that we hadn't told anyone we were going to discuss. The original topic was the committee hearing on the assassination of President Andrews. I did a little digging around, and a source told me that Barker was behind this."

"Senator Barker? His mentor?" Warner asked, not sure he believed what he heard. "Why would he do that?"

"Seems there is a power play happening among the Phenom Five," Harrigan suggested. "The stories didn't match up, and I took that to Jenkins. He gave the name of the admiral and details the offensives that the admiral lied about. It all matched up, so I went with Jenkins's version all the while telling my bosses that I was running with Barker's version. I convinced them to go live, with some help from Senator Jenkins and Senator Mercer. I know for a fact that my bosses are a part of Mockingbird. When I was looking into the operation, they killed that story quickly; it left me suspicious. A source I can't name told me that someone in the government was keeping Mockingbird alive. Jenkins, who is chair of the Intelligence Committee, thought it was dead. Jenkins reported to me that his predecessor had ordered its demise. He now knows otherwise now." Harrigan took a swig of his whiskey to settle his nerves.

"All the big broadcasting companies have people involved in this operation?"

"Yes.".

Warner took another sip of his whiskey. "This Mockingbird thing needs to be one of our first stories. Are you interested in working for me?"

"Yes," Harrigan confirmed, nodding his head.

"What do you need?" Warner asked.

"A team I can trust to start with,'' Harrigan responded. "And access to Senators Barker and Mercer and the CIA director."

Warner smiled. "Going after the big fish right away—I like that." Warner paused, finishing off his whiskey in one long gulp. "It might be wiser to get some of the smaller fish on board first."

Harrigan smiled. "Oh, I'm getting them on the line as we speak."

"Well, then, I suppose the only thing we haven't talked about is your contract." Warner opened a file that was to his right. He pulled out a stack of papers and put them on the edge of his desk. "I'll get us some more Jack while you look over that contract."

{IV}

Washington, DC

"It's time," Mercer said. He sat down and motioned for Jenkins to sit as well. "You need to close the committee and get back out on the campaign trail. McNair can hurt you more now that he'll be out campaigning for president. We can't do anything else now in regards to Stevens. Take your findings, summarize them, and send them to the attorney general with a request to have Stevens and the others stand trial."

"Do we know that will happen?" Jenkins asked, the doubt apparent in his voice.

"Make it a talking point of your campaign—how no one has taken the blame for the assassination. You know how to make that work. The attorney general is refusing to bring charges against someone in his own party. You know how to spin this. It gives us the moral high ground," Mercer coached.

"I want to see him stand trial," Jenkins responded, feeling defeated.

"Bobby, look, the Republican Party is still in shambles, but they are starting to regroup. With only a few months before the conventions, they have organized under a new ticket. The latest polls show a huge distrust of both parties. However, you have a higher approval rating despite Barker's attempt to ruin you, and, honestly, this last accusation of you ordering Nikki's assassination isn't playing all that well." Mercer sat back in his chair. "It's our election to lose, and we will lose it if we don't take advantage of the disarray in the Republican Party now. You need to be out there, and you need to hammer home that they are ducking the responsibility to have Stevens stand trial. They should be the party with the trust issue, not us."

Jenkins knew Mercer was right. "I'll close the committee this afternoon. Are the impeachment proceedings going to continue?"

"Technically, they can't because Stevens is no longer in office," Mercer stated. "Sullivan is going to make a speech about Stevens's cowardice, for lack of a better word, in the House tomorrow."

Jenkins shook his head and looked down. "So, Stevens gets a pass."

Mercer smiled. "Not if you send your evidence to the attorney general and we pressure him to pursue Stevens in a court of law."

"We both know that his placement in that mental institution will prevent him from standing trial. He will put in a plea of not guilty by reason of insanity and be cleared. Hell, the AG will probably note that and not even bring charges." Jenkins stood up. "This was an exercise in futility." He started to leave Mercer's office.

"Then introduce a bill to restrict the power that the insanity defense grants," Mercer added quickly. Jenkins turned around to look at Mercer. "Announce it on the campaign trail."

"I'm not a lawyer, Daniel. You are," Jenkins quipped. "How would I do that?"

"Currently, the burden of proof is on the government. Change that. Make the defendant prove that he or she is insane with clear and convincing evidence. Right now, the government has to prove beyond a reasonable doubt the insanity. Shift that to the defendant and limit what the specialist or doctors can testify about on the stand." Mercer watched Jenkins as he processed what Mercer was saying. "I can have one of my aides draft up a copy. Why don't we co-sponsor the bill and we'll bring Sullivan on board as well."

"Would it be constitutional?" Jenkins asked.

"We can write it so that it would withstand the appeals process. I'm sure of that," Mercer declared. "It may not get us Stevens, but it will prevent this from happening again. Besides, Stevens wasn't insane when he put the plot in place."

"I'll co-sponsor that bill," Jenkins confirmed before he walked out the door with that familiar, sly smile on his face.

{V}

Washington, DC

Later that afternoon, Jenkins gaveled the select committee to order. McNair wasted no time in calling on the chair, but Jenkins did not acknowledge McNair's calling out to him. "The chair has a few statements," Jenkins said, looking at McNair, who sat back in his chair.

"As you now know, Mr. Stevens is no longer in the Oval Office, removed from power via the Twenty-Fifth Amendment by President Blackwood. It seems Mr. Stevens—"

"He should still be addressed as President Stevens, as all former presidents are," McNair corrected Jenkins.

Jenkins paused, not reacting to McNair. Instead, he emphasized his first words in defiance of McNair's comments. "Since we have confirmed the assassination plot with three witnesses who were a part of the conspiracy, I am, therefore, closing this investigation as Congress is now without power to bring justice. I will forward the evidence, testimony, and depositions to the attorney general for review and consideration for legal action to be taken against those who executed this most heinous crime. I adjourn this committee. Good day." Jenkins struck the gavel three times, the sound echoing throughout the room. He stood and walked out of the committee before anyone could stop him.

Jenkins walked down the hallway and into his office. Without saying a word, Chris pointed to the television. On the screen, reporters had cornered Barker outside of his Senate office. Jenkins stopped to watch the interview, sitting on the edge of Chris's desk.

"Would it be fair to say that you mentored Jenkins after his election to the Senate?" One reporter shouted and then shoved his microphone into Barker's face.

"Yes, that would be a fair statement," Barker agreed.

"You are also a big supporter of his campaign for president. Did you see anything that would have pointed to Jenkins ordering Ms. Charbonneau's assassination?" another reporter called out.

Jenkins looked at Chris with confusion. "Where is this coming from?"

"McNair stopped to talk to reporters outside the committee room. He brought up his assertion that you ordered the hit again and that you dismissed the hearing to prevent the truth from being disclosed."

Barker stopped and looked at the reporter. Jenkins held his breath, waiting for Barker to sink him and his career. "Look, the campaign trail can have its tense moments. Were there times when I saw Senator Jenkins and Ms. Charbonneau disagree? Of course I did. Ms. Charbonneau decided on her own to expose the Sipes tape, and I'm sure Senator Jenkins wasn't happy about that decision. Ms. Charbonneau has a lot of questions to answer. McNair has put forth an interesting twist on the situation. I would like to see Ms. Charbonneau extradited so that we can have a more thorough explanation."

Barker reached for the doorknob of his office door just as another reporter shouted, "Do you think Jenkins tried to have her killed?"

Barker paused. Jenkins waited for the ax to drop. "Senator Jenkins is a lot of things, but I don't think he would have ordered the assassination of the love of his life. Now if you will excuse me, I

have some calls to make." Barker disappeared behind his office door.

Jenkins was shocked. His mouth dropped open in disbelief. Did Barker just save him? And at what price did Barker's comment cost him? What did Barker know, but more importantly, what did

Barker want? Harrigan had warned him that Barker had all kinds of intelligence due to Operation Mockingbird. Jenkins cocked his head. "You son of a bitch…" he whispered, his voice trailing off as his mind started to pull together possible scenarios. "What evidence do you actually have and what have you made up?" Was this another ploy to get back in charge of Jenkins and his campaign? Jenkins sat on Chris's desk thinking of his next move. He desperately wanted to be free of Barker and his control.

"Still no comment, sir?" Chris asked.

"For now," Jenkins confirmed. "I need to figure out what game he is playing." Jenkins walked into his office and placed a call to Senator Mercer. He asked if he could stop by Mercer's home that evening.

Jenkins arrived at Mercer's home, walked up to the front door, and rang the doorbell. Mercer ushered him inside the house. The two men walked to Mercer's study. Mercer crossed the room to the bar and poured Jenkins a scotch. He poured himself vodka and tonic. Mercer handed the scotch to Jenkins and sat down across from him. "Do you have any idea where McNair got Nikki's assassination tip?" Mercer asked.

"Not anything I can back up with facts at this point."

"You saw that some of the reporters are saying it's Connors who gave the intelligence to McNair," Mercer stated.

Jenkins took a sip of his scotch. "I hadn't heard that. I don't think that's true." He thought for a moment. "But if Barker wanted to throw someone under the bus to keep any suspicion away from him, he would do that to Connors and never regret it."

"I agree," Mercer said. "I think this is a power play by Barker. What I don't know is who did try to kill Nikki."

"I don't know either. The CIA is still investigating, but they are not any closer to disclosing any information about it. My contacts in the UK tell me they are no closer either. I'll call Jack Kensington in the morning."

"Let me know what he says," Mercer added. "You are better at this intelligence game than I am, but tell me, who would want to kill Nikki? And why would they try to kill her *after* she exposed the tape? It doesn't make sense. If it were Stevens or you or anyone in power here, wouldn't it make more sense to kill her *before* she exposed the tape?"

"Yes, it would make more sense to do it before." Jenkins took another sip of his scotch. "Unless, of course, your whole purpose for doing so was to frame me."

Mercer studied Jenkins. Mercer's thoughts took him to a more elaborate plan. What if Jenkins wanted Nicole dead? Could he orchestrate this whole scenario to make it look like he was framed? Mercer shook his head. "It's getting hard to keep track of all the players in this."

Jenkins knew what Mercer was thinking. He stared at Mercer and didn't blink an eye. "I didn't do it." Mercer acknowledged his comments with a simple nod. "Thank you for believing me."

Mercer smiled. "I am sure what Nikki did hurt you deeply. I can see that you still care for her."

"I still love her," Jenkins corrected. "I never wanted to see her hurt. And for God's sake, I could never kill her." Jenkins bowed his head and looked at the floor. "I also know that I have lost her." Mercer could see Jenkins was visibly shaken by his confession. Jenkins downed the rest of his scotch and set the glass on the table. He cleared his throat. "All that aside, without some hard evidence, I have no idea how to refute this accusation." Mercer nodded his head. "Making the case that I didn't do it without evidence makes me look pretty guilty."

"I agree," Mercer took another drink. He stood up and retrieved the scotch bottle from the bar. He set it on the table next to Jenkins.

"No, thanks," Jenkins said. "The last thing I need is to be picked up on a drunk driving charge."

Mercer chuckled. "You're right." He removed the bottle and placed it back on the bar. "How can I help?" Mercer walked back to his seat.

"I'm not sure right now," Jenkins replied. "Until I have that figured out, I'd stay away from me."

Mercer appreciated Jenkins's attempt to keep him out of the spotlight. "Just let me know what I can do."

Jenkins stood up and walked to the door. "Thanks for the drink and the support. Hopefully, I'll be in touch soon with some answers."

CHAPTER SIX

End of May 1980

Inverness, Scotland

Afer their meeting with Tony, Sean and Nicole drove to Inverness, a city in the Scottish Highlands. After spending a few days searching the areas outside the city, they secured a small furnished cottage in the country. Sean had decided that the time had come for Nicole to learn to protect herself. He was determined to teach Nicole how to shoot a gun if it was the last thing he did. Given the resistance Nicole was giving him, he was beginning to think that it just might be the last thing he ever did!

"You don't have to buy a gun," Sean said, sitting at the kitchen table looking at Nicole who was sitting with her arms folded.

She rolled her eyes at Sean's comment. "I don't like guns."

"I'm not asking you to make love to the bloody thing," Sean wanted to shout, the strain evident in his voice. "Nicole, you need to protect yourself in case something happens to me."

Nicole paused. "Don't say that."

Sean looked down. "I'll give you a scenario where learning to shoot a gun would be helpful to you. Will you just hear me out?"

Nicole nodded. Sean was at first taken aback by her agreement. "OK, let's say Kent finds us here and he manages to shoot me or keep me at bay by breaking my legs or something—"

"Stop it!" Nicole said, her face showing the hurt the thought was bringing her.

"Just listen," Sean pleaded. "I'm not here or not able to help you. As much as the thought of Kent killing me or breaking my legs to keep me from helping you makes you hurt, you need to think of this. Do you have any idea how much the idea of Kent getting to you, capturing you, and abusing you before he ultimately kills you torments me?"

Nicole's anger subsided. She had never stopped to think about the possible scenario that Sean now placed in front of her. "I'm sorry. I haven't thought about that."

"You need to learn how to protect yourself. I know you don't like guns, but you need to learn how to shoot one at the very least. I also would like to teach you some basic fighting skills including how to use a knife." Sean could see Nicole softening to the idea. "Come on, tell me that you don't think that the fighting skill training couldn't be a little fun." Sean's mouth curled into a provocative smile.

As hard as she tried, Nicole couldn't help but return his smile. She wanted to have the last say, though. "Just hope you never really piss me off one day."

Sean laughed. "I'll be careful." He stood up and grabbed some cans that were sitting on the counter by the back door. "Let's go."

After securing their jackets, they moved outside. Sean set the cans down on a short stone wall that circled the cottage. He took Nicole by the hand and measured a short distance back from the targets.

He looked around the countryside. He had picked this particular cottage because he knew that he would be teaching Nicole the skills to help her regain her confidence. He removed his Beretta from its holster and took aim at one of the cans.

"You want to aim the gun at the center of the can," Sean looked at her. Nicole was looking out over the land. "Nicole, please."

"What is that?" Nicole asked, pointing at an animal off in the distance.

Sean sighed. "A cow, I guess. I don't care." He took Nicole and placed her in front of him. With one arm around her waist and his other arm that held the gun extended toward the target at Nicole's shoulder height, Sean pulled the trigger. The bullet struck the can, which flew up in the air and off the stone wall. The loud noise caused Nicole to recoil.

"That's the first thing you need to get used to," Sean said, holding her tight to keep her from moving away from him. "Look where I'm aiming. Look down here along this line." Sean tried to position her. "Nicole, please cooperate." Sean was starting to get angry at her lack of focus.

"Damn it, Sean," Nicole cursed. She grabbed the gun out of Sean's hand. She pointed it at the second can and shot the gun. It struck the can, just off center. "I never said that I didn't know how to shoot a gun. I said I don't like the damn things."

She forced her way out of Sean's grip who stood there in shock. She stood, braced, and then shot the third can. As the can rose slightly in the air, Nicole squeezed the trigger again, striking it just before it fell behind the stone wall. She turned, looked at Sean, and handed him the gun.

Sean was still speechless. He looked at Nicole, the questions apparent on his face. He shook his head, trying to clear it. He started to mouth one of the questions, but he just couldn't get the words to come out in the order he wanted.

"When it is 1964, and you are a white woman in Mississippi looking for the bodies of three men who were killed by the Klan, you take your protection seriously. I learned to shoot a gun then. One of the agents taught me." Nicole waited before she continued. "I was sick and tired of sexual harassment that started all the way back to my days at Harvard Law School. The bullshit started up again in Mississippi. One of the agents thought I would get more respect if I knew how to handle a gun. The sad thing is he was right." She looked Sean in the eyes and repeated herself. "Dark nights out looking for the three CORE members, one of whom was black, resulted in every supremacist wanting to make sure I knew my place. I never said that I didn't know how to use a gun." She walked past him, brushing his shoulder. "I said that I don't like them. I thought that part of my life was over." She kept walking and returned to the cottage.

Sean watched her walk away, realizing how much he didn't know about the woman he loved. He turned to look at the one remaining can. He shook his head, still surprised. "Amazing," was all he could mumble before he shot the last can twice. He replaced the gun in its holster and walked back to the cottage. "And don't be thinking you aren't getting a gun now, my love," he muttered as he walked toward the cottage. "You bloody hell will be getting a gun."

{II}

Puy-l'Évêque, France

Maggie wondered why she always invoked God's name when she climaxed. She didn't believe in God. Of course, this upset her mother who was a devoted Catholic—in spite of the fact that her mother had broken one of the commandments and a few of the religion's man-made laws. Maggie despised her mother and the man who had caused them both pain. It angered Maggie that her father would never know her mother's suffering over the years. She cursed at herself for even thinking of her mother at this moment. She detached herself from Kent, who was lying spent beneath her. Maggie laid on the bed, looking up at the ceiling of the gorgeous chateau in which she was now living. She wondered if she played her cards correctly if she would be worthy of all the Serpent had acquired.

Kent's breathing started to slow. He had never experienced anyone as good in bed as Maggie. It was not love. Kent had never experienced love, and even in his current state of mind, he wouldn't have recognized it if he had. He was just happy that this blonde-haired vixen with an insatiable appetite had wandered into his life. He had a weakness for blondes. He knew very little about this woman, and he didn't care to know anything more. If there came a day when he needed to dispose of her, not knowing the details of her wants and desires would make that task easier. He was intrigued that Maggie didn't want to know more about him. He questioned if she was simply fulfilling her bodily need just as he was.

Maggie sat up and grabbed her robe. She wrapped it around her as she walked to the bathroom to take a shower. "The market will be closing soon. Should I pick up the mail too while I'm in town?"

"That would be great. I have some correspondence to look over," Kent replied. There was no exchange of feelings toward one another, no need to embrace and hold each other. In Kent's mind, this arrangement was perfect.

"Do you want anything in particular from the market?" She asked as she dropped her robe to the floor of the bathroom in clear site of Kent. She eyed him as she ran her hand up her inner thigh. She bent over to run the water in the tub, well aware her tease had piqued his interest again.

Kent gave her a grin and shook his head. He had work to do and calls to make. He grabbed his underwear and trousers. "Grab whatever you like," he said while he was dressing. "I'll be in the study. Let me know when you are leaving." He zipped up his trousers and walked out of the bedroom. He smiled mischievously as he gave one last thought to the image of Maggie in the shower. This life was worth the time he spent undercover and being interrogated by SIS. He felt like he was finally in control of his life and he had everything he ever wanted. Well, almost everything. Sean and Nicole were still alive. His mood turned dark as he thought about them. In his mind's eye, he recalled the scene at the beach house. Nicole had teasingly played with his mind that night. He played out a scenario in his head where he ripped her from Sean's arms and made Sean watch him rape and murder Nicole. All the years he had to pretend to love Sean like a brother enraged the hate within him. Sean would pay for his gilt-edged life—a stark contrast to Kent's life.

The running water in the shower brought Kent back from his dark, deleterious thoughts. He shook his head to clear it and walked down the hall to his study. He closed the door and walked over to the desk. He noticed there were messages on the answering machine. The Serpent's business required a secure phone line and the privacy of the office. He would wait to listen to the messages—

no doubt propositions for the Serpent to consider—until Maggie had left.

Maggie finished dressing and picked up her purse. She walked down the hall, knocked on the door knowing it was locked and announced she was leaving for the market. Kent responded with a quick response that told Maggie he was busy with the work of an assassin. She looked inside her purse ensuring she had money and left the chateau for the market.

Puy-l'Évêque, which translates to "Bishop's Hill," was a quaint small town nestled above the Lot river. Saint-Sauveur was the main church, sitting on the hill and built into the town wall to strengthen its defense in the fourteenth through sixteenth centuries. The city had fallen into the hands of the British during the Hundred Years' War. The town was attacked by Protestants, who were fighting for King Henry IV in 1580 during the Wars of Religion. Marks of the king's cannonballs fired into the walled city are still visible on the exterior church walls. The remains of an old Roman road were still noticeable in places. Through time, the small town with a little more than two thousand residents expanded from its perch above the Lot down the mountainside to the river bank.

The Serpent took pride in the family-owned vineyards that surrounded the town. Winemaking was a cover that Kent intended to keep. The three vineyards were contracted out to and maintained by three different families. The Serpent took a small percentage of the wine profits in exchange for their work. The three families lived on what they could make in the wine business, which varied from year to year depending on the weather. Puy-l'Évêque was part of the Cahors wine region and grew Malbec grapes. The Malbec grapes produced a single-variety wine. Barges would arrive on the Lot River, where the wines would be loaded and shipped to the Bordeaux region for distribution and sale.

Puy-l'Évêque was a perfect town in which to hide. Its small population was happy with its relatively isolated life. Only one national road, D811, went through the town and the townspeople preferred it that way. The river, the D811, and one railroad station suited them just fine. The pace was slow. The farms around the town provided an excellent choice of in-season vegetables and a wide variety of cheeses. There were local bakeries and butchers. Life was good in this small town.

Maggie walked down the hill from the chateau that sat midway between the river and the old walled town. When she got to town, before heading to the market, she made a detour to a little bistro that had a public phone. It had been several weeks since she had last checked in with Elliot, who had been Sean's contact at SIS. She walked to the back where the public phone hung on the wall and placed her call.

"Hello, dear brother," Maggie said when she heard Elliot's voice. "Is there any news on our other brother?" Maggie was referring to Sean.

"All is good with him," Elliot replied. "How are things with you?"

"It's all good. We're hitting it off very well. It's still in the early stages, so I must be discreet. As far as I know, we'll be hanging around this place for a while." Maggie knew the Serpent had informants in the town. She knew she had to be cautious. She didn't want to come right out and say that the Serpent didn't have any travel or jobs planned at the moment. "All that may change in a few weeks. It depends if we can locate our other brother."

Elliot smiled for a moment. Even if he knew where Sean was, he wasn't about to let Maggie or anyone else know. He did find it interesting that Maggie asked about Sean. He noted that on a piece of paper in the folder he had pulled out of the file drawer when he heard Maggie's voice. "Call again when you have the chance or when he accepts a contract. Thank you for calling. Take care."

"You too, my lovely brother," she added with a hint of sarcasm in her voice. Elliot made another note in the file regarding her tone. Maggie walked out of the bistro after thanking the owner. She continued to the market where she picked up fresh vegetables, a variety of cheeses, and some meat. This was all she could manage to comfortably carry back to the chateau. It would last them a few days. If Kent decided to accept a contract, she might need to use the excuse of driving to the store for more food and place another call to Elliot to report Kent's travel plans. After retrieving the mail from the post office, she returned home within a few hours, not rousing any suspicion on the part of Kent.

{III}

Inverness, Scotland

"If I had a gun, you'd be dead," a woman, who appeared to be in her early fifties, whispered just loud enough for Sean to hear. Nicole and Sean had ventured into town to pick up some milk, bread, wine, and various meats in the grocery store. Restocking of the shelves and the banter of the clerks could be heard in the next aisle over. While still attractive, the woman had clearly led a hard life. But from the crow's feet around her eyes, a few wrinkles along her upper lip, and the gray hair that highlighted her dishwater-blonde hair, the woman was in excellent shape. Her clothes were formfitting, and it was clear that she prided herself on her muscle-toned body. Without the wrinkles and the spray of gray hair throughout, she could pass for someone a number of years younger.

She was standing behind Sean, who slowly moved his hand to his gun in its holster. Nicole had not heard what the woman said, but noticed Sean's deliberate hand movement. She looked at the woman who winked at her and put her finger to her lips indicating she wanted Nicole to remain silent. Nicole thought that odd and her brow furrowed with confusion. "Now, turn around and give your old friend a big hug!"

At first, Sean could not place the woman, who began to laugh and threw open her arms to hug him. Her laughter gave Sean the best clue. Sean retracted his hand from his Beretta and tilted his head while asking, "Gillian?"

"Yes!" Gillian confirmed, taking Sean into her arms and pulling him close. In her late forties, Gillian Webster looked older than her age but had not lost an ounce of strength. She twisted Sean side to side. "I think the last time I saw you, you were sixteen! You haven't changed a bit."

"It has been a long time," Sean confirmed, retreating from the hug, a bit embarrassed. "And you are far too kind. I don't think I've aged as well as you. What are you doing in Inverness?" Sean took a quick look around to see if their actions had attracted any attention. His eyes came to rest on a smiling Nicole with her arms crossed in front of her. He could tell she was wondering who this woman was.

"I've lived here since 1955," Gillian responded.

"I wondered where you had gone. I remember seeing you at Geoffrey's graduation, and then you just seemed to disappear."

"Yes, I left London shortly after that," Gillian confirmed. "It wasn't possible for me to stay there any longer, but I kept tabs on you and your brother." Gillian's attention seemed to waver as she thought briefly about that time. She mumbled, "You and Geoffrey were so kind to me." She shook her head to clear it and changed the subject. "What brings you to Inverness? Work, I bet."

"No. It's just a short visit." Sean raised an arm to indicate he wanted Nicole to join him. Nicole walked toward him, and he brought her to his side in an embrace. "This is Nicole. She's from the United States and has never seen the United Kingdom—"

"Well," Gillian frowned and lowered her voice. "She'll be seeing a lot more of it now that she has asylum." Gillian winked. Sean, surprised that Gillian recognized Nicole, took a quick look around the store. "Relax, Sean. No one of any importance ever drives this far north."

Sean finished his quick sweep of the store and found that Gillian was right. The store was virtually empty of shoppers. Sean changed the subject, thinking back to when he was a teenager. "Weren't you Jack Kensington's secretary back in the day?"

Gillian hesitated. "Yes, that's right." She smiled and, adding a hearty laugh, she continued, "You had quite a crush on me back then." She nudged Sean with her elbow, giving him a wink. Sean began to blush, knowing that Gillian was right. "Ahh…see! I knew you had a thing for me!" She looked at Nicole. "It was great fun to tease him back then." Nicole joined Gillian in laughter as Sean tried to control his inevitable blushing. "That was a great time. I was having a ton of fun back then."

Gillian was very happy to see Sean and clearly still enjoyed teasing him. She thought it might be a good opportunity to hear more about the people she had truly loved but had to leave. Gillian knew better than to ask about the people she had worked for in a public place, especially Jack Kensington. She had read the story of Sean's wife and child in the newspaper, and while the paper didn't mention Sean's occupation, she had guessed he had joined SIS as he had pledged. Jack was always filling Sean's head with swashbuckling tales of secret agents. Even when Sean was young, it was apparent that he didn't get along with his father. Also,

Gillian's hug revealed to her the shoulder holster and gun. Gillian quickly deduced that Sean and Nicole's visit to Inverness was not pleasure. "Let's get together, shall we? I would love to hear all about you and your family. I never get any visitors, and I would just love to spend some time with you both."

Against his better judgment, Sean agreed. Before parting ways, Gillian wrote down her address, and they settled on a date and time for their visit. Gillian's home was not very far from their rental. After an awkward hug good-bye between Sean and Gillian, they each returned to their shopping. Upon arriving back at the rented cottage, Sean unloaded the car while Nicole started putting the groceries away.

The cottage itself had a total of four rooms. There were two bedrooms, a bathroom, and the kitchen/living room area. The living room was a nice size complete with a fireplace and stone wall, which gave the cottage a very homey feel. The kitchen was open with a table separating the two rooms. The only sound was the eerie wind that seemed to constantly produce whistling sounds as it swirled through the trees and around the buildings.

"Shall I begin dinner?" Nicole called to Sean, who was in the bedroom.

"Not yet," Sean walked back into the living room. "Let's have a cocktail first."

"Well, I'm not going to promise dinner gets cooked if we are going to start drinking," Nicole joked.

"I'll help," Sean replied. "I'd just like to sit for a while."

"OK, what do you want to drink?" Nicole asked.

"I'll get us gin and tonic. Sit down, I'll bring it over." Sean moved to the kitchen as Nicole walked to the couch that flanked the fireplace.

Nicole sat down, picking up the remote for the television that was on the coffee table in front of her. She flipped through the channels until she found the local news report. She turned the sound down so that it just provided background noise. "I hope you don't mind; that whistling wind is enough to make my skin crawl."

"No," Sean said as he finished making their drinks. He walked over to the couch, handing one glass to Nicole. "There must be a front moving through." They toasted, clinked glasses, and each took a sip of their drink.

"Wow," Nicole said. "You must have really needed this."

"Is it too strong?" Sean asked, innocently. "I can get more tonic if you like."

"No, that's OK," Nicole responded. "I think I'm just out of practice." Sean smiled. "You may be making dinner by yourself." Nicole watched Sean as his thoughts took him elsewhere. "So, tell me about Gillian."

Sean looked at Nicole. "That's who I was just thinking about." Nicole gave Sean a look that told him she knew that. Sean marveled at her intuitiveness. "I don't remember much about her. I know that she was Jack's secretary at SIS. Dad and Jack have been friends for a very long time. Dad was in the House of Lords by then. Jack had quickly worked his way up the intelligence ladder, making it clear he wanted to be the director. Dad was all for that and helped in any way he could. Gillian was probably in her twenties back then. She has never looked her age, and she had this particular way about her. She wasn't gorgeous. Actually, she was very average looking, but she had the best sense of humor, and when you are a horny teenager, her smutty mouth and teasing were intriguing. She knew I had a crush on her. She flirted with me just to see me blush." He paused. "She was fun, and I will always remember that provocative laugh. Although something had changed the last time I saw her. We were all celebrating Geoff's graduation, and she was very serious, almost sad. Thinking back on it, I suspect she and Jack were having an affair." Sean's mind drifted off in thought. "I remember an awkward moment a few months prior when I walked in on them…having a moment. We were all at Dad's country estate." Sean paused, starting to smile, "It was probably no more than a kiss, maybe a passionate one, but it was certainly embarrassing for them both and bloody awkward for me."

"Probably something you don't want to mention when we visit," Nicole suggested, her sense of humor evident in her voice.

"At different events or gatherings at our home, Gillian would be there, especially if Jack was there. Jack's wife was there as well. It makes sense now, why Gillian would spend most of her time talking to Geoff and me. If Jack or his wife came into the room, she became very nervous and would find a reason to usher us to another room. Dad always thought it was sweet of her to be looking after us." Sean paused as he thought for a moment. "It was probably a month or two later that she vanished. There was no explanation given to us. Being sixteen, I didn't ask what happened to her."

"So I gathered," Nicole chimed in before taking another sip of her cocktail. "I can say that I'm not particularly happy that she recognized me."

"Yes," Sean cleared his head of the past. "That concerns me as well." Sean took a drink, letting the gin warm his mouth before swallowing. "I hadn't thought about just how recognizable you would be."

"Do you think we're safe?"

"We are for now. We need to be prepared. Who knows where Kent has informants."

{IV}

Washington, DC

"Kevin Thompson would like to see you," Chris said into the phone and then replaced the handset to its cradle. "Go on in."

Thompson walked into Jenkins's office and to the chair in front of his desk. Jenkins was finishing a sentence he was writing and motioned for Thompson to sit down. When he finished, he looked at Thompson.

"Remember you asked me to follow up on the McNair information that Harrigan gave you?" Jenkins nodded his head. "There was nothing there. I've been to the courthouse, looked through old records, every place I could think of, and found nothing. Are you sure this happened in DC?"

"I don't know that for sure," Jenkins replied truthfully. He noticed Thompson's dejected demeanor. "Don't feel so bad. Harrigan called and said he couldn't find anything either." He looked down at the paper on which he was writing finishing the additions to a speech he was giving in a few hours.

"I don't know what else to do," Thompson started. "We can't get a subpoena to look through the files at Rosen, Shafer, and Pruett. We don't have probable cause."

Jenkins looked up. "What did you say?"

"I said we couldn't subpoena the law firm's files."

195

Jenkins began to smile. "That's it!" he exclaimed.

"I said we could not—"

"I heard you," Jenkins interrupted as he opened his desk drawer and grabbed his key ring. "I have a feeling that would lead to a dead end as well."

"Why are you so happy?"

"It was Nikki. She is the source."

"OK…" Thompson said, still not following Jenkins.

Jenkins found the key he was looking for on his key ring. "With Nikki's records, I don't need a subpoena."

"Well, technically…"

"I don't have to say where I found them." Jenkins stood up and grabbed his suit jacket off the back of the chair. He began to put it on and walked to the door. "Are you coming?"

"Are you kidding?" Thompson questioned Jenkins, as he stood up to follow Jenkins out of the office. "Senator, wait!"

Jenkins stopped just as he reached for the doorknob. He turned and looked at Thompson. "What's the matter, Kevin?"

"You can't go over to Nikki's condo," Thompson declared. "What if the press sees you enter? You pay me to do the investigating. Let me do my job."

Chris looked up from his work at Jenkins. "Kevin's right, sir."

"Let me go have a look around. If I find something, I'll let you know, and we can figure out what the next steps are. Don't get your hands dirty on this," Thompson added.

Jenkins knew Thompson was right. He detached the key from the key ring and handed it to Thompson. "Upstairs in her bedroom on the right side of the bed is a nightstand. Pull the drawer out, flip it over, and you'll find the key to her files taped underneath."

Thompson wanted to laugh. "I'm not even going to ask how you know that."

Jenkins smiled. "She told me—"

"I said I didn't want to know," Thompson interrupted.

"In her files somewhere is the combination to her safe," Jenkins continued.

"OK, now I'm curious. Does Nikki know the combinations to your safes?" Thompson asked.

"No."

"So, why was she so giving with her information?"

"It was part of an argument. Nikki thought if she told me hers, I would tell her mine." Jenkins smiled and raised his eyebrows.

"I bet she was furious," Thompson joked.

"She was. Bring whatever you think will help us." Jenkins thought how genius it was for Nicole to plant this evidence. He also wondered how she knew Harrigan would come to him with the information. He couldn't wait to hear back from Thompson.

{V}

Washington, DC

The attorney general issued a press release that resulted in a packed conference room. The press conference was to address the possible prosecution of former President Stevens and his accomplices. The rumor was the attorney general, who had been appointed by Andrews, would show no mercy.

He entered the room promptly at nine o'clock and placed a leather notebook on the podium. As he opened the notebook and scanned the room, the reporters took their seats. The room became quiet without any prompting. He looked down at his notes and cleared his throat. Off to his right were four assistants who had accompanied him, standing attentively, arms full of papers, and waiting patiently for the attorney general's instruction. He motioned for them to start distributing the papers and the assistants sprang into action, each taking a section of the audience as planned.

"Good morning," the attorney general started. "I will not be taking any questions, and my assistants are handing out printed copies of what I'm about to address." He waited for the assistants to finish before he launched into his announcement. "The Office of the Attorney General has reviewed the evidence submitted to us by the Senate Select Committee formed by Senator Robert Jenkins. We have conducted some additional interviews with the parties in question and find that we owe it to the American people to press charges. Those charges are as follows: President Mark Stevens is charged with conspiracy to the murder of President Andrews, first-degree murder, and treason. Representative Davis is charged with conspiracy and treason. FBI director Michael Jefferies is charged with conspiracy, first-degree murder, and treason. Joseph Engle is charged with conspiracy and treason. The reason Engle and Davis are charged with conspiracy and treason is that they had no direct contact with the assassin but contributed money needed to secure the services of the assassin. Their payments went directly to Sipes. Jefferies provided the contact information and Stevens ordered the assassination. However, we are still considering an additional charge of murder. More information is available in the packets. We see no other path available to us, and we take no enjoyment in bringing these men to justice. The trial dates will be established quickly thanks to the evidence collected and provided by the committee. In the coming days, there will be an announcement regarding the trial dates. That's all I have for today. Thank you."

The attorney general closed his leather notebook, tucked it under his arm, and left the room as the reporters shouted questions. The news reporters would hound the Justice Department for clues over the coming days. Questions would be asked and suspicions raised, making one wonder if the media was attempting to sway public opinion. The attorney general and his staff would endure much scrutiny in the coming weeks, but they were prepared. There was too much evidence not to pursue these charges.

CHAPTER SEVEN

Beginning of June 1980

Inverness, Scotland

S ean and Nicole arrived at Gillian's house, a few days having passed since their chance meeting at the grocery store. Sean's intuition was running wild—he wasn't sure why. He had voiced his concern earlier to Nicole, who tried to reassure him that it was probably just nerves in regards to seeing someone he had not seen in years. Sean dropped the subject, knowing that his intuition was rarely wrong.

They exited the car and walked to Gillian's door. Sean glanced around the grounds and even swayed off the path, taking a look at the sides and part of the backyard. Nicole gave him a quizzical look but knew that he was in full agent mode and smiled at his concern for their well-being. Satisfied that he couldn't see anything suspicious, he rejoined Nicole at the door.

Nicole rang the doorbell, taking Sean's arm. She didn't like seeing him this nervous, and it made her feel uneasy. She felt Sean's shoulder holster and gun as her hand brushed past them. Ever since the explosion at Peter's cottage, Sean only removed the holster and gun when he slept. Even then, the gun was within reach.

Gillian opened the door with a huge smile, giving them both a hug.

She had an apron on, which was covered in flour. Sean and Nicole did their best to avoid the flour but failed in the end. It was obvious that she had been baking. The aroma of freshly baked scones and clotted cream filled the air. For Sean, it brought back childhood memories. His mother would rise early on cold mornings to make the scones and clotted cream for breakfast. Along with the scones came bits of a more traditional breakfast including eggs and a breakfast meat, but it was the smell of the scones that Sean woke up to and thoroughly enjoyed, almost too hot to eat without burning his tongue. "Come on in! I need to grab the scones from the oven. Have a seat; I'll be right back."

"Can I help you?" Nicole asked, dusting the flour off her jacket.

"No, everything else is on the table." Gillian ushered them to the table in the back of the main room. Sean looked around the small, furniture-laden home. He surmised that it was a two-bedroom unit, and when he was content that no one else was present, he walked over to the table.

He motioned for Nicole to move away from the seat she was about to sit on as it would give him a better advantage to see both the front and back door and most the windows. Nicole gave him a disapproving look, as she was certain that Sean was overreacting. Sean shot a look back at her. It told Nicole that he wasn't in the mood for any back talk.

"The scones smell wonderful," Sean said. "They remind me of my school days."

"It's your Mum's recipe," Gillian announced as she walked in from the kitchen with a tray containing the scones, clotted cream and a pot of tea. Gillian served the tea and then sat down. "Margaret gave it to me."

"What's this?" Nicole asked, pointing to the clotted cream.

"It's clotted cream, dear," Gillian responded. "Don't tell me you've never had it."

"I've never had it," Nicole bantered with an intrigued smile on her face.

"Clotted cream is cow's milk, cream actually, that is scalded, never stirred, during the heating of it. When it starts to clot, it is removed from heat and left overnight to cool."

"So it's like cream cheese?"

"Cream cheese? Oh, no, not at all," Gillian said, wrinkling her nose. "I tried that once. I didn't like it." Gillian spooned some of the cream from its dish and put it next to the scone on the plate that she handed Nicole. "Give it a try, love, and if you don't like it, I'm sure Sean will finish it."

Sean smiled at Gillian's comment. "How did you know this was one of my favorites?"

"I think your dad mentioned it a few times. I can't remember really." Gillian thought for a moment. "It might have been during my time working for Jack Kensington. I used to bring these scones in for us to enjoy in the office. Your father must have been there a few times and enjoyed them during their meetings. That must be it."

They chatted for a while around the table, enjoying their tea and scones. They talked about Sean as a teen and Gillian teased him about the crush he had on her. She confessed she had fun teasing him and watching him blush. Nicole enjoyed hearing about the antics that Gillian played on Sean.

Gillian was not shy in any way and continued to be forward with her questions. She mentioned that she had often offered advice to

Jack, an action that did not go unnoticed by several other secretaries. From Gillian's telling, she was a Renaissance woman in a much more genteel age. Women in the workforce at that time were seen and not heard. The feminist in Nicole admired her for her courage; however, Nicole was about to find out something that would cause her to admire Gillian even more.

They moved to the casual sitting area in the front of the cottage and sat down. Sean was becoming even more curious about Gillian's disappearance hearing about how closely she had worked with Jack. As they became comfortable in their chairs, Sean asked, "Gillian, if your work relationship with Jack was so outstanding, why on Earth did you leave?"

Gillian lowered her head for a quick second. She looked up again and, with a hint of regret, she addressed Sean. "No one has ever known that reason; not even Jack. You see, Jack and I were involved outside the office." Nicole smiled as Gillian said that remembering Sean's comments from a few days ago. "I became pregnant in the winter of 1955. I never told Jack, but I was so in love with him. I asked him if there was any circumstance where he would leave his wife for me."

Sean stood up and walked to the window. Looking outside, Sean recalled the many women Jack Kensington had taken to bed over the years. Jack married for status, not love. Everyone knew it. Well, everyone except Peter—until Sean blurted it out one day.

Gillian continued. "We had a wonderful last night together. Jack fell asleep at my flat. We woke the next morning. When I asked again if he would leave his wife, he assured me that he would never do so, even though he said he would the night before. Of course, now I understand that 'yes' was in the throes of passion." Gillian had not stopped smiling since their arrival. But now, her face turned somber, and she seemed to age before Nicole's eyes.

The light that was present had left Gillian. Her voice revealed a disdain that grew over the many years she had endured without the man she loved. "It was clear I made one awful mistake. I fell in love with Jack and wanted him for myself. I thought he loved me, but it became clear that I was expendable."

"So, you left to have the baby?" Nicole asked. Sean turned to face Gillian when Nicole asked her question.

The disdain was even more evident as Gillian replied, "I'm Catholic, love—of course, I had the baby."

Nicole found that comment a rather interesting dichotomy. Gillian was sleeping with a married man, breaking one of the Ten Commandments, yet she wouldn't abort the child produced from the sin. Were there degrees of sin? What was the justification that went through Gillian's mind that said it was acceptable to sleep with a married man? What stopped her from committing another sin? Nicole was no prude, and she certainly had broken some Catholic laws—if she had been a Catholic or possibly even the least bit religious. She had grown up attending Protestant services only on occasion with her parents. Her parents instilled in Nicole a set of morals that she mostly adhered to in her childhood years. However, the day her parents died in a car accident was the day she turned her back on religion.

Nicole's mind took her back to that time. She saw herself pleading with the pastor of the church they infrequently attended, begging him to lay her parents to rest. The pastor told Nicole he couldn't because her parents were not members and they didn't give money to the church. Nicole's aunt, her father's sister, stepped in, taking a leadership role. Her aunt, like her father, was very spiritual and she helped Nicole at a time when her whole world had crumbled. The aunt had the bodies of her parents cremated, and she held a memorial at Nicole's childhood home. Afterward, Nicole and her aunt traveled from their Midwestern town to spread the ashes at the various vacation spots her parents had taken Nicole over the years.

She got a perplexed look on her face when she thought back to the time she was shot. She remembered seeing her parents, Carol, and even her aunt, bathed in white light. She hadn't given the vision much thought until now. How long were they all there in that glorious light? Was she dreaming or were they actually there? There were rays of different colors; all the colors of the rainbow reaching out and beckoning her. It was a calm and pleasant feeling, and she didn't want to leave. Thinking back to that experience, it felt strangely odd now.

Gillian mistook Nicole's facial expression as a judgment on her actions. She calmly said, "Don't judge me, love."

Gillian's voice brought Nicole back from her thoughts. "Oh, no!" Nicole expressed emphatically. "I'm not judging you at all. I was just thinking back to something that happened to me when I was younger. I'm sorry. It had nothing to do with you or your circumstances."

"My daughter is the best thing that ever happened to me. I truly believe that God has a plan. And while I still pray for forgiveness of my sins," Gillian pointed to a framed photo of her daughter on the fireplace mantel, "I know my daughter is the best gift I could have ever received."

Sean moved from the window to look at the photograph. He stopped in front of it, and he understood instantly all the warnings his intuition had brought him. In the photo was a beautiful young lady with blue eyes and long blonde hair parted in the middle. Her eyes twinkled with happiness, and her build was slight but muscle toned. Sean had seen her before. "What's her name?" Sean asked trying to hide his animosity.

"Margaret, but we all call her Maggie," Gillian informed them. "I named her after your dad's secretary. She was very helpful to me at a time when I had no one."

Sean's back was to Gillian and Nicole. Nicole noticed his body stiffen slightly. He closed his eyes. Yes, it was definitely Maggie, and Maggie was teaming up with Kent. She was supposed to be gathering information and garnering Kent's trust. She was supposed to be the agent that SIS could count on to take out Kent if he got too out of hand. Sean opened his eyes, which flashed a familiar anger as he looked at the photograph again. He could hear Maggie's voice flirting with him in Charlie's office. "And Jack Kensington doesn't know he has a beautiful daughter?"

"No, he doesn't know." Gillian heard the hint of the anger that Sean was trying desperately to conceal. "I don't want him ever to know, Sean. Is something wrong?"

Sean ignored the question. Nicole looked at Sean's hands. One of them was clenched so tight it was turning red. She started to become concerned. Still looking at the photo, he asked, "Is she here in Inverness? Where does she work?" Sean had managed to make these questions seem like a genuine inquiry and not a cross-examination.

"No, she left Inverness after graduation. She lives in London and works for an advertising agency. She's not a model, mind you. She works behind the scenes on accounts, I think she said. In any case, she told me that the advertising market is so competitive that she can't talk about her work. She wrote me a while ago and said that her new project is taking her abroad and that she would write and call when she could." Gillian smiled at the accomplishments of her daughter. "I'm so proud of her."

Sean tried not to scoff at Gillian's last comment. "Does she know who her father is?"

"Yes, of course. There was no way we were ever going to cross paths again, so I told her when she was in her teenage years. There was a bit of resentment and anger that we both needed to work through, but after a few weeks she let it go and was back enjoying life. She is that way, you know. She's like a butterfly, flitting here and there and brightening all she touches." Nicole couldn't tell if Gillian was intentionally brash. Her voice had a sweetness to it, but there seemed to be an underlying hostility. It was as if Gillian was trying hard to convince not only Sean but herself that she wasn't holding a grudge.

Sean almost got sick at the butterfly comment. His intuition was telling him that Maggie wanted revenge. He swallowed and gathered his senses. He looked at his watch and announced, "We need to leave." He looked at Nicole, who knew not to counter what he said. Sean turned to face them. "I'm so sorry, Gillian, to rush off like this, but there is something I must attend to this afternoon." He stepped toward Gillian to give her a hug. Gillian stood up and wrapped both arms around Sean. The photograph that Sean had been studying was now exposed.

Nicole glanced at the photograph and quickly let out a low but audible gasp. She gave a small cough to cover the sound and cleared her throat. She stood and walked over to hug Gillian. "Thank you for the tea and scones. I'm not sure I'll get used to clotted cream, though." They embraced briefly, and then Sean took her arm. They walked to the door and said their goodbyes a second time.

"Maggie will be so happy to know that you've stopped by," Gillian said as Nicole walked outside the small house, followed quickly by Sean.

Sean turned and looked at Gillian. "You've mentioned me to her?"

"She knows all about you, Geoff, Peter, and Jack. You were all my life back then. The stories I told were like fairy tales to her. She loved hearing them."

Sean gave the best fake smile he could give her. "Right," was all he could muster.

"Good-bye and thank you again," Nicole interjected, albeit the thank-you sounded a tad bit disparaging.

Gillian smiled back and exclaimed again how happy she was to have seen them. Sean asked her not to mention the visit to Maggie, but he knew that would not be the case. They turned and briskly walked to Sean's car. "Foolish woman," Sean whispered angrily. They arrived at the car, and Sean opened the car door for Nicole. She didn't make eye contact with him as she slid into the passenger seat. Sean waved to Gillian, who was standing in the doorway, as he reached the driver's side, opened the door, and got into the car. He started the engine and tried his best not to peel away from the curb as quickly as he wanted.

Nicole looked over at Sean. She watched him as he put miles between Gillian's house and themselves. With each mile that passed, the familiar, intense behavior that Nicole first witnessed at the beach house in North Carolina started to soften. She knew better than to talk to him when he was in this mood. She knew he was forming a plan and she didn't want to interrupt his thoughts. As they approached their rented, quaint cottage, Sean seemed to relax enough for Nicole to talk to him.

"I don't understand what's going on here, Sean."

"That makes two of us," Sean confirmed. "But we aren't staying in Inverness. We can't risk that."

"Where are we going?"

"The more I think about it," Sean started with a small hesitation in his voice, "I keep coming back to London."

"It is a big city," Nicole said with a smile. "Sometimes it is easy to get lost in a big city."

"That's not why I want to go there," Sean commented. "If Jack doesn't know that he has a daughter, there's a possibility that Maggie isn't..." his voice trailed off.

"Are you saying that she may want to hurt Jack?" Nicole asked in surprise.

"That could be a possibility," Sean suggested. "And she just might be thinking retribution beyond Jack."

"Who? You and your dad?"

Sean was frustrated. He didn't know enough, and that was eating away at him. Every nerve was on high alert, and every impulse was telling him to run. His intuition was telling him he needed to tell his father and Jack about Maggie. They arrived at their cottage, and Sean turned off the engine.

"Sean?" Nicole prodded.

"I don't know, Nicole. Something just isn't feeling right."

Nicole nodded her head, indicating that she understood. "Let's get packed and get out of here."

Sean smiled at Nicole's willingness to trust him completely. They got out of the car and walked into the cottage. They packed quickly. Nicole made some sandwiches and packed a few drinks. The fewer stops they made on the way to London, the better. She couldn't help but wonder if her asylum was limiting their choices.

Sean placed all the bags into the car and returned inside the cottage. He saw the worried expression on Nicole's face. She finished placing the food and drinks in a small bag and looked up to see Sean looking at her. She smiled faintly when Sean caught her eye.

"Ready?" Sean asked as she walked toward him carrying the bag.

"Yes."

"It will be all right," Sean told her reassuringly. "I just feel like I need to warn Dad and Jack."

"I know," Nicole replied.

After getting into the car, Sean looked at the cottage and the surrounding landscape. Nicole was doing the same. Their eyes met, and Nicole tried to smile again. "We don't seem to stay put very long," was all she could manage to say.

{II}

Atlanta, Georgia

Harrigan was a fighter. He wasn't born with a silver spoon in his mouth, and he didn't land in the anchor chair directly from college. In truth, no one does, but his high standards and hard work earned him the respect of others as he worked his way up the ranks of his chosen profession. He started out in the trenches of the Vietnam War, covering tide-turning offensives from the foxholes with the American soldiers. He later traveled to Afghanistan to do an in-depth report on the Mujahideen. Harrigan caught the eyes of the network bosses, and when their beloved anchor stepped down, Harrigan won the support of the public for his honest, direct approach, strength, and ability to humanize a story. Harrigan, like Jenkins, had watched men die in defense of the rights secured by the Constitution. He appreciated those men's courage and respected their sacrifice. He loathed those who took advantage of their privileged upbringing and their lack of compassion for the common man.

Harrigan was watching the campaign coverage and was impressed with the changes Jenkins had made in his speeches. Harrigan had to admit that Jenkins's speeches were now reflecting Jenkins's beliefs, and it reminded him of Jenkins's Senatorial campaign—the successful campaign that, years later, would land him in the middle of the mess that resulted in the GOP's disarray. Harrigan was very doubtful the overanalyzing, dry, and serious Blackwood could rally his party behind him. McNair, the flamboyant and charismatic Irishman, was having more success. McNair had no problem attacking Jenkins. McNair's problem was the press, along with the average American citizen, who was not interested in what McNair was saying.

Harrigan now had a little apartment in Atlanta. He was working closely with the crew of the little start-up cable news network. Harrigan's experience both in front of and behind the camera was desperately needed. He had done what Warner told him to do: he formed a team consisting of those he trusted the most. One of the producers from his old network joined him. Harrigan had mentored some college journalism students in Washington who were due to graduate in a few days. Two of them had finished their exams and decided against attending graduation, excited by the offer to work with Harrigan at the start-up. The third graduate would be joining them in a few days.

Harrigan looked around the newsroom and saw mostly young faces. The veterans were either producers or anchors that Warner was able to steal away from some of the most prominent news agencies. He liked the feel of this network. It felt like the Wild West of the news. Harrigan worried that their youthful zeal might get them in trouble, but he hoped the cooler heads of the most experienced producers would keep that from happening.

"Hey, Steven," a young woman called from the receptionist desk at the front of the bullpen. "You have a package here."

Harrigan walked over to retrieve it. After thanking her, he headed to his office and closed the door. He looked at the envelope and noticed there was no return address. He opened it up to find the closed-door summarization of McNair's attempted murder and an illegal drug charge. Also in the file was McNair's arrest record, courtesy of Chief Bailey, and his admittance record to Saint Elizabeths Hospital. Harrigan sat down as he read the notes, complete with the judge's name, the prosecutor's name, and a clear note that McNair's counsel was Tony Shafer. However, a black marker obscured what followed Tony's name.

Included in the summary was the list of exhibits—the evidence gathered by the police. The high-price escort's name and the illegal substance used that evening were listed as well. All Harrigan had to do was contact her and get a statement, or even ask for an interview, to start the wheels in motion. It was almost too good to be true. Then he remembered his conversation with Jenkins about the mysterious woman who informed him of McNair's indiscretion. He paged through the remaining documents and looked again at the envelope. There was nothing tying this package to Washington DC, let alone Jenkins. The postmark indicated the package was mailed from Montana. Harrigan scratched his head.

He thought about what he had in his possession. He knew that Jenkins was also not born with a silver spoon in his mouth and that Jenkins earned everything he had achieved. He wondered if Jenkins could be trusted and how honest Jenkins truly was. Was Harrigan willing to risk working with Jenkins to expose McNair? Would his actions aid yet another corrupt politician, or would he be helping to facilitate a change that could ultimately alter the expectations the voting public had of their politicians? Did Jenkins mean to bring the change that had been called for in the past twenty years or was it just another empty campaign promise? Call for change, get elected, and then return to business as usual was the commonality regardless of which party gained power.

He picked up the phone and dialed Jenkins's Senate office. When Chris answered, Harrigan identified himself. He told Chris that he knew Jenkins was in California and asked if Jenkins could call him when the senator got a chance. Chris agreed to pass on the message.

Harrigan locked the information in his desk and returned to the business at hand. Warner was scheduled to tour the facilities at two that afternoon. World News Network was due to go live in twenty-four hours, and their opening story still needed polishing. The eruption of Mount Saint Helens in Washington state had occurred on May 18th, and WNN had sent a camera crew and reporter to cover the effects of the eruption. The last eruption of a volcano in the contiguous forty-eight states had been in California in 1915. Mount Saint Helens killed fifty-seven people, and WNN created a memorial slideshow of those who had lost their lives in the eruption. As Mount Saint Helens continued to spew its lava in the following two weeks, an interesting story was developing on two men listed as killed in the eruption. A WNN reporter managed to track down one of the men listed as killed—who was still very much alive—and interview him. After initially reporting one of the men missing, the person who reported the man being interviewed as missing was now claiming they had made no such report. People always loved a little mystery and scandal dashed with drama.

Another in-depth story WNN was focusing on was the 1980 Olympics. Moscow was hosting the Summer Olympics, but a boycott was imminent. With the USSR's invasion of Afghanistan earlier in the year, the United States along with its allies debated over the last two months whether to participate in the games. Ultimately, sixty-five nations would not send their athletes to the games. WNN had teams in Moscow to report on the political atmosphere there. There was a news team in Iran to discuss the kidnapping of the US ambassador and his death that had occurred in February. It would also report on the coup attempt and the killing of Afghan President Tariq. The report would tie these events to the ousting of the Shah of Iran, weakened US-Iran relations, and finally the invasion of the USSR into Afghanistan. It would paint the picture of two Cold War adversaries utilizing two developing nations as their pawns in a power play to secure oil rights and how the everyday citizens of these two countries were affected by these powerful nations' association with jihadists. These two powerful nations, the United States and the USSR, also did not realize just what their naïve meddling would create for future generations.

The third story dominating the debut of WNN was the attorney general's progress on the murder, conspiracy, and treason charges against the four remaining conspirators. WNN reporters would also be following the campaigns of frontrunners Jenkins and Blackwood, as the conventions were just around the corner. Harrigan hoped to obtain an interview with both men. He had called both campaign managers yesterday and was waiting to hear back from them. He had also called the British government with a request to interview Nicole Charbonneau. He wondered if he would hear anything back on that request. The new information he had just received, if he could confirm it, would also provide additional feature stories for the new, fledgling network. Harrigan knew from all his experience that the earth-shattering news stories presented themselves on their own timing. He just needed to be patient.

{III}

Los Angeles, California

Jenkins was doing a live phone interview in his hotel before heading back to Ohio for one last mad-dash campaign effort to win the state. His lead over Douglas Stanford in California was in the double digits, but Ohio was a tight race. Fred Whittaker, his campaign manager and a trusted friend, wanted to spend the day before the June 3rd primary swinging through Ohio's cities, which typically voted Democrat.

Whittaker was in the room as well, listening to the phone interview on an extension. Jenkins was in a chair, staring at the muted television as he listened to the interviewer prattle on about subjects for which the interviewer knew very little. Jenkins had shown patience throughout the interview, giving his stock answers and lowering their content to the level of the interviewer so that he and his listeners could grasp it.

Then it happened: the interviewer decided to go off script. He decided to ask the one question that could cause Jenkins to lose his temper. He asked about the accusation that Jenkins had ordered the assassination of his ex-girlfriend. Jenkins looked at Whittaker, who could see Jenkins's face turning red with anger. Whittaker moved his hand in an up-and-down motion, indicating that he wanted Jenkins to calm down.

Jenkins took a deep breath. When the interviewer was done casting judgments with false evidence and innuendo, Jenkins calmly said, "I'm not sure what planet McNair is on right now, but Nikki was the love of my life. And if I take all of your theories to heart, then why wouldn't I have had her killed before she exposed the tape? McNair's accusation makes no sense. After she exposed the Sipes tape, my leverage to blackmail people, as McNair put it the other day, disappeared. Who am I going to blackmail now that the secret is out? Not one person. Everyone who was involved in that conspiracy is either dead or removed from office. There is absolutely nothing to gain from—how did McNair put it?—shutting her up."

The interviewer confirmed that McNair said that would be Jenkins's response. He then asked about extraditing Nicole to the United States.

"She has asylum in the United Kingdom. She will not be extradited; she is not a spy. If anything, she is a whistleblower, and I don't believe in persecuting anyone who has the courage to do what she did. Frankly, someone used Nikki because they were not brave enough to expose the tape themselves." Jenkins paused and laughed when the interviewer suggested Jenkins was that person. "No, it wasn't me. It was her old boss and a friend of Norman Sipes. He put her in the middle of this, and for that, I'll never forgive him." Jenkins listened to the follow-up question. "His name is Tony Shafer." Jenkins grinned when the interviewer reminded him that Tony was dead. "No, he is very much alive. In fact, I had a meeting with him a while back." He paused. The interview as if Tony staged his death. "I think you should ask him that."

And that was the new piece of information that would cause a new spin on the story. The next forty-eight hours would be spent searching for Tony Shafer, resulting in the focus being directed away from Jenkins. Whittaker smiled at how slickly Jenkins had planted the information. Jenkins couldn't care less how the press would treat Tony. He was sure that Tony deliberately made Nicole the target with his actions. With this new twist, Jenkins wanted to close down the interview. "Thank you so much for having me on your program. I'm running behind schedule a bit and need to get on a plane." He paused, listening to the interviewer. "I appreciate that," Jenkins responded to the interviewer who said Jenkins had his vote. "Remember to vote on June 3rd. I need your and your listeners' support. Thank you." Jenkins hung up the phone.

"Nice," Whittaker said. "Do you even know where Tony Shafer is?"

"Nope, and I don't care," Jenkins said as he stood up and stretched. The phone rang, and he picked it up. It was Chris. He informed Jenkins that Harrigan wanted to speak to him. Jenkins told Chris to call Harrigan back and tell him he would call him first thing in the morning.

Jenkins arrived in Ohio in the early morning, followed by only a few hours of sleep in a hotel bed. The time on the plane was spent discussing strategy and possible candidates for the vice presidency. He had asked for a wake-up call earlier than usual so that he would have a chance to talk with Harrigan. Coffee was delivered to his room, as he had requested, fifteen minutes after the wake-up call at five thirty. He drank a cup of coffee, and when he felt he was awake enough, he dialed Harrigan's new home number that Chris had given him. "Good morning, Steven."

"What time is it?" Harrigan asked in a sleepy voice. Harrigan had been asleep.

"Six o'clock," Jenkins informed him. "Chris said you wanted to talk to me?"

"I was hoping we could do this in person," Harrigan huffed as he sat up in bed. "It's about some information on McNair that was sent anonymously to my office."

Jenkins smiled. "Really?"

Harrigan remained silent for a moment as if he was waiting for

Jenkins to inquire what the information contained. When Jenkins didn't speak, Harrigan began. "It has to do with the information a source had given me. I couldn't find anything about it at the time."

"Do you need something from me?"

"Where did you get this information?" Harrigan asked accusingly.

"I don't believe I have ever seen it. I won't comment on something I haven't seen," Jenkins dodged the accusation. Jenkins was not going to confirm any suspicion that he sent the package.

"Can I report the information to you and ask for comment?"

"That sounds like something the press would do," Jenkins advised, shrewdly.

Harrigan thought for a moment. "I don't have the information here with me. How do you want to play this?" He knew that Jenkins sent the package to him. He also knew that Jenkins was never going to admit to that. "Would you come on my show and we can talk about your candidacy, and I can ask some questions on the information?"

Jenkins knew Harrigan was in Atlanta. He grabbed his calendar. "I won't be back in Washington until the evening of June 3rd. There is something I want to do before I'm on your program and I would need for the interview to be done remotely. My schedule is packed, and a trip to Atlanta is out of the question. Would the fifth work?" Jenkins asked.

Harrigan thought about his schedule. "I believe so. I'll call Chris after I check my schedule to confirm. And we can set something up with our affiliate there in Washington so that you can do it remotely."

"That sounds perfect," Jenkins confirmed. "I will talk to you when

I return." Jenkins hung up the phone. He poured himself another cup of coffee and then dialed Senator Mercer's number. "Good morning, Daniel."

"Bobby? Is everything OK?" Mercer asked as he looked at his bedside clock.

"Yes, everything's fine," Jenkins said. "I have a busy schedule today. I was just wondering if I could meet with you the evening of June 3rd."

"Yes, of course."

"And then, if you could, schedule a meeting with Barker in your office for the morning of June 4th."

"What should I say it is about?"

"Well, let's mislead him a little," Jenkins replied with a sly grin on his face. "Tell him that you have been talking to me about vice presidential candidates and you have convinced me to reconsider."

Mercer sat up in bed. "Are you serious?"

Jenkins chuckled. "No, not on your life would I ever consider him. It will all become clear tomorrow evening. In the meantime, just have some fun setting him up for once."

Mercer smiled. "Remind me never to piss you off."

Jenkins smiled again. "It's not a wise thing to do. I will see you tomorrow evening." Jenkins hung up the phone and started his day with a much-needed shower to help rejuvenate him. His day consisted of campaign stops and speeches. He was the Democratic front-runner, and the polls showed that he could win the primary election by a landslide.

{IV}

London, England

"Dad," Sean called as he walked into his father's house in London. It had taken them about nine hours, including a stop, to travel to London from Inverness. In Nicole's estimation, Sean drove like a madman, but thankfully they arrived without incident. She was glad that she had packed the sandwiches and drinks. Nicole had to beg Sean to stop once, and since the car needed refueling, Sean relented. "Dad," Sean called again, as he walked into the living room. "Dad, where are you?"

It was just after nine o'clock in the evening. Peter was sitting in the dining room, entertaining his guests. He stood to meet Sean when Sean entered the room. Nicole was not with him—she had headed to the nearest bathroom. Peter's heart stopped for a second when he didn't see Nicole. "Sean, what's wrong? Is it Nicole? What happened?"

Sean turned around to see that Nicole had not followed him into the room. "She's with me; she's fine." He turned and took a few steps into the living room. "Nicole?" he shouted.

"I'm in the bathroom, speed racer," Nicole called from the hall.

Sean bit his lip at Nicole's tone and nickname for him, trying to suppress his laugh. He turned back around to face Peter when he noticed the dining room full of people. "I'm sorry. I didn't realize you had company."

"Yes, well, we're meeting about some parliamentary business. Sean, can this wait until later or even morning?"

"Yes, of course." Sean was still shocked to see all the guests, who were staring at him like he had lost his mind. "Do you mind if we stay over?" Sean leaned into his father and added quietly, "And can you have guards placed around your flat?"

Peter hesitated. He wasn't sure he wanted Sean to overhear the conversation among the guests. "Sean, couldn't you stay at Geoffrey's?"

"I don't think that would be a good idea," Sean cautioned.

Nicole had entered the room and was walking up to join them. Sean looked at her. "Dad has guests."

"Yes, I gathered that when I saw all the cars on the street," Nicole countered, smiling that Sean had missed that. Her presence piqued the interests of the guests in the dining room, and they started whispering to one another. Nicole moved closer to Sean and took his hand.

Peter thought of Elizabeth and realized that Sean was probably right. Geoffrey typically had his hands full even without Sean introducing Nicole to her. "Well, you know where the bedrooms are. We still have a bit to do here."

"Thanks, Dad." Sean turned from Peter. Sean led Nicole up the stairs to the bedrooms.

Peter returned to his guests, who were now chatting among themselves about the scene that had just occurred. "I do apologize for the interruption," Peter said over the babble. "Where were we? Oh yes, talking about how the populace would react to a member of the House of Lords becoming prime minister."

The group of men, who consisted of the members of both houses, turned their attention back to Peter's question. While there was a precedent for such a thing, it hadn't occurred since the 1960s. And then it didn't last long before a vote of no confidence occurred. Before the sixties, a prime minister from the House of Lords preceded the world wars, and after those wars, the attitude of the populace wasn't favorable. Each of Peter's guests remarked that they felt the reaction of the people would be very negative. On the other hand, it also depended on how well liked that Lord was. Peter listened intently to each alarm or question voiced. The night ended with no clear direction to take. Peter would have to weigh all their information and decided if the risk was worth throwing his hat in the ring. He also wondered if he was too old and if he should put forth Geoffrey as a candidate instead.

As he bade goodnight to his guests, Peter's thoughts turned to his other son and Nicole. He shut the front door, turned to walk up the stairs, and headed down the hallway to Sean's old childhood bedroom. He smiled when he thought about how Nicole had so much ammunition of Sean's juvenility in the room at her disposal. She must have had quite good fun teasing him.

They were still awake when they heard three light taps on the door. Sean got up out of the chair, putting down a favorite book he had started to read, trying his best to ignore Nicole's comments of various items. As he walked to the door, he realized that he hadn't read anything for pleasure in quite some time. He opened the door, with Nicole walking up to greet Peter.

"Would you like to talk now?" Peter asked.

"If you have a few minutes, yes," Sean confirmed. "I am sorry for crashing in like that, Dad."

"It's quite all right, Sean," Peter responded as they all walked back downstairs. "Actually, it was nice to know that you are seeking my help. That hasn't happened in a long time."

Sean smiled. "I guess things have changed."

Peter was going to comment but felt it was better to stop while he was ahead. He didn't want to start another of their endless arguments. "What can I help you with?" He asked as he sat down on his favorite chair in the living room, motioning to Sean and Nicole to do the same.

"We were in Inverness," Sean divulged.

"Inverness, so that is where you decided to steal away," Peter commented. "Why Inverness?"

Sean thought for a moment. "It was as far north as I could take Nicole and keep her asylum," Sean confessed. "There was no other reason really. When we arrived, we found a cottage to rent, and I never imaged that we would run into anyone we knew."

"But you did."

"Yes," Sean confirmed. "Dad, you aren't going to like hearing this because it involves Jack. I can spare you the details if you like and just ask that you call Jack and set up a meeting with him. There is something he isn't aware of, and he needs to know about it."

"Obviously whatever this information is, it also threatens us. Otherwise, you would not be here," Peter responded. "Tell me what happened."

Sean told Peter about their meeting Gillian. Peter smiled at the sound of her name. He remarked that she was a delightful young woman. It made Sean wonder if Dad had ever strayed or even if he had been with Gillian himself. Peter caught his son's quizzical look and assured him that that had never happened. Sean was relieved to hear this and continued with his story. He mentioned Maggie, Gillian's daughter with Jack, and how Maggie was sent to spy on Kent. "Her orders were to become intimate with Kent—his lover."

Peter sat for a moment, taking in Sean's story. "Do you think that they may be seeking some sort of revenge on Jack?"

"Possibly," Sean responded. "But her contact at SIS should be aware that she may turn, and they could have the beginning of a double agent on their hands."

"Or worse," Peter said. Peter had now shifted gears and was thinking as the chair of the Intelligence Committee. "Wouldn't you agree that Maggie might see this as an opportunity to train and someday become the Serpent herself?"

"That is also a possibility. I didn't train Maggie, Dad. I don't know anything about her, but my gut says this is bad. When I met her in Charlie's office, it was very clear she wanted to work with me." Sean smiled as he recalled Nicole's reaction to Maggie. Nicole frowned, well aware of what Sean was thinking. "She was even flirting with me."

Peter grinned. "I'm sure you took that right in stride." Neither Sean nor Nicole missed the tongue-in-cheek humor. Sean chuckled while Nicole rolled her eyes, shaking her head. "I don't understand, Sean. Why can't you call Jack?"

Sean swallowed. "Because I'm no longer an employee of SIS as far as the books are concerned."

"But you have your gun there." Peter pointed to Sean's shoulder holster. "And I'm assuming you have your license to kill."

"Yes," Sean confirmed. "I'm on one of Jack's special…" His voice trailed off, not sure what the correct word was. "Teams."

Peter's brow furrowed as he processed Sean's comment. "I see." Because of Peter's chairmanship on the UK's Intelligence Committee, he knew what Sean was referring to, and he wasn't sure that it was a good thing. "So you cannot contact anyone at SIS, including Jack?"

"He would prefer that I didn't contact his office."

"I'm not sure I understand, Sean," Peter said perplexed. "How are you to provide and obtain intelligence if you can't contact anyone at SIS? This arrangement seems counterproductive."

"Dad," Sean said scooting forward on his chair. "I'm a special case. My mission is only to kill the Serpent if he comes after us. I'm not supposed to hunt him down. I'm not really to have any contact with SIS at all."

"Jack's using you as bait. You know that."

"Yes," Sean confirmed. "However, we don't know how quickly Kent will try to hunt us down again."

"I would think my cottage in Guildford is a vital piece of information to be considered. He tried to kill you there," Peter reminded him annoyingly. "Sean, you can't be out in the field without any intelligence or a contact from which you can obtain information. That's suicide, and you know it."

"My plan wasn't for him to find us," Sean confessed. "And we would have been fine. Maggie changes all of this."

"I would think so," Peter agreed. "We aren't going to get anywhere tonight with this. I'll call Jack in the morning and have him come here first thing. We need to figure out a way to keep you both safe." Peter stood and walked to a cart in the corner that contained his liquor. He motioned to Sean and Nicole. Both indicated that they would like a drink. He poured three glasses of gin. He handed Sean his and Nicole's drink before he sat back down. "I have some other news that you should know before you talk with Jack. It concerns the assassination attempt on Nicole."

"There is new information?" Sean asked. He looked at Nicole, who leaned forward to set her drink on the table that separated Peter from them.

"Yes," Peter started, "it appears that they have confirmed that it was Bobby who ordered the assassination. In fact, the US news agencies reported on it the other day."

Nicole sat quietly. Sean looked at her, surprised there was no verbal reaction at the accusation.

"Who accused Bobby?" Sean asked.

"McNair announced it in a press conference. It was very strange. Blackwood announced his run for president and McNair as his running mate." Peter looked at Nicole. "Then McNair made the assertion that Bobby was responsible for your attempted assassination."

Nicole cocked her head in skepticism. "Brian McNair?"

"Yes," Peter responded, steadfast in his reporting of the incident.

Nicole was dismayed. She didn't like how the turn of events had placed Jenkins at the center of her attempted assassination. She searched her thoughts and feelings before she announced with all the confidence she had, "It wasn't Bobby."

"Nicole," Sean interjected. "You have to admit that Bobby had the means to execute this quickly. He had the access, and he has the connections."

"Jack said that the information from the tests indicated that a Marine sniper executed the order," Peter added. "This particular sniper is typically used by the Joint Chiefs of Staff. The sniper usually works in the Middle East…"

"I would like to talk to Bobby," Nicole said, looking at Sean. "In fact, it's rather important that I talk to Bobby."

"Why?" Sean asked.

"I planted some information with a reporter about McNair. I was hoping that Bobby could use this information, but obviously, he hasn't put it all together," Nicole explained. She saw Sean's confusion turn to anger.

"You did what?" Sean asked, the disbelief evident in his voice.

"Don't be angry," Nicole pleaded. "It didn't concern us, and it was meant to help Bobby piece things together. Obviously, it wasn't helpful, or we wouldn't be having this conversation."

"I can't believe you acted on your own, without informing me," Sean stated. "I thought we were in this together."

"I'm sorry. You're right. Things got a little crazy after the explosion," Nicole admitted. "We are in this together, and I shouldn't have done it. It was a long shot—"

"What was this information?" Sean interrupted, still fighting back his anger.

"I cleared McNair of an attempted murder charge a few years back. There were drug charges as well. McNair was blocking Bobby during the hearings, and I thought it would help him. It had nothing to do with us."

"I can't even begin to tell you how angry this makes me," Sean started, trying to keep himself from yelling. "That one call—"

"Two," Nicole corrected. She determined if Sean was going to be angry at her, she might as well get it over with in one sitting.

"Two?" Sean asked. Sean looked at his father, who was sitting quietly trying his best to stay out of the argument. Peter took a sip of his gin, making it clear to Sean that he was not going to speak. Peter looked as if he were watching a tennis match, complete with his eyes darting between Nicole and Sean with each verbal volley.

"I had to call the reporter back because where I reached him wasn't an appropriate place for us to talk."

Sean closed his eyes. "Do you have any idea how much danger you put us in?" Sean didn't wait for an answer. "Damn it, Nicole! I'm trying to protect you!"

Nicole didn't respond immediately. "The information didn't pertain to us, Sean. But it is important for Bobby to know this. As I said, they obviously weren't able to find the information. Since Kent's attempt on our lives happened shortly after that, I doubt what I did helped him at all."

"It could have confirmed we were there."

"Possibly, but not likely," Nicole insisted. "In any case, I am asking now that we talk to Bobby."

Sean raised his eyebrows, exhaled a breath, and turned his head looking away from Nicole. He shook his head in disbelief.

"Sean—" Nicole started.

Sean stood up and walked away from Nicole. He shook his head again. "I can't believe you did this."

"I am sorry," Nicole offered. "I should have discussed it with you."

"YOU THINK?!" Sean yelled. He ran his fingers through his hair and rested his hand on the back of his neck as he processed the information Nicole had just shared. "You did this to help Bobby. You did this without even thinking about the implications of your actions." Sean shook his head again and looked up at the ceiling.

Nicole waited for Sean to process the anger and hopefully move past it. After a few minutes of silence, she said, "I don't know this for sure, but there is a possibility that someone else is using this information to get back at Bobby."

"Our concern is not Bobby's campaign," Sean snapped. "Or even his life for that matter."

"You're overreacting," Nicole stated.

"I don't think so," Sean shot back. "I trusted you. I never kept a secret from you. I didn't act behind your back. You have no idea what you have set into motion with this foolish act." Sean started to leave the room.

"I'm calling Bobby, and I want you on the extension," Nicole demanded.

Sean stopped. "Why are you doing this?"

"Because I care about us," Nicole asserted. "I care about all of us."

Sean shook his head. "Until I hear from SIS and until we can truly figure out who tried to kill you, you are not calling Bobby." Sean looked at Nicole. "We'll talk with Jack in the morning, and after that, we'll discuss the next steps." Sean started to walk away and then turned to face Nicole again. "I have so many questions running through my head right now. I would never have thought that one of them would be if you love Bobby more than me." Sean saw the effect his last words had on Nicole. "I'm going to bed. Good night."

Nicole watched Sean leave the room. Peter stood, walked over to Nicole, and gave her a quick kiss on the cheek. "Sean doesn't trust people readily. He's hurt. My advice is to choose who you want to be with, Nicole. You can't love two men."

"I don't love, Bobby. I've always loved your son," Nicole responded quietly. "But I do care for Bobby. He needed this information. If he doesn't have or if he hasn't put the two together, this will end up with my attempted assassination on his hands. I won't have that."

"I'm afraid I can't help you, my dear," Peter replied. "Good night."

"Good night," Nicole responded, disappointed. She sat downstairs for most the night thinking about her actions and Sean's reaction. She thought about Jenkins and wondered how he missed the clue. She hoped that he would put the pieces together and do so soon.

{V}

Washington, DC

Jenkins arrived at Mercer's home around six o'clock on the evening of June 3rd. Anne Mercer greeted him at the door and led him to Mercer's study. She asked if Jenkins had had anything to eat, to which Jenkins replied he had not. Anne left for the kitchen to prepare a sandwich for Jenkins.

Jenkins watched Anne leave and for a second wondered how Mercer got Anne to be so respectful of his business. His thoughts turned to Nicole and how he would have to bluntly ask her to leave the room. Louise Barker and Anne Mercer understood they would have no say in any matter discussed. He wondered if Mercer discussed any business with Anne even in private.

Mercer entered the study and saw the contemplative look on Jenkins's face. "Is anything wrong, Bobby?"

Jenkins shook his head. "No, I was just thinking how Anne seems to show no interest in your work."

"The result of years of training," Mercer joked, with a quick chuckle. He became more serious. "In the beginning, she did want to know everything, but after a few incidents that weren't pleasant for her, she began to show no interest. It has its price—the non-interest that is. There's a wall between you and your wife, always. Along with that wall comes some form of isolation. There will always be some secrets between us. She has things that she keeps from me too." Mercer sat down behind his desk. "This life takes its toll on personal relationships, but there is no one I would trust more than Anne."

Jenkins acknowledged Mercer's comments with a quick nod. "I fully understand what you're saying."

There was a knock on the door, and Mercer stood to open it. Anne had returned with a plate and a drink. A ham sandwich with cheese, lettuce, and tomato along with some potato chips filled the plate. In her other hand was a glass of cola.

"If I remember correctly, you aren't that fond of pickles," she said, setting the food and drink on the table next to Jenkins. She handed him the cloth napkin she had draped over her shoulder.

"That is correct," Jenkins responded. "Dill pickles are not one of my favorite foods." He looked at the plate of food realizing how hungry he was. "This is wonderful. Thank you so much, Anne."

"You are quite welcome," Anne replied as she started for the door. She stopped halfway, turned, and asked, "Bobby, have you heard anything from Nikki?"

Jenkins had just taken a bite of his sandwich. He held up his finger in a polite gesture asking for her to wait until he swallowed. "She is quite well," he finally said. "As you know, she has asylum in the United Kingdom."

"Will she ever be able to return?"

"Anne," Mercer said, feeling like Anne's questions were beginning to invade Jenkins's privacy.

"I just miss her," Anne responded defensively. "I didn't realize how much I liked her until she disappeared from our lives."

Jenkins looked down and then back at Anne. "A sentiment I can fully comprehend."

Anne's face showed some horror as she realized if anyone was missing her, it was Jenkins. "Oh, Bobby! I'm so sorry."

"It's quite all right," Jenkins assured her. "I think those days are over. While I'll always love Nikki, it seems quite impossible for us to be anything more than friends."

Anne looked at Jenkins. "If you truly love her, then you shouldn't give up so easily." She shifted her weight to her other leg and folded her arms. "I wouldn't have taken you for a quitter, Bobby." Her husband cleared his throat, which was his way of telling her to leave the room. Anne caught the signal. She raised both hands in the air, indicating that she didn't mean to pry into Jenkins's personal life. "All I'm saying is that maybe Nikki needs to be reminded of all you have to offer. That includes how you always seemed to put her first." Anne turned and left the room.

"You will have to forgive Anne," Mercer said. "Despite everything, she is a hopeless romantic."

"I imagine that can be quite a struggle for you," Jenkins responded, coldly.

"At times," Mercer confirmed. "Now, what did you want to talk about?"

Jenkins finished another bite of his sandwich before responding to Mercer's question. "I have in my possession information that

McNair faced an attempted murder charge of a high-priced escort some years ago. Additional charges consisting of possession and under the influence of an illegal drug are also part of this evidence."

Mercer's brow furrowed. "Are you sure? I've never heard of any such incident."

"Oh, I'm sure. I'm very sure," Jenkins confirmed, confidently. "I have the arrest record as well as a summarized note that details the plea bargain that occurred in a certain judge's chamber. Tony Shafer was McNair's attorney." Jenkins could tell that Mercer was putting together the pieces.

"You think Barker is blackmailing McNair."

"Yes."

"And part of the blackmail is to say you ordered Nikki's assassination attempt."

"Yes," Jenkins confirmed. "I have all the information we need to put Barker in his place finally. That's what tomorrow's meeting is about."

"Can I see the evidence?" Mercer asked.

"At tomorrow's meeting," Jenkins replied.

Mercer sat for a moment. "Who gave you the information on McNair?" Jenkins sat quietly. "You know Nikki could be disbarred for this."

"Nikki isn't involved in this. Harrigan said he had a source, who he wouldn't name. I didn't ask him who it was. And you, of all people, know how powerful information can be in this town, whether it is the truth or not." Jenkins paused. Mercer gave him a skeptical look. "I haven't talked to Nikki. She kept copies of the cases she worked on in her home office. I have a key to her condo." He stopped, not wanting to voice the rest of the story.

"So it was Nikki?"

"I didn't say that," Jenkins countered. "Let's just say that the source is reliable. I have no way of knowing who Harrigan's source is—who I do know happens to be a woman. Again, he did not reveal his source's name."

Mercer smiled. He thought for a moment. "The information on McNair will be easy enough to explain, especially since you said you have the arrest record."

"Yes," Jenkins said. "Thompson retrieved the record a few days ago. He has a good relationship with Chief Bailey."

"Our meeting with Barker is at ten in the morning," Mercer informed Jenkins. "I don't mind saying that I'm uncomfortable with not knowing all the details, Bobby."

Jenkins finished his last few potato chips, wiped his hands with the napkin, and smiled at Mercer. "I'll see you then. Thank you for arranging the meeting." They walked to the front door, where they bade each other good night. Jenkins was looking forward to sleeping in his own bed, but not before he made a victory speech for winning the primaries that had occurred earlier in the day. He had his campaign manager arrange for that to happen in front of the Jefferson Memorial. He wasn't sure why he did that; it just felt right.

CHAPTER EIGHT

June 1980

WASHINGTON, DC

Jenkins was walking over to Mercer's office with the evidence he needed for the meeting with Barker. A few reporters kept pace with him, asking questions about the attorney general's statement and the charges. Jenkins expressed that he felt the charges were justified and that he hoped the trials would help to mend the divided nation. He hoped that this was the first of many steps that would return the governing process to a more transparent and honest system. As he reached Mercer's office, he thanked the reporters for their company on his walk. The reporters laughed at the senator's pretentious gratitude. Jenkins smiled as he opened the door to Mercer's office and disappeared inside.

Mercer's aide stood, knocked on the inner-office door, and opened it for Jenkins to enter. Barker was already waiting, having arrived a few minutes before the ten o'clock meeting time. At first, this made Jenkins feel uneasy. He looked at Mercer, who looked up from a paper he was reviewing. He placed it aside and greeted Jenkins. He motioned for him to take a seat in the empty chair that flanked Mercer's desk. Jenkins sat down and placed the folder of evidence on his lap.

"Can we begin now?" Barker asked impatiently. "I do have work to do."

Barker's annoyance told Jenkins that Mercer had not engaged Barker in his absence. "I bet you do," Jenkins rebutted sarcastically.

Mercer gave a little smile, wondering how much pleasure Barker's former prodigy was going to receive from this meeting. "Larry, what we have to say doesn't have anything to do with offering you the vice presidency."

"That's good," Barker started, "I don't want it." Barker stood to leave.

"Just a minute," Mercer called to him. "We aren't done." He motioned for Barker to sit down. "Go ahead, Bobby."

Jenkins looked at Mercer. He had so many things he wanted to say. The thoughts flooded his head, and he didn't know where to start. Jenkins cleared his throat and decided to ask the question that had bothered him most since the discovery of this information. "Would you like to start by telling us why you ordered the hit on Nikki?"

Barker looked at Jenkins. His breathing started to increase while he tried to keep his blood pressure and anger in check. "I had nothing to do with that," he spat out. "McNair seems to think it was you, with good reason I might add."

Jenkins tried not to snicker. Instead, he gave a devious smile and said, "Only because you are blackmailing him. It's over. I don't know all the information you obtained over the years as chairman of the Intelligence Committee, but I do know that you are continuing to run a little operation called Mockingbird. That's going to stop." Barker didn't react. His breathing had steadied but was a bit quicker than normal, and his neck and face were turning red. He reached up and loosened his tie as Jenkins held up the folder. "I have here the evidence you used to blackmail McNair. You used this information to make McNair accuse me of Nikki's attempted murder. McNair never went to trial per se, although he did appear before a judge. I had a hard time getting the police record, but I did secure it." Jenkins pulled out the police report. "I know you obtained this information through the CIA via Mockingbird. Thanks to my ties to the intelligence community, I also know that you bribed one of the Joint Chiefs. You used his access to have a sniper take a shot at Nikki."

"He's making this all up," Barker pleaded with Mercer. "I had nothing to do with it."

"Continue, Bobby," Mercer commanded. He took the arrest record from Bobby and peered over to see what else was in the file.

"Why would I give a shit about that bitch?" Barker snapped, his evil eyes narrowing to look at Jenkins. Barker used this look too often, and Jenkins was not intimidated.

"When you gave the command for Nikki's assassination, we were still a couple. You had a heated argument with Nikki in South Carolina. You threatened her life. Do you think that she wouldn't have told me about that?" Jenkins placed the opened folder on Mercer's desk. Jenkins pointed to each document going over the contents. "You see, we have you. All the evidence you used to bribe both the joint chief and McNair."

Barker's complexion went pale, and his breathing became shallow as Jenkins held up each piece of evidence. When Jenkins finished, he sat back and crossed his legs.

Barker looked at Jenkins. "What do want? Now that we each have something on each other, there's no reason we can't form a new alliance."

Mercer was the first to speak. "I don't want a new alliance. I want you to remain quiet throughout the rest of this election cycle. If you do so, we won't target your seat. In fact, we may find you a position in Jenkins's administration." Barker looked at Mercer. "But if you open your mouth or if you bribe one more person, so help me, Larry, I will take your ass down. Do you understand me?"

Barker sat for a moment. He was caught, like a rat in a trap. He did order the hit on Nicole. He disliked her immensely. He didn't like how Louise acted whenever she had been around Nicole. He knew killing Nicole would allow him to become the mentor to Jenkins that he was before she came into Jenkins's life. He knew he would have been Jenkins's vice presidential pick. Now all of that was gone. He was defeated. All the information that he obtained through Mockingbird seemed to be useless. Barker pointed to the folder. "What are you going to do with that information?"

Mercer closed the folder and handed it back to Jenkins, who placed it on his lap, his hand never relinquishing its grip. "It's out of my hands," Jenkins said. "A reporter came to me with the information, initially. I asked him to give me a few days to confirm it. The reporter will disclose McNair's unfortunate evening with the high-priced escort. I doubt he'll be on the ticket much longer. It also will be leaked that I was in no way connected to Nikki's attempted assassination. The reporter is just waiting for my call. Also, he is doing a series of special investigative reports—one of them is on Operation Mockingbird."

"Are you crazy?" Barker yelled. "You can't let him do that!"

"It all depends on how much we need to control you," Mercer added. "The decision is yours. There is nothing we can do about the news reports."

Barker sat for a moment. "Can you keep my name out of it?"

"That depends," Jenkins replied.

"On what?"

"How much you step out of the limelight," Jenkins declared. "I don't want to see your name or face on the news. I don't want you stumping for me, and I don't want your so-called help ever again." Jenkins understood how dangerous a caged animal could be. "I have more than this on you," Jenkins added. "Don't make us use it. Don't make us expose a scandal that ultimately stains your illustrious career," Jenkins warned, the distaste for the word *illustrious* evident in his tone.

"Go back to your office, Larry," Mercer said. "I hope you heed this warning."

Barker stood up slowly. He walked to the door, and before he turned the knob, he looked back over his shoulder and hissed, "Fuck you both." With that, he walked out, slamming the door behind him.

Jenkins looked at Mercer. "What do you think he'll do?"

"I have no idea. Just be ready with the information about Nikki," Mercer said. "Tell the reporter to go ahead with the story on McNair. Let's do our best to keep the story on how much disarray there is in the GOP."

{II}

Atlanta, Georgia

Harrigan sat behind the news desk in the new studio of the World News Network. In front of him was a small stack of papers, which contained his handwritten notes on the stories he was going to present. Everyone was running around, except for one man. Warner was standing still next to one of the three cameras in the studio that afternoon. When he caught Harrigan's eye, he simply smiled.

It was two minutes to air. The sound tech walked up on the stage and wired Harrigan. He clipped the microphone on Harrigan's lapel and assisted Harrigan in clipping the bulky power pack on the news anchor's belt. The wire ran up his back and inside his suit jacket. Into his ear went the earpiece that would provide cues from the producer who was sitting in the control room in front of Harrigan. The stage manager shouted orders above the chaos. Cameras were moving, searching for a better position as instructed by the producer. Harrigan cleared his throat as he watched all the young and anxious personnel scramble.

"As Murrow use to say," Harrigan announced. "'Steady.'"

"One minute to air," the stage manager called out. "Get out of the picture!" He yelled at another person who was standing off to Harrigan's left. Slowly, within thirty seconds, the soundstage went quiet. The manager started his countdown and then pointed to Harrigan.

"Good afternoon and welcome to World News Network," Harrigan began. "It's been a long, interesting journey to this point. The development of cable television and the creativity of Theodore Warner have merged to produce what we hope will be an informative, thought-provoking, and entertaining network. WNN has but one mission, and that mission is to provide you, our viewers, with all news, all the time. You might be wondering if there is enough news to fill the airwaves twenty-four/seven. I suppose if you thought, as we have for so many years, that all news around the world fit nicely into a thirty-minute segment, then your answer might be no. However, those of us who were employed by those networks were constantly frustrated with the amount of news that did not get reported. Newspapers had the ability to report more than an on-air news show. As our lives have become more complex, and the demands of today have increased, the consumption of news via newspapers doesn't seem to be a viable option. WNN is an experiment. We don't know if we will have an audience that can sustain our budget, but we are willing to give it a try." Harrigan looked down at this notes. "We won't be just reading headlines. We'll be providing more of the story. We will be interviewing as many sources as we can and as many sources who are willing to join us. We will do our best to accurately, in-depth, and truthfully report the news both here at home and abroad."

Harrigan looked at the monitors. He saw his colleagues waiting in different areas of the world. "We have bureaus around the world, and we'd like to introduce you to our team of reporters who will be bringing you the latest developments. We'll start in Tel Aviv, Israel, with Candice Jones. Candice, in March of 1979, Egypt signed a peace treaty. The Sinai Peninsula became part of Egypt, and the Gaza Strip is now under Israeli control. How has this treaty been received?"

Candice Jones waited as she listened to Harrigan finish his question. She was an attractive woman, and her business attire was topped off with a customary scarf worn to conceal her hair. "Hello, Steven, and I have to say first that I am looking forward to reporting from this region. It's a wonderful day!" She gave a smile as she heard Harrigan confirm her statements. "I'm standing in Gaza right now, and the mood is one of extreme caution. The tension is so thick. It is almost palpable."

As Candice continued her report, the camera was off of Harrigan. He shuffled through his papers. When Candice finished, he thanked her for her report and moved on to introduce the next reporter. The final stop on this world tour was the United Kingdom with the news desk located in London. Douglas Newkirk was the anchor, another incredible steal of talent by Warner. He was waiting patiently for his cue.

"Steven," he started in his almost stuffy, proper English accent. "I must say that I am utterly giddy at the thought of working with you and with this new enterprise."

Harrigan wanted to laugh, but he stopped short. Newkirk always had a way of taking an ordinary statement and puffing it up to make it sound important. Through his smile, Harrigan returned his kind statement of gratitude.

"The big news here today is that the prime minister may be facing a challenge. There is a rumor that the Conservative Party will be tabling a motion of no confidence." The Labour Party had control of the House of Commons and was able to keep the no-confidence motion at bay until recently. The prime minister's position on some contentious legislation had proven to be a bitter pill, and the populace was growing anxious. A series of strikes by the unions and industrial disputes had put the population through some very rough times. Newkirk explained all of this to the viewers.

"If the members bring a vote of no confidence, who would be the frontrunners for a new prime minister?" Harrigan asked.

"This selection is quite different than your election process in the United States," Newkirk started out. "It has more to do with the position of the parties in the House of Commons. The prime minister has to answer to and maintain support of the House. Without that support, it would be very hard to maintain one's position as prime minister. So, having said that, if the no-confidence vote succeeds, and the prime minister is removed, the Sovereign appoints the person who would likely have the support of the House. Normally this is the leader of the largest party in the House of Commons. This process is further clouded by the moves of the Labour Party lately. There are some polls that suggest that Peter Adkins may take the lead of the Labour Party and apparently is interested in becoming the next prime minister."

"Isn't he in the House of Lords?"

"Yes, he is. There is some history that bears the leadership of the British government residing in the House of Lords, but recent history has seen that position retained in the House of Commons. So, there is a precedent," Newkirk advised. "Of course, we are getting far ahead of the process, but I will add that Lord Peter Adkins just may be the charming leader the Labour Party is looking for right now to steady the ship."

"Thank you, Douglas," Harrigan responded and turned his attention back to the viewers. "Now you have met the key players around the world who will be at the forefront of our reporting. There are many reporters and staff whom you will undoubtedly become familiar with as time marches on here at WNN. I will be one of many anchors here in the United States. We need to pay a few bills with a commercial break, but when we come back, I will start with a report on the current campaign and a news story exclusive. I hope to see you back."

After a few seconds, the stage manager shouted, "And we're out for thirty seconds."

"Great job, Steven," Warner said, walking up to shake his hand. "We're off!"

Harrigan shook Warner's hand. "Thank you, sir."

"I'm off to a meeting," Warner said as he turned and walked away.

"You're not staying for the next story?" Harrigan called. "That doesn't bode well for keeping the interest up."

Harrigan was joking, and Warner knew it. He waved his hand above his head and walked off the soundstage. Harrigan laughed at the gesture. He knew Warner's attention span was short. Harrigan looked down at his notes while the stage manager announced they had ten seconds, counting down until they were live.

"Welcome back," Harrigan said. "This next story was researched by me, with the help of sources who shall remain anonymous." He paused, looked at his notes, and carefully thought of his next words. "This election year has been atypical, to say the least. That word probably doesn't adequately describe the chaos that this country has been enduring. One president was assassinated, which lead to another president resigning and being pursued by the attorney general for treason, conspiracy, and murder. Knowledge is power in Washington, DC, and the dissemination of knowledge can swiftly swing that power. Never in my years of journalistic pursuits have I witnessed anything like this."

"A few decades ago, the Central Intelligence Agency launched an operation they called Mockingbird. The purpose of this operation was to use the media, reporters, and high-ranking corporate officers of the major networks to spread propaganda. In others words, the CIA was controlling the story, not just the news media. Do you ever wonder what happened to 'freedom of the press'? This next story tells you about the origins of Mockingbird, how it operated, and investigates whether it is still in use today. Take a look," Harrigan said as the tape began to roll.

Harrigan's story began with the establishment of the operation and how Mockingbird grew to become an enormous, well-funded project. The story disclosed the controlled meddling at the highest level of the CIA. The CIA director was in charge of the distribution of information and identifying the news person or media to announce that information. While mostly used to control foreign affair stories, there were indications that politicians were part of the leaking process as well. One such case involved Senator Joseph McCarthy in the 1950s.

J. Edgar Hoover, the director of the FBI, was jealous of the CIA's power and began to investigate certain individuals including the CIA director's right-hand man, Frank Wisner, the former head of the Office of Strategic Services. Hoover's investigation provided information that many had been active in "left-wing politics." That information was passed on to McCarthy, and the witch hunts began. McCarthy referred to the CIA as a "sinkhole of communists" many times.

With Hoover and the FBI feeding information to McCarthy, McCarthy became feared by many and at the same time egotistical. He felt he was untouchable and, for a long time, that appeared to be true. Fearing that the CIA was losing its authority and with many of the CIA employees being called out by McCarthy as communists, Wisner unleashed Mockingbird on McCarthy. Very reputable and respected journalists began to release a barrage of negative coverage on him. This tactic was only one arm of Operation Mockingbird, but it was a very effective one. McCarthy's witch hunt ended with his censure by the Senate, one of only a few senators to ever attain this disgraceful disciplinary action.

Operation Mockingbird would be employed in overthrowing governments, misleading the public via news reports on wars, and had an arm dedicated to foreign policy initiatives. It reached the highest level of the news media, some presidents, and chairmen receiving pay for diverting or burying news stories. There was no person too high or too low that this operation couldn't touch. In the 1960s, knowledge of this operation started to appear in books.

In the late 1960s, the CIA director announced that this controversial operation was coming to an end.

Harrigan's story didn't include all the dirt on Barker—just enough to show the public that Mockingbird was still alive and well. It reported on the McCarthy, Hoover, and Wisner years. It included a piece on Jenkins's live appearance on *Newsweek Tonight* and how Barker obtained the information on Jenkins. Toward the end of the piece, Harrigan announced a new piece of information that no other network had.

The story ended with information about McNair's attempted murder of a high-priced escort while under the influence of cocaine. Harrigan showed the arrest record that was obtained by Thompson. However, at the request of Senator Jenkins, it did not show the actual paperwork he had obtained out of Nicole's files. Instead, Harrigan typed out certain key phrases. Harrigan simply noted that these came from a source who would remain nameless. He only added that the call came from overseas. Harrigan felt that tidbit added a bit of mystery to the story.

Harrigan waited for the red light on the camera to illuminate. He paused for a moment, unsure of what to say. Finally, he spoke. "Operation Mockingbird started out as a propaganda tool but fell into the wrong hands. It makes you wonder just who is running this country." He paused. "We'll be right back."

The soundstage was silent.

{III}

Washington, DC

Jenkins was sitting in his office with Thompson and Chris beside him. They had just finished watching Harrigan's story. Jenkins wasn't surprised by it—he contributed to the story and had given Harrigan direction. He wondered if being the source of the story made him the new Barker. His position on the Intelligence Committee gave him more power than most committees. Its close rival could be the Ways and Means Committee. He never really thought about it, and he found it odd that he was thinking of it now.

Thompson was the first to speak. "Holy shit," he said. "How do you dial that back?"

Chris wanted to laugh at Thompson's reaction but didn't. "C'mon Kevin, you mean to tell me you never thought something like that was going on?"

"I worked at the FBI. The joke there was you never knew which cover-up would trip you up. My advice was: if you got your ass chewed out, you tripped onto something."

Jenkins stood up. "Chris, will you give me some time with Kevin?"

"Yes sir," Chris said as he stood, turned off the television, and left the room closing the door behind him.

Jenkins moved back to his desk. He motioned for Thompson to sit across from him. After Thompson had sat down, Jenkins started. "Kevin, if and when I become president, I'm going to need people I trust in certain positions. Your work has been flawless and above reproach. I'd like to float your name for FBI director."

"What?!" Thompson almost shouted. When the shock of Jenkins's statement settled in, he cleared his throat and said, "I'm sorry. That came as a complete surprise. Sir, no one knows who I am. I don't think that would go over too well during the confirmation process."

"I'm not worried about that," Jenkins dismissed the concern. "Look." Jenkins sat forward resting his forearms on his desk and folding his hands. "We can put your résumé together, add that you've been doing investigations for me. I know that Senator Mercer has appreciated your work as well. With my backing and Senator Mercer's, it shouldn't be a problem."

"I hardly think I'm qualified," Thompson protested.

"I think you are more qualified than you think you are. You have the one thing that makes your appointment most appealing right now: you're honest, and there is nothing in your past that can hold you hostage. Your background is clean, and I can trust you." Jenkins studied him for a moment. "I need you in that position."

"You realize that if I managed to be confirmed, I couldn't owe you any favors," Thompson said bluntly.

"I would expect nothing less. Just don't do any favors for anyone else in Congress," Jenkins added. "Do we have a deal?"

"Wouldn't that be doing you a favor?" Thompson retorted with a wink. "If you want to float my name, I won't turn it down." He shook his head in disbelief. "I can't see how anyone would confirm me, but you would be the ones wasting your time."

"It won't be a waste of time," Jenkins countered. "They confirmed Jefferies, and I'm still trying to figure that one out. Work on your résumé. Chris can help you with some other information we'll need to pull together for the confirmation. All of this is hypothetical, of course. I've got some other things to attend to now."

As Thompson opened the door, Chris was standing on the other side about to knock on it. "I think you need to watch this, sir," he announced as he walked to the television set and turned it on. "When they come back from the advertisement, Harrigan will be speaking to Senator McNair via telephone."

Jenkins put down the piece of paper he had just picked up. "That was quick." Jenkins wondered if Barker had tipped McNair off. Jenkins noticed his phone's main line was blinking. His intuition told him it was Mercer. "Senator Jenkins, how may I help you?" He was correct; it was Mercer telling him to turn on WNN. "It's on. I'll call you back."

Jenkins fully expected that McNair would respond to the uncovering of his secret. He just wasn't sure what the hotheaded Irish American would say. McNair rarely reacted with substantial truth to back up his accusations. He always believed whatever he said to be truthful, a handicap that the press enjoyed exposing. It wasn't that McNair flip-flopped more than other politicians. It was more his lack of caution that hung him out to dry. There were times when the Republican Party considered him a loose cannon and high-security operations were kept from him if there was a belief that McNair couldn't keep his mouth shut. Jenkins had to admit to himself that his appointment to the Intelligence Committee made no sense to him, especially when Jenkins spent most of his time covering for McNair's mistakes. In Jenkins's opinion, if there ever was a person who fit the definition of the word *inept*, it was Brian McNair.

Jenkins walked over to sit in front of the television. Harrigan introduced Brian McNair, and the interview was off and running.

"Senator," Harrigan began. "I understand that having your personal life exposed in this way would be very upsetting. But I did contact your office a few days ago to inform you of my findings and to obtain a statement from you. I left a message with your aide."

McNair was quiet for a moment. "That's beside the point. Who gave you this information? Who is your source?"

Harrigan gave a little smile. "I'm not obligated to share my sources, Senator. You know that. Have I reported any false information? Were you charged with attempted murder of a high-priced escort?" Harrigan wrote something on a piece of paper and waved for an off-camera staff member to retrieve it from him. "And Senator, before you respond, I've just asked my producer to call the former escort."

McNair cleared his throat. "She told you this? She's lying."

"No, she was not my source. Is it true that you met with Judge Pierce in closed chambers and the indictments disappeared?" Harrigan paused, waiting for McNair's reaction. "The arrest warrant was very difficult to find, but thanks to my source, it was retrieved. I must say whoever you hired to cover your tracks did an excellent job. If not for my source, its discovery might not have occurred."

"I'm telling you here, and now, I did not make an attempt on her life, and I did not enter a drug rehab program at St. Elizabeths. I was in Hawaii with my family during those weeks."

Harrigan tilted his head feigning confusion. "So, you are telling me that you took a four-week vacation to Hawaii in the middle of a work session in Congress?"

McNair was doing a fine job of hanging himself. "I don't believe Congress was in session at that time."

Harrigan looked down at his notes. "Yes, it was." He read the dates off to confirm. "Senator, you are President Blackwood's vice presidential candidate, don't you think we, the people, deserve to know the truth about our representatives?" Harrigan placed his finger on his earpiece. "And we do have the former escort on the phone standing by."

McNair knew his indiscretions were now exposed. "I have no further comment."

"I have only one more question. Former President Stevens is now residing at St. Elizabeths. Did you facilitate his stay or help in any way with those arrangements?"

"I have no further comment at this time," McNair abruptly hung up the phone.

"Senator?" Harrigan asked. "It seems Senator McNair has left our conversation." He turned his attention to the high-priced escort who was waiting on the phone to speak. Harrigan explained that they would not identify her by name. When she confirmed the incident and the cover-up, Jenkins turned the volume down on the television.

"Looks like Blackwood will be looking for a new vice president." Jenkins smiled. "Let's get back to work."

{IV}

London, England

As promised, Peter called Jack Kensington in the morning, and Jack agreed to meet at Peter's house on his way into work. It was a little out of Jack's way, but Jack knew Peter never requested his presence unless it was important. Jack arrived before Nicole and Sean awoke, so Peter poured Jack a cup of coffee and asked him to have a seat in the dining room. Peter walked up the stairs, knocked on Sean's room and informed them that Jack was waiting for them downstairs. Sean was amazed he had slept so long and so deeply.

After a few minutes, Sean and Nicole joined Peter and Jack in the dining room. Nicole opted for tea, never being much of a coffee drinker. After Peter's housekeeper obtained their breakfast orders, which included a proper "fry-up" for Peter, Sean, and Nicole, she returned to the kitchen to get started. Jack had eaten earlier and was quite satisfied with just his coffee.

With the breakfast orders keeping the housekeeper busy in the kitchen, Sean and Peter got down to business and informed Jack of Maggie's identity. It was hard for Sean to ascertain if Jack was embarrassed that they knew of his affair or if he was angry that they knew.

"A daughter?" Jack questioned, visibly shocked at the news. "You saw her picture in Gillian's home?"

"Yes. Gillian told us as we were leaving that she told Maggie all about you, my Dad, Geoff, and me. She said that Maggie loved hearing about us."

"She said it was like a fairy tale to Maggie," Nicole added. "That can be taken one of two ways, of course. She either hates you for denying her a loving family, or she did think that it was a fairy tale. Since Maggie was so eager to meet Sean and work with him, one could conceive that she is trying to achieve a position that she thought was not available to her."

Jack didn't say anything at first. "When Gillian left, I had no idea she was pregnant. The weeks leading up to her abrupt departure she questioned me a few times as to the possibility of me leaving my wife for her. It all makes sense now. I told her as unfaithful as I had been, my wife was just as unfaithful. We didn't marry for love. I married for the position, and Mary's family preferred me to her other suitor," Jack acknowledged. He looked at his longtime friend. "Peter, I feel I owe you an apology."

"Whatever for?"

"I know you thought I did marry for love. I know you didn't know about my infidelities."

"Oh dear God, there was more than one?" Peter's question revealed his surprise. He was quite willing to forgive one affair, but to continually repeat what Peter felt was inappropriate behavior was a bit of a stretch.

Sean couldn't help but laugh at the flabbergasted tone in his father's voice. Nicole kicked him under the table, which made Sean stop laughing, reach for his shin, and give her an unappreciative look. These actions were not missed by either Peter or Jack.

"It's quite all right, Nicole," Jack said. "I'm sure Sean would appreciate not being kicked under the table again." He turned his attention to Peter. "Yes, Peter, there were many. I envied the relationship you had with Brighid. I didn't have your upbringing, so I had to marry into it. I have always appreciated and was grateful for everything that you made possible starting with our friendship during the war. There are a lot of things that you made happen for me, including talking to my wife's parents on my behalf and making her marrying me acceptable. I hope you don't think I was using you because I wasn't."

"But you aren't ashamed of your behavior?" Peter asked.

"No, I'm not. It became clear early on that my wife was not going to be as supportive as you. It also became evident that she never broke off her relationship with her beau from school. Considering her parents' distaste for that bloke, I was an easy solution." Jack looked at Sean. "How many know about my affairs, Sean?"

"I'm not sure many do," Sean advised. "You know I did. I sometimes intruded because of the information I needed to get to you. You were my mentor and a friend when I first started at MI6. I could not have done what I did without your help. I didn't tell anyone if that is what you are asking." Jack tilted his head, unsure if Sean was telling the truth. "Jack, I could have used that information many different ways. You are still head of MI6 because I didn't. We had an alliance, and I don't undermine alliances that can benefit me or this country."

Jack accepted Sean's response. "Do you think Maggie is going to come after us?"

"I think you need to treat her as if she was a double agent," Sean stated. "It may turn out that she just wanted to be close to those whom she has heard about growing up, but we don't know that for sure."

"What does your gut say?" Jack asked, taking a sip of his coffee.

Before Sean could reply, the housekeeper arrived with breakfast. She put the tray down on the buffet and placed a plate in front of Nicole, then Peter, followed by Sean. She poured coffee and tea before leaving. She closed the door behind her, and the conversation continued.

"My gut says that Maggie has her own agenda," Sean cautioned.

"So you do think she may be seeking revenge," Jack confirmed.

"Let's look at it this way; you grow up in Inverness, hearing your mother talk about a man she loved. This man wouldn't leave his wife for the two them. Gillian never told you she was pregnant. She's a devout Catholic, and she wouldn't abort the child. Gillian disappears, scorned and humiliated thinking that you didn't love her enough to make that dream world she lived in possible. Gillian obviously thought that you would leave your wife. When you said you wouldn't, she had no option except to disappear. Not only was Maggie denied a father, but Gillian missed out on the life she wanted with you. I would say there is more than enough evidence to warrant Maggie being a double agent. Have Maggie and Kent worked together before? Have they ever met? Did she help him escape?"

Jack shook his head. "I don't know."

"I think someone should be looking into that," Sean replied. "Yes, I do think she will become a double agent. I do think that she'll persuade Kent to train her. And I do think, at some point, she may try to kill you."

Nicole had been eating up until the last sentence. She placed her knife and fork down on the plate and picked up her teacup. Her trembling hand did not go unnoticed. Two thoughts came to her mind. The first was the ability of these men to callously discuss someone's murder. She felt she would never understand how they could do that. Nicole then wondered if Jack would send Sean on a mission to kill Maggie. The thought of Sean not by her side made her extremely nervous. She placed the teacup back down on its saucer without taking a drink. She didn't look up from her plate, but she could feel that they were all looking at her.

Peter was the first to speak. "Needless to say, this concerns us all. I have to say, Jack, that I'm not thrilled at the prospect of Sean and Nicole being out there with no connection to MI6. They need the benefit of intelligence that your agency can afford them."

Jack agreed. He looked at Sean. "Do you want to go after Maggie?"

Sean was surprised by the question. "No."

"Sean," Nicole started, "are you sure? You're not just saying that because of me?"

Sean turned his head slowly and looked at Nicole. "I don't want to be in the field. I don't want to go after Maggie."

"Why not?" Nicole pressed. "Is it because you would have to," her voice lowered, "be with her? You know, I mean *be with her.*" Nicole imagined the procurement of information and trust involved sexual relations with one's enemy. She swallowed. "If you want to do this and that's the only reason—"

"Nicole," Sean interrupted. "I don't want to be in the field again. I have had enough of that life, the deceptions, and I honestly don't think I could function as I have in the past knowing you were here, somewhere, without me." Nicole gave a faint smile. "It's out of the question," Sean said looking at Jack.

"Without being an agent, Sean, I'm not sure how I can get you the intelligence."

Peter sat forward, placing his arms on the table. Sean started eating his breakfast again. "I think I may have an idea."

Sean stopped a forkful of food midway to his mouth. He put the fork down on the plate and looked at his father. "Am I going to like it?"

"I don't know. Are you willing to hear me out?"

Sean looked at Nicole and then at Jack. "Yes, let's hear it."

"You could become an ambassador." Sean's brow crinkled at the wild solution. "Jack, how many of our Ambassadors are former spies?"

"Well, I think it is more accurate to say that the spouses are usually the spies," Jack jested. In a more serious tone, he said, "Besides, I can't identify them and shouldn't comment on that. Let's just say that many more of them are not involved in the intelligence-gathering profession."

"Let me get this straight: you would make me an ambassador, and I could still keep my license to kill and my gun?"

"Well, you may not need either of them. Being an ambassador, you would have a security detail and your residence protected. I'm sure we could negotiate acceptable terms with the right countries," Peter explained.

"You know, Sean, Peter's idea is worth thinking about," Nicole added.

"There's only one problem that I can think of right now," Sean said, looking at Nicole. "Nicole can't leave the United Kingdom."

Peter smiled. "There is such a thing as diplomatic immunity."

"That only applies to family members," Sean reminded Peter.

"Not necessarily," Peter implied, a sly smile on his lips. "Nicole could be your attaché."

Sean looked at Peter. "An attaché?"

"Yes, your assistant or member of your diplomatic staff," Peter clarified. Peter could tell Sean was not convinced. "Oh dear Lord, Sean, you work for MI6. It's not like we couldn't get her a fake identity. There are such things as wigs and all that."

"Excuse me," Nicole interceded. "I'm not particularly sure that being the ambassador's attaché makes us any safer. The Serpent assassinated my president. He had a detail of Secret Service around him, the DC police force secured the surrounding buildings, and the FBI was also helping. If all that can't keep the president safe, what makes you think your security forces can?"

Sean was still staring at his father. "It depends on where they send us."

"Meaning?" Nicole asked.

"The kind of protection is dependent on the country and what is negotiated with that country. We could live in a virtual bunker."

Nicole looked down. "And the White House isn't a bunker?"

"He was shot on his way to the Russian Embassy," Sean corrected. "And that was the Serpent's first trip to the United States."

"Nicole," Jack started, "you are correct. Nothing is one hundred percent fail-proof. We can't promise that we can always keep you out of harm's way. You've already been shot. But, doing this provides a better chance of keeping both of you safe. Peter is also correct. Sean running around the United Kingdom as a one-man security team with no intelligence information or contacts at his disposal is not going to work forever."

"If I have access to intelligence information, we'd have a better chance of escaping both the Serpent's and Maggie's bullets." Sean sat back, wiped his mouth with his napkin, and looked at Nicole. "President Andrews's assassination was successful because of a number of reasons. One was that the Serpent paid two Secret Service men to hold the president for that final shot that killed him. The other was that the FBI director was in on the plot. The third was complacency. We don't have the luxury of being complacent."

"You'll do it then?" Peter asked.

"I didn't say that," Sean shot back quickly. "I need to think about this. I need to work through some scenarios to make sure I haven't missed anything." Sean stood up. "I gave you the information you needed to hear, Jack." Sean extended his hand, and Jack accepted it. "Thanks for coming over. We'll be in touch." Sean turned and left the room.

Nicole looked at Jack and then at Peter. She thought for a moment and then said to Jack, "The day we went to Gillian's—I haven't seen him that uptight in a long while. You need to understand that, Jack. He does think that Maggie will be a detriment and that whatever operation you have her in, well, he thinks and strongly feels the operation is compromised."

"Don't think for a minute Nicole, that I don't take him seriously. He was our best agent. He could be again. I respect his not wanting to go back in the field." Jack leaned forward. "But this needs to be said: as long as you and Sean are alive and Kent knows you are alive, Kent will hunt you."

"Then maybe we should die," Nicole responded. "Maybe there is a second option besides the ambassadorship: we fake our own deaths and assume new identities."

Jack thought for a moment. "I think Sean could do more to benefit us by being an ambassador." He looked at his watch. "I need to go. I have a security briefing in a half hour." Jack stood and started for the door. Peter followed Jack to the front door, they embraced, and bade each other good day.

Nicole followed but was a few steps behind the gentlemen. She smiled faintly and said, "Thank you for coming over."

Jack could see her concern. "I'd do anything for Sean. He is like the son I never had."

"I can see that," Nicole said. "I hope you have a good day." Nicole wasn't close enough to Jack to hug him, so she just gave a quick wave as she folded her arms. Jack returned the wave and left the house. Nicole turned and headed for the stairs. "I'm going up to talk to Sean."

Peter acknowledged Nicole's comment and watched her ascend the steps. He called up after her, "I'm heading off to the office in a few minutes. I won't interrupt to say good-bye. Hopefully, I will see you both tonight at dinner."

"Have a good day and thank you," Nicole said as she continued up the stairs. She stood outside the bedroom for a moment before entering. She opened the door and walked inside. "Are you OK?" She asked as she closed the door.

Sean was looking out the window and turned to look at her. "Yes, are you?"

With a couple quick, abbreviated nods of her head, Nicole indicated she was. She moved to the bed and sat on its edge. "You were out of the room when I gave another possible option." Sean turned slowly. Nicole paused and looked down at her hands. She was nervously picking at her fingernails. "I suggested that we could fake our own deaths," Nicole offered. "Another option to that…" Nicole swallowed, knowing this option would set him free from her. "You could fake my death, and you could then do what you felt was best."

Sean stood there, shocked by her last sentence. He didn't know how to react. His face showed his confusion as his mind quickly flashed questions. Did she want to be free of him? Did she not love him any longer? "I don't understand. What do you mean what's best for me?"

"I mean it would free you up to go after whomever without worrying about me. Or you could start a new life if that is what you wanted." Nicole could see she was still not making sense. "After last night, I thought you might not want me around."

Sean stood there for a minute trying to decide if he should be mad at Nicole or laugh at her nonsensical logic. He gave what appeared to be a combination of quickly aborted laughs and a huffing noise produced by the expelling of his breath. He turned his head and looked at the wall, not focusing on it. He turned his head back to her and walked over to sit beside her. He took hold of her left hand and whispered, "I would still know you were alive and I would still be worried." Nicole lowered her head looking at her hand in Sean's, her cinnamon-red hair hiding her smile. "Please don't think for one minute that my reaction has anything to do with you being a burden or preventing me from doing what I want to do. Yes, I was mad at you last night. I still am. But I am also still madly in love with you."

Nicole looked Sean in the eyes. Her eyes began to tear up. "I am so sorry."

"I know you are. I love you, Nicole. Never doubt that."

"I'll always speak with you first before I do anything like that again. I didn't realize that I could have compromised our location and safety."

"Thank you," Sean said. "And you know I wouldn't think of doing something without talking to you first."

"What are you talking about?" Nicole teasingly shot back. "Since when have I ever had a say in where we are going?"

Sean's mouth dropped open in disbelief. "When have you not had a say in that?"

"Excuse me," Nicole quipped with a playful tone in her voice. "Would you like me to list them? Bobby's beach house for starters—"

"Right," Sean interrupted. "Forget I asked that question." He heard Nicole's stifled laugh. "You know, faking our deaths or even the death of just you isn't an option. It still means hiding out and wondering if Kent would discover the truth. We would be in the dark just as much as we are now."

"Sean—" Nicole wanted to disagree.

"Hear me out, Nicole, please," Sean pleaded. "As an ambassador, I could obtain clearance to have the intel on Kent and Maggie briefed to me. We would know their every move, and we could stay one step ahead of them. We would request a special detail of bodyguards, and we would live in a compound under the protection of the highly trained military."

"It sounds like jail," Nicole offered. "It sounds like Kent is controlling our lives. Where would we go?"

"I don't know. There are probably things we need to understand and training to undergo, of course. I'm sure Dad would have this all planned out. We'll talk to him at dinner and see what he has to say."

"Do we have any say in this?" Nicole asked.

"I'm sure we do especially if Dad hasn't fully developed his plan," Sean replied. "And if it doesn't feel right or if it feels too risky, I think we can walk away. We would be no worse off than where we are today." Sean hugged Nicole. "We have to take this one step at a time. I do know this: I can't keep us safe if I don't have access to intelligence."

Nicole could see his point. "What happened to your plan 'he'll find us'?"

"He did," Sean confirmed. "And I had no idea he did until it was almost too late." Nicole nodded her head in agreement. "Does this mean we agree? Should we go the ambassador route?"

Nicole lifted her head from Sean's shoulder to look at him. She started to smile. She appreciated how he included her in this decision. She felt like a partner. Two rather insignificant questions to him were very significant questions to her. They made a world of difference. "As long as we work together and never keep secrets from each other then I agree."

"We'll tell Dad tonight at dinner," Sean confirmed. A hint of displeasure flashed across Sean's face. "He's going to be insufferable about this. He has been prodding me to be an ambassador since I was a teenager."

Nicole couldn't help but laugh.

"Nicole? Sean?" Peter called up from the bottom of the stairs. "Can I have a moment of your time?"

Sean and Nicole walked down and joined him in the living room. Peter was sitting in his favorite chair with a smirk on his face. Nicole looked at Sean who was just as confused as she.

"What is it, Dad?"

"It seems that Bobby deciphered what you wanted him to figure out after all, Nicole." Peter began. "I was just informed by Margaret that information on McNair was reported to the American people on this new cable television network called World News Network."

"What information?" Nicole asked.

"That he was charged with attempted murder of a high-priced escort. A chap named Steven Harrigan had a live phone interview with McNair. He also mentioned a drug charge, but the interview didn't go into that detail. It seems when Harrigan informed McNair that they had the former escort on the phone, he hung up. They then confirmed the story via telephone with the escort. I would venture to say, McNair's actions ruined his chance at the vice presidency."

"Don't sound so melancholy, Peter," Nicole said sarcastically. "He committed a crime, and it should have been dealt with when it happened. Tony was McNair's lawyer but backed out of attending the meeting in the judge's chamber, delegating it to me. I had no problem exposing this, especially if it helps Bobby."

Peter put on his coat. "Now the question becomes, what else do you have on your politicians? More importantly, how will Bobby use it in the future? The last thing your democracy needs is a dictator as president with endless access to damaging information to laud over representatives' heads whenever he wants to."

It was Nicole's turn to smirk. "And don't think for one moment that hasn't already occurred countless times in America's history."

Peter gave her a sardonic smile. "Well played."

"Yes, indeed," Sean added. "If they ever reveal you as the source, though, you know you could be disbarred."

Nicole looked at Sean. She knew that could be an outcome of her actions. "I doubt I will ever be a lawyer again. I'm beginning to doubt that I'll ever be in the United States again," Nicole retorted. "If Bobby is going to turn the country around, he needed that information. It levels the playing field for Bobby. I hope he does what he promised us back in Kansas."

"I do too," Sean concurred. "He seems to be well on his way."

{V}

Washington, DC

Fred Whittaker was an older man in his sixties and reminded Jenkins of his father. He had served in World War II in the Pacific with a special force whose primary objective was intelligence gathering. Jenkins knew that skill would come in handy in the current political environment. Whittaker was trustworthy, and the two worked well together. Short in stature, Whittaker was a barrel-chested, muscular man who looked younger than his age. He dressed impeccably, thanks to a doting wife. More importantly, the Washington insiders respected him. This presidential campaign was Whittaker's first, and at any other period, that may have been detrimental to a candidate. Mistakes irritated Whittaker, which seemed to be too commonplace on Jenkins's current campaign for his liking.

"Is he in?" Whittaker asked Chris as he walked into Jenkins's office.

Chris could tell that Whittaker was not happy. "I'll let him know you are here," Chris picked up the phone and buzzed Jenkins. "Mr. Whittaker to see you, sir," Chris nodded. "Yes sir." He looked at Whittaker as he hung up the phone, stood, and moved to the door. "You may go in."

"Thank you, Chris," Whittaker said as he breezed past him into Jenkins's inner sanctuary. "Morning, Senator."

"Morning, Fred," Jenkins greeted Whittaker as he extended his hand over his desk. Whittaker shook the senator's hand and then stood in front of the chair, waiting for Jenkins to sit first. Jenkins motioned for him to sit as he took a seat. "Are you practicing for the Oval Office?" Jenkins asked jokingly.

"It's called respecting the office, sir," Whittaker replied. "Have you seen the newspapers?" he asked, holding up the paper in his hand. "McNair is saying that you leaked the information to Harrigan and the accusation made by WNN is untrue." The press was having a field day with McNair in the days following Harrigan's story.

"I assure you I did not leak the information to Harrigan," Jenkins asserted. "And I don't think we need to be focusing any more attention on that story."

Whittaker threw the paper on the vacant chair next to him. "Very well. The convention is coming up soon. Preparations are being made, and we are vetting those seeking the opportunity to speak."

"Good," Jenkins responded. "When can I expect to see a list of possible speakers?"

"Next week," Whittaker replied. Jenkins acknowledged his comment with a quick nod. "Is there anyone that you don't want speaking at the convention?"

"Barker," Jenkins replied. "I welcome anyone else."

"It will look odd not having someone as powerful as Barker speak for you, especially since he was instrumental in kicking off your campaign."

Jenkins was looking down at a piece of paper while Whittaker was speaking. He looked up at him as he finished his sentence. "No Barker," Jenkins said sternly. "He is not to come anywhere near the convention. Do you understand?"

"Yes sir," Whittaker confirmed. "What can I tell the press if Barker starts making waves?"

"He won't," Jenkins replied.

"What if he does?"

"Then we tell them that he leaked the information on McNair," Jenkins declared, irritated.

Whittaker showed the shock on his face. "Did he?"

Jenkins's head bobbed between a yes and no answer while he spoke. "In a roundabout way, he did."

"What do you know?" Whittaker demanded.

Jenkins just shook his head. "You're not inside yet. If we need to get into it, we will. Trust me, Barker won't be a problem." He looked back down at the paper he was reading.

"Have you been thinking about candidates for the vice presidency?" Whittaker changed the subject. "We need to start leaking names to the press to get a read on who plays well."

"Yes, I have been thinking about candidates. I'd like to float a couple of names, including Senator Patricia Samuelson." Jenkins looked up again when he didn't hear Whittaker react. "What's wrong with Samuelson?"

"I just don't think we should push too much," Whittaker countered. "I'm not sure it is the right time for a woman vice president with all that has happened."

Jenkins took in his campaign manager's comments. "I didn't say I was selecting her. I said I want to float her name to see if we get a bounce."

"You already have that demographic in your pocket, if I may say so," Whittaker reminded him. "Your good looks and Southern charm locked that one up."

"Are you suggesting that my good looks and charm are the only reason women are voting for me?"

"No sir."

"You better not be," Jenkins cautioned as a smile crept across his face.

"I'm just suggesting that another demographic needs our attention. We can do that with the right vice presidential candidate."

"Which demographic is that?" Jenkins asked.

"African Americans," Whittaker stated.

"Are you serious?" Jenkins questioned, somewhat astonished.

"You find that surprising?"

"Yes, I do. Are you suggesting that the country is ready for an African American vice president and not a women vice president?"

"No," Whittaker countered. "I'm suggesting we float some names and we talk about your voting history on certain legislation. I also suggest that we have some prominent figures—"

"I don't like the way you're pandering this."

"I'm not pandering."

"Yes, you are. I have always been a supporter of the black community going back to and including my pivotal vote on affirmative action. I have a great working relationship with the African American women's movement, speaking at several events over the years." Jenkins sat back in his chair. "Are you implying that somehow my Southern accent and the fact I'm from North Carolina make me weak when it comes to civil rights?"

"Yes," Whittaker confirmed. "We looked at your record. You

haven't attended one African American event in your home state during this campaign."

Jenkins looked at Whittaker with a small amount of anger in his eyes. "Who is going to expose that fact?"

"McNair," Whittaker revealed. "We heard he plans on talking about it tonight on one of the big three networks."

"I am beginning to hate politics," Jenkins said, the disgust evident in his voice. "McNair has been dropped from the ticket. We don't need to react to his bullshit. And it is pandering."

"Call it what you want, sir, but it is what it is," Whittaker responded. "You're weak here."

"Now, I suppose you want me to go and speak at some event to show that I'm not weak here," Jenkins barked.

"And float some names," Whittaker quipped.

"It doesn't look like we're doing this because McNair is falsely accusing me of being weak on civil rights?"

"He's not calling you weak on civil rights. He's saying you're a bigot because you won't campaign in North Carolina for African Americans."

Jenkins looked at Whittaker, his nostrils flaring with anger. In truth, Jenkins was not a bigot, and he did support the African American community in his home state. "He does understand that I was a state senator when the integration of the school systems was being discussed and implemented. I supported, planned, and worked with the black community on that issue. He does understand that my record in the state Senate shows my undying support of African Americans, does he not?"

"Obviously, he doesn't—"

Jenkins slammed his fist down on this desk and stood up. "Damn it, Fred. You do!"

Fred didn't stop speaking, he just raised his voice over Jenkins. "—And the nation doesn't know either. McNair will brand you a bigot on television."

Jenkins started pacing. His anger was still visible. He took a deep breath and placed his fists on his desk, leaning forward. "So what do we do?"

"We float some names today. We put together a political ad with soft money—"

"No soft money."

"Sir—"

"No soft money!" Jenkins reiterated. "I won't be beholden to someone who I don't know. I won't find out in my first year in office that John Doe from some corporation gave me money to say that I wasn't a bigot," Jenkins said sternly. "If we don't have the money to do this, then we ride out the storm."

"We have the money," Whittaker said. "It wasn't about the money; it was the appearance."

"The appearance of what?" Jenkins asked. "I have nothing to hide on this. Maybe I haven't spoken in my home state because I was never asked. Have you even thought of that?"

"No sir," Whittaker replied. "Were you never asked?"

Jenkins thought for a moment. "I can't remember," Jenkins responded. "Float some names and whatever else you think needs to be done with the funds we have available."

"Yes sir," Whittaker agreed. He started to leave.

"And Fred," Jenkins called after him. Whittaker turned to face Jenkins. "I want to see the names first."

"Yes sir," Whittaker confirmed before leaving the office.

"Dear God, I hate this part of politics," Jenkins moaned to himself, as he plopped back down in his chair.

CHAPTER NINE

October 1980

Atlanta, Georgia

Harrigan was standing in the office of his executive producer at WNN. He was not alone as the other anchors of the twenty-four-hour news network were all called in for a meeting. WNN had been on the air for four months now. It was now autumn, and the conventions were months old. Blackwood didn't appoint a vice president after McNair's indiscretions disgraced the ticket. Instead, he used the convention to nominate his new sidekick. Blackwood presented a few names and the delegates at the convention rallied around an up-and-coming politician who was a representative in the House. Kenneth Stanton was from Kansas, and he had a lot of energy. He was very vocal about the direction of the Republican Party, leaning farther right than McNair or Blackwood. He was a devotedly religious man and always stopped short of declaring out loud his closely held belief that America should be a Christian nation. Although a relatively small percentage of the GOP felt as Stanton, the party's knee-jerk reaction to McNair's sins set the stage for the growth of their religious platform, or at the very least the party overcompensated with pandering to the religious right. Stanton's voice and ideas were hard for the Republicans to ignore, and since the party was scrambling to unite, no one took a minute to access the damage the party leaders may have been inflicting in regards to the GOP's future.

Jenkins's pick for vice president was a long but common process. Six candidates' names were mentioned at the convention including Patricia Samuelson's, who Jenkins admired and wanted on his ticket. Strongly advised by the DNC and Whittaker, Jenkins decided to allow the convention process to aid in his decision. Samuelson was a strong supporter of Jenkins's platform and had appeared on many talk shows in support of him. It was a close race, if you could call it that, between Senator Samuelson and Reginald Jones, an African American representative in the House. In the end, Samuelson won the spot. She was from Massachusetts and could carry the northern states where Jenkins wasn't polling as well as his party liked. After the conventions, the four candidates hit the road for the final stretch of campaigning.

WNN had secured the rights to host one final debate a week before the election on November 4th. The two presidential candidates' staffs agreed upon the format. A panel of three WNN anchors would ask the questions, while management decided that Harrigan would be the moderator. The panelists consisted of Stacy Hardwick, a female who co-anchored the prime-time edition of the news; George Smith, Hardwick's African American co-anchor; and Jeff Dixon, an investigative reporter known for his knowledge of foreign affairs and policy.

Each candidate would have two minutes to respond to a question. The panelist could ask a follow-up question, and each candidate would have one minute to respond. Closing statements would last two minutes per candidate. The point of contention in Harrigan's mind, since he was the moderator, was the one minute for each candidate to challenge the other candidate.

"I'm just not sure how we will get through all of these questions in a ninety-minute debate," Harrigan emphasized. "Is there a limit to how many challenges they can have per question? If not, we won't get past the first one."

"He has a point," Hardwick added. "They should have a limit. Make them pick and choose which topics they are going to challenge. Otherwise, we will be in a constant loop of rhetoric."

"And I think the challenge time should be limited as well," Smith chimed in. "One minute to challenge and a one-minute response."

"What about a rebuttal to the challenge answer?" Harrigan asked.

"They will find a way to work that in," Smith replied.

"This is like telling kindergarteners the rules of the playground," the executive producer said in frustration. "We go through all this trouble, and we'll be in chaos within five minutes. Wouldn't it just be easier to say 'play nice'?"

Harrigan laughed. "I think I'll say that just before I throw it over to the panel for the first question."

"Are these questions set?" The executive producer asked while he looked over the final list. "And do the campaigns have the list of possible topics?"

"Yes to both questions," Harrigan confirmed. "Other than this challenge thing, I think we're all set."

"I'll get on the phone with the campaign managers and make sure we have that agreed upon by noon tomorrow," the executive producer said. "Thanks for all your hard work on this everyone. I look forward to our first debate tomorrow night."

"Try and get some sleep," Harrigan said, as he and the rest of the anchors got up to leave the executive producer's office. "I know it's exciting, but we have to be on our toes." Everyone agreed as they exited the room and returned to their own offices to lock up their desks before leaving.

{II}

London, England

Nicole and Sean were walking back from the Underground to the flat they had secured just down the way from Parliament. Sean was in training to become an ambassador. It wasn't exactly training, but more coaching that his father wanted to provide him. Peter also wanted Sean to acquire relationships with certain members of both houses and the prime minister since he would need their help during his ambassadorship. The so-called training was just one continuous coming out party for Sean. While everyone knew Peter had two sons, Sean seemed to have dropped off the map when he entered MI6. Geoffrey and Peter rarely spoke of him, and when they did, they said he was off traveling. The little white lie wasn't too far from the truth as tracking Saverio the Serpent did require lots of traveling.

It was after midnight when they reached their small, stylish one bedroom flat. Earlier in the evening, Sean and Nicole had attended a private function of the embattled prime minister. A vote of no confidence was going to occur. It was only a matter of weeks before it happened. Sean had remained quiet most the evening, although he did speak at length with his brother, Geoffrey. It seemed Peter was resigned to the fact that putting his name forward for the PM position was not likely. A few months back, he had started supporting Geoffrey for the position. In those months, it was clear that Geoffrey needed to deal with his wife's drug abuse. Elizabeth had met Nicole only once, but it was more than enough. She watched the interaction between Sean and Nicole and carried on so badly that evening it became clear to Geoffrey that he needed to do something. This evening, Geoffrey's frustration was raw and palatable. In Sean's mind, he could still hear Geoffrey saying, "She's just daft." Sean didn't know what to say other than that Elizabeth did need help and he would be happy to assist Geoffrey if he could. He also told Geoffrey that the intervention needed to happen soon. It was then that Geoffrey revealed to Sean that he had already arranged for her to move to Nightingale Hospital two days from this evening. Sean could only agree that Geoffrey was doing the right thing. Nightingale would surely help her.

Nicole drew a lot of attention from the stodgy English politicians the whole night. While she was quiet on the way home, she had no problem providing her opinion when asked at the party. She acknowledged that her awareness of the United Kingdom's politics was limited; however, that did not stop them from engaging her in conversation. Nicole found it fascinating that they were interested in hearing her point of view and wondered if this was common. While on the way home, she thought about how many women were in the House of Commons (a small number, but slightly more than in the US House of Representatives) and how involved they were in key positions. She decided that if the country had a queen, it made for a more accepting public of the role women could play in government. The differences between the United States and the United Kingdom were fascinating to her. Little did she know that discrimination found many female victims. She only recalled bits and pieces of the suffrage movement from her studies at Vassar.

"You are awfully quiet tonight," Nicole called from the bedroom as she changed into her pajamas. "Are you all right?"

"I'm fine." Sean poured himself a gin. "Would you like a gin?"

"With tonic," Nicole said as she walked back into the living room and sat down on the couch. Sean walked over to her and handed her the gin and tonic. "Thank you. Would you mind if we turned on the television?" Nicole asked as she looked at the clock. "Bobby's debate is due to start."

Sean reached for the remote and turned the channel to the BBC. The BBC had chosen to pick up the debate feed of WNN. They both grabbed their drinks and sat back on the couch with Sean placing his arm around Nicole.

Harrigan got the cue from his stage manager. The candidates were standing at their podiums now, and the crowd was settling into their seats. An occasional call for each candidate came from the audience as Harrigan prepared to speak.

"Pay close attention," Nicole said to Sean. "If you want to learn to speak *'politician,'* these two are the ones to learn it from." Sean squeezed her, acknowledging her comment.

"Good evening," Harrigan began. "Welcome to the WNN presidential debate being broadcast from Georgia State University in Atlanta. We would like to extend our thanks and gratitude to the League of Women Voters for their sponsorship and unending work to provide a voice for women. My name is Steven Harrigan, and I will be the moderator for tonight's debate." Harrigan described the procedure, which included that both candidates would be asked the same question and their responses timed. A follow-up question could then be asked and also a challenge question. Each candidate had one minute for the follow-up question and any challenge questions. Harrigan informed the candidates that he would interrupt them when their time was up, so he encouraged them to keep their answers direct and on subject. He advised them that a red light would illuminate on their podium when their time was up. "We realize this is an unsettling time. Our nation faces a period of rebuilding trust not only among our citizens but the people of the world. Mark Stevens and his accomplices are on their way to justice with their trials starting in the coming weeks. We must look ahead and focus on the many issues plaguing our country that certainly were not the focal point in the past six months. Our debate will center on domestic, economic, foreign policy, and national security topics. I won't guarantee that there won't be other topics that surface depending on your comments." The crowd chuckled at Harrigan's last statement.

Harrigan introduced Stacy Hardwick, George Smith, and Jeff Dixon. "President Blackwood won the toss and will go first. Before I have Stacy ask the first question, just a quick reminder to the audience that you are to remain quiet during this debate. Please hold your applause to the end. Thank you. Stacy, you have the first question, which deals with foreign policy."

Hardwick was an attractive brunette in her early forties. She had worked overseas and provided investigative reports for most of her career with one of the big three networks. Well respected for her work, she was actively mentoring other women in the field of journalism. While her television image portrayed her as kind as she was knowledgeable, she could cuss like a sailor and hold her drinks with the best of them. "Good evening, President Blackwood," she started.

"Good evening, Ms. Hardwick," Blackwood responded with a condescending tone in his voice. Jenkins noticed it and looked up from his notes. He looked at Blackwood and then at Hardwick. It was noticed by her as well, but she gave it no gravitas.

"Mr. President, the Middle East is becoming a hotbed of terrorism as well as the many small wars funded by both the United States and USSR. We have had Soviet aggression into Afghanistan. If that aggression were to move into other Persian Gulf countries, a very real threat would exist. One threat could be a disruption of Persian Gulf oil to this country. We are woefully unprepared to aid and sustain any kind of powerful force in that region. How would you address further Soviet aggression into other countries in the Middle East?"

Blackwood had taken notes during her question as did Jenkins. They both wanted to make sure they could address the question fully without omission. "Thank you, Ms. Hardwick, for that question, and it's a very good one." The tone this time was less noticeable, but Hardwick gave an awkward nod of her head and a weak smile in acknowledgment. "As always, the United States would like to provide a path to world peace. However, in some cases, that just isn't possible. I would only use our forces abroad as a last resort. We are guardians of the free world, so when it is necessary to flex our muscle, we need to rise to the occasion." Blackwood was in a difficult situation. The Soviet Union had marched into Afghanistan and was still there today. Olympians missed out on the summer games as a protest to the Russian invasion. Under the Andrews and Stevens administrations, the USSR set its sights on Iran and was making gains in that country, which resulted in the fall of the Shah and the current hostage situation. There was nothing either candidate could do except acknowledge that their attention was on other pressing issues. "It is unfortunate that we tend to react versus control the circumstances in the Middle East. My predecessors, unfortunately, did nothing to stem this aggression. We are in a situation where we need to beef up our military and deploy them to Saudi Arabia and other countries who wish us to defend their interests and ours."

"Did he just say that he is going to start a war in the Middle East?" Sean asked Nicole.

"Basically," Nicole commented. "Did you see Bobby look at him?"

"I saw that double take," Sean said. "I think he was wondering the same thing."

There was a follow-up question to that before Hardwick turned to Senator Jenkins. "Good evening, Senator. The same question to you." Hardwick repeated the question to Jenkins, who checked his notes, marking off each point he wanted to make.

"First of all, I would like to extend my gratitude to the League of Women Voters and WNN for this debate," Jenkins began.

"The difference between a career politician and someone not ready for prime time," Nicole said. "Bobby's well prepared—look at how calm he is. Blackwood looks like a deer caught in headlights." Nicole looked at Sean. "That's where your MI6 training is going to come in handy."

"Also, I hope Mr. Harrigan will take into account that I'm from the South and my Southern drawl can be considered a disadvantage in timed debates," Jenkins added with a smile on his face. The panel and audience laughed. When the audience calmed down, Jenkins began. "Since I don't have much time left, let me get directly to the point. Where I differ from President Blackwood is that I truly believe any involvement in the Middle East should not include putting our young men in harm's way. Diplomacy should be exhausted before that occurs. We should be seeking out a conversation with the Soviet Union, not threatening them. We have voiced our strong dislike for their invasion of Afghanistan by boycotting the Olympics, and our allies joined us in that boycott. That was only a start. However, where this policy is failing is in our lack of follow-up with clear dialogue on what not only the United States expects of Russia, but what the UN and our NATO allies expect of Russia. Included in that dialogue should be the toppling of the Shah of Iran and its government. Our hostages are paying a high price for their freedoms and ours. We owe it to them to focus on a dialogue that holds the USSR responsible for their actions and reinstates the Shah at the earliest possible date. If the Vietnam War and the Korean War have taught us anything, it is that we should have a full and comprehensive understanding of the atrocities as well as clear and concise objectives before we put one advisor or one soldier on the ground. We cannot afford to take our eyes off the playing field. Our world is expanding and the gains made over the years has advanced many civilizations. The tensions in the Middle East are at an all-time high, and the United States has multiple interests in the region. However, that should not drive our foreign policy. If our interest is only oil or energy, we need to put plans in place that lessen our dependence on foreign oil. That isn't just true for oil but for all products. It is becoming a global marketplace, and I won't deny that, but we need policies that protect our country and our citizens."

"I'm never going to be that smooth," Sean stated, rubbing his forehead with his free hand. "Did he answer the question?"

"Neither did, really," Nicole said, shaking her head. "It takes time, and you'll have plenty of help."

"I have a feeling I'm not going to make a very good ambassador," Sean replied. "I am way too impatient and too honest."

Nicole smiled. "Well, I'm sure that the first place they'll want you to serve will be a relatively calm country."

"I hope so."

Smith was up next since neither candidate challenged the other on that question. "Mr. President, the decline of our cities has accelerated the rise in crime; strained race relations; and seen poor and or failing public education systems, abnormally high poverty rates, and the decline of services to the public. As president, what would you do in the next four years to reverse this trend?"

The camera zoomed in on Blackwood revealing the tiny beads of sweat on his forehead and upper lip. He hesitated for a moment, unsure of how he wanted to start. "I have talked with a number of congressmen who have the same idea. This idea is to create a development zone. The burden of running or establishing this zone would fall under the jurisdiction of local governments and the national government utilizing tax incentives and private sector sponsors of the programs. We would allow the local government to identify these zones based on the percentage of people on welfare or unemployed. The tax incentives would create jobs for these people. There have been a few of these development zones already established as a test, and the results look promising."

Smith was not impressed. "Mr. President, blacks, and non-whites populations are increasing in number in our cities. Many feel the hostilities from white people, who may be preventing them from joining the economic mainstream. There are racial confrontations in schools, on jobs, and in housing as non-whites strive to attain the American dream. Can you tell us what future America looks like under your administration in regards to a multiracial society?"

Blackwood shifted his weight to his other foot and slid his left hand into his trouser pocket. "I believe in it. I'm very optimistic that we can overcome any adversity that may exist. When I think back to how divided this country was when I was a child, I know we have made great progress. There is so much more to accomplish, and the development zones I mentioned previously is a start to that. One thing I know for sure is that my administration will seek input from all races and not ignore their ever-growing presence here." Blackwood looked at Jenkins when he spoke the word "ignore." It was a pointed slap at what Blackwood's campaign was advertising as Jenkins's weakness. The camera cut to Jenkins whose only reaction was to smooth out his tie while he waited for his turn. Blackwood continued to paint himself as the candidate who would work for all the citizens. "Some of us chose to ignore the racial problem, and some claim it doesn't exist and has not existed. We will have equal opportunity for all people in this country, despite our differences."

Smith waited to see if Blackwood would go a bit further in the few seconds he had left. Smith was hoping that Blackwood would provide a glimpse of a plan he would use to ensure that equal opportunity he spoke of, but Blackwood provided no key steps or plan. It was an awkward silence. Smith cleared his throat and then directed the question to Jenkins.

"I must say it saddens me that President Blackwood did not take the time to research the many programs and stances that I took during my term in the North Carolina Senate to help all the people of my state. I also kept many promises I made during my campaign for my U.S. Senate seat. At the national, state, and local level, the government was very concerned and in deep despair about the rapidly deteriorating conditions. These conditions were present not only in the central city but also in our small towns in rural areas. I would like to take this opportunity to educate those watching here and at home on the various programs on which I worked. Let's put this dog to bed right here, right now. While in the state Senate, I initiated with fellow colleagues a very successful program of urban renewal. This program led to higher employment and the use of those additional income taxes—a percentage of those taxes went directly into funding this program. As a result of the additional income taxes, there was no need for a state tax to fund these programs and grants were obtained as well. As president, I would look at this program and determine what changes would be needed to apply this nationwide. With the institution and benefits of the windfall profits tax, we could have a forty-three billion dollar budget within ten years. A portion of that tax could be diverted to help those seeking the American dream. A portion of that same tax could be spent on transportation systems. This expenditure not only would help inner-city residents obtain better-paying jobs, but it would also lessen our dependence on oil. We need to understand that not everyone owns a car or can afford to own a car, but most are willing and able to work. How do we make this happen? All it takes is an amendment."

"I'm sorry, Senator, your time is up," Harrigan interrupted.

Jenkins playfully shook his head. "It's my Southern drawl, Mr. Harrigan. I apologize."

Harrigan laughed and so did some in the audience. "I assume you aren't apologizing for your Southern drawl?"

"No sir. I'm apologizing for going over my time for that question. The possibilities excite me very much."

"I never realized how great Bobby is at this," Sean said. "Does he give lessons?" Nicole smiled at Sean's comment.

Smith asked his follow-up question. Jenkins was writing some notes down while Smith talked. "I'd like to address two things. First, my opponent took a swipe at me as does his current campaign advertisement insinuating that I have never spoken with the black community in North Carolina." He turned and looked directly at Blackwood. "President Blackwood, neither have you. I will add here that I have visited areas of North Carolina and the deep South that you have not. I have held the hands of battered women of color and been to services of men who have been victims of racial violence. I have seen firsthand the devastation that hate causes. I will not stand for it. We have a long way to go, and we should not be dividing our cities into zones, as your plan suggests, that label their inhabitants as outsiders. I have a lot to learn, and I know from experience that all I have to do is ask and I will receive assistance. I will engage those who seek to be engaged in this conversation." Jenkins turned back to the audience. "My second point, more direct to your question, Mr. Smith, is that we are a nation of refugees and immigrants, many of whom fled their mother country for freedom. The common bonds we share are those freedoms. It holds our country together, and it is our strength. It is my pledge to the American people that regardless of your race, creed, or economic circumstance, you will be represented in my administration. The time has come to put an end to racial and gender divides. It is time to embrace our differences and realize the strength of those differences. I pledge to create an administration that represents the melting pot that is the United States of America."

There were questions on the double-digit inflation that the United States was currently facing. Dixon asked questions on foreign policy and national security. Sean watched the debate, trying to take mental notes on how to address the questions and he wondered if he would ever sound as polished as these two men. Nicole dozed, her head on Sean's shoulder. The ninety-minute debate continued with much stating of fact and fiction. Sean nudged Nicole awake when Dixon began the last question.

"I think we would be remiss if we didn't address America's growing dependence on foreign oil," Dixon started actually forgetting that the dependence on foreign oil was addressed partly in the first question. "Through the CAFÉ standards, a bill sponsored by Senator Jenkins, and along with other conserving measures taken by the public, the US reliance on Arab oil as a percentage of total imports is much higher today than it was in 1973—the year of the Arab oil embargo. A substantial loss of Arab oil could plunge the United States into a depression. There was a major push by Mr. Sipes, CEO of Sipes Oil Company which is an American-held oil company, to drill in the ANWR. Senator Jenkins, your stance on that is clear. Stevens and Sipes clearly felt threatened enough by all of this to order a sitting president's assassination for his reversal on a bill that would have allowed drilling in the ANWR. The question is this—"

"Oh, good, for a minute there, I thought we might need to time you," Jenkins interjected with a hint of a joke in his tone. It drew laughter from the audience.

Dixon smiled and waited patiently for the laughter to die down. He looked at Blackwood. "Mr. President, can development of alternative energy resources without damaging the environment be done, and what will it mean for American families' steadily higher fuel bills?"

"My opponent is for raising your fuel bills," Blackwood started.

"I am?" Jenkins interrupted, his brow furrowed in confusion.

"Yes, you are," Blackwood fired back. "You are in favor of higher fuel bills for both our cars and household costs." Jenkins shook his head, not entirely sure where Blackwood was going with his comments. "You are falsely scaring the American people with the cry of America being energy poor. We are energy rich. One-eighth of our total coal resources are utilized today, and 22,000 coal workers are out of a job mostly due to regulations in regards to the mining of it or the burning of it. My opponent has his fingerprints all over the Clean Air Act."

"God forbid that we should be able to breathe in the future," Jenkins interjected.

"Senator," Harrigan interrupted. "You will have your say when President Blackwood is finished."

"Thank you," Blackwood said to Harrigan. "We need to reduce our dependence on foreign oil by drilling for oil here at home. We have much to explore as only two percent of the oil in the Continent Shelf has been touched. My opponent lobbied for seventy percent of the lands taken out of the 'multiple use' designation, which has oil just waiting for us to tap into it. We could end our dependence tomorrow, and I won't be shy about doing so." Blackwood seemed to be so mad that he didn't realize his response lacked the polish of his earlier answers. Perhaps it was the mention of the assassination in Dixon's question or the way that Jenkins interrupted him.

Jenkins waved his hand once at Dixon. "I don't need the question repeated." He turned to Blackwood. "Excuse me, Mr. President, for trying to ensure that future Americans will have clean air to breathe. Not only do I want our grandchildren and their grandchildren to be able to breathe, but I also want them to be able to enjoy and explore the natural beauty of our country. Picture this," he turned back to the audience. "You are now a grandparent living in the east, and you travel to Florida to the Gulf of Mexico with your son or daughter and their family. You drive there in your oil-and-gasoline-powered car, which still guzzles less than ten miles per gallon with its big, powerful v12 engine. Yes, I said v12, because the car manufacturers were not being held accountable to the CAFÉ standards. The air is so thick with pollution from the coal and the car emissions because we thought that the corporations would be responsible. Well, shame on us. After spending a large sum of money on gasoline because the Arabs have us literally over a barrel—an oil barrel—you arrive at the Gulf. Now, we are playing catch-up as the rest of the world has been developing solar and wind renewable energy, so we hurriedly built oil rigs in the Gulf to drill for the oil that my opponent talked about. You remember the pristine white sand that was so hot it almost burned your tender feet. You grab your granddaughter's hand and head for the beach, but it's no longer white. It's black, with tar from the oil platforms that are hazily outlined just off the coast. There's very little beach left because the burning of fossil fuel has resulted in higher temperatures around the globe. The emerald-green water of the Gulf of Mexico is now dingy brown. The sparkling water is no longer. It is replaced with a pungent thin layer of oil and gasoline, drifting onto the beach from the oil platform just offshore. There are dead birds and fish littering the beach. The stench is beyond words." Jenkins paused a moment to let his imagery sink into the heads of the audience. He shifted his weight to his other foot, his prosthetic leg starting to cause him some discomfort. "Some would say I'm melodramatic with my description. But I don't think I am. I have witnessed and investigated an assassination that was born out of greed. It was not our dependence on foreign oil or President Andrews's reversal of drilling in the ANWR that killed him. It was the greed of five men, all of whom had ties to corporations. This greed is blinding and all-encompassing. If it goes unchecked, it will surely destroy us and all that this country stands for. Capitalism is astonishing, but greed is the disease that will topple this country, as it almost did this past year. Make no mistake about it: greed was the motivator, not our dependence on foreign oil."

Nicole smiled at Jenkins's statement. She wasn't sure when the old Senator Jenkins she admired had reemerged, but she was glad he was back. "That's the Senator Jenkins I remember. I think that just won him the election."

"I need to get some sleep," Sean said looking at the clock, astonished at how late it was. "It's after two."

Nicole sat up as Sean clicked off the television. Sean stood and walked to the bedroom, followed by Nicole. As Sean proceeded to the bathroom, Nicole slid under the sheets and quickly fell asleep.

{III}

Atlanta, Georgia

Blackwood raised his hand, indicating that he wanted to challenge Jenkins's opinions. Harrigan acknowledged Blackwood. "Senator Jenkins, just to be clear, are you saying that all corporations are untrustworthy?"

Jenkins smiled. "Now, Mr. President, you know better than that. I am saying that capitalism is a wonderful economic system. The problem is when capitalism overreaches into government affairs. The assassination of our president is a very good example of that. In a way, it was a coup, and we were very lucky to have discovered it—discovered isn't the right word. It was the actions of certain people who brought it to our attention. I'm not saying all corporations are untrustworthy, but greed is a powerful aphrodisiac. As the corporation's profits grow and the market share begins to weaken, greed begins to surface. I believe it is the government's role to ensure that one corporation doesn't have a monopoly. For capitalism to remain healthy, corporations need competition. It is government's role to guard against monopolies and ensure public safety, as it has done in the past. We are starting to see competition in some markets deteriorate. The Sherman Antitrust law is receiving many challenges. To be clear, competition is necessary for a healthy democracy."

"Thank you, gentlemen, that is all the time we have for questions," Harrigan interrupted. "You will each have two minutes for your final statements. President Blackwood will be first."

Blackwood quickly flipped to a paper that was located behind all his note papers. He took a drink of water and started his statement. He talked about his vision of America and the work he had done over the last four months restoring not only his party but treating the wounds the country endured during the last year. He thanked Jenkins and his committee for their hard work and their unbiased findings. Blackwood talked about the need to reduce inflation so that the middle-class would be able to save money and spend it on vacations and other luxuries. He outlined his policies and hopes for the next four years if he were the people's choice.

"Thank you, Mr. President," Harrigan stated. "Senator Jenkins, you have two minutes."

"Thank you, Mr. Harrigan, Ms. Hardwick, Mr. Smith, and Mr. Dixon. I would also like to again thank the League of Women Voters and WNN for this opportunity to present my views on the very important topics we discussed this evening. And thank you to the audience both here and at home for listening." Jenkins paused as he gathered his thoughts. "I truly believe that we are at a crossroads. Our world is expanding, and the United States is opening to a new and ever-broadening global economy. While my opponent acknowledges that inflation exists, I have yet to hear one proposal on how to fix or even contain it. I've only heard he wants to make sure that you can afford a vacation or some other luxury. It seems odd that vacations and luxuries are being discussed while the basic needs of the middle-class are being ignored. We need to understand that our current economy is very susceptible to outside influences because of a number of reasons. In short, to strengthen the United States economy, we need to stimulate job growth, improve the industrial makeup of this country, and ensure that the energy—specifically the OPEC price increase—cannot affect so radically our consumer price index as it has since 1974. We need an industrial strategy that is diverse and not so dependent on energy. Manufacturing jobs are vital, and we need to be an innovator as well as a producer. There are many strategies that my administration will be investigating. Our national security is another area where our attention would be well placed. With my experience on the Intelligence Committee and my connections throughout the world, I will be in a unique position to respond to any threat. The Middle East is becoming a force to be reckoned with and is a complex situation. Only through dialogue and understanding will we be able to reach for peace. Terrorism is a growing threat, and we need to address this as well. We need to bring our hostages home, and if elected, that will be the first duty I will address. Equal rights for women and people of color are also important, and you heard me outline policies that I will introduce to achieve equality for all." Jenkins paused for a moment, knowing he had a small amount of time left. "Two minutes is hardly enough time to address all of the challenges facing this great nation. Over the last year, our government has been distracted by five men and their need for absolute power. I compared this earlier to a coup, and it was very close to that. I believe this incident is a wake-up call to the American people. It is time to bring the people back into our governing process. This election is one of the most crucial elections since the beginning of our country. We can no longer afford to be blasé about our choices and our involvement in our political process. Corporations should not be the only voices heard. There have been many confessions during the last year and corruption has been exposed. If we don't address this problem, it will only get worse—and I'm afraid, become accepted as part of the political process. We need to examine this and corral it before it is too late." Jenkins paused, mostly for dramatic effect. "I have served my country both in the military and as a senator. Now I would be honored to serve my country as president with your support and participation. I hope that on November 4th, you will vote for a promising future by selecting me to represent you, the people of the United States of America. Thank you, and God bless America." Jenkins looked over at Harrigan as the crowd started to applaud.

"This concludes our debate. Our gratitude to the League of Women

Voters," Harrigan said, talking over the applause that was growing. "Please remember to vote on November 4th. Thank you for watching and good night."

The majority of the crowd started chanting, "Jenkins!" and began to rush to the stage. Jenkins smiled as he walked over to Harrigan, shook his hand, and then he shook each of the panelist's hands. Blackwood followed Jenkins's lead. Then, Jenkins walked to the edge of the stage and started shaking the hands of the audience members. This move made the Secret Service very nervous, and as the picture faded on television screens, the agents were seen moving into positions to guard both candidates. After a few minutes, Jenkins waved to the crowd. A louder cheer erupted, and Jenkins placed his hand over his heart. He waved again and then walked off stage. Jenkins was pleased with his performance, and the grin on Whittaker's face confirmed that his campaign manager was as well.

CHAPTER TEN

November 1980

London, England

Peter didn't look up when Sean walked into his office. "You're late." A note he was writing required his attention. An important vote regarding Afghanistan and the UK's involvement was pending. Peter was determined to have his say and support Geoffrey's stance, which was to back NATO's position requesting the withdraw of the USSR immediately.

"Sorry," Sean replied. "We were over at Geoff's late last night. Elizabeth is finally getting the help she needs. Geoff was feeling a bit down."

"Yes, I had a meeting," Peter said. "Thank you for keeping him company last night."

"After all that she has put him through, I marvel at the love he still has for her," Sean said as he took a seat to the side of his father's desk. "Do you think the no-confidence vote will come soon?"

"Yes. It will probably occur in the next week. Plans are in place, and Geoff will be put forth to serve." Peter was proud of his sons. "Jack dropped off the latest intelligence for you." Peter handed him a folder.

Sean took the folder and immediately began reading it. Now that he had been receiving intelligence briefings for the past few months, he was able to determine if Kent was making a move to try and assassinate them. Most of the intelligence from Maggie was spot on, and it seemed that she was performing her job satisfactorily. There was no evidence that she was acting as a double agent, but there was no information given to Maggie concerning Sean or Nicole. She occasionally asked about them, but she received no specific information. Sean noticed a notation that Kent would be traveling to Germany in the coming weeks. Sean started thinking about that destination.

"Dad," Sean started, "isn't there a conference of high-ranking officials going to take place in Germany in a few weeks?"

Peter looked at Sean. "Yes, it is a trade meeting, I think. Why?"

"Kent is going to Germany," Sean advised. "I'd double security around our people. Would you like me to suggest that to Jack?"

"No, I will," Peter stated. "Good catch, Sean." Peter picked up the phone to call Jack and relayed the message. Sean continued to read the intelligence report during his father's conversation. "Jack said that he was a step ahead of you, but thanks you for your confirmation."

Sean closed the folder after reading the last page of the report. "Thanks," he said as he handed the folder back to him. "What's on the schedule for me today?"

"I think I've given you everything I know about being an ambassador. You've cultivated relationships with other parliament members. I think you are ready for an assignment. The prime minister called this morning asking if you were ready and I told him that I thought you were. I have arranged an appointment. It might be best if Nicole could join us."

Sean stood up and buttoned his suit jacket. "What time is the meeting?"

"In about an hour," Peter told him.

"I'll meet you at his office," Sean said as he left.

Peter, Nicole, and Sean arrived at the prime minister's office at the same time. Shortly after, they were escorted into his office, taking seats across from an empty desk. The prime minister was running late. Sean looked around the office, noting various neatly placed pictures and books. Nicole was doing the same, wondering why she was even in the meeting. Peter picked at what he thought was a piece of lint on his trousers, but upon closer inspection, he determined it was a snag. He sighed at the discovery, knowing he shouldn't pick at it any longer. After a few moments of awkward silence, the prime minister arrived, opening the door to his office while finishing a command to his secretary.

"Lord Peter Adkins," the prime minister started. Prime Minister Wharton was an older man, having served his country for the last fifty years between the House of Commons and his current position. "Thank you so much for coming, and I'm sorry to keep you waiting. Hello, Sean and Nicole." He shook each of their hands as he spoke their names. He moved behind his desk, sat down, and motioned for them to retake their seats. "Sean, I'm told you are ready to start your diplomatic service."

"Yes sir," Sean confirmed with as much confidence as he could muster.

"It's all quite simple, really," Wharton reassured him. "Have you decided, Peter, what he is to be called?"

"Called?" Sean asked perplexed.

"Your title," Peter informed his son. "Yes, Lord Sean Adkins, the Earl of Guildford is appropriate."

Sean looked at his father. "Is that title necessary?"

"Yes, it puts you in a position of authority," Peter insisted.

"But Dad—" Sean objected. Nicole looked over at him. It never dawned on her that Sean and his family had some amount of royal blood coursing through their veins. She found Sean's employment at SIS to be even more astonishing, given his royal title.

"Really Sean, you have had the name since birth. I don't see what the fuss is about," Peter declared with a confused look on his face. "You might as well get used to the idea that you will be called by the name you have despised since your teenage years."

The prime minister was trying hard to hide his smile. "Yes, well, Lord Sean Adkins, the Earl of Guildford, it is then." He picked up a pen and wrote down the name on a piece of paper sitting in front of him. He then signed the paper, placed it in a folder, and handed the folder to Sean.

"What is this?" Sean asked.

"Those are your credentials. Before you are officially an ambassador to the country you are serving, you need to be accepted. You present those papers to the leader or president of the country, who will utter some formal words and welcome you to his country. It's all for show. You'll get your picture taken, and they will probably have some official welcoming. It marks the beginning of a relationship with the government entities of the country in which you will be serving."

"And that country is…?" Sean inquired.

"Oh, sorry," Wharton started, "no one told you? We had an urgent need to withdraw our ambassador in the USSR. You are going to replace him."

"Russia?" Nicole questioned.

The prime minister gave a weary look at Nicole, not at all liking the tone in her voice. "Yes, you will be going to Moscow. The Russians accused our last ambassador's wife of espionage."

Sean shook his head. "Well then, sending a former MI6 agent should make them feel better."

Wharton paused for a moment. He didn't appreciate Sean's sarcasm. He looked down at a paper in front of him as he composed his thoughts. He looked up and said, "Sean, have you dealt with the Russian government during your tenure with MI6?"

"No, not with the government per se."

"Then I don't think it will be a problem. I'll speak with Mr. Kensington about any possible conflicts. In most cases, as you know, our agents are identified with numbers. There is no link to you by name. I think it is perfectly safe. As it should be our embassy is well protected. It was unfortunate that the wife of the ambassador was foolish with her actions." The prime minister directed his last remark to Nicole as a warning.

"When are we to report?" Sean ignored Wharton's last comment.

"The current ambassador and his wife have already left. I don't see a problem with you taking some time to get things in order before you leave. How does the middle to end of November sound to you?" Wharton was looking at a calendar. "I understand there is some work to be done regarding your identity," he said looking at Nicole.

"That's correct," Sean interjected. "We'll need some help from the agency with that."

"Yes, well, I suggest you better get busy."

"I made some calls this morning," Peter said. "They need Nicole and you to be at Vauxhall Cross this afternoon.

"When you arrive in the USSR, Colin Stewart will be assisting you. He is the acting ambassador until you arrive, and what the previous ambassador's chief of staff. You'll find Colin to be a great help." The prime minister stood up, and all three followed his lead. "Thank you for your service, Sean. We look forward to working with you."

They all shook hands with the prime minister and left his office. Sean and Nicole departed for SIS headquarters, and Peter went back to his office.

Jack met Sean and Nicole in the front lobby when they arrived. He greeted them both with a hug before they all headed for a conference room.

"It's customary that we give the incoming ambassador to our adversary countries a briefing before they depart. We can do that today while some assistants work on Nicole's disguise," Jack said as he opened the door to the conference room.

"That would be great," Sean agreed as they walked to some chairs and sat down. Jack sat next to the phone, and he called for the necessary people.

"I know that this might seem a bit unnerving," Jack started, "but really, Russia is very safe. Our embassy there has our most trained forces. I suggested you for Russia, Sean. The Serpent has had very little interest in working with the Russians."

"You mean, Saverio had very little interest. I'm not sure that is true for Kent," Sean corrected.

"We have no intelligence that suggests that Kent has worked with the government there," Jack confirmed.

There was a knock on the door. Jack instructed the three assistants to enter, and before they knew it, the assistants had swept Nicole out of the room.

"She'll be fine," Jack reassured Sean. "Let's get started."

Nicole followed the three people (one male and two females) down the hallway as they discussed the possibilities of concealing her identity. Nicole listened to the conversation, quite sure she didn't like the idea of wigs and other cosmetic changes they were discussing. They arrived at a room full of the very things they were debating.

"Have a seat, dear," the male assistant said. "I think she would look better as a blonde." He turned to Nicole. "Would you like short hair?"

"You're not cutting my hair," Nicole stated adamantly.

"No, we wouldn't think of it," the male assistant replied. "We're talking about a wig. Let's try them both on!" It was as if they were playing dress up, and they were giddy about the prospect of changing Nicole's appearance.

When they were through, they escorted Nicole to another office area where a passport was fabricated listing her as Sean's attaché. Strangely enough, they kept her first name. They explained that it would be easier for all to remember. They changed her last name to Spencer. She had her picture taken, and all the necessary paperwork created, signed, and readied for her new life.

With her papers and disguise intact, they escorted her back to the conference room. She walked into the room and looked at Sean. Her cinnamon-red hair was hidden under a long-haired blonde wig. They had changed her clothes due to the extra ten pounds they added around her midsection. They showed her how to apply her makeup to make her look at least five years older. She was given a pair of thick-rimmed glasses to wear as well. She was holding a small travel bag, which contained the cosmetics she would use and instructions on how to use them. The whole training experience was overwhelming.

Nicole's eyes darted from Sean to Jack. She wanted to cry. Throughout everything—the ordeal with the Serpent, losing her best friend, almost being abducted by the Serpent on that stormy night in North Carolina, being shot and recovering from that wound, and now not being able to return to the United States, Nicole had always held onto one thing: her identity. It was the last thing she was clinging to, and now that was being ripped from her. She felt lost with nothing to ground her. She fought all her life to be Nicole Charbonneau and, in a matter of minutes, that person was erased. She hated what they had created; she hated every blonde hair and every extra pound they strapped to her. She wondered if death would have been preferable. For the rest of her public life, would she be known as Nicole Spencer? She swore to herself that would not be the case.

Sean just stared at her with dismay. He knew underneath the disguise was the woman he loved, but he couldn't imagine they could make her look so different. He was astonished and didn't know what to say. He could see the tears welling up in her eyes. They had turned his beautiful, attractive Nicole into a prudish, demure, older woman that he would not have noticed when walking down the street. "It will be okay," Sean said, offering his hand to her. He realized this was the objective of a disguise: to create someone the opposite of what they truly were.

"You only need to be in this disguise when you are in public," Jack added quickly.

"I'd rather not be in it at all," Nicole shot back. "Is this necessary? Who knows me in Russia?" she pleaded.

"We don't know," Jack replied. "It's more to keep your fellow Americans at bay. If you can get them to rescind the extradition order, you could travel as Nicole Charbonneau for all we care."

Nicole looked down then back up at Sean. She knew there was no hope of that until possibly after the election and then only if Jenkins won.

One of the female assistants moved forward with her folder and handed it to Sean. "Here are her papers. Her new name is Nicole Spencer."

Sean looked at the assistant. "As in the Earl of Spencer's family?"

"Well, no," the female assistant confessed. "We didn't think of that."

Sean took the folder and thanked the assistants even though he was perturbed at the last name chosen for Nicole. Jack sat back down at the conference table—an indication they were not finished. Sean motioned for Nicole to sit beside him.

As Nicole walked by him, Sean slipped his arm around her waist, pulling her to him. He whispered in her ear, "I still love you." It was exactly what Nicole needed to hear. She tilted her head, so the top of it caressed Sean's cheek without saying a word. They moved to their seats. Sean browsed through the folder and then handed it to Nicole. He noted her new passport, urging her to put it in her purse.

"As you know, Sean, the Soviet Union is very active in Afghanistan," Jack said. "We are interested in any intelligence in regards to that situation. Also, the war between Iraq and Iran is still raging. Any intelligence in those areas would be a great help to us as well."

"I'll probably need another update before I leave," Sean responded. Sean stood and shook Jack's hand. "Please include information on Kent's and Maggie's movements in the intelligence briefings I receive." Jack nodded his head in agreement. "Is there any special clearance for my gun and license to kill?"

"You're not traveling there as an official agent, Sean. You'll have both your gun and license, just as before. Any reports you file to MI6 will be done with your OO5 codename. The Foreign and Commonwealth Office will need to clear your gun. As for your license, I'm going to pretend I didn't hear you bring it up." Jack had a crooked smile on his face. "I do believe you own your gun. I trust you have the necessary paperwork for it."

"I do," Sean confirmed. "I think that is all we need right now."

The three walked to the lobby where they wished each other well. Nicole shook Jack's hand as did Sean. They left the building and walked to Sean's car.

"Sean," Nicole started, "is there any way we could go to the United States before we travel to Moscow?"

"Why? What for?" Sean asked, confused.

"I was thinking I might as well sell my condo," Nicole said. "It doesn't look like I'll be going home anytime soon. And it would test out this disguise. If I get caught, I'd rather get caught in the United States versus Soviet Union."

Sean smiled. "And we know someone who could help us out."

"Well, there is that."

"I'll see what I can do," Sean said. He kissed her forehead. "But first, we have to do some shopping. That dress is horrid." They both laughed as Sean started the car.

{II}

Puy-l'Évêque, France

Returning from an assassination, Kent boarded a train in Paris after arriving at Charles de Galle Airport. He had called Maggie and asked her to pick him up at the Gourdon train station. Kent was not in a particularly good mood even though this job had paid well. The lack of alcohol in addition to the food he was not accustomed to eating left him feeling sick and weak. In the two weeks while on the job, he ate very little. The local cuisine looked horrible and tasted even worse.

Kent had been in negotiations with this client for months, and the price the equivalent of a million dollars finally convinced him to accept. Kent flew to the Middle East to kill the son of a wealthy and prominent Saudi Arabian oil tycoon. The son had insulted another family, also just as wealthy, by spurning the arranged marriage to their daughter. As part of the son's last days as a bachelor before the scheduled wedding, his friends had escorted him to Cannes. On a side trip to the French countryside, he met, fell in love, and quickly married a young French woman. The woman was very common; her family had no wealth. Her family was not thrilled with the prospect of their daughter marrying a man she had just met, but when they heard how rich their new prospective son-in-law was, they gave their approval.

When Ahmed Kattan brought his beautiful French bride home, his father was very angry. The father knew the wrath of the spurned family would be harsh and no amount of money or power would satisfy them. Ahmed's father was right, and the spurned family contracted Kent for the kill.

Ahmed spent the remaining days of his life happily in love with his new French wife. The two Arab families never spoke and never appeared in the same place at the same time. As far as Ahmed knew, his father had settled with the other family by arranging an audience with the family to apologize; he truly thought that they had forgiven him.

A contact of Kent's informed him of Ahmed's schedule upon his arrival. In keeping with the Serpent's habit of leaving no one alive who could identify him, Kent retrieved the schedule from a designated location. He communicated with the spurned family and his contacts via telephone. Kent knew this was for his protection as much as theirs. He arrived in Arab clothes and left the country that way. Every detail was planned out.

The morning of Ahmed's death was typical. The family ate breakfast together, prayed together, and then went on about their business. It was a little after one in the afternoon when the Serpent's bullet found Ahmed's forehead. He died instantly in the market where he was buying his bride a gift.

Kent retrieved the money a few days after that, leaving the country undetected. Intelligence reports contained just a couple sentences about the assassination pending ballistic reports. It only mentioned the assassination because of Ahmed's family's position in Saudi Arabia.

Kent was glad to be home and couldn't wait to indulge in vices forbidden in the Muslim country. He instructed Maggie to have plenty of food and drink available. He planned on celebrating, and Maggie was also part of his planned celebration. He noted that he had never been so miserable. Kent vowed never to step foot in the Middle East again for less than two million. A smile came to him, however, when his mind replayed the actual killing. He now understood Saverio's lust with taking a life. It was a power Kent enjoyed exercising as much as Saverio. He could only imagine what it was going to be like to kill Sean and Nicole.

{III}

Raleigh, North Carolina

Election Day had finally arrived. Jenkins was tired from all the travel and constant campaigning, and he was looking forward to a day of relaxing—as much as possible—with his parents while waiting for the results to come in. Although he had butterflies in his stomach about the impending outcome, he felt he had done his best. He waved to the reporters who had camped out to catch him voting, and he chatted with them briefly. His parents accompanied him to their local polling place. His mother proudly held the arm of her son as he escorted her to the waiting limousine surrounded by the Secret Service agents. The agents also flanked Jenkins as he attended to his civic duty of voting.

Even though the Secret Service had guarded him for months, Jenkins still was not used to it. He found them to be a nuisance and restricting his movements. He preferred Thompson by his side, but that would possibly be coming to an end soon. Thompson waited by the limo and opened the door for Jenkins's father, mother, and Jenkins, who gave one last wave to the crowd and reporters. Jenkins had floated Thompson's name for the next FBI director and received little pushback when his colleagues reviewed Thompson's credentials. They liked the idea of someone familiar with and who had worked inside the bureau being in charge.

When everyone was inside their vehicles, the motorcade headed to Jenkins's childhood home, where his parents still lived. He remembered fond childhood encounters as they drove past the schools Jenkins had attended. He thought about how long he had worked to achieve all he had accomplished to date. He thought about how odd time was; how time erases some pain, but allows other wounds to remain open. He thought of Nicole and how different the day would be if she were by his side. He thought of his journey to this very moment. His fate was now in the hands of the Electoral College and the voters. He would not allow himself to think that he would easily be victorious.

They arrived at the house, and, upon entering, Jenkins saw the staircase where he used to sit late on Friday and Saturday nights to listen to his father's war stories. He smiled as he recalled his youth during which he was certain his father was a real-life superhero. He suppressed a chuckle, remembering when he was old enough to realize that the stories he had heard were embellished and depleted of the real war wounds and deaths of fellow soldiers that his father most certainly witnessed. That thought brought him back to his own war wounds. He quickly walked into the living room, removing his suit jacket as he pushed his demons back into the shadows.

"Don't worry so much," his mother said as she walked up to him, her French accent still noticeable after all the years. "Ce que sera sera." She smiled at her son and wondered if he still knew the meaning.

"What will be, will be," Jenkins interpreted. He kissed his mother's forehead. "I remember."

His mother continued to the kitchen to make some coffee and prepare a snack for all the dedicated agents who were surrounding their house. Jenkins smiled as he listened to her ramble on about how they must be hungry and all the fuss made over her son. He walked to the fireplace and looked at the family photos framed and arranged in a certain order. He stopped when his eyes reached a photo of his older sister. He missed her so much. He wondered if she would be proud of him. His thoughts moved to the horrible day when his parents received the news that she had been shot and killed at a civil rights demonstration. The campus of her university held the passive protest. As the number of protesters grew, the peaceful demonstration turned violent. Caught in the crossfire, a single bullet hit her, and she lay bleeding to death. Jenkins remembered his pain and the promise he made to her. He recalled how her death helped him through his SEAL training. That promise gave him a purpose, one he was still serving to this very day. His hand was resting on the mantel just below the picture. He brushed his finger along her cheek and gave thanks to her. She was his inspiration at his darkest times.

After an hour, Chris arrived at the house with some papers that needed to be signed. Jenkins received phone calls from colleagues and friends who wished him well. He wondered if Nicole might call, but then remembered she didn't have his parent's phone number. He was grateful for Nicole and Sean's help in releasing the tape to the public. He knew there was no stopping Nicole after she fled to Paris and ultimately London. The three formed an alliance and her counsel regarding his involvement in the Vietnam mission that he discussed on *Newsweek Tonight* was perfect. Mercer was a big help as well, and Nicole's counsel to seek Mercer's help to thwart any interventions was priceless. He knew he would be indebted to them both for a very long time. Jenkins felt he had very few true friends. Friendship was a casualty in the life he chose. However, he knew the Nicole and Sean were friends, and he was thankful for them.

Jenkins rested most of the day. He conducted a few phone interviews. He worked on his delivery of the two speeches. Of course, he preferred the acceptance speech. His mother prepared his favorite home-cooked meal. One would think the meal would be North Carolina barbecue, but it wasn't. Jenkins did enjoy a good barbecue, but he preferred his mother's Coq au Riesling recipe. The chicken was fall-off-the-bone tender, and the spices tickled his taste buds in a way he could not accurately describe. The aroma lingered in the air throughout the day aiding in his walk down memory lane. At dinner, his mother implored him to say the blessing, prompting everyone to join hands. He ended it with, "I have so much to be thankful for; those here in the room and for those not so close but forever in our hearts." His mother squeezed his hand.

The polls were beginning to close. Joining Jenkins at the house was Whittaker, Chris, his campaign press secretary, and a few others who worked so hard on his campaign. At his campaign headquarters in Raleigh, a crowd gathered waiting for his arrival.

Jenkins retreated to the living room and turned the television to WNN. The now familiar face of Steven Harrigan at the anchor desk materialized. Polls were beginning to close on the East Coast, and projections from exit polls would soon be announced. Jenkins felt more anxious now—something he didn't think possible—compared to how he felt earlier in the day. He stood behind his father's oversized leather chair, his hands resting on the corners of it. He noticed he was holding his breath when Whittaker walked up and put his around Jenkins's shoulders.

"We did everything we could, Bobby," Whittaker said. "We left it all out on the field. I'm proud of what we did and what you said. You should be proud too."

"I am," Jenkins responded. "But that isn't calming down the butterflies." Whittaker gave a half-hearted laugh and tugged Jenkins to and fro. Whittaker knew exactly what Jenkins meant. Jenkins returned the nervous laugh and said, "The campaigning is over, and now it is up to the people. This isn't beauty contest."

Whittaker looked at Jenkins with confusion. "This isn't a beauty contest? Well, it helps to be likable—which you are—I would like to think that your position on issues and the Democratic platform has a bit more to do with it." Whittaker released Jenkins and walked over to sit on the couch. "If it were a beauty contest, we would have included a bathing suit rally. I'm sorry, but I don't want to see you in a bathing suit, and I believe the voters don't want to either." His attempt at levity worked as they all laughed as they moved to various open seats.

Jenkins father moved alongside Jenkins on the way to his favorite chair, he tapped Jenkins on the side of his shoulder. In his hand was a glass of scotch. "This might help those butterflies fall asleep."

Jenkins took the glass. "Thanks, Dad." He took a sip of the scotch as he father sat down and turned his attention to the television. "It's funny. I never thought I'd hear myself say this. When I started this campaign, the only acceptable outcome was for me to win. Now, I keep saying to myself, if I lose, please don't let it be embarrassing."

Whittaker looked down, then back up at Jenkins. "As I said earlier in the day our own polling shows we are doing quite well."

"Yes, so you've said. We'll see if those polls are correct."

Harrigan introduced a few political experts that would provide commentary throughout the night. Since no results were available to announce—the first polling places were to close in fifteen minutes—the pundits added to Jenkins's anxiety. They discussed every possible option including how Jenkins could lose. All of these scenarios were presented to Jenkins earlier in the day, but they came from his staff and didn't sound as cold and harsh as they did now. Jenkins took another sip of his scotch. He walked over to the chair where his mother was sitting and sat on the arm of it. She offered her hand to Jenkins, who gladly took it into his.

It was a torturous fifteen minutes before the first projections were announced. Just before Harrigan broke into the banter between two of the pundits (one Republican and one Democrat), the Republican pundit said, "I don't know whose polling data you been looking at, but my data suggests that Senator Jenkins doesn't have nearly the votes to win."

Just as the Democratic pundit was about to speak, Harrigan raised a finger to silence him and said, "Gentlemen, we have projections to announce." He swung his chair around to face the camera that was now adjusting the shot to show Harrigan on the left side of the screen and the graphic of the state and a photo of the candidate they were projecting as the winner. "Based on exit polling, WNN is ready to call the state of Kentucky for President Blackwood."

It seemed like the air went out of the room. Jenkins looked down before he looked at Whittaker. Jenkins had spent a fair amount of time in Northern Kentucky, making sure he made stops there whenever he visited Southwest Ohio. He reminded himself that they did spend more money and time in Ohio. No one could ignore the historical fact that no presidential candidate won the presidency without Ohio. Still, Jenkins couldn't help but think this was a bad omen.

"It's early, Bobby," Whittaker reminded. "It's only Kentucky, and we didn't target them as much as we did Ohio. If we lose Ohio, then I'll worry."

On the heels of Whittaker's comment, Harrigan then proceeded to announce Indiana, Georgia, Vermont, and Virginia for Blackwood. With each announcement, Jenkins looked at Whittaker. Jenkins shook his head as his spirits began to fall. His mother squeezed his hand to reassure him. He gave her a weak smile as he stood up. He released her hand and started to bring the scotch glass to his lips. He said, "That's forty-nine electoral votes for Blackwood to my zero."

"I continue to stand by my previous statement," Whittaker replied, but Jenkins could tell even his confidence was wavering.

Off-camera, the Republican pundit could be heard chiding the Democratic pundit in a whisper. Harrigan, who was privately rooting for Jenkins but would never admit that out loud, said, "And in the South, the great state of South Carolina casts its eight Electoral College votes to Senator Jenkins."

It was small, but at least it gave Jenkins a start. He gave an agitated exhale of breath. His displeasure at being forty-one votes behind Blackwood was evident. With sarcasm, Jenkins said, "The people are speaking." He drank down the rest of the scotch and walked into the kitchen. He put the glass in the sink and turned back around to see Whittaker leaning against the kitchen door frame with his arms folded.

"I'm not too old to turn you over my knee, young man," Whittaker stated with a hint of a joke in his voice. Jenkins looked at him, not at all appreciating Whittaker's comment. Whittaker could see his attempt to lighten the tension didn't work. "Of for God's sake, Bobby, how many states are there? This was only six of them. Five of them were long shots from the beginning. We knew this." Neither man's facial expressions changed. "If you thought that you were going to win every state, then I apologize for not addressing that scenario when I started to work for you. It is only in very rare circumstances does a candidate sweep the nation. Hell, Bobby, FDR didn't win every state."

Jenkins looked down as a smile crept across his face. "I just didn't expect the first five projections to be for Blackwood."

"We are still OK. We've got a long night ahead of us. I don't see a reason to panic until after eight," Whittaker turned to walk back into the living room. "Are you going to join us?"

"In a minute," Jenkins walked to the refrigerator. "Would you like a soda?" Whittaker was happy that he would not have to remind the senator not to drink too much. Either way, Jenkins would have to make a public appearance. Jenkins saw Whittaker's relief. "I'm not that stupid." The two men returned to the living after Jenkins had opened his soda bottle.

The rhetoric continued between the political pundits for an exasperating twenty-five minutes before they next projections were ready to be announced. Whittaker reminded Jenkins that this small group of three states whose polls were closing at seven-thirty in the evening contained two states that were very important to the campaign. One was Jenkins's home state, and the other was Ohio.

Harrigan turned to the camera and announced they had more projections. He announced West Virginia voted for Blackwood. Jenkins just closed his eyes. He was beginning to believe that Blackwood would be the candidate with the landslide victory. He wondered what he had done wrong. Why was his campaign polling so off base? He began to think what he could have done differently. Was Barker's influence at the start hurting him? Or did the change in direction after he fired Carson hurt him? And then it happened. Jenkins was standing next to Whittaker. No one in the room was speaking.

Harrigan began, "Polls are now closed in Ohio and in Senator Jenkins's home state of North Carolina. WNN is projecting that Senator Jenkins will win both of these states."

A cheer went up from everyone in the room. Whittaker hugged

Jenkins. His mother stood and clasped her hands together placing them to her lips. His father clapped then reached over to hug his son. There were cheers and smiles on the lips of Thompson, Chris, and his press secretary.

"That brings Blackwood to fifty-six Electoral College votes to Jenkins's forty-seven," Harrigan stated.

"We're on our way now!" Whittaker exclaimed.

At eight o'clock the polling places of seventeen states closed and the winners announced. Of those seventeen, Jenkins won twelve which resulted in Jenkins taking the lead in the Electoral College vote. He was eighty-one votes ahead, but half the nation was still voting. Jenkins was far from winning the election and needed eighty-six votes to reach the two hundred seventy to win the election. The next big block of projections wouldn't occur until after nine o'clock.

Chris was fielding phone calls from news stations asking if there were any changes to the plans that were put in place hours ago. Would Jenkins be heading out to his headquarters in Raleigh at the pre-arranged time? Would the vice-presidential candidate be joining him? Chris was confirming their plans and made no other statements.

Samuelson and her husband arrived at Jenkins's childhood home at half-past eight. Jenkins greeted them, and both exchanged their relief at having a slight lead at this point. Jenkins expressed his gratitude to Samuelson for her campaign efforts. He also told her that he enjoyed working with her and hopefully they would continue to work closely no matter the outcome. Samuelson echoed Jenkins's sentiments.

At nine o'clock, Jenkins walked back from the kitchen where he had retrieved a glass of water. Everyone was engaged in conversation: Samuelson was talking in French with Jenkins's mother, Chris was talking with Whittaker and Thompson, his dad was spinning his swashbuckling war tales to the press secretary who was making notes for what Jenkins construed would be included in a future speech. Jenkins observed the room, and he noted the pride that was replacing the anxiety he felt earlier. They had all worked hard, and he was thankful for the people that surrounded him.

Harrigan began to announce the results. He projected Kansas a win for Blackwood. This was a surprise to everyone. The Republican pundit claimed Kansas went Republican because of the way Jenkins had left in the midst of his campaigning there and never apologized. While the Kansas voters may have been a bit put off by the last minute cancelations, Jenkins was sure he and his staff apologized for the incident. Louisiana was chalked up to Blackwood. That was not a surprise as Jenkins's campaign pulled money from the state after it was clear Blackwood had a double-digit lead that never wavered.

Over the next fifteen minutes, Harrigan announced state after state as a win for Jenkins. Then, at nine-thirty, Harrigan said, "We are now projecting that Senator Jenkins has won Texas with its twenty-five electoral votes. This puts the senator over the needed two hundred and seventy votes. Therefore, we project Senator Robert James Jenkins will be our next president."

Papers were thrown from the hands of the Chris and Whittaker as everyone cheered Harrigan's pronouncement. In the midst of all the cheering and hollering, Jenkins was hugged by his parents, Samuelson and Chris. Whittaker, Thompson, the press secretary and Samuelson's husband all had the opportunity to embrace or shake the hand of the president-elect. The laughing and congratulations continued for a few minutes.

Remote coverage from the campaign headquarters was shown on WNN. The stark contrast of winning and losing was apparent in the separate reports. The party was in full swing at Jenkins's campaign headquarters. The reporter could only file their report due to the celebrating. Blackwood's headquarters was solemn.

Jenkins changed into his navy blue suit and was preparing to leave his childhood home for his campaign headquarters when the phone rang. Chris announced it was Blackwood and handed the phone to Jenkins.

"Congratulations, Bobby," Blackwood started. "You ran an exceptional campaign. I hope that you can unite this country and keep your promises."

"Thank you, Mr. President," Jenkins replied. "I could use your help in Congress. Will we see you in two years?"

"I haven't decided yet," Blackwood confessed. "I'm sure the party will be beating down my door."

"I've always appreciated that I could reach across the aisle to you. We've accomplished great things in the past working together," Jenkins remarked. "You tried your best, sir. Unfortunately, the mountain was a bit too high."

Blackwood smiled at Jenkins's comment. "There was a lot to overcome, but we will get the party glued back together again."

"I'm sure they will look to your leadership to help accomplish that, Danny Boy." This was Jenkins's nickname for Blackwood when he needed his help. Blackwood's mother was of Irish descent, and Jenkins was present once when he heard Blackwood's mother call him by that name. Hearing Jenkins say it with his Southern accent always made Blackwood laugh. "This country needs at least two strong political parties. You need to help lead them back," Jenkins urged. "While we both have our flaws, they amount to nothing compared to some of the others in our parties." Jenkins was referring to Barker, among others.

"Yes, that is true. May I be blunt, Mr. President-Elect?" Blackwood asked with a bit of trepidation in his voice.

"Of course," Jenkins replied. He preferred bluntness.

"You are aware of Barker's blackmail of McNair, aren't you?"

"Yes."

"Are you aware of the special op—"

"Yes," Jenkins interrupted. "Barker and his information will not be a concern. We can't afford any more loose cannons."

"Thank you, Bobby," Blackwood replied. Jenkins could hear the relief in his voice. "The sooner, the better, as many in my party are angry and may lash out at your inconsistency of dealing with powerful politicians who misuse their influence."

"Ahhh, Danny Boy, you are putting that far too politely." Jenkins had a little laugh in his voice. "I'm well aware of the rumblings. But understand that there is plenty of dirt on both sides. I don't think either of us wants to get caught digging in the dirt pile." It was a warning. Jenkins, thanks to Nicole's files, now had many indiscretions he could leak or use at any given time.

"No," Blackwood agreed. "No, we don't."

"Thanks for the call," Jenkins started. "I'm heading down to give my speech now. I wish you all the best."

"As do I, Mr. President-Elect," Blackwood said and hung up the phone.

Jenkins held the receiver for a few seconds, reflecting on the conversation. It was clear to him before Blackwood's call that he needed to ship Barker off to some far-off ambassadorship. He was too popular in his home state of Texas to lose his Senate seat. But he couldn't send him someplace irrelevant as that would draw too much attention. He decided that talking to Mercer would be his best approach, but he would think about Barker in the morning.

He had a victory speech to give now. It was time to celebrate.

CHAPTER ELEVEN

Mid-November 1980

Washington, DC

After the election, Jenkins moved his office to Blair House—a tradition followed by previous presidents-elect for varying lengths of time before their inauguration. Jenkins chose to use Blair House for meetings and planned to move into the residence two weeks before he was to be sworn in as president. He owned his condo in Washington and had no intention of selling it while in office.

Chris fielded many calls in the days following the election. But there was one in particular that he was impatiently struggling to keep secret from Jenkins. The day had finally arrived.

Sean laughed at the perplexed look on Chris's face when he walked into the foyer of Blair House with a blonde woman on his arm. Her large sunglasses obscured much of her face. Her coat and gloves were fashionable, but Chris began to wonder where Nicole was. Chris looked out the door for her, but only saw the limo driver who was walking back around the car to the driver's side.

Nicole leaned over and said, "It's me, Chris."

Chris's head snapped to look at her when he heard her familiar voice. "Nicole? What happened to you?"

She laughed. "In case you forgot, I'm wanted in this country," she whispered.

Chris had forgotten about the extradition order filed by McNair, as had most of Congress. In fact, the two agencies that had not forgotten were the FBI and the CIA. "Well, we'll see what we can do about that," Chris announced. "This way," he said as he led them to Jenkins's office.

Nicole held back, allowing Sean to move to the doorway. Chris was about to open it when Sean shook his head. He wanted to surprise his friend. With Nicole out of view, Sean opened the door and leaned against the door frame staring intently at Jenkins and waiting for him to look up.

After a few seconds, Jenkins felt the draft from the open door. It was strange that Chris would open the door and not announce someone. The last time this happened, Barker had greeted him. He slowly looked up with only his eyes. When he saw Sean, he threw his pen down and rose to his feet. "Sean!"

Sean smiled and moved toward him, preventing him from seeing Nicole. They hugged and exchanged pleasantries.

"Congratulations, Mr. President," Sean greeted his longtime friend along with a handshake and hug. He intentionally left off the "elect" when he addressed him.

"Thank you," Jenkins replied. "Please, call me Bobby."

Sean shook his head. "I'm afraid I can't do that."

"Sure, you can," Jenkins returned. "I insist."

"Well, maybe when we are alone, and I'm not meeting with you officially."

"Officially?" Jenkins questioned. "I don't understand."

"I'm the new ambassador to the USSR," Sean declared.

Jenkins smiled and laughed. "Are you serious?"

"Very," Sean replied. "Oh, excuse me. My attaché is with Chris. I'd like to introduce you." Sean walked to the door and waved his hand for Nicole to enter. Chris followed her to the door—he wanted to see the look on Jenkins's face. "I'd like you to meet Ms. Spencer."

Jenkins's face showed his puzzlement. Was Sean in the United States without Nicole? If so, where was Nicole and was she safe? Jenkins was under the impression that Sean and Nicole were in a relationship. As this Spencer woman entered, Sean slipped his arm around her waist and kissed her cheek. Jenkins took another look at the woman before he offered his hand. His voice revealed his confusion even though he was trying hard to accept the situation. "It's very nice to meet you."

Nicole smiled, took Jenkins's hand and gave a quick curtsy. She had removed her sunglasses before she entered the office. Earlier in the day, she had applied the makeup as taught, making her appear years older than she truly was. As she told Sean, if she could fool Jenkins, she knew then that her disguise would work.

"No, uh," Jenkins started, "you don't curtsy. I'm not a king." He kept looking at her.

"She's a little weak on the protocol, but there are plenty of people at our Russian embassy who will help with that," Sean said.

"Yes, of course," Jenkins replied. "Sean, where's Nicole? I assumed you two were in a relationship. Aren't you? Is she going to Russia with you?"

"Of course she is going to Russia with me," Sean confirmed.

"Then where is she?"

"Aren't you forgetting the extradition—"

"I have," Jenkins interrupted. "But it never was a serious threat."

"Serious enough that your intelligence agencies made inquiries," Sean responded.

"Chris," Jenkins called, looking past his two visitors. Chris was smiling, content that he was not the only one who hadn't recognized Nicole. "We need to get that rescinded. Can you get to work on that?"

"Yes sir." Chris didn't move from the door.

"Now," Jenkins prodded. Chris acknowledged him with a nod of the head but did not move. Jenkins was becoming irritated with his aide.

"Oh, thank God," Nicole said, as she reached up and removed the wig. Her cinnamon-red hair fell and caressed her shoulders. "It's about time."

"Nicole?" Jenkins said as a smile crept across his face. Her makeup was still confusing him. He thought for a minute that all she had been through in the past year must have aged her. Chris laughed as he closed the door to Jenkins's office.

"Congratulations, Bobby," Nicole said as she moved toward him. They embraced. "I'm so happy for you," she whispered in his ear.

Jenkins held her close and tight. He delighted in her breath caressing his neck and her nose nuzzling his ear when she spoke. He turned his head and whispered, "Thank you. I couldn't have done it without you."

They held the embrace a little longer before Nicole broke it off and returned to Sean's side. Jenkins watched her wipe a single tear from the side of her eye. He knew she still cared for him. The realization made him grateful, but he also knew he had indeed lost her.

"You will take care of this extradition," Nicole confirmed.

"Yes. I'll do that right away. I'm sure Blackwood will do me one favor and do it quietly. So, you are going to Moscow with Sean, or was that made up as well?"

"No, we are going to the USSR," she confirmed. "I'm here to sell my condo and take care of a few things."

Jenkins moved to his desk, urging them to take a seat when he suddenly remembered— "Oh no," he said. His face went pale. "Can you change where you are to serve, Sean?"

"No," Sean's confusion was evident. "What's wrong?"

Jenkins sat down, followed by Nicole and Sean. "We just announced this morning that Barker is *our* new ambassador to the

USSR."

"So?" Nicole said. "I doubt that we will be running into him frequently."

"Nicole, you don't understand. He was behind your assassination attempt," Jenkins declared. "My sending him to Moscow is a penalty and isolates him. Harrigan's information and your note, as well as your files, lead me to believe that he ordered it. I have no concrete evidence that would stand up in court—"

"What note?" Nicole asked.

"The note you wrote about his threat to kill you after a quarrel in South Carolina," Jenkins explained. "Kevin and I determined that it might have been a note you wrote to clear your mind. He found it on your desk."

"Oh, that note," Nicole deadpanned. "I meant to shred that."

"So he didn't threaten you?" Sean asked.

"Oh no, he threatened me," Nicole confirmed. "I just didn't think he would do it."

"Well, we announced that he would be our ambassador to the USSR this morning. He has no other option but to accept, which he did," Jenkins confirmed.

"Bobby," Sean began. "Are you sure you want him in Moscow? The Russians are pretty active in areas that would threaten US interests."

Jenkins smiled. "So, you're still working for MI6 after all."

"I'm acting on behalf of my government as an ambassador first. With the Soviet's activity, I would expect to spend time with my NATO allies exchanging information and discussing any possible actions we may take." Sean winked at Jenkins. His implied message was understood.

Jenkins sighed. "Now you see my dilemma. Barker holds a lot of secrets, and he has a lot of power. I couldn't just dismiss him to an insignificant country without arousing some curiosity. I'm afraid I'm stuck with this decision." He looked at Nicole. "I wish I would have known. You understand that I can't reverse this decision, don't you?"

"Yes," Nicole replied. She looked at Sean. "I'm not afraid of him, Sean."

"Here I thought we might get down to only one person wanting you dead," Sean joked. He looked at Jenkins. "Being an ambassador has its perks. Our embassy there is well fortified."

Jenkins nodded his head. "And if any intelligence shows Barker is moving against either of you, let me know." He looked at Nicole. "Even if it is just another argument or your intuition."

"I hope you'll do the same," Sean countered.

"Absolutely," Jenkins assured them. There was a knock on the door. "What is it, Chris?"

Chris opened the door only enough for him to see into the office. "Senator Mercer is here for your ten o'clock meeting." He closed the door as he addressed the senator. "He'll just be a minute, sir."

Nicole pulled her hair back and swirled it on top of her head. She swung the blonde wig into place, stood, and gave Jenkins a wink.

Sean stood and extended his hand. "We'll see you soon. Drop a note when the cancellation of the extradition occurs."

"Will do," Jenkins said, not releasing Sean's hand. "Take good care of Nicole."

Sean smiled. "I will."

Jenkins walked around the desk and hugged Nicole. He wondered if it would be the last time he would see her. "Take care of yourself. I hope we'll get to see each other again."

"I'm sure we will, even if it is just official functions," Nicole whispered. She didn't want to chance Mercer hearing her voice.

"Thank you for the tip about your files," Jenkins said, still holding her tightly. Nicole smiled at the confirmation that he knew that she was the source. "If you ever need anything, call me."

Nicole stepped back, gave him a quick peck on the cheek and in a low voice added, "I still consider the three of us an alliance. Maybe we can make some positive changes in this world."

"Hopefully we already have." He walked with them to the door of his office. "Safe travels, Mr. Ambassador," he said as he opened the door. Nicole walked out first, not saying a word and assuming her role as Sean's attaché. Sean followed her. "Senator Mercer, allow me to introduce Her Britannic Majesty's Ambassador to the Russian Federation."

The senator extended his hand. Sean shook it while he said, "Lord Sean Adkins, Earl of Guildford at your service, Senator." Jenkins looked at Sean when he spoke his title. Sean could read his mind. He knew the thought of Sean's royal lineage had never crossed Jenkins's mind.

"It's an honor to meet you," Mercer started. "Wait, are you Lord Peter Adkins's son?"

"Yes," Sean confirmed as Nicole moved to the door. "I am one of his sons. Geoffrey is my brother and is in contention for the prime minister position."

"Your father is a very good friend. I heard a lot about Geoffrey, but very little about you."

"Yes, well," Sean started as he moved to the door, "I was a bit of a playboy, and my father didn't approve of my lifestyle. If you'll excuse me, I'm late for another appointment. Have a good day, Mr. President-Elect, Senator," Sean said with a slight nod of the head. He opened the door and allowed Nicole to walk out first. He followed her out.

"I hope he'll be able to handle Barker," Mercer said as he and Jenkins walked into the office. Jenkins looked at Chris, smiled, and closed the door behind him.

{II}

London to Moscow

By the time Sean and Nicole were ready to leave for Russia, it was the end of November. There was another briefing for Sean, and thanks to Jenkins, Nicole was happy to return all the pieces of her disguise back to MI6. Sean argued that the disguise might deter Barker and Kent, but Nicole would not hear it. She calmly explained to Sean that with everything else she had lost over the last few years, her identity would not be one of them. Like Sean, she wasn't going to let fear dominate her life. They were moving to Russia, and she was going as Nicole Charbonneau. She refused to discuss it any further.

The flight to Moscow was uneventful. They arrived at the embassy on December 1st. Colin Stewart greeted them at the airport and escorted them to their limousine surrounded by a security detail. Stewart was the epitome of efficiency and organization. He had requested a few moments of their time when they arrived at the embassy.

"Here are the most important communiqués and the intelligence briefings that have been forwarded since leaving London." Stewart handed Sean several envelopes. Sean noticed the intelligence briefings were still secured. He looked at Stewart.

"I don't have the clearance to open those," Stewart responded to the unasked question. "As chief of staff to the previous ambassador, he felt the less people knew, the better."

"For the last month, you haven't been receiving intelligence that could affect your stay here, and you didn't open these?" Sean questioned.

"We were very hopeful that there was nothing important in those envelopes," Stewart said.

"Well, I'll have a look at them and let you know," Sean replied while shaking his head. He was impressed that Stewart respected his clearance, but felt the gesture was a bit foolish. He made a mental note to check into Stewart and, if possible, get him the appropriate clearance. "Is there anything else?"

"After we had received the communication that you were arriving today, I took the liberty of arranging meetings of the staff here and also important people in Moscow," Stewart said. "Those meetings start the day after tomorrow."

"Thank you." Sean could tell that Stewart was uncomfortable about something. It was as if he had another question but was hesitant to ask. "Is there something you'd like to know, Mr. Stewart?"

"Yes, well, forgive me, sir," he began. "I'm not familiar with the role of your attaché." He looked at Nicole. "Will Ms. Charbonneau require an office and staff? And what purpose will she be fulfilling?"

Sean smiled. He looked at Nicole. "Ms. Charbonneau will be working closely with me," Sean said. "We haven't discussed her role yet, so, we'll get back to you on the other arrangements."

"Very good, sir," Stewart acknowledged.

Stewart then escorted Sean and Nicole to their residence in the same building as the embassy's offices. On the way there, he pointed out various offices and introduced them to staff members who happened to be available. It was a longer journey in time rather than distance. It was quite clear to Sean and Nicole that the staff, particularly Stewart, was very happy to have a new ambassador. Sean made a note to look into the previous ambassador and his actions. He got the distinct impression the previous ambassador had behaved like a pompous dictator. After an hour and a half, they finally arrived at the residence.

Stewart opened the door, handed Sean the keys, and said, "I'll allow you to explore your residence on your own. The bedrooms are on the left. Your suitcases are in your rooms." He smiled and bade them farewell.

Nicole was looking up at the tall ceilings and the decorative walls. "Thank you, Mr. Stewart," she said in awe of the artwork that adorned, well, everything.

"Yes, thank you," Sean reiterated. "I'll see you in the morning then."

"Very good, sir," Stewart said as he closed the door behind him.

Sean handed her a key and placed the other on his key ring. Nicole did the same as she continued to scan the elegant foyer. "Is the whole place like this?"

"I don't know," Sean replied, heading for the bedrooms. "I've only just arrived here." Nicole noted his flippancy and gave a lighthearted but sardonic chuckle. Sean continued to the bedrooms, opening the door to the master. "Well, our bedroom is just as extravagant." He noted his two suitcases and the absence of Nicole's. He walked to another bedroom, which was across the hall—there they were. He picked them up and carried them to the master bedroom. He turned, wondering what Nicole was doing. He walked back to the foyer.

When he entered the foyer, he saw Nicole reading a small notecard. She was standing by the circular, carved wooden table in the center of the room. Displayed on the table was an antique porcelain vase that contained two dozen yellow roses. Sean had noticed the roses upon entering and brushed them off as a thoughtful gesture by the staff to welcome them.

Nicole did not look up from the card when Sean entered the room. She was deep in thought. Nicole recalled her conversation with Geoffrey, whose bid for prime minister had succeeded, and Peter at Peter's flat the night before leaving London. She had told them how excited she was to be starting a new life now that the past two years provided some sense of closure. With the conspiracy exposed and the trials almost finished, Nicole explained that her role in that was complete. She noted that Stevens was still in the mental hospital. His trial was pushed back due to the pending legislation that Jenkins and Mercer were pushing through to make the burden of proof in regards to an insanity plea rest with the defense. Jenkins would be assuming office in January. The hurt and loneliness she felt as a result of Carol's death were easing. She had survived two attempts on her life and was now with the man she loved. The alliance between her, Sean, and Jenkins was intact, and for the first time in two years, she felt safe and secure. She explained that she was looking forward to this new adventure in Russia and was hopeful about the future.

Nicole's anger grew as she read the notecard a second time. The card read:

> *"Nicole, You have enemies near and far. I will never forget about you. –Kent"*

Her face flushed with anger. Nicole picked up the antique vase, bringing her arms back to throw it.

"Nicole, wait!" Sean yelled. "It's a rare, antique—"

Sean was too late. Nicole finished her motion hurling the vase at the wall to her right. The vase shattered into pieces, falling to the floor. The roses landed scattered on top of the demolished vase. She didn't care about the vase or the flowers. The message from Kent didn't scare her. It confirmed that she was being hunted, and she had been hunted before—in Mississippi during her fight for civil rights as part her work with the Department of Justice. Even during those rough times, she didn't allow anyone to take her power.

She still had the notecard in her hand. With a mixture of determination and anger, she walked toward Sean, who had an astonished look on his face. As she reached him, she thrust the notecard into his hand, brushed past him, and continued on to the master bedroom without saying a word.

Sean read the note and then cursed to himself. He knew then there was a mole in MI6—how else would Kent have gotten the information so quickly? He recalled the intelligence communiqués that were still unopened. He walked back to the master bedroom to open and read the letters, hoping they might contain some clues. When he reached the bedroom door, he saw Nicole sitting on the bed.

Nicole looked at Sean. "How hard is it to get a gun in Moscow?"

Sean grinned and walked to his suitcases. He picked up the smaller of the two, put it on the bed, and opened it. He reached into the suitcase, retrieved the gun permit document, and a Beretta. Placing the permit under the gun, he tossed both onto the bed within Nicole's reach. She looked at him confused. He opened his suit jacket and showed her his Beretta which was still in his shoulder holster. "An early Christmas present for you," he said. "I was hoping you'd change your mind. There's a practice range located within the embassy compound. I suggest we check it out in the morning."

"Yes, thank you," Nicole said. She reached for the gun and started to examine it. "That's a brilliant idea." She gathered her resolve and vowed to not let Kent stop her—no matter what.

A NOTE FROM THE AUTHOR

It has been so much fun writing this trilogy! Now I will embark on to the next set of books featuring the adventures of Nicole, Sean, and Jenkins. I envision the Blind Series as trilogies. I am researching and creating the next trilogies as this book launches.

As I researched *Blind Influence*, *Blind Persuasion*, and *Blind Alliance*, it was amazing to me how little times have changed politically. A lot of campaign promises made in the 1980s are still given lip service today. Little progress has been made toward those promises—on either side of the aisle. In fact, the only progress our representatives in Congress can claim is the divisiveness of this nation due to their rhetoric. Less rhetoric, more substance, and courage to do what is right is direly needed.

When I began writing this series, I expressed to friends that I felt the 1980s were a turning point for our government. Throughout the eighties, on through the nineties, and up to today, the split in the United States has grown exponentially. The underlying question that started me on this journey was: "What if one drastic thing had occurred back in the 1980s, that put us at an obvious crossroads, and one politician had the courage and finesse to lead, where would we be today?"

These first three books cite numerous things that did occur—including Operation Mockingbird. The next books will include historical events as in this book. However, my characters actions may take an alternative course. I hope you will join me as we explore an alternate and yet parallel universe.

Thank you for your continued support. You can find me on social media (Facebook and Twitter) and the Blind Series website: http://blindseries.lindafisler.com/ where you can sign up for newsletters. The website also contains deleted scenes from the books and blog posts about any number of things. I wish you all the best.